JAMES CRUMLEY'S
ONE TO COUNT CADENCE

I am the eldest son of generations of eldest sons, the final moment of a proud descent of professional killers, warriors, men of strength whose only concern with virtue lay in personal honor. But I still misunderstood a bit that day, I still confused being a soldier with being a warrior. That small, mean part of me which had wanted to care about rank and security and privilege was dying, and with the death of order began the birth of something in me monstrous, ah, but so beautiful. My heritage called, and though it would be many long moons before I answered, the song had burst my cold, ordered heart and I hated in the ringing sweep of the sun, and I lived.

ONE
TO COUNT
CADENCE

JAMES CRUMLEY

VINTAGE CONTEMPORARIES
Vintage Books
A Division of Random House
New York

FIRST VINTAGE CONTEMPORARIES EDITION, June 1987

Library of Congress Cataloging in Publication Data
Crumley, James, 1939–
One to count cadence.
(Vintage contemporaries)
I. Title.
PS3553.R7805 1987   813'.54   86-40468
ISBN 0-394-73559-5

Front page photo copyright © 1984 by Lee Nye

Manufactured in the United States of America
10 9 8 7 6 5 4 3 2 1

for my Mother and Father

and for Charlie

It was written I should be loyal to the
nightmare of my choice.
> *Joseph Conrad,* Heart of Darkness

And I will call for a sword against him
throughout all my mountains, saith the
Lord: Every man's sword shall be against
his brother.

O

Thus will I magnify myself, and sanctify
myself; and I will be known in the eyes
of many nations, and they shall know that
I *am* the Lord.
> *Ezekiel 38:21,23*

Fuck 'em all but nine—
Six for pallbearers,
Two for roadguards,
And one to count cadence.
> *Old Army Prayer*

ONE TO COUNT CADENCE

HISTORICAL
PREFACE

It's funny how stories get around. Just the other day
Captain Gallard mentioned that one about the car.
He hadn't spoken for several minutes, but had sat,
staring out my window toward the sixteenth green
running his fingers through his curly hair. When he
finally spoke, his voice was low, drifting far from the
Philippines, all the way back to Iowa and his childhood, as he told me about the mythic automobile of
his youth.

You know the story: the car, the big, fancy one
you've always wanted and dreamed about, is for sale
in a nearby city (always the city) for twenty-five
dollars. They always tell that part first, as they told
Gallard about this Lincoln in Des Moines. Then the
eternal catch: an insurance salesman died in the car
on some deserted road; died, then rotted, and the
stench has seeped into the very metal. "And you
know how death stinks," he said to me, hands in his
hair again, those hands (farmer's hands, short and
flat and strong, the tips of the middle two fingers on

the right hand pinched off in a corn picker long ago), not at all the hands of a bone surgeon.

"I even saved the money," he said with a wistful smile. "But I didn't go to Des Moines. I don't know why. It wasn't the stink so much—no one would smell it but me as I roared up and down those gravel roads at night—but I couldn't figure out how to get a girl in it, and you know cars are no good without girls. So I didn't go," he said, leaning back and chuckling. "Didn't get the girl I had in mind either. At least not then." He laughed again, smiled, then let his eyes wander back to the golf course and the two girls working on the green a short way down the hill across the road. The two were short, stocky mountain girls, Benguet Igorots, hips wrapped in many skirts and feet bound in oversized tennis shoes. They resembled those foolish and energetic dolls with weighted bases which when hit always swing up for another punch. But that wasn't what I saw reflected in his eyes, not them, no, nor the bright green fairway fringed in dark pine, nor the city of Baguio misty and lost in the distance, none of these, but the long delicate snout of that mythic Lincoln.

In my not-so-distant youth the car was a Cadillac for one hundred dollars (even dreams are subject to inflation, I suppose) in San Antonio. A doctor, so the story went, had driven into the nearby cedar hills, then blasted a neat hole ringed with brain tissue through the top. I also dreamed, and also failed to follow, though not for so sensible a reason as Gallard. I was simply afraid it wasn't true, and I certainly didn't want to find out. I still hear of the car, though, as I'm sure you do. A Thunderbird in Los Angeles. A Corvette in Atlanta. A Jaguar in Boston. The cities, the cars change, but not those dusty boys in small towns, nor the dream. I'm sure of that; but no longer am I certain if we dream of the power and beauty of the machine or of the stink. Perhaps, and some say for sure, they are the same, but I don't know. I just know the dream is real. Somewhere back in America grown men—doctors, lawyers, corporation chiefs—waste their fluid into the metal, decay and drip, drip, decay and fall, so you and I might dream—and be fooled into a nightmare of death and a cold wind over an open grave.

Gallard doesn't care for me to talk like that, and when I told him how I felt about the dream car, he accused me of seeing all myths, thus God, as a conspiracy. When I answered "Certainly," he accused me of a lack of seriousness. I reminded him that only the day before he had said I was too serious. He maintained that both accusations were valid. "Do you see evil everywhere," he then asked, "or just reflect it?" (I remember Joe Morning asking me the same question once.)

Gallard cares for me, tends my mending arm and leg, carefully X-raying the leg once a week to check the pin. He claims the X-rays are really a plot to sterilize me, and I agree. But all this time he is really searching for another wound, a festering, dripping sore he thinks he smells. He hasn't discovered it yet; but I'll tell him someday. Like a sly old coyote around poisoned meat, he circles, retreats, holds his hunger. But soon the blood and flesh will be too much in his nose, and he must eat or go mad. Maggots purify an open wound, or so I'm told, and I don't suppose I'll really be well until the day Gallard eats the blood of my friend, Joe Morning, on these pages he gave me to record upon. "Therapeutic,"

Gallard calls it. "Madness," say I. But he is a doctor in the full sense of the word and he cares for wounds.

He smelled it quickly, perhaps even that first day I arrived at the Air Force hospital on Camp John Hay near Baguio. I don't recall very much about the Med-evac flight from Vietnam—a bulky pain in my whole right side, a forest of gleaming needles, a constant plain of white faces. Then the plane approached the island of Luzon. At first the land was a speck, then a dot, then it grew into a disturbing blot on the pure surface of the ocean, a green-black imperfection in a blue universe. Soon it became an eruption, a timeless monster raising itself painfully from the silent depths of the Mindanao Trench, slime oozing down its steeply ridged back, circled in a froth of white where the sea boiled at contact. Closer, I felt the aged beast must reach up for the plane and brush it away like a troublesome gnat, and I was afraid, again, choked and blinded by fear, but as suddenly as it came, the fright disappeared, the world tumbled back to its rightful place. Slime grew back to thick jungle, and froth eased into restless waves napping at the mountains' feet, and I . . . and the sleeper back to his grave.

Again awake as the plane approached Baguio, I glimpsed the stark arrogant mountains tripping and falling among themselves, tumbling into the waiting, self-righteous valleys, and then the soft plateau resting above the gigantic disorder. Everything spoke peace: the quiet green fairways trimmed out of the deep black of a tropical evergreen forest; the thousand dazzling blue-eyed swimming pools winking and glittering among color-dazed gardens and quiet homes.

But I wasn't fooled. I still crouched in a radio van where grenades had scattered death like flowers; still hugged a ragged, skinny old man with blood blossoms adorning his chest. Like all warriors come home, I wasn't sure where or when the fighting stopped, nor did I know the difference between night and day. Then eyes, coal-black and curious above a patient green mask, said, "Take it easy, son." And so, for the moment, I submitted.

Many drug-weary days later, while I was still silent, Gallard came to ask after me. When I didn't answer, he raised his eyebrows almost to the black curls drifting over his short, square forehead, asking again with his face. I nodded toward the casts on my arm and leg, toward the traction apparatus, and shrugged as best I could. He shook his head slightly as if to say, "Okay. Take it easy. I'll be back another time." A wise man, I thought, as he left.

More days with my eyes shutting out bare walls the color of clabbered milk, off-white, way off. The sunlight, rich and golden at the window, ran like rancid butter on those walls. My eyes closed often in self-defense, but found little peace in the darkness. Instead there were the visions, the dreams of a drunk sleeping in the chewing-gum filth of an all-night movie house, slipping in and out of scattered light and darkness until the shadows of his mind match, in a clever and evil way, the shadows on the screen. When he leaves, if ever, he has no memory of sleep. I had only the blank, white faces of false concern.

I ate the hospital's surprisingly good food, submitted to the daily rituals of bath and bed-change, took their shots when they gave them, and endured in painful silence when they didn't. "Is man such a stranger to agony that he must hunt for the Garden with a needle," I say to the two nurses who drug me, Lt. Light and Lt. Hewitt. One laughs; the other thinks it is a famous quotation. Lt. Hewitt once said to an orderly at my door, "Battle fatigue," and shook her hollow head. I laughed, an obscene, barking bellow. Lt. Hewitt, or Bones as she is known, smirked and quickly left. To tattle, I supposed. Regulations permit only Death and doctors above the rank of captain to laugh in this hospital.

Gallard came soon afterward and asked after me again. Silence had begun to bore me, but I wasn't ready to talk yet. I wanted him to really want to know, so I said:

"Curious instruments aren't the keys to Heaven, sir, nor for that matter, to my heart, either."

"They, of course, weren't meant to be," he answered as he exited.

I laughed again, softer, and rang for the nurse. She raised my bed, but not quite high enough for me to see out my window comfortably. I lifted my body and a sudden wave of black discs floated at me. My head seemed airborne also, and the discs enlarged and drifted closer, then suddenly covered my eyes with a quick bright shock and I fainted.

Climbing up from the faint, more symbolically than physically, I quietly labored out of the sea of self-pity. My nose filled with the smell of fresh-cut grass, heavy and a bit too sweet, like watermelon, and the tart needles of pine, and the unmistakable mixture of make-up, sweat and perfume which meant woman. I focused on the blue, sweetly wrinkled eyes above mine.

"Hello, lovely," I said, and touched her cheek. She blushed, her face like a rose nestled among her pale short hair. Lt. Light had a large body, but her face was a small, timid oval above it. She was small breasted, but perfect in the legs and hips. I hadn't noticed before. She always hunched forward as if afraid her height might offend, and this small touch made her uniform seem less than the armor the other nurses wore.

"It seems you're all right," she said.

"I suppose the script calls for me to say, 'Well, you're pretty much all right yourself,' and you are, in spite of the script, all right."

"What do you want?"

"A cigarette?" I asked, and she gave me one and a light.

"Anything else?" she asked with the match cupped in her hand. "And if you say what the script calls for, I'll bust your head."

"It might be worth it."

"It might," she chuckled. She had sounded as if she really did want to know if I wanted anything else.

"You might stay and talk."

"I can't."

"Not right now?"

"Not anytime. You're an evil-minded enlisted man and I'm an officer and a gentleman," she said with a bit of a smile. But then back to business: "You sure you're all right?" She turned to leave as I nodded, and the hesitant way she carried her head struck me again. I wanted to straighten that back and lift that delicate face to the sun.

"One more thing," I said.

"Yes?" she asked very solemnly. She could change so quickly. Like all defenseless things, she was too ready to be hurt.

"Your name?"

She smiled again, and then did it perfectly, never thinking Lt. Light would be enough. "Abigail Light."

"Abby?"

"No."

"Gail?"

"No. Abigail," she said with a flip of her head, smiled again as if pleased by the sound of her name, then left. She had spoken her name in an old-fashioned way, musically important and not to be cheapened by a nickname, a name from a time when names mattered. Abigail Light. How much nicer than mine, I thought, mine which resembled an ominous rumble of thunder on a spring day. Jacob Slagsted Krummel. Slag Krummel.

I lay back in bed. My body, so lately and violently taught its vulnerability, forgot the pain, the violation. I stretched against the aches and pains of inactivity, scratched some of the smaller scabs on my right side, and decided I would live after all.

I examined my surroundings: my room; those sour walls; an uninviting porcelain-enamel framed bed, complete with an array of mechanical devices to push, pull, twist and turn, so that it might have been a place to get sick rather than well; two windows on the west wall, raised halfway and partly covered by age-yellowed roller shades, with panes of glass too clean to be less than sharp.

Out the windows is another story. In the distance sits the city of Baguio, summer capital of the Philippines, a multi-colored maze spread over half a dozen soft hills. Much nearer, lodged at the edge of a rise, is the Halfway House, a low and massive log building with an umbrella-spotted terrace slightly behind the ninth green. The tenth and eleventh fairways are across the road to the left, but I can't see them, nor the twelfth, and only the back edge of the thirteenth green because all this is hidden by the rise on which the fourteenth tee sits. The fourteenth fairway is straight with a slight down-slope for two hundred yards, then the plane of the land tilts left for the next one hundred yards just where a well-hit slice will run downhill into the evergreen rain-forest mixture of rough. Then the fairway is level for another thirty yards to where the raised green is banked against the side of the hill with two small traps at the fore-lip. (I once drove the right-hand trap with a good drive and lots of downhill run, but Morning thought I had paid my caddie to drop the ball there. He always was a hard man to convince.) There is a road about twenty yards above the green, and a graveled path on this side of the road leading directly toward my window. The path forks between the road and the hospital, one fork leading toward the hospital past my window, and the other toward the fifteenth tee off to the right. No one seems to walk toward my window, though.

My nostalgic lingering over the view was not without reason. There had been times when that small golf course had been our only refuge. We would come up when the heat and debaucheries of the plain had clogged our spirits, up to the mountains, to the sun and the afternoon rains. Cool air and solitude, fresh vegetables and virtue, golf and moderation, and the mountains stretching toward the sky. These things had brought peace to us then—but I wondered if they could pacify me now, now that I was alone with my memory, my history, now pinned with a wing I couldn't carry.

Less than three months before, Cagle, Novotny, Morning and I had stood on that very circle of green which so occupied me when I saw it again, stood healthy and laughing as the sun ate the morning mists. And as I thought of them, the sudden life in my veins became quick guilt, and all I had to do to see them again was close my eyes.

Black and white, black and white, stark black and

white. A negative world undeveloped by dawn. A roar of all sounds lashed into one and no single cry can lift its pleading arm above the clamor. Novotny's healthy tan now blasted gray, his fatigues still starched, but he has a crazy black part through his stiff white hair. Cagle, small hairy body dancing in skivvy shorts, jerk, step, jerk, jerk, as blood spurts from his chest. And Joe Morning, Joe Morning, his strong length folding forward in a quick nervous bow as if someone important had just ended his life.

I opened my eyes and they were gone, and they were there, and there was not a thing I could do about it. I slept.

A nurse and a Filipino orderly woke me at ten for a bed-change and a whore's bath. They managed to do it without making me pass out from the pain. The clean sheets were stiff and cool against my back, and the bath had left me feeling clean for a change. I might be clean, but my right leg, after two weeks in a cast, smelled as if it had crawled in there to die. I asked for a barber and, oddly enough, one came from the hospital shop. He cleared away the stubble, trimmed my moustache and gave me a haircut.

Clean, shaven and rested, I refused to remember, and thought life would be wonderful if I could get a drink. In my nightstand drawer were several letters, one from my father with a fifty-dollar money order in it. I just glanced at the letter, catching a few lines here and there, something about his understanding that I wouldn't have any money in the hospital. It seemed that some rear-guard orderly in Cherbourg had stolen his money when he had come back from Bastogne with pneumonia in December of '44. Whatever his reason, Thank God, I thought, because I didn't have any money.

Lt. Light cashed it for me on her lunch hour, then

I collared the orderly when he came back to pick up my lunch tray. He squirmed and complained a bit, then became so businesslike that I knew this was a regular business. I gave him enough scrip for a black-market fifth of Dewar's, and promised him another five when he brought it to my window that evening.

With nothing to do all afternoon except wait for that magic bottle, I read my mail. One was from my ex-wife, and opened with a small chapter on how nice it was that we were able to be friends even after our divorce—which wasn't quite true, but it sounded nice when she told her friends. Then she chatted about all the fine work she was *involved* in among the Negro population of Mississippi. She spoke of Mississippi as if it were Madagascar, but I knew that in spite of the fashionable nature of her "idealistic commitment" as she called it, she was really a good-hearted woman in the best sense of the word, and most of the time I was sorry that she had left me. She also managed to hope that I wouldn't get mixed up in that mess in Vietnam, and quoted the objections of a brilliant and dedicated young man she worked under. I wasn't quite so sorry after all. She had been writing me for almost two years now, telling me how she suffered for my bitterness and bias, but she wasn't about to give up, even if I never answered. In a drunk moment some months before, I had dropped her a postcard with one word on it, "Nigger-lover," but I had forgotten to address it. I often wondered who received it; it was a photo of a Negrito pygmy.

My father's letter was the usual thing: it had or hadn't rained, and the ranch was or wasn't doing well; one of my younger brothers had done something to make him wonder why a man bothered to continue the family name (this time Claude, the youngest, had tried to ride a Brahma bull in a rodeo, and had been hooked in the mouth before he got out of the chute, and the old man had to cough up two hundred bucks for a dental bill, and that reminded him, parenthetically, of my first and last, ha, attempt at the bulls, when that bastard bull, named Sara Lou for some obscene reason, had eaten my lunch at the Tilden rodeo, cracked half a dozen ribs, broke my left arm, and left me with a four inch half-moon memento on my left cheek, and goddamn hadn't that been funny); he wished I would get out of the Army because it was a shame to waste my education, but a man had to do what he wanted or never be happy, and the Army wasn't really so bad, or he didn't remember it being so. The last thing he mentioned (last so I wouldn't think I had caused him any grief or worry) was the telegram and letter about me being hurt. It took a while, but I finally understood that he thought I had been injured in an aircraft accident.

An aircraft accident, they were calling it. Well maybe it was. Surely the good old Army brass couldn't admit that a little bitty batch of Vietcong had dropped in on the 721st Communication Security Detachment and its three-hundred-thousand-dollars worth of equipment on our first night of operation; dropped in and knocked hell out of us. Not even the American Congress was supposed to know we were in Vietnam, so how could the VC know? I didn't know then how many casualties the 721st had taken, but I had seen enough to know that it had been bad. A plane crash. Shit.

And here I was, shot in the arm and leg by an American first lieutenant three hours after the attack was over. I hadn't been angry yet, partly because I had done a foolish thing, and partly because I had not thought about it. There were others dead, and I counted myself lucky to be alive, fortunate enough not to bitch about the conditions of being alive. But anger is easier than reflection, so I paced the afternoon remembering every stupid officer I had ever known, and learned to hate them all over again.

After evening chow Ramon and I handled our transaction at the window. I had a snort, then hid the bottle under my pillow, and tried to sleep until taps. I, fool that I was, wanted a peaceful drink without any nosy nurses bothering me.

It must have been three o'clock before I awoke. My leg hurt, my head ached, the scabs on my side itched and my mouth tasted like the inside of a tennis shoe. Like a wounded crab I managed to pour a large amount of tepid water on my nightstand and a small swallow in the glass which I drank without drowning. Now was the big moment, the drink I had been waiting for all day. Mellow Scotch to sooth an angry soul. It tasted like shit. Strange how that taste cuts through romantic notions.

I choked on the first swallow and spit half of it on my bedclothes. Three more fast sips, then I rested, waiting for a little numbness. I wondered why I objected to being drugged with drugs, but not with alcohol. Matter of middle-class taste, I supposed. Another sip, then a swallow, then a real man-sized drink. It didn't make any difference; I still gagged each time. I rested again.

A delicate chill had touched the air, and it seemed too heavy and damp for the mountains. Slight rustlings and tiny chirps like drowsy questions peeped through my window from the two pines. Past the trees a misty fog slept in the hollows, solid and white under the moon, gauzy and glistening beneath the street lamps. I searched the drifting mist, waiting for the Scotch to nudge me into that magic world outside my window, but I quickly began to feel silly:

like a midnight rendezvous that doesn't come off, and by one o'clock you are tired, cold and wish to hell you had never come, and hate the day you met her. And as I thought of a woman, supposing one to be just what I needed, I wondered what a climax in traction might be like. In my shape? Why not? Anything Fredrick Henry can do, I can do better. But then she came, the one I had been waiting for. Pale and delightfully breathless, a virgin reborn in the cobweb tangle of moon in her hair, her mouth opening like a flower under mine. . . . As if by magic I was drunk, the cold air bubbling in my nose, the hot kiss of Scotch in my belly.

For fifteen minutes I laid waste to those fifteen hundred famous virgins whoever they were. Within the next five minutes I banished evil from the house of man, smashing mine enemies with my virtuously white right claw. I shot a little more time trying to say "white right claw." I had had love, virtue and honor, so I tried wine again, and drank seriously for a while. But it all amounted to—within half an hour I was drunk and bored, securely immobilized, without a soul to talk to me, to see me, or even pity me. Just me, alone in the dark, with half a bottle left and too many hours until dawn. But even boredom lacked constancy. My mind ranged the wide world of all incoherencies. I was grief-stricken and appalled by my survival; then certain that it was only my due as the fittest. There was much guilt, then bountiful thanks, for the death of Joe Morning.

All things are possible on dark mornings, and by the time dawn revealed the troubled corners of my room, I hated, hated Lt. Dottlinger, who I had never liked anyway, and then the bastard shot me . . . well. I dug a pen from the nightstand drawer and signed my own cast, scrawled FUCK YOU exactly over the hole in my thigh. I wanted to write SLUTFINGER, as Dottlinger was known in the 721st, but was too tired.

Dawn is one thing, daylight another: I had several drinks during the difference. Sleepy groans announced the new day in the wards. All ambulatory patients were being awakened to make their beds and sweep and buff under them. If any managed a hundred-and-one degrees or a traction cast, they could sleep ten minutes longer. I thought this no way to treat sick men, so transferred hates from Dottlinger to the hospital. I was mad. (I say mad, in the literal sense, neither to excuse nor to account for the following adventure.)

Lt. Hewitt came in. Poor Lt. Hewitt carrying her lack of flesh. She was always bright and cheery, her uniform so starched and white it glittered like an angel's wing, her smile all teeth and well-brushed gums, as if to say, "Look at me! I don't care that I'm ugly and skinny. Oh, see how well I'm holding up! See!"

"Good morning, Sgt. Krummel," she sang as only she could. "And how are we this fine morning?" She held the thermometer out like a stick of candy. As I tried to answer her, she stabbed me under the tongue, and crowed, "There we are!"

"Where?" I mumbled.

"Now who's autograph is that?" she asked as she saw my sign. "Now, that's not very nice, Sgt. Krummel," she said, stiffening her back and propping her fist on what passed for her hip. "Just what is it?"

I spit the thermometer at her and answered, "A valentine?"

She was not amused.

"A proposal?" I offered. Her fist skied off her hip. Probably not angry before, she certainly was now,

thinking I was making fun of her. "Sure," I hurriedly
said, trying to make it all into a joke, "The closer to
the meat, the sweeter is the bone. Leap in here and
we'll make the beast with two backs." I didn't think
her father would mind. I laughed. I should not have.

"You son of a bitch! You smart-ass son of a bitch!"
she screamed, then punched me right in the nose.
With her fist like a large, bony knuckle. My nose
started bleeding and that, for some sanitary reason,
made her even angrier. She hit me again. On the
nose. She must have smelled the liquor because she
stepped back and accused me, "You've been drinking. You're drunk, aren't you? Aren't you?" Her voice
screeched like chalk on a blackboard and made my
teeth ache.

"A man's gotta have a little fun in this shithole."
The blood had dripped through my moustache into
my mouth, so I spit on the other side of the bed.
Bones hit me again. In the eye.

"Hey, will you cut that crap out?" I asked.

She hit me on the nose again. I debated hitting
her (one of my ancestors, so it was told, had once hit
a woman, but she had had a knife after him), so I
decided not to. I spit a mouthful of blood on her pure
skirt. It splattered the white cloth like dark sin,
and I could not have hit her hard enough to make
her jump back the way she did. A dirty trick, I
admit, but better than hitting her. Also easier.

"You've ruined my uniform!" she shrieked. "You'll
be sorry! You'll pay for that! And this too!"

I reached under my pillow and had a drink on
that.

"Don't you throw that bottle at me! Don't you
dare."

God knows I wouldn't have. No telling what she
would have done to me.

"Get out of here, you silly bitch. Get out and let me die in peace."

"Don't you threaten me!"

"Ah, shit . . . Hawww!" I shouted, then threw the bottle in the opposite corner. She screeched and ran away like a wounded goat.

It was so quiet after she left that I could hear an occasional early golfer driving off the fifteenth tee and snatches of conversation and laughter from the fairways. The morning seemed fresh and bright, the air clean, and I wished I were playing golf out there instead of hell in bed. Then I was sorry I had thrown the bottle away because I wanted another drink. The one I'd had was working like magic in my stomach; better than coffee or food, it had awakened me.

Then Sgt. Larkin, the male nurse, rushed in, pushing a rattling tray of hypos. He was a short, stocky, hairy man who tried to give the impression he had seen everything. But he had not seen me.

"Okay, son," he said, "Take it easy. Everything's going to be all right." He advanced, needle held like a knife in his hand, and reached for my unbroken arm. "This'll make everything all right."

"Then you take it. Keep off, man." I jerked my arm away.

"Okay, buddy, let's stop with the games." He had a low level of patience. He tried to make his voice cold and military; but I didn't give a shit for that now.

"Butt out, Larkin. Get that damned needle away."

He reached again, and I slapped the needle out of his hand. The swinging of my arm released something in my blood, something hot and clean. It hardened into a calm, mean thing, clear and clean now, and I liked it.

"Okay, bud, we're through with the games now," he said, preparing another dose. "I don't want to break your other arm, but you're gonna get this one way or the other."

"Don't talk so much, tough man. Get on with it." I felt a smile like a dare on my face. Larkin hesitated, then shook his head as if wondering what there was to be afraid of. I caught him with a stiff thumb in the windpipe as he leaned over the bed. Not too hard. Not too easy either.

He staggered backwards, his hands pleading at this throat, his eyes praying to me, then crashed into his tray. It danced drunkenly away on two legs, bounced off the wall, then swayed, throwing its glittering mad burden across the floor, then rolled slowly back towards Larkin. He gurgled and moaned, tossing.

"Don't fuck with the Phantom," I said, and he heard me before he passed out. The spasm in his larynx relaxed, and his breathing started again. But I didn't pay too much attention. Christ was a carpenter; he could afford to forgive his enemies; I'm a warrior, and can't.

It was quiet again, and I rested, testing the air with my bleeding nose. I pitied Bones for a moment, wondering how I might apologize. But kindness never really repays cruelty, I thought, Let her hate me. That might be the kindest thing of all. But then I laughed as I wondered what poor soul might rattle Bones together some day. "What a mess," I whispered. "What a silly mess." I was sure that somehow this was all Morning's fault. Maybe the bastard was going to haunt me. I might have offered his ghost a drink of blood or Scotch, whatever its preference, but the Air Policeman Bones had called came in.

He was so tall and strong, his face nearly all jaw under the shadow of his cap. His mouth was compressed into a thin, unbent line, and he stood as if he might challenge the gods of war themselves; but he was a soldier, not a warrior. All show and slow to boot.

"All right," he said, sharply. "What seems to be the trouble here." He had glanced at Larkin and the scattering of glass with a look which said "inoperative" and dismissed them from his mind. "You there! What's going on here?" He addressed an imaginary point where my head would have been if I could have stood.

"Me? Geez, I don't know. I just work here."

"You, fellow."

"Say, sonny, ya'll tilt that there sombrero back jest a scrunch so's Ah cain sees ya'll's eyeballs. Ain't likely Ah'd talk with a man, if'n Ah cain't sees his eyeballs."

He snapped to attention. "Cut the lip, huh."

"You taking me in, airman?"

"No," he answered in all seriousness. "Just going to hold your arm while they stick a needle in it. I've handled you nut-house cases before."

"Oh, really. Well, let me show you something before you start handling this nut-house case," I said, holding up my left hand. "See that hand, sonny. That's a real mean hand. Registered with the police in seven states as a dangerous weapon. See those calluses on the side there, and on the fingertips. That's a killer's hand, son. You'd best watch it."

"Ha, ha. You been seeing too many movies, fellow."

"Perhaps, perhaps so, young man. That may well be the case. But the visualization of a dream certainly does not alter the essence of its reality; it enhances the reality."

"You really are crazy, aren't you? I guess you look sort of crazy."

Ah ha, I thought, a nonbeliever, a discounter of

dreams. And a warrior must dream. "I'm warning you, watch that hand."

"You better stop going to those movies. You're liable to get hurt," he chuckled as the doctor entered, brisk, impatient, another blessing in hand.

"Away! foul son of Priam or be split asunder," I shouted, waving my arm. "And the smoke of your pyre will trample the night like the hot, raging breaths of a stallion and the flames lick the sky like the hounds at his flanks."

"Jesus," the doctor said.

The AP laughed and stepped to the side of the bed. "Okay, sir, I'll handle this crazy bastard," he said, smiling just enough to bend the line of his mouth. I sneered, bunched my arm on my chest. He reached for it, then hesitated and shook his head like Larkin, then reached again.

But it wasn't there. It had sped like a spear into that soft spot below the sternum, in, in to the knot of nerves, and quivered there. His eyes opened in the shadow of his visor. I had only intended a poke, a tap to let him know that I could, but my arm raised a soul of its own and spoke to something in mine. Again, swifter than thought, strengthened with a short grunt of nervous energy, my hand rejoined the battle. The AP's mouth opened, though not in laughter, and the upper half of his body tilted over the bed. I raised the cast-bound arm, serious now, and swung, remembering a Paiute ghost dancer granted invulnerability by Wovoka, a Bulgarian under Krum seeking a Byzantine skull for his drinking cup, remembering every violent image dredged from the limitless memory of man, and the ghosts lent me strength. I took him on the side of the head above the ear. His cap flew away; his head and shoulder crammed against the wall, shattering plaster. He shivered in a spasmodic dance, then his eyeballs, visible now, rolled, and he joined Larkin on the floor.

I, purged, lay back to ease my ragged breath. Then the pain came from my leg, twisted and sucked my soul back into the void, and I went thankfully away.

There was a bird, a woodpecker, standing on my head, pecking my nose. I clenched my eyes and rolled my head, but he kept up that incessant pecking. Each one came as a bright flash, tapping me out of the peaceful darkness. Goddamned bird. He wouldn't get off my nose. He pecked exactly where it had been broken once, right in the tenderest spot. I strained to get my hands on him, but they would not move. Then a phrase from a bad Tennyson sonnet jumped into my head, something about a "still-recurring gnat." But it wasn't a gnat, it was a vulture. . . . Then I woke.

Another Air Policeman, same size, etc., leaned over me, hitting the bridge of my nose at perfectly regular intervals with his billy, very light blows, only slightly heavier than a raindrop. He was good. No matter which way I turned my head, his baton was waiting there to keep up the beat. Tap! Tip!—ha, you Tap! missed Tap! that one. Tap! But only that one. Jesus, I thought, this is getting damn repetitious. I pictured an unending line of APs waiting outside the room. Surely twelve trials would be enough, I laughed to myself, But will this ever stop? Does a wave ask the circle of the sea for the shore? I laughed. Straps held my arms and I moaned. But the beat still went on. With a chant now, to my open eyes, "Tough guy. Tough guy. Tough guy." I snarled at him, a growl, a lion harassed by the beaters: "Yaaaawwwwllll!"

The cadence stopped blinding my eyes, and I saw

that he had stepped back. He was older, tougher than the other one, and informed me in a quiet voice how happy he would be when I recovered from my injuries, probably self-inflicted, and I could come visit his friends and he in their stockade. I snarled again, snapped like a hungry hound. He leaned solicitously over me, smiled clean teeth, and pleasantly intoned, "Tough guy." His baton captured my attention as he rapped me gently in the crotch, almost tenderly. Then a bit harder, and the ripe, spreading pain and nausea began to flow, in, then out, leaving a great hollowness in my guts.

"One more time," he murmured.

Doctor Gallard came later, came with his portable X-ray and his concern.

"How's the leg?" he asked as the technicians laid sheets of lead covering on my chest. He asked only about the leg. "I came as soon as I heard . . . about the incident. You didn't hurt that leg, did you? Surely hate to go back in there."

"I don't know."

"Why is your nose bleeding?"

"Lt. Hewitt popped me one this morning when I made what she called advances toward her."

"It shouldn't still be bleeding."

"I sneezed."

Gallard glanced at the AP, then back at me as if to say I probably deserved worse than I had received. "Go ask the nurse for some ice and a cloth, corporal."

"I'm supposed to guard him, sir," he said, nodding at me. Like all warders, caged men frightened him more than free ones.

"I think I can prevent him from biting me, corporal. Go on."

"I don't know, sir. He's a mean one, he is." He chuckled.

"Don't mock your betters," I said to him, "lest they notice you."

"You guys never learn, do you?" He stepped toward the bed.

"The ice, corporal."

"Yes, sir."

Gallard did not speak while the AP was gone, and made him wait outside when he came back. "You feel it's your right to rape and pillage?" he asked, cradling the back of my neck with the ice.

"Achilles called rear-guard soldiers wine sacks with dogs' eyes and deers' hearts."

"So what? You haven't seen enough war to even know what it's about, and yet here you are raising more hell than a regiment of Marines."

"I knew, now I know. Besides, small things lead to bigger ones without anyone's help. Acorns and oaks and all that crap. I wanted a drink. This came of only that. Takes two to make war. Things grow in this crazy world."

"Of course," he said, digging his hands into his hair as if searching for something very small and incredibly important. "So?"

"Not an excuse. Just what happened, that's all. It was my fault, but I'm not going to say I'm sorry, or say I won't do it again. I want to be left alone, and I will manage to be left alone."

"Victim of an undeclared war, huh? Fighter for right and humanity? Killer of small, hungry men."

"I was raised for a warrior. What else would you have me do?"

"That's your problem, not mine."

But you want it to be, I thought, And it will.

He finished with his business and went away.

I sang softly into the afternoon, sang to the green grass and sky, to the bright, burning haze of the sun, "Joe Morning, Joe Morning, where have we come?"

1

BASE

"This is a strange outfit, Sgt. Krummel," 1/Sgt. Tetrick said on that morning I first arrived in the Philippines in the late summer of 1962. "Unusual. Different. We're a small outfit, less than seventy men. It really ought to be good duty, but somehow it ain't. The work's too easy, and these kids get bored, and when they're not bored, they're pissed off. Their bowels jam up or run like crazy because of the work schedule, and their sleep is always screwed up." Tetrick stood and shuffled his way over to the trick schedules. His feet were still tender from a case of jungle-rot he caught in Burma during the war. He was careful never to put a foot down any harder than necessary. He explained that the 721st Communications Security Detachment had only an Operations Section and a small Headquarters Section of cooks and clerks since most of the administration and personnel work was handled on Okinawa. The men in Operations, "Ops," were divided into four tricks of ten men. Each trick worked six days, 0700 to 1600, then had a seventy-two hour break; six swings, 1600 to 2400, then a forty-eight hour break; and then six mids and another seventy-two hour break.

"Your trick is on break now," he said, "and they're all in Town—that's what they call Angeles—drinking and whoring and anything else they can think of to get in trouble. Town is bad. Three-fourths of it is off-limits forever, two-thirds of it after 1800, and all of it after 2400. But will they be back before curfew? Shit, no. They got to run and hide from the APs and laugh about how much fun it is. And if they can get knived by a *calesa* driver or run over by a jeepny or drown in a sewer for all I know—or care." He shrugged, sighed, then walked back to his desk and continued, "But somehow all the bastards will get back in one piece just in time to wash off the crud, shave, brush their teeth maybe, and get to the three-quarter before it leaves for the Ops Building." He shook his head and folded his long arms, then stared at the rain beyond the half-screened passageway. "It rains all the goddamned time, too."

1/Sgt. Tetrick, ex-marauder, twenty-two years service—the last twelve as a first-shirt—was of medium height, but because of his heavy, sloping shoulders and long arms, seemed much shorter. A little hair adorned his head, a gratuitous bit of sun-bleached fuzz circling from ear to ear and no more. This too was another small reminder of Burma, but he wore his baldness as if it were dictated by military expediency. A golf tan, his single vice, didn't cover the rich ocher-yellow malaria stain on his skin.

"But they're a good bunch, damnit," he said quickly, out of his reverie as if the distant bugle he heard had stopped. "And it's our job to keep them out of the stockade—damned Air Force calls it the Confinement Facility—and the hospital so they can do their work." He glanced back at the rain and shook his shining head again. "You just can't run an Army outfit on an air base anyway. Damned airmen don't blouse their boots and wear baseball caps and bus-driver uniforms. Shit." He shuffled behind his desk. "You were in an infantry outfit on your last hitch?" he asked, already knowing the answer.

"Six years ago."

"Long time to stay out. How come you came back in?"

"Like you said: it's a long time."

He dropped it. "Don't expect this to be like a line outfit. Not at all."

"I didn't."

"I don't know what it is," he said, "but it ain't soldiering."

Tetrick continued explaining the 721st Com Sec Det as he deftly handled my paperwork. His voice was roughly concerned, even irritated, but still tender as he spoke of the outfit; like a Nebraska farmer whose four grown sons had left the land for the cement and money of the city, leaving only his swollen hands to toil in the land of *his* father: he could not understand, but his dust-thickened voice kept whispering, "God love 'em. God love 'em." The Army had not issued Tetrick a wife, as the saying goes, but it had these sons. And me too, for that matter. Everything I needed from the supply room— bunk, mattress, field gear—had already been carried to my quarters on the second floor. Tetrick apologized for not having any regular NCO quarters, then added that he liked for his trick chiefs to bunk with the men. I was pleasantly surprised when I was assigned a houseboy, a young Filipino who, for five pesos a week, would clean my quarters, take care of my laundry and shine my boots, etc. Enlisted men also were allowed houseboys and even the KP was pulled by Filipino workers. It all seemed very British, darkly faithful Indian batman and all that, but the houseboys were all hard-core finger-popping black-marketeers, already more Western than Oriental. Tetrick then took me in to meet the company commander, Capt. Harry Saunders, and the executive officer, Lt. Dottlinger. The lieutenant merely grunted and squeezed my hand, giving me the impression that he didn't care for me before he met me. It took longer to meet Capt. Saunders.

Capt. Harry, as he liked to be called, came from Brunswick, Georgia, and his lifetime ambition was to win a medal of some, of any, sort, then retire to home and become a Republican. All this, and the additional "u" in his name, was to prove that he was more than a redneck kid who had gone to college on a football scholarship, arriving with only a single pair of shoes, tennis shoes at that. In spite of all his posturing, he was a happy, shambling bear of a man whose only real fault lay in the unsophisticated nature of his dreams. He had a tendency to say "men" in all capital letters, but he had an easy, open-armed way and a smile which said he truly loved everyone in the world. Except his wife. And Lt. Dottlinger. Capt. Harry seemed pleased with me, mainly because I was both a Southerner and a "collegeman."

"A master's degree, huh?" he said several times. "How about that, Sgt. Tetrick? How about that? We damn well need more NCOs with a college background in this outfit. They seem to get along better with the men. What's it in?"

"Sir?"

"Your degree."

"Soviet Studies, sir."

"Well, how about that? I'll bet you're the only sergeant in the whole Army with a master's degree in Russian . . . what was that? History?

"Yes, sir."

Capt. Harry went on and on about the degree until I wished that I had not listed the thing on my 201 file. There was a painful irony in being faced with my own vanity, in being asked why, with the degree, I had reenlisted. "A man's wife leaves him for the civil-rights movement, for an ideal not another man, then it is certainly no wonder whatever he does," I often told myself. But no one else. No, nor Capt. Harry when he asked that day.

I accepted their good luck wishes, and left, again asking "Why?" as I had for the two months of basic and the six months at Fort Carlton. But I had no answer, and perhaps wanted no answer. I had the rain and the random barracks noise and time . . . time clicking past like a pale young whore popping her gum behind too bright lips, endlessly unconcerned and unsatisfying, hopelessly desirable.

The 721st resided in a single two-story concrete building. The mess hall, the day room, orderly and supply rooms, and quarters for the First, Supply and Mess Sergeants filled the first floor. The second contained fifty two-man rooms divided by a long hallway. Each room had an outside wall of adjustable aluminum louvers and an inside wall of wooden ones. The rooms were quite large and, except for the usual bareness, were not too military in effect. No metal foot- or wall-lockers

knifed the space. Instead there were two large closets, a gray
metal table with two office chairs, and a three-quarter-bed-size
bunk.

My cot sat next to the adjustable louvers, lengthwise to
catch any breeze. I had never seen one of the new, larger
bunks before. Ordinarily only the Air Force used them. I
dropped my gear on the floor, kicked off my shoes, stripped
out of the heavy green wool uniform I had been shrouded in
for two miserable days on the MATS flight from California,
and then stretched out on the bunk. None of those thin, cotton-
lumpy racks the Army called a mattress, but a thick, foam
rubber one to hold my weary bones. Yep, Sgt. Tetrick, I
thought, scratching one foot with the other, This is a strange
outfit. All I need now is a swimming pool and a spot of sunshine to be a real recruiting-poster ground pounder. Hoping
for some sign of the sun (it had been raining since my flight
arrived), I cranked open one set of louvers. The rain still
fell heavily, but across the street a small building was visible.
I hadn't noticed it when I ran from the jeep to the barracks,
but there it was, my swimming pool. Not exactly mine, but
right across the street, and I could use it anytime. Okay, I
thought, If the sun comes out, I'll just take a goddamned
swim. It didn't, so I unpacked my gear, showered, then slept
through evening chow.

I awoke after sundown. The rain had disappeared into a
mist which gathered in fuzzy balls around the street lights.
My watch had stopped. Across the hall I heard the whirr
and click of a record changer and very faintly the opening
bars of *Bolero*. The hall was empty, quiet and solemn, as if
everyone had gone away. I knocked and entered when a voice
said, "Come in."

A very tan young man in his shorts sat on one of the cots,
resting his back against the wall and a writing pad on his
knees. He had one of those clean muscular bodies in hope
of which ten million little boys eat Wheaties, skin the color
of butterscotch pudding, crystal-white teeth flashing in his
quick grin, and one left leg entirely masked in scar tissue. A
burn, obviously, puckered and crisp-bacon brown scrambled
with rotten off-white. (A bucket of roofing tar had been

dumped on his leg from atop a new supermarket in Laramie, Wyoming one summer.) A magnetic deformity which drew a curious eye, a lingering look, perhaps even a poke with an inquiring finger to see if, like a burnt marshmallow, the outside would crumble and reveal a soft, sticky white core. The rest of his body seemed so perfect as if to compensate for that leg.

"Seven-thirty," he said cheerfully when I asked for the time. He paused. "You Sgt. Darly's replacement?" I nodded. He paused again, then did a good thing: he stood up, reached out a hand, and said, "Tom Novotny."

"Jake Krummel," I answered, though "Jake" sounded odd in my mouth after so many years of being "Slag." Never Jake, but always Slag, I no longer had the self-confidence or, more likely, conceit, to introduce myself by that audacious nickname. (All this a waste of time, though. I exposed my real identity the first time I got drunk.)

He offered me a smoke, handling the ritual of the pack and matches as if he had just begun smoking, though he had been for years. I think he realized how odd a cigarette looked in his healthy face. He and I sat on opposite bunks, exchanging the amenities of strangers to the increasing volume of the music.

Novotny reached to the only odd piece of furniture in the room, a chest-high mahogany cabinet, and eased the volumn down. The cabinet was rich Filipino mahogany, with carved jungle scenes on every flat surface which, when examined very closely, revealed a large number of couples, triples and daisy-chains in various stages, states and forms of—intercourse is not strong enough; fucking too crude for the artistry of the carving; copulation too limited; so I choose—cohabitation, for the figures did forever live in the wood. I had to laugh: a sexual stereo system able to handle LPs, 45's and 78's, tapes, AM-FM radio and Freudian nightmares.

"Hey, is this setup yours?" I asked.

"Naw. Belongs to Morning. Matter of fact, this isn't even my room. I just come here to write letters to my girl," Tom said. "She likes classical music."

A nice thought, I mused as I rubbed the wood. Three shelves above were filled with paperback books, perhaps arranged too neatly, too organized by subject and author. Dostoevski, of course, but no Chekhov or Tolstoy. Sartre, but no Camus. Just a shade off-center of what I would have chosen. Too French, too black, and too avant-garde for my tastes, the books still made me want to talk to their owner.

"What's this guy's name?"

"Morning. Joe Morning."

"He on my trick?"

"Yeah."

"Seems to read a lot."

"Yeah. Says he writes poetry too, but I haven't seen any of it. He spends too much time in Town to do much of anything else."

"Say, are you on my trick?"

"Sure."

"Tetrick said you all were in Town."

"Didn't go. Go to Town 'cause I'm tired of base. Sometimes I stay on base 'cause I'm tired of Town. Ain't new anymore. Only so many ways a man can get laid."

"I wonder," I said, touching a wooden maiden who clutched a small and hairy object to her crotch which I assumed to be a monkey, "after seeing this thing. There may be something new under the covers." We chuckled together in that easy way which told both of us we would be friends.

It pleased me that Novotny did not seem ill at ease or in any way treat me as a sergeant, and at the same time we understood that the moment would come when I would have to tell him to do something or other which he did not want to do. If he respected me, he would do it and not, as others would, dislike me for the accidents of time and place which made me his sergeant. The months at Fort Carlton in training school had been unpleasant because I had been a barracks sergeant, a bad barracks sergeant, too easy at first, then too hard later when the man tried to take advantage of me. I had no business being a sergeant anyway. I was just a guy who had stayed in the reserves for the hell of it and the money (and maybe because I hoped I wouldn't miss the next war as I had the Korean one). That lack of experience, and my attempts to be intellectual about something which isn't, caused me much trouble. There is no rationale about orders: they have to be given and taken, but never can make much sense if thought about. Given a choice, I would have preferred to forge my tiny link on the chain of command out of mutual understanding of and respect for the necessity and value of discipline, but men who defied God certainly were not going to bow to any abstract discipline. But oddly enough, my foolishness was going to work in the 721st because the men were good. Not all, I guess, but enough. Like Novotny: good men whatever their educational or personal differences.

As our conversation faltered, I asked Tom about a place to eat on base.

"Say the food is okay at the NCO Club," he said, giving me an out if I wanted it.

"No club tonight."

"Pretty fair steaks at the Kelly Restaurant."

"Where's that?"

"I'm going up, if you want to come along."

"Sure. What about your letter? I'll wait if you want to finish it."

"Fuck it," he laughed. "She'll marry some prick before I get stateside anyway. Get ready."

As we walked down the hall to the central stairwell to call a cab, I was again struck by the quiet, the sense of desertion, but as I moved between those rooms, those walls which could not hold even a breeze, I realized they provided an unusual privacy for enlisted men. People were behind those walls—signaled by a muffled laugh or cough, a book falling from sleepy hands, a radio humming, a bunk groaning under a restless sleeper—privately behind them. I could not remember a single moment during my first hitch of being alone in the barracks, not even in the latrines.

"You people live good," I said.

"Ain't home," Tom said, turning into the stairwell.

The Kelly Restaurant was exactly what you would expect on a military installation: the second-best eating place in any small American town where the Baptists and Methodists gather to exchange weather complaints, clothing compliments and pessimism, a warehouse of scratched and chipped formica and cracking plastic, except the Kelly Restaurant served Japanese beer in liter bottles.

"The steaks were okay," I said as Tom and I were on our fourth or fifth bottle, "but the waiters were surly as hell."

"Fuckers," he said, grinning so hard his cheeks bunched into tight little balls of leather. "Real shits. Don't tip 'em, they pick your pocket on the way out." He raised the tall green bottle. "Banzai!" We drank to that. "Crazy little Japs," he said, "Tried to win the war." He shook his head without shaking his grin at all. "If they'd a give this stuff away free, they could a walked on the drunks from San Francisco to Cincinnati. Wouldn't be no wars if people drink more."

"Just be sloppier. Huh," I said as an airman second and his date strolled past our table, "That wouldn't be a bit sloppy." The airman turned around, but I smiled at him, and he turned back around.

"Leech bitch," Novotny said.

"Who?"

"Fucking leech. Dependent child. Sixteen years old and already given the clap to thirty-seven guys."

"You know her?"

"Comes to the pool all the time to make us holler. Ain't hollerin' yet. Only airmen mess with leeches. Below our principles."

"Might be all right."

Novotny straightened up, dropped his grin, and very solemnly said, "Man might as well be a lifer as screw a leech." He paused, concerned, "You ain't no lifer, are you?"

"Lifer?"

"Taking twenty?"

"Shit, I don't know. . . ."

"What the hell you doing back in the Army anyway?"

"Shit, I don't know. After my wife left me, I. . . ."

"Woman trouble. Knew it," he interrupted. "Soon as I laid eyes on you, knew it. Woman trouble. You know I'm the only guy been here long as I have hasn't got a Dear John. Only one left. Seen 'em all go down. Woman trouble. Spot it a mile away." He shook his head. "What you need is a seventy-five cent love affair, fellow."

"Is it that cheap? I don't have a pass yet, anyway." All new personnel had to be on base fifteen days before they were allowed a pass.

"No, no. This's different. Over at the Airman's Club. Six bits. No nookie, just true love and dancing. Be my guest."

We settled the check, then walked through a drifting mist toward the barn-like tin building which housed the Airman's Club. Our voices and laughter rang in the cool, damp night, clear and echoing along the glittering black streets. The soft halos of the street lights wavered in easy breezes and jeeps and trucks hissed politely past. I remembered, remembered those Friday nights in Seattle, Ell and I wandering home from weekly hamburgers and beer at a neighborhood bar; madcap rainy evenings that seemed to dance to our laughter, alone and together, untroubled as never before or again, wet and cold and happy as when we were children. And later tipsy and steaming under the shower, slick and soapy, and we could never wait, never.

Novotny danced and furiously danced with his seventy-five-cent-love-affair until I expected his bad leg to fly off and tumble right up to the bandstand, felling potted palms as it went; but it seemed as able as his other. Able enough to play football, he explained, and added that the season would start soon and anyone who wanted to play could go over to the Agency outfit and sign up. The three Army units—Agency, ACAN and the 721st—had one team among them.

"We really tear up airmen," Novotny said, sitting down while his girl caught her breath—my affair had long since left me to my sullen silence. Novotny had that same strained grin again, as if he did not intend to wait for the season. "I hate this fucking place, but we get a good club like last year—won the base championship—and it's okay. Football season goes real quick, bam bam bam, then six more months and I'm going home. Back to the ZI, the Zone of Interior, the Land of the Big PX, multicolored staff cars and concrete barrios. No more PI for this GI. I'm going civilian-side."

All the way back to the barracks he explained why I too would soon adhere to the motto, IHTFP or I Hate This Fucking Place. At the time I wondered what there was to hate, though I later understood that it was the time itself, the slow, inexorable murder of the time, the boredom of escape, the pure nihilism of the peace-time soldier, suffering not only the contradiction of terms "peace" and "soldier" but that of "time" too. But I didn't hear what Novotny was saying then: I had my own enemy, blacker and vaster than time—memory, or history as it is popularly called. I named it my enemy then, hating it as the Roman soldier who pierced Christ's side must have hated Him. Salvation is a hateful thing: surely the memory of man proves that.

No, I didn't hear the pain in Novotny's voice, the grinding agony of having no meaning. I fell asleep, thinking, Surely soldiers gripe in Heaven . . . no one understands the reward for virtue . . . only the penalty for guilt. Then I dropped away to visions of a scarred leg dancing alone in the desert, a vast stone leg pursued by a girl-child, pretty and pink, but when she caught it, her hands rotted black and fell away as my father's voice tolled, "My name is Ozymandias, king of despair: / Look on my works, ye warrior and king." (I always dream what I've read, though changed in my mind as if I'd written it. A mighty conceit.)

Later that night I dreamed of home, a cool spring morning, soft and fresh. As I walked to my car, the sweet air tickled my face and sprinkled goose-bumps with a quick shiver among the sun-white hair of my arms. The chill, pleasant and deep, touched with excitement, caused me to pee in the thick grass where the washing machine emptied. It was right, the sky open and blue and the long run of the pasture glistening clean and dark green with the dew, and the patch of grass curled and thick, and all this mine, and the sky and the fields and the grass, all mine, and me, young and king in the heart of her.

The stream, golden arch into the tight grass, sparkled and slowly rolled, then I too, like a wisp, toward the dark tangled hairs flew. As I drifted, the grass bore my Ell, my first, naked and green in the sudden night, arms and shining legs lifted. Then finished, easily I rested in her, lovers on the patchwork fiber of my back seat, my car half-hidden in a low brush thicket, and I lost in her, in the ease and softness of her under the wide sky of night, my Ell, my fallen breath cupped in the curve of her neck. But quickly she whispered of things wet, warm, and dangerous, of spermy traps, and I leaped away to clutch the condom bloated with the tinkling afterthought of a pee. The thin walls burst, flooded the shame of my waste across the moonlight plain of our loins. I cried in guilt for she saw . . . and woke crying in fear of the loneliness too she must have seen. *Else why she should love me?* I asked half-dreaming as I crawled from the damp bed.

I stripped the bunk, flipped the mattress, and wandered to the latrine to shower. Back in the room I smoked, leaning against the screen. *I wonder if John Wayne ever peed the bed?* The stretch of a grin on my face only eased the mood for a second.

Ah, you crazy bastard, Krummel. What are you doing here? *Came to laugh. You dream of being a warrior? Seems to me you pee the bed and cry for yourself.* What else should I do? *You could have been anything?* I wanted to be everything. I couldn't decide. I always got to places too late. *Now you've learned the worth of a limited choice.* No, I just made the wrong ones. *So now you wait for a war like a fool? Why not start your own? You know your history. You need nothing else.* Whatever I say, you'll say I'm just afraid, which I am. I can only be what I am. *And your history, your memory as you call it, dictates what you must be?* Yes. *You wandering purposeless fool, out of time and place, remembering wars that never happened, heroes that never died much less lived.* I couldn't stop dreaming of a better time, of honor and heroism and virtue. Where else can I find them? They told me that is where they were, cast in the fires of battle. Maybe they're right in some way they don't understand. *Maybe you're a fool?* Maybe.

I watched the rain suck at the curling blue smoke, the mourner's rain, chokingly heavy and black, and the glittering drops plummet to earth, to earth and who knows how much farther.

The next morning Sgt. Tetrick gave me a guided tour and lecture on Clark Air Force Base, Philippines. Clark Air Force Base lies on the central Luzon plain in the province of Pam-

panga near the city of Angeles. It is bordered on the west by
the Bambam river which skirts a heavily jungled range of hills
and on the east by the Manila-Baguio highway. Clark is one of
the largest bases in the Far East. It provides runways and
support facilities for countless jet fighters and bombers which
guard Southeast Asia against China, or for American business
interests, or against the Eskimos, depending on your politics
and memory. The base, in its turn, is also guarded. A strong
hurricane-wire fence encloses the entire base. The fence, as
any other important facility of the base, is also closely guarded
by the Air Police, Filipino constabulary and Negrito pygmies.
The APs patrol the perimeter in jeeps and three-quarter-ton
trucks, armed with Browning automatic shotguns, subma-
chine guns, carbines, rifles, pistols, and angry German Shep-
herd police dogs. The APs shoot on sight, usually forgetting
the warning shots, and quite often kill, not only thieves and
infiltrators, but expensive dogs and each other on occasion.
When an AP kills a Filipino intruder, he is quickly court-
martialed, found guilty, fined one dollar, given a carton of his
favorite smokes by an apologetic major, then flown back to the
states on the next flight. The Filipino constabulary, being
indigenous, suffer no such inconvenience. They are merely
required to reimburse the government for each round of ammunition expended that does not find a human target. They
seldom miss; ammunition is expensive. The Negritoes, true
pygmies, live mainly in the hills except for a small group
which resides in cardboard, tin and board shacks near the
back fence. They are famed for their unreasoning love of
Americans, their righteous hatred of Filipinos and Japanese,
and their action against the Imperial Army of Japan during
World War II. Their favorite trick, since they are able to stalk
and hunt quite well, was to quietly remove every other man's
head in a Jap barracks or bivouac at night, placing it on his
chest so that his comrades might find it the next morning.
This usually disabled the whole unit: those who weren't sleeping forever never slept again. In spite of these gruesome
tricks, the Negritoes are jolly little folk in their gray uniforms
and silver badges, bare, dusty feet and bush hair only half
hidden by helmet liners, and faces split by smiles twice too

large for men only four-feet-six. They perform their work in the highest of spirits and with the greatest of efficiency.

However, the base loses approximately $140,000 in theft and pilferage each month. In a single night eighteen hundred iron crosses were lifted from the military cemetery for scrap iron. On another, five two-and-a-half-ton trucks and six jeeps were stolen from a motor pool and driven on boards over that high, well-patrolled fence. Still another time an imaginative thief stole a fireman's uniform, then a fire truck to go with it. He drove the truck out of the station with siren and flashing lights going full blast, raced the five miles to the Main Gate as seven Air Policemen stopped traffic for him.

Tetrick pointed out all these events should have been expected once the Army allowed their personal Air Corps to become something he called the "Air Farce"—unfairly, I'm sure. "Three old ladies with blowed-up rubbers could take this place," he grunted.

If the base, as we agreed, existed only because intelligent thieves were leaving something for next time, the base didn't seem excited about the danger. Conditions were calm, situations normal at the seven swimming pools, the PX shopping center, the Officer's and NCO's and Airman's clubs, the veterinarian's office and the golf course (where every Tuesday and Thursday afternoon Tetrick baked his bald head and managed to get drunk before the sixteenth tee). The residential sections were as cool and unruffled as if they were in Indianapolis and Vietnam on the dark side of the moon. Everywhere was order, lawns just so high, geometrically trimmed hedges and trees, clean sidewalks, uncluttered roadsides. As Tetrick drove me around base, I was reminded of the just completed campus of a mammoth junior college in Southern California. "I don't know what it is," Tetrick said again as we drove toward the Main Gate, "but it ain't soldiering."

About half a mile from the gate, just as I could see the guardhouse through the heat haze, Tetrick swung the jeep left down a side road toward a distant group of large frame buildings. "Central Exchange," he explained. "They keep the scrip there," he said, referring to the Military Payment Certificates, MPC, Scrip, or Funny Money as it was called, which was paid instead of green backs as a courtesy to the Filipino economy. "When what's left of the Huks don't steal it. They got $60,000 three years ago. They'll be back when it runs out." He turned left again about half a mile from the Exchange on a gravel road leading toward a square, windowless building. He parked next to the double hurricane fences with the challenging barbed wire strands leaning out along the tops.

"This it it," Tetrick said as if it were. "Seven hundred twenty-first Communication Security Detachment Temporary Operations Building." He pulled a security badge out of his shirt pocket and gave me a temporary one. At the gate he waved to the guard on the roof of the building, then inserted his badge into a waist high slot in a black box next to the gate. "That checks the badge. If it is right, a light comes on up there and he opens the gate." A buzzer sounded, and Tetrick opened the gate. "The second won't open until the first is locked again." Another buzz and we were in the compound. As usual the grass was just so, the sidewalks bordered in neat, ankle-high hedges, and a yard-boy, a jolly-eyed, bent, old man peeking from a floppy straw hat, leaned on a hoe. I glanced back at the elaborate gate system, at the yard-boy, then at Tetrick.

"Don't let it trouble you," he chuckled. "The girls in Town know more about what we do than we do." He opened the steel door by inserting his badge in another slot, then led me into the electronic murmur of secrecy. Behind me I noticed that the old man had, with polite discretion, turned his back.

I took the ease of the afternoon after Tetrick's tour, swimming and resting in the sun. The pool was mine except for a middle-aged dependent wife sitting on the edge of the pool, three loud children, the golden-fuzzy lifeguard, and two airmen. The woman alternately heaved one massive leg then the other through the water as tiny whirlpools in the chlorine-tinted water sucked vainly at her massive flesh. She sat under the lifeguard stand and chatted with golden-fuzzy. She seemed to be trying to peek up his trunks, and he down her blue suit, though why, I did not dare guess. The children were hitting: each other, the meek waters of the kiddie-pool, me twice with rubber toys, and their mother for attention. At times all three balled at her passive shoulders, yammering and pounding their flesh of flesh. Mrs. Leech would shrug, laugh and shake her brown hair like a starlet, and fling the children away like so many dirty drops of water off an angry dog's back, then turning up to golden-fuzzy again, grin up his skinny leg. The two airmen were quiet. One spent the whole afternoon rubbing iodine and Johnson's baby oil into his already brown-black skin, while the other swam the length of the pool twenty times at an eight beat crawl, rested for five exact minutes, then swam again.

From the towel I communed in the broad open plain, bowing to Mount Arayat, the lifeless volcano squatting like an altar on the level distance, a ruined memory of ancient sacrificial fires, the tip of its cone crumbling into a snaggle-toothed decay as hordes of jungle clamored upward, hand over fist, pulling down the tired slopes. It was told that Huk bandits and headhunters shared the distant giant, secure in his hairy trunk, lost to man and his reckoning of time.

At five it rained for eleven minutes, sudden heavy drops, and at five-thirty the sun disappeared into a deep purple mass of clouds rising soft and curved against a shell-pink sky. I paused to watch the sunset, the purple reaching for black, the pink easing to purple, as I strolled back from the pool, toasted, hungry, tired.

After a silent meal I laid out a uniform, read for a bit, then dozed, awaking to the tickle of laughter, talk and the ringing of bottles. Never having been one to either stuff wax in my ears or tie myself to a mast, I slipped into my trousers and nosed down the hall toward the open door of Novotny's room. As I passed, he called an invitation to me for a beer. I nodded, guessed that I would, and went on to the latrine.

As I entered, I nearly stumbled over someone crawling toward the urinals. He had that odor and slept-in look which I assumed to be Town. In spite of the dirt, the stubble and the glasses, he appeared to be a clean-featured young man of perhaps twenty or twenty-one, handsome in a tall, muscular manner, but his unkempt face hung like a bad smell over his dirty clothes. I offered to help however I could. He stared at me for a moment as if he knew who I was, then looked very bored with me.

"I'm Marduke the Mandrill and I play the mandolin with my mandible, baby, and I'm all right," he said, holding up his right hand to show me the bloody, swollen knuckles. His voice, like his face, did not fit: his words were carefully enunciated, formed like bricks to be used in the construction of a Tower of Philosophy, absolutely undeniable. "Except for my left mandible, man," he continued, examining the right hand under a pursed mouth, "I seem to be limping on it. I'm a cripple, you know, a fucking cripple, and there is no home in the American Army for a cripple crutch or a cripple creek or any other kind of deformity. Sorry about that, man. Suppose I'll just be limping on home now," he finished, crawling under the sinks toward the far end of the latrine, singing, "We shall overcome!"

He seemed happy and harmless (he had a great ability to seem), so I left him alone. As I left, I heard him shout, "Overcome! You've heard of overkill? Well, this is Overcome! Sperm whales of the world, unite! We shall overcome!" Then laughter mixed with the spasmodic gurgle of vomit. Then: "And the angel of the Lord thrust his sickle into the earth, and gathered the vine of the earth, and cast it into the great wine press of God's wrath." I shook my head and walked back to Novotny's room.

If I had any questions as to the stability of the men of my trick after my encounter in the latrine, Novotny's room answered them. They were, to the man, crazy. They called it "going Asiatic." Six or seven drunks—they didn't stand for counting—packed the room like an overcrowded cage of underfed monkeys. They chattered, they laughed and shouted in high, tired voices, they snatched squatty brown bottles of San Miguel beer from a waterproof bag filled with ice and drank them in quick selfish gulps as if afraid they might be stolen before finished. I accepted the offered beer and sat on the bunk next to Novotny.

"There's a drunk crawling around the latrine," I said.

"Don't sweat it. That's Mornin' and he gets like that some-

times. He's our demonstrator and Freedom Fucker." He
snipped off the ends of his words with the tight little grin of
the night before.

"Well, he said he was all right. Except for his left mandible," I said, holding up my right hand.

"I don't give a shit who he calls it," shouted a small fellow
suddenly dancing in front of me. "Don't care at all, just so he
keeps decking them flyboys away. Deck 'em away, away!" he
said, slamming a fist into his other hand, ignoring the beer he
held. Foam sparkled in his heavy black eyebrows and beer ran
down his cheeks. "Saved me from that airman, he did. Swept
him off my back like a fly. Boom! Swish!" Another fountain of
beer. "Might have killed me, mac," he said, holding his collar
away from his tiny neck to expose six or eight blood-crusted
scratches.

"Airman tried to give him a higher asshole with a rum
bottle," Novotny explained casually. "Then Mornin' got the
airman. That's what they're doing back so early. APs don't
understand that sort of shit."

"Sgt. Krummel," Novotny added, thumbing at me.

"Cagle, mac," the small one said, holding out a hairy little
hand.

"Caglemack?" I asked, shaking it.

"Just Cagle," he said, wrapping his whole tiny face around a
cigar. He continued dancing like a doll on a string, a leg this
way, an arm that, and all the while his black little moustache
wriggled and squirmed as if trying to crawl off his upper lip
into his mouth. "Boom!" he shouted, whirling to the other side
of the room. "Swish! Fly, flyboy, fly!"

I listened to the recounting of the three days, the new fuck
at so-and-so's, the arguments, Levenson's tumble into the
creek—he was pointed out as the naked, dreamy one in the
corner, nonchalantly nude—the fight again, Franklin's walk
past a girl with the clap without catching another dose, and
what a wonderful, awful Break it had been, hadn't it? Their
frenzy increased with each beer. They asked more than three
days could have: life, love, and happiness.

After a couple of beers I went back to check on Morning. He
was sitting on the lip of the shower stall, leaning against the

frame, and beating his head on the tile, singing again, but the song was too soft to hear.

"Hey, you need a hand?" I asked. He was hitting his head quite hard against the tile.

He stopped, but still sang. He sighed, and looked up calmly. He seemed tired, looked haggard. Just that second it came to me that he was not as drunk as he wanted me to think, but drunker than he realized.

"I didn't mean to kill my brother, you know," he said in a quiet, normal voice, a very collegiate voice which might have advertised fraternity blazers on the radio. "I didn't mean to." He had been crying.

"Sure, buddy, I know," I said, helping him to a sink. I ran cold water over his head for several minutes before he raised his face to the mirror. He stared at his reflection, then dried his glasses and said, "When I was a kid, I used to lay in bed after they made me turn the light off, used to lay there and make faces in the dark until I had one I thought was pretty good. Then I'd run to the bathroom and flip on the light to see it in the mirror." He paused, replaced his glasses—Army glasses with colorless rims which should have seemed out of place on his face, but they gave him a bemused, scholarly dignity—and looked at me. "Now I come down at night to make sure I'm not making a face, just to be sure." He shook the water off his hands, glanced once more into the mirror without expression, then walked slowly out.

Back in Novotny's room, another beer in hand, I told him what Morning had said about killing his brother.

"Ain't got no brothers. Just drunk again," he answered.

"Morning's my friend," Cagle chimed, "but he's a lousy fucking drunk sometimes."

"How do you know?" Novotny asked, his grin sly.

"What the hell you mean, 'How do you know?'" he answered, mimicking Novotny's clipped words and grin. "I've known him since basic, that's how I know."

"Bullshit," Novotny said calmly, challenging the world.

"What do you mean, 'bullshit!?'" Cagle's voice was high and shrill, and he stomped his foot. "Huh?"

"Never seen him drunk when you weren't too, you little hairy fart, so how the hell do you know how drunk he gets. And speaking of lousy drunks, who was it beat up that jukebox? and who can't go in the Tango anymore 'cause they don't pay for their beer? and just who the hell did the APs find under that Flip's house at three in the morning?"

"You never seen a woman so ugly. I couldn't believe that guy was really going to screw her, even if she was his wife. I had to see," Cagle said, smiling at the memory. "Didn't get written up, so fuck you, Navaho, and your pinto pony too."

"Keep away from my woman, piss ant," Novotny laughed and turned to me. "Ask the Beetle there," he said, pointing at Cagle, "how many times he's fallen on his fucking head and busted up an eyebrow. Everytime something hits the floor, everybody stands up and says, 'Okay, where's that fucking bug? Got to take him back and get his goddamned eyebrow stitched up again.'"

"There's a man knows a fine scar when he sees one," Cagle said, pointing at the four inch half-moon on my cheek. He showed me the crosshatching of thin white scars hidden in his brows. "How about . . . ."

"Oughta take up a collection to buy the Beetle a crash helmet for drinking," Novotny interrupted.

As the hours passed I began to feel some responsibility as trick chief to get everyone to bed for a little sleep before 0645. How should I play sergeant, I asked my beer bottle. An authoritative hint: "All right men, six o'clock comes pretty early!" A fawning plea: "Okay you guys, let's break it up, huh? Get a little beauty sleep, you know, ha, ha." Or a Listen-I'm-one-of-you-boys-and-I-hate-to-say-this-but-we-better-hit-the-sack sonnet. Perhaps just stand, flex my muscles, curl the ends of my moustache, and order, "Stop this shit." By the time I finally decided to hell with them and that their sleep was their business, the gathering ended as neatly and naturally as I could have hoped. The three-day frenzy was over for them, and the six-day drag just beginning. Letters they had meant to write, sleep they had hoped to catch up on, and last-Break resolutions never to go to Town again were all lost chances.

Fatigue muffled their "Goodnight, shitheads" and fogged their red-rimmed eyes and wrapped around them like tattered old blankets.

From my bunk, as I had a final cigarette and the night breeze stroked me, I heard Morning's record player from across the hall. A high, thin female voice drifted easily around a guitar, sounding very small in the night.

2

OPERATIONS

The job of the 721st involved a sort of reverse spying for the Filipino military establishment on themselves. They provided us with schedules and frequencies of transmissions in certain areas, and we recorded the messages—Morse code groups by typewriter (mill) and voice on tape—and then the Filipinos checked for security violations by individual operators. These violations were nothing so dramatic as giving information to the enemy (nonexistent, anyway), but were usually on the order of one operator (op) saying so long to another op when he was being transferred or discharged, or the transmission of a message in the clear when it was supposed to be encoded. This was supposed to be a foolproof scheme to double-check on their communications security—but things proof against a fool are seldom of any help against a clever man.

Joe Morning was clever. If he thought he might be recording a violation, he would manage to lose the signal at just that moment. He claimed no desire to punish some hapless Pfc in another army making even less money than he. After the newness of the work wore off, I tended to agree with him, just so it didn't happen too obviously; but at first I stayed on his back once I found out what he was doing. It was to his credit, I suppose, that he admitted what he was doing without being accused.

The afternoon of the first day I discovered his game with the static and security violations. I was checking copy-sheets, filing the necessary carbons and placing the originals in the attaché case the Filipino officer would pick up at 1530. I noticed that most of the copy was quite good for the day-trick, when interference was heaviest, except for Morning's which was spotted with marks of ((((((*GARBLED-GARBLED-GAR-BLED*)))))) (((QSA NIL QSA NIL))) ((HERE NIL MORE HEARD—QSK 5 × 5)). I checked his next scheduled transmission on the extra console, and although the op had an unusual style of keying, he was so loud he might have been next door. Morning's copy was again spotty. I thought perhaps he might not be a good Morse op, but later in the afternoon I watched him copy, with two fingers, a Chinese Communist (Chi Com) propaganda station sending 35 words per minute clear text Spanish. Morning copied without a mistake, almost without effort; he was a fine op. Only Novotny might be better. Morning stayed with the Chi Com a few minutes into his next schedule (sked). When he finished with it, I mentioned something about the quality of his copy earlier in the day, hoping he would understand that I knew what he was doing.

"Well, Sgt. Krummel, I had both ends on that sked," he said, pointing to the copy I was holding, "and this one fellow's wife is expecting her first and the other guy's wife has had six kids, so he was telling him not to worry. They were talking in clear text, but it just didn't seem right to bust a guy because he gets excited about his wife having a kid. More people should care about their wives that way." He answered me as if there could be no question about it. (He had the ability of never sounding wrong—not in any pushy way, but purely in his self-possession and confidence that he knew the truth.) It pleased me that he had confessed without being accused, but it left me in the position of either letting him get away with it or being against expectant fathers.

"Okay, Morning, but watch that sort of thing or there will be more than a father to get busted." Already he had me on shifting ground. "I don't like waves, and I don't like trouble, and that kind of shit makes for stormy, stinky waters." Who was I kidding? I was hooked. I didn't know quite how much just yet.

"Sure. I will. I'm really sorry," he said frankly, "but that guy was so damned excited, so worried, I just couldn't get him in trouble." Morning smiled, and I remembered hearing the quivering urgency of his keying when I had listened and now understood those handfuls of dits and dahs he had so frantically been throwing on the air, then I smiled too.

"God, it's taken him eight years to make corporal, and with a kid he's going to need the extra money," Morning said, at ease now that he knew I wasn't going to push him. His voice was friendly; he was talking to me, not my stripes.

"I thought they were talking about kids?"

"Yeah, this time, but I knew from before. He has such an odd fist, I can always tell when he's working. I remember when he made corporal. He broke into clear text then too. But he doesn't usually do that. He's really a good op, Sarge."

"Remind me to give the net to someone who isn't a member of the family, Morning. Jesus."

"He's being transferred to an automatic Morse net next month." Morning couldn't keep from grinning, and he knew neither could I.

"Well, goddamn, I guess you Dear Abbys are going to miss him and his family troubles," I said to the Trick in general. "I'll see if the chaplain's office doesn't need some extra help. Or maybe I can let you all open a home for unwed mothers in your spare time."

"Need something exciting around this fucking place," Novotny growled, "and I reckon unwed mothers would be just the right thing." A few chuckles followed, then they turned back to their work, not yet sure of me. It isn't easy to trust the man who gives the orders.

"Sgt. Krummel, I'm really sorry about the trouble. But you get so damned bored around this place, and thinking of the guy on the other end of this business as a buddy makes things pass easier. No one likes to be a sneak and a tattletail to boot," Morning said. "But I am sorry."

"Forget it. And don't tell me about the Chinese spy you keep in business because his mother's sick. Don't tell me."

"If I don't tell you, how will you know?"

"I don't want to know. Anything."

There was never any more trouble. I kept Morning on the higher echelon nets where the ops were more careful and on the training nets where the ops were sloppy and mistakes and violations came every sked. In spite of the smoothness of that problem, Morning always had the ability to get me mixed up in his crap. Never again, I said, walking back to my desk, Never again. But I was already holding my breath, waiting for the waves. (Morning would have said that my involvement with him was as much my fault as his, which is true. He was my fault. But I took care of that in Vietnam.)

The operating section of our building was contained on a single ground floor room, with most of the space taken up by electronic equipment and desks, but with a small area left open for the trick chief's desk, coffee pot and weapons' rack. The Detachment officers, as opposed to the company officers, a major, two captains and four lieutenants, had offices, for some never explained reason, underground, reached by an outside stairwell. They occupied these holes only in the daylight and seldom bothered with the actual operation of the Det unless an unusual problem arose. I quickly learned that work on the ground floor could proceed untroubled by the "Head Moles" as they were called. This peace was increased by a warning system installed in the air-conditioning unit by the Trick radio-repairman, Quinn. When a badge was inserted into the key slot which opened the front doors, the compressor coughed shyly. With this early warning system the men relaxed in a way unusual for enlisted men so near officers. My only real duty was to be sure that the Sked Chart was met and copied in all the bullshit sessions, the word games and general gold-bricking which made up the bulk of the hours. I settled that quickly: "Any op I catch missing skeds loses his pass for seven days, no questions asked." I got everyone's pass except Quinn's the first two days, then signed the three-day passes for the Break as if I had forgotten. The Trick understood, but they weren't my Trick yet.

The Trick and I seemed to work well in the beginning—

more credit to them than to me. They were a good group. Only Quinn and Peterson had not been to college, which might have been unusual for the Army as a whole, but was about the average for the 721st. None of the men were draftees dislodged from their life plans, but all had enlisted, probably because their lives were already out of joint. Only Collins had finished college; the others had flunked out or quit. Any one of them might, and did, cause God knows what trouble in Town, but only Franklin would at Operations. He was an unhappy kid who had gone to MIT on a math scholarship, then been ejected for peeing in a main lounge on Mother's Day. He never caused any real trouble because he, alone, thought my return to the Army a gallant gesture: a big, fat finger to the world. He liked that.

We worked well together then, the Trick and I, but it wasn't like later when we would march down the streets of Town ten men strong, and they would sing "We are Krummel's Raiders / We're rapists of the night / We're dirty son of a bitches / And rather fuck than fight!" That was fine.

Oddly enough it was through Franklin, rather than my first friends, Novotny, Cagle, and Morning, that the Trick and I became united. The seventh night of my first set of mids Franklin came to work drunk. Nothing unusual. In fact at least half of the men came to every mid-trick a little bit drunk. And Franklin had been having problems with his family since he had written a letter home telling about his being busted for indecent exposure—peeing in the street; everyone did it, but not on AP jeeps—and that he was in love with a Filipino barmaid, a nice girl who didn't work in the rooms out back, a lovely girl, and he couldn't believe she loved him. He had acne, a dead-white skin and long, greasy blond hair. The Devil as a juvenile delinquent. His parents had replied to his honest confession and plea for understanding with a Dear John asking him not to return home, ever. Franklin was nineteen and believed it. The first thing he did was seduce the girl, first with a cigarette, then a drink, then a trip out back. He stayed drunk for a week afterward, but had caused me no trouble, until this night.

He passed out. I saw him resting his head on his mill, and I shook him to remind him of his next sked. The swivel chair rolled toward the wall, dumping him at my feet with a thump I felt through my boots. Cagle turned around and said, "Goddamnit, Franklin! If I told you one time, I've told you a thousand, to leave those fucking kites alone." He helped me lay him between the wall and console, then copied Franklin's sked.

Morning, who acted as if he had invented mitigating circumstances, checked with me. "You going to turn him in, Krummel? If anyone's had a tough deal out of life, that poor bastard has."

"Morning, I don't care if all you sons of bitches sleep. Forever." I left Franklin to sleep it off. Several bad jokes were made to ease the tension, then everyone went about their business.

Around 0400 Cagle dropped through the trap door which led to the roof and shouted that a jeep was turning down our road. Lt. Dottlinger was the Officer of the Day. If he didn't kill Franklin right then, he was sure to stick him in the stockade and prefer charges. Being the able leader of men that I was, I didn't know what to do. But the Trick looked at me. It would be my decision. I tried not to think, but grabbed Franklin's shirt front and dragged him over to the ladder. Morning helped me lift him to the roof. Cagle let Dottlinger in the gate, then followed us down the ladder and took his position.

Dottlinger entered to an "OH, no!" sigh of the compressor. He had been passed over for captain twice, and when the lists came out once more without his name on it, he would revert to his former enlisted rank of sergeant which he hadn't really made but was a gratuitous benefit of OCS. He loved being an officer, and looked for chances to seem efficient.

"Sgt. Krummel," he said, returning my greeting, "What are those men doing out of uniform?" Several of the men had removed their fatigue shirts.

"Operations policy, I understand, sir. The men on the midtrick may remove their shirts while inside the building."

"Not when I'm Officer of the Day, Sgt. Krummel."

"I'm sorry sir, I didn't know. You men get your shirts on. And button up those flapping pockets." Dottlinger didn't like the pockets bit. He wanted to do it. He suspected me for finishing college. He hadn't made it.

Morning was copying very intently, and had not stopped to put on his shirt, though he heard me.

"That man is still out of uniform, Sgt. Krummel."

"He's copying, sir. He has a sked."

"I want his shirt on now, sergeant, right now."

"Yes, sir." I waved at Novotny to relieve him. He plugged his cans into Morning's console, and picked up the man at the end of a line as Morning slipped out of his chair.

"Ahhhh," he moaned, shaking out the muscles of his back as if he had been copying for hours instead of seconds. "Oh, hello, Lt. Dottlinger. How are you tonight? Or this morning, I should say. Haven't seen you in quite some time, sir." No trace of insolence in his voice. Nothing Dottlinger could hang a feather on.

"Get in uniform, Morning."

"Sir?"

"Your shirt. Get it on."

"Sir, we're allowed to remove our shirts on mids."

"I don't want excuses, soldier. Get in uniform." Dottlinger was red.

"Am I under arrest, sir? I don't understand. A phone call from home, sir? Tell me."

"What? Don't be silly. Get your shirt on—now!"

"You had me scared there for a minute, sir. I was sure it must be trouble." Morning started to walk away.

"Morning! Get your shirt on!"

"Yes, sir, right away. But I've been copying for over an hour and I ah . . . need to go to the latrine, sir."

"Now!"

"Yes, sir!" Morning fumbled with his sleeves, put the wrong arm in once, then buttoned one button too high, then one too low, and all the time jumping from one foot to the other. As he undid his pants, he shouted, "Jesus!" and ran for the latrine, his shirt tails flapping and his pants tumbling around his ankles. He ran like a man trying to hold a balloon between his knees. He didn't have any shorts on and the men laughed at his bobbing, bare white ass. He came back shortly, relieved, stretching and sighing, "Sorry about that, sir. But I just couldn't wait another second."

Dottlinger was twice as red in the face now, and he slapped his ball-point pen in his hand as if it were the swagger stick he couldn't carry any more. "Why aren't you wearing shorts, soldier?" he burst out. Levenson, our red-headed, freckled faced Jew, popped from behind the antenna patch panel, grinning like a weasel, giggling in his high-pitched voice, then ducked back as Dottlinger turned.

"Sir?" Morning asked.

"The Army went to great trouble to issue you underwear, and gives you a clothing allowance, so why aren't you wearing shorts?" He shook his pen at Morning. "Don't you have any, soldier?"

"Yes, sir. Yes, sir, I do."

"Why aren't you wearing them?"

"I always wear them for inspections, sir. Always."

"I don't care about inspections. Why aren't you wearing them now?"

"It's quite personal, sir, and I'd rather not discuss it in front of the other men, if you don't mind, sir." Ordinarily Dottlinger would have understood personal modesty, but not now.

"I don't care what you'd rather not do—I want to know why, soldier!"

Morning ducked his head and mumbled something.

"Speak up!"

"They crawl . . . they get in the. . . ." He even managed a blush. "In the crack of. . . ." He seemed overcome by shame. "The crack. . . ." Not a sound.

Dottlinger sighed, and for a moment I had visions of him ordering all pants dropped to check the shorts situation, but he caught hold of himself. "Morning, don't let me catch you without shorts again." Levenson giggled. You could see the resolve in Dottlinger's face to get Morning. "You think that's funny, Levenson."

"Yes, sir," he answered.

Dottlinger started to say something, then paused as if to say, "What can you do with a crazy bastard who sits around naked all the time in the barracks." He knew he had been taken for a ride, and a weary, familiar one at that. He looked like four o'clock in the morning. His face told of years of being the kid chosen last for the ball games, a fox first caught, a never successful hound, the kid who could never keep up, and he was behind again. He stayed a while longer, checking the building, listlessly searching for dust or dirt in a place cleaned and inspected three times a day. When he came up from the offices below, he said to me, "I believe the area under the major's desk could use some wax and a buffing, Sgt. Krummel, especially where he puts his feet. If you'd take care of that, please . . ." he said walking toward the door.

Petty bastard, I thought, no longer quite so understanding. "Yes, sir, I'll get the shit-house mouse on it right away."

He turned back. "I'd prefer if you didn't refer to the Operation's orderly in that manner, Sgt. Krummel. This is not the old Army, you know. We realize that profanity exhibits a vocabulary deficiency, and I don't think a man with a master's degree should suffer from that particular problem, do you?"

"You're quite correct, sir. Not that particular problem."

"Well, goodnight, sergeant. Ah, and don't neglect the major's desk."

"No, sir. The major's desk. Yes, sir."

As the heavy door slammed behind Dottlinger, Cagle slipped from his chair and up the ladder as quickly as a monkey to let him out the gate, then lowered Franklin through the trap. He was still out. Novotny lodged him in his chair and slapped his face with cold water until he came around. He woke, mumbling, "Fuck 'em, goddamnit, fuck 'em," then staggered to the latrine. He returned in better shape, his eyes puffy but awake and a silly grin on his face.

"Jesus Christ, it's four-thirty," he said, stretching his arms and yawning. As he rubbed the back of his neck, he found a few pieces of gravel. "Hey, where'd this come from?" Novotny explained. "You guys did that for me? Jesus. . . ." He started to say something smart, then stopped. "Jesus. Thanks. . . . Thanks." He started to cry, bewildered tears. "Nobody ever . . . ." He stammered, then sat down and put his headsets on.

I put things in order, caught up the hourly log, then grabbed a can of wax, a mop and the buffer out of the utility closet. I took an hour on the major's floor, waxing and buffing until the tile was as shining hard and brittle as my anger.

When I went back upstairs, everything was clean and glistening except the floor, and Franklin was waiting for the mop and buffer. "I'm sorry, sarge," he said, taking the gear from me, "I promise you, if it ever happens again, I'll turn myself in. Promise. Thanks."

"Don't sweat it, kid. It won't happen again," I said, admiring the immaculate room. *You, Krummel, you got troubles? A Trick-ful.* It was different now, easier and more relaxed, like a family, now that I had pulled Franklin into the Trick by his shirt front, stepping into the living room myself. We knew where we stood, for better or worse: together.

But Joe Morning and I were friends from the beginning. Perhaps it was as simple as two men just liking the look of each other, or as complex as covering hate with love. We looked somewhat alike, enough so that we often passed for brothers in Town, except for our coloring, Joe fair and I dark, and our noses, mine hooked and crooked as sin, his straight as an arrow. I affected a ferocious, drooping moustache, and Morning his scholarly spectacles. We stood the same six feet, but I was thirty pounds heavier than his 195, and I suppose it was the size which started us.

"You ever play any football, Sgt. Krummel?" he asked on his fourth trip to the coffee pot that first morning at work. I could tell he wanted to say something, to start a conversation, but he didn't, so I waited.

"I played a little in college."

"Where?"

I told him. He had heard of the small South Texas school. They had been NAIA contenders two seasons before.

"You play on that team?" he asked.

"No. I was at the University of Washington by then." We went through the routine about what I was doing in the Army, and then I pulled a quick history out of him. (Actually no one ever had to pull anything out of Morning. He told everything, which is a nice way to lie.)

He had been born in Spartanburg, South Carolina, but spent

his first ten years or so in Phoenix, then back to Spartanburg for the rest of high school. He went to a large Southern university as a single-wing tail-back and Accounting major until he changed to drinking and Philosophy in his second semester, which he continued until he was expelled in his junior year. Then he commuted between Phoenix where he sang folk songs in a bar and the South where he sang in demonstrations, until, so he said, an Alabama judge, at Mrs. Momma Morning's request, sentenced him to three years in prison or the Army on an assault charge. Morning had forgotten how to passively resist. He took the Army as the greater of two evils, gave the judge as a reference on his security clearance application, and after nine months at Fort Carlton, he came to the 721st. (The Alabama judge bit was only half a lie, and Joe Morning told it with such skill and a great ability to laugh at his troubles, that everyone, including me, believed it. Only Quinn ever suspected, and he was crazy. Even as I know the truth, I still think Morning told a fine story.)

Morning was open and friendly with me from the start, as he was with nearly everyone, but I never knew quite what to make of him in the early days. Surely he hated the world order, the capitalist system, the American miscarriage of democracy, the slavery of the Army, the Philippines, Clark Air Base and the 721st; but not necessarily in that order, because his moods would change. But I don't think he hated any single man. He would rail for hours against Southerners, but would defend the other Southerner on our Trick, Collins, to any and all comers. But to the South in general he shouted, "Freedom Now! Fuck understanding your particular problems!" It was the same with Filipinos: he thought them thieving, sneaky bastards. But each trick he risked a court martial for some Filipino private he didn't even know. Morning hated Christians, particularly Catholics, but he would defend the Catholic Church against the accusation of holding back education three hundred years during the Middle Ages; and he probably knew his Bible better than any man I knew, but he hid his knowledge, and only shouted verses of damnation when he was crazy drunk. His friends never knew quite where he stood, but they did know that Joe Morning would do anything they asked, and seldom ask anything of them. When he did, it was with such great shyness that no one could refuse him. He was thoughtful to boot and kind in the bargain, and easily forgave the thoughtless and unkind acts of his friends. He could be cruel, moody, but he endured these things with a wry, self-effacing humor which took the bite out of the bitterness. Ordinarily he was a happy, perfect drunk, but once each month or so, he would lose control in a wild, insane night, and cry and fight and scream and beat his head on the floor till no one knew who or what he was. . . .

Such was Joe Morning, Joseph Jabez Morning, hanging between the sun and the moon, a man of great tides. Like all men without roots, direction or patience, he was a revolutionary, not a rebel but a revolutionary, a destroyer, a reacher for all or nothing for anyone. (It would be easier, so much easier, this history I record, if Joe Morning could have been a bad man, an evil heart, but he was good, and in his misguided virtue drove me to the evil of excess and even to murder, and in the end passed the avenging, burning, falling stone of revolution to me.)

He came to me the morning of Franklin's salvation and asked, "Sgt. Krummel, the Trick is having a Roll Call in Town today, if you'd like to come." Roll Calls were for the men, and no trick chiefs allowed unless asked by the men.

"Thank you. I'd like that."

3

TOWN

By the time I ate and walked up to my room, the Trick had already changed out of their uniforms and gathered in my room.

"What's the hurry? I'm going to shower first," I drawled.

"Shower!" they screamed. "What are you? a preacher? You don't shower before you go to Town!"

Outvoiced, I reached in the closet for a pair of slacks.

"What are you? Got a date or something? You don't wear slacks to Town." They were dressed in Town clothes, that is, everything from shoes to shorts which could be ripped, stolen, or shit on for all they cared. I tried a pair of Levi's.

"What are you, a new guy? No Levi's, no blue jeans off base!"

I took another pair, light brown, a knit shirt and a pair of buff Wellingtons, and sat them on the table. "Okay, troops, out," I said, opening the door. "You just wait in the Orderly Room, I'll be right down. As soon as I shit, shower, and shave."

They grumbled, but they left, and were waiting in the Day Room, playing pool and shuffleboard when I came down.

"So you're lovely, Sarge," Cagle said, "but Town is all used up by now." It was 0745.

"I hear you're going to Town," Tetrick said from behind his

desk. He handed me the sheaf of three-day passes. "Make 'em sign out." His face was pale and bloated from a hangover, but he smiled. "They'll take care of you until you can take care of them. I hope. But watch yourselves. Capt. Saunders is going stateside for six weeks, and Lt. Dottlinger will have the Company. He don't like guys who go to Town. So stay clean."

"You guys don't let him fall in love," Tetrick shouted as we left.

Lt. Dottlinger was coming in, his OD armband still crinkling his shirt sleeve, as we tumbled out front to wait for the cabs to take us to the gate. He answered our quick salutes with a crisp touch of ball-point pen to cap bill and a grim, brimstone eye.

Angeles, in spite of its reputation as a minor version of heaven, was a collection of bamboo huts, wooden, tin-roofed buildings, dusty streets, open sewers, and seventy-five or eighty bars. It wasn't quite as modern as a Mexican border town, which it very much resembled, nor as dirty as a large city slum. The streets always seemed festive in a way, filled with people, dogs and pigs wandering without the help of crosswalks or traffic lights. I liked the look of the people. They were cleaner than I had been led to expect, and without that wolfish, greedy glare of the citizens of Columbus, Georgia or Fayetteville, North Carolina or Kileen, Texas.

Our cabs stopped in the center of Town where five streets intersected. Three kiosks were around the plaza, three of the half-dozen or so enclosed ones. The others, and there seemed to be hundreds spotted around Town, were open to the weather. It was explained to me that kiosks were for serious drinking, since the barmaids were indecently nice and wouldn't even meet an American eye on the street. The whores were in the bars or in houses. Trick Two, my Trick, usually gathered at the Plaza.

We filed into the narrow, high room, jammed ourselves around an elongated horseshoe bar on small, hard bamboo stools. Venetian blinds held off the early morning sun around one long and one short side, and three Edwardian fans ladled the air above the bar, buzzing and stirring as much breeze as

fat, lazy blowflies. A huge hulk of chrome and plastic commanded the scene from a niche high in the end wall, content-
edly bubbling, watching over her foolish children.

"Roll Call, mama-san," Morning said to the large, middle-
aged owner of the Plaza.

"Aaiiieeee," she giggled, taking her glasses off. "Take business to Chew Chi's." She sat her glasses back on her face as if
they might protect her as Trick Two sat down.

"Too early," said a heart-faced girl behind the bar. Her smile
exposed a front tooth circled in gold-fill which formed a small,
white heart on her tooth. She and two other girls gave everyone a cold, thick San Miguel and a utilitarian tumbler of such
thickness it might be used for anything from weapon to an-
chor—and it was. Beers were neatly poured, then Morning
pulled a crumpled sheet of paper from his pocket, and began:

"In so much as this is a world we didn't make, filled with
dangers we refuse to understand, we of Trick Two do hereby
withdraw ourselves from the arms race, the space race, and
the human race for these next three days; and being the finest
of fellows, comrades and carousers, humbly raise our glasses
in defiance and bow our heads in shame, and here do solemnly
swear (or affirm) to drink until the moon falls from the
heavens, the heavens on our heads, or we, fat chance, on our
asses.

"Agreed?"

"Aye!"

"I shall read the roll of the honored and infamous alike."

"Thomas Earl Novotny," Morning intoned.

"Aye," growled Novotny, then stood and poured the beer
down his throat.

(Novotny, the cowboy, hated the Army so bad that when he
made Specialist Fifth Class he would change out of uniform
rather than eat in the NCO mess area. But he was a good
soldier. Perhaps he just didn't like people telling him what to
do.)

"John Christopher Cagle." He choked halfway down, but
finished his glass.

(Cagle, the monkey, the dancer, the nervous mover. His
father was a chaplain, a major in the Air Force who believed,

according to Cagle, God to be a combination between General
Eisenhower and General Motors. "That Great Used Car Salesman in the sky," Cagle used to sing. He had been expelled
from Indiana University his senior year for trying to break
into the Kinsey Institute of Sexual Research's pornographic
collection, and had been in trouble ever since. The Company
had long since given him up so long as he hurt no one but
himself and his eyebrows. His greatest triumph came when he
returned from thirty days' leave in Japan. He stepped off the
plane wearing a Japanese private's uniform, carrying a samu-
rai sword and sporting a goatee. But he never told anyone how
he got on that plane.)

"Doyle Quinn."

"Ha!" Quinn shouted, "Now the serious drinkin' begins!"
and tossed down his beer.

(Quinn. His steady shack, Dottie the bowlegged whore,
cared for him and hid his shoes so he would be faithful, but
nothing worked, so she tried suicide from the second floor of a
nipa hut and became Dottie the bowlegged whore. But none of
this made the slightest impression on Quinn. He was a sly,
dark Irishman from the City, tough and wild, never caring if
the sun came up. A false tooth set in his jaw had been broken
in a fight, leaving only the gray, metallic core, and Quinn
didn't bother to have it fixed. Born to streets and alleys,
poverty and race riots, his laughter had acquired a stony,
mocking edge to it which said, "I've seen the whole mess and I
don't give a shit for it, so let's have another.")

"David Douglas Franklin."

"Ha!" he snorted and snarled like his idol, Quinn.

(His parents thought they had brought the wrong baby
home from the hospital, and in shame never had another. Mr.
Franklin was a typewriter repairman and his wife cashiered in
a restaurant in Bristol, Connecticut, and their son had an IQ
upwards of immeasurability. They prevented him from reading until he was four by slapping the *Reader's Digest* out of his
hands. They thought he wanted to tear out the pages. They hid
him in a back room when friends came to play bridge because
he always won. Once they discovered that he wasn't a freak,
Franklin went on display throughout the neighborhood. He

finished eight years of school in two, then missed four years
because he wouldn't go, then two more because he failed when
they made him attend school, but managed to finish with his
original class which was all he wanted, anyway. His father's
finest moment came as he decked the school psychologist for
suggesting that the child might have family troubles. I once
heard Franklin say, "I rather be dumb than have acne.")
Morning called the rest of the names, and they drank.
Samuel Lloyd Levenson, the Jewish weasel, red-headed, frec-
kle-faced, giggler, always naked in the barracks, but he would
make it. William Frank Collins, he was called Mary, crewcut,
pug-nosed American boy, mild segregationist, biology teacher,
husband and father from Florida. Carl Milton Peterson, our
kid, known as the Gray Ghoul for his thin, shallow face and
mild manners, son of a Bemidji, Minnesota service station
owner. Richard Dale Haddad, looked Jewish, had an Arabic
name, but claimed to be Spanish, he was an operator, a big
man in the blackmarket, balding at twenty-three like any other
good young executive. Then Morning called my name, then
his, and after he drank, he passed the list to me, and I called
the names and we drank, and we all called the names until
they answered no more.

At high noon: Cagle, Morning, Novotny, Quinn, a one-
legged guitar player and pimp named Dominic who claimed to
be a veteran of the Spanish Civil War, a Filipino homosexual
hairdresser called Toni dressed in full drag, and me, who
claimed by this time to be the last survivor of an Apache
attack on Fort Dodge, Iowa. The other guys had platoons of
empty bottles doing drill before them, while I couldn't even
keep my scraggly squad in a good line of skirmishers. I
thought those other bastards had been stealing my bottles just
to emasculate me, but I couldn't catch them. The faster I
drank, the further behind I got, and while my nose was nearly
in my bottle, the others were too sober to trust. I suppose I did
well, considering I took on the Trick's hard-core Townies. San
Miguel ran about fifteen percent alcohol, and took getting used
to.
    At least I wasn't the only drunk. Peterson had simply dived

out of his stool at 1015. Novotny took his money, and carried him out to a *calesa*. Outside he found Collins throwing up in the street, so he sent them off to the Trick's apartment to sleep. Levenson had roared away to the Factory for a quick three-peso piece, with Franklin right behind him. Haddad had gotten angry at Mama-san because she wouldn't let him do another flamenco on the bar like he did last Roll Call, so he left too, stamping and clapping and shouting *Olé*.

Finally the rest of us counted up our bottles, paid and said goodbye to Morning's two Filipino friends. As I stepped into the sunlight, the heat, the brilliance, knocked me silly. It was the light of the day that would never be night. Nothing, not the hand of God, nor the mere spinning of the earth, could put out that fire in the sky. We wandered down the street, the middle of the street, dodging our way through the sea of dusty gold.

"Sgt. Slag," Quinn said, "you look a little bit drunk."

"Nonsense, knave. It's these chuckholes in the highroad which cause me to use this particular peculiar gait. Chuckholes, my fellow. Indeed."

He laughed wildly, almost braying, his tooth flashing like a spark, and slapped me on the back.

"Avast there mate."

He laughed again. "You're okay for a fuckin' college guy. You might make it."

"And you also, kind squire, are a fine bit of a gentleman, a yeoman tiller of the soiled and a reveler."

We turned a corner somewhere. I could see the world. A wrinkled old woman, her graying hair wrapped into a bun, tended two baskets by the edge of the sidewalk. She squatted motionless, sucking on a black cigarette, the fire in her mouth, taking smoke with each breath of air. One basket held *baluts*, the nearly-hatched duck eggs which Filipinos considered delicious, and the other, small ears of corn toasted on coals.

"Haven't we met somewhere before, young lady. Perhaps Newport. Or was it Saratoga?" I was saying as Novotny came back to get me.

"Not her, man. She's worn out." The old woman hadn't moved. Smoke wisped around her small leathery nose each time she breathed.

"Ah, but she's beautiful. Don't you see? There's character in that face, those delicate wrinkles cut by the sharp knife of time. The dignity of age. . . . 'It little profits that an idle king,/By this still hearth, among these barren crags,/Met with an aged wife. . . .' "

"You buy *balut*," she asked suddenly, the con shining in her eyes as she looked up.

"Yes, mother, those who hustle, live. Yes." I paid twice the price, and walked away with Novotny, the egg warm and firm in my hand, begging to be thrown.

"You drunk?" he asked.

"I?"

"What are you going to do with that? Not going to eat it, huh?" he asked as I pitched the egg in the air.

"I had to lose my cherry sometime," I answered, tossing it higher and higher. It broke in my hand and a warm, stringy fluid dripped between my fingers. I squeezed it and the juice spat on the street and rolled up a fine film of dust. In my hand the shell pieces revealed the yellow, matted feathers of the stillborn duckling. I picked the shell away. The body lay in my hand like the victim of a shipwreck. I dropped the mess in the gutter and wiped my hand on my pants.

"What's all that about?" Novotny asked.

"Huh? Oh, it was a symbolic expression of the nihilism inherent in all human searches for pleasure, coupled with the paradox that pleasure is the basis of conservatism, the enemy of nihilism."

"Bullshit."

"Exactly."

He and I caught up with the others at the Keyhole, a quiet, dark bar with a few cushioned lounge chairs. I sat down in one, drank two more mouthfuls of beer, then passed out.

I awoke on my face. A button on a lumpy, raw-cotton mattress bit into my cheek. As I rolled over, I saw myself in a large mirror which hung at an angle over the narrow bed. Also reflected was a small naked girl sitting backwards on a chair next to the bed.

"Hey," she said, smiling, "you wake up now, huh? Good. Time to go soon. Good you wake up now."

"Who're you?" My head hurt and I was still whoozy.

"TDY."

"Huh?"

"TDY. Temporary Duty. Tanduay Rum. TDY. Best puck in all Town. You look in billfold."

I did, expecting all my money to be gone. All but ten pesos of it was and there was a folded note. "Dear Fucking Newguy: Sleeping in the streets, bars, or latrines of Town is expressly forbidden by CABR 117–32. There was a party at the apartment, so you couldn't sleep there. I took your money. The room is paid for. The Alka-Seltzer is for your stomach and head— TDY for your soul. When you're ready she'll show you the way to the apartment. Good Morning."

I looked up. TDY was standing next to the bed, holding the foil package like a gift in front of her hairless crotch. Her smile had a what-the-hell reflection in her eyes, and her body was young and slim; but she wasn't attractive, or even pretty or cute. I wondered if Morning was playing a joke. Me, sleep with that obviously disease-infested child. Why her feet were even dirty. And she had no clothing that I could see except for a soiled, limp blue dress hanging on the doorknob like a dishcloth. No shoes either.

"You like TDY, yes?"

"Yes, but I like Alka-Seltzer too." I climbed off the bed, took the packet from her, and went to the sink. The room was small, square and furnished with a bed, chair, sink and the mirror. A single unscreened but shuttered window exposed a length of cracked, vine-crawling wall. The room was stripped for action. I took the seltzer, washed my face and walked back to the bed to put my boots on.

"We puck now," she said, laying her small hand against my shirt. "Joe Morning say TDY no have heart of gold, but silver pussy." Her hand slipped under the knit shirt and lay flat against my stomach. It seemed so tiny, so painfully childlike. I was ready to react if she tried to grab my crotch as if it were a moneybag, but she did not stir. Just that tiny hand warm against my belly. "We puck now?" It was not a question of time she was inquiring about, but of her and me and the universe. She undressed me, then with a giggle pushed me on the bed, turned me over when I bounced, and jumped astride my back. She lay there for several minutes, quivering, rubbing her belly on my butt, kneading the muscles of my neck and shoulders, and whispering small kisses across my back. She stayed that way until a sweat broke between us. Each time I tried to turn over, she bit me, not playfully but hard, then continued. Then she turned me over, lay on my chest with her back, and began all over again. She placed my hands on her little breasts and held them and rubbed them and shivered against them. She caught my cock between her legs and held it. The sweat broke sooner this time, and when it did, she slid and moaned and moved and held me tighter between her legs. Her body was so small against mine, and in the mirror, it seemed most deliciously black on the white space of me. My hands looked like water-whitened jellyfish stinging at her breasts.

Then she flipped over and threw herself against me, her body skittering across mine, and clamped her mouth to mine, splitting my teeth with her tongue, her tiny hands clutching our faces together. I could feel the expectant hunch of her on my stomach, but she was too short to breach the gap. She sprayed kisses over my face, in my ears, warm and flickering like the summer rain. But her head crept slowly down my chest as her rocking crotch searched, found and took me as if I were the gift, and cradled me preciously. She sat up and back, her hands on my chest, and gave as much as she took.

The motion was slow and easy for a time, graceful in her control, then faster. She closed her eyes, then bared her teeth, then faster, her hands sliding against my chest. And faster still, her toes dug into the mattress, riding in quick little punches. She grabbed my neck, pulled my face to her, to the small hot slaps of her breasts. My body bent in a circle, a hard, fleshy ring around her, and she the tiny missing link completing the arc—and she pumped like a runner's heart. I understood about the silver, the quick sliding silver, and that single hoping arm reached and all my blood fled to my feet in the wake of her motion, then exploded up the aching chimneys of my legs.

I lay empty, only now aware of her greedy contracting spasms, wondering if she had really had a climax. (In the months to come I understood that she always did, and always would. She liked to fuck. She wasn't obsessed with it, or manic about it, she just liked it. She was obsessed with movies. She always cried afterwards, thinking GIs expected it. I never heard one complain, though, now that I think about it. Maybe she knew more than we thought.)

I woke when she climbed off the bed. Her eyes were puffy, but she smiled like a child on her birthday.

"I ride on top," she said, " 'Cause . . . cause you too . . . big." She meant heavy. "And so you can watch in mirror."

My back ached, I was nearly raw and my head still hurt, but it had been a long time since I felt quite so good. I had forgotten how nice love without complications can be.

"I forgot to look," I said from the bed, watching her prop one foot on the wall and pee in the sink. I had to laugh.

"You should look," she said when she finished. "Room is fifty centavos more for mirror." She turned around. "How come you laugh?"

"Because you're beautiful."

"You put me on."

"No. Never."

"TDY not pretty."

"No. But you're beautiful."

"What you mean?"

"Beautiful like God, like an angel."

"Shame," she said, but she smiled.

"And I promise to look in the mirror next time." She laughed.

As I dressed an afternoon thunder shower flashed heavy rain in the sun. I opened the shutters, and smoked, waiting. The rain eased into large, splattering drops against the bright washed green of the vine, then ended with a roll of thunder like applause after a fine performance, and TDY and I left.

The world sparkled, spotless in the slanted rays of the sun. Water splashed like laughter from the glimmering puddles in the bronze street as *calesa* ponies sauntered past, and beggar boys marveled at the tickling ooze of mud between their toes as shy-eyed gum-and-flower girls disapproved from shaded doorways. They were happy, so easily impressed by a passing storm. Even TDY giggled and danced around me, splattering my unconcerned pants.

"What took you so long, man," Morning asked as TDY and I met Novotny, Quinn, Cagle and him on our way to the apartment.

"He sleep long time," TDY answered for me.

"Not too long, I bet, with that little Indian around," Novotny said, laughing. Quinn reared his head, rolled his eyes and spit wild snorts of laughter after the racing black clouds. Cagle grinned sleepily, then shut his eyes and leaned against the wall.

"Yeah," I said. "And thanks, too. I think I'll pass out again. . . ."

"That's for sure," Quinn interrupted.

". . . so I can wake up all over."

"She's something else," Morning said, rubbing his hand down her back and across the pout of her butt. "Pure silver under there. Pure." TDY laughed and arched against his hand, purred and tilted back her head. Morning asked if she wanted a beer.

"I go home, Joe. Clean up house," she said. "See you Mr. Moustache," she said, switching her butt against my leg. She pulled one end of it. "You tickle pussy sometime, huh?" She giggled and skipped down the street.

"Okay, where's home for that sweet little girl?" I asked. "Just in case you guys aren't around when I ah, pass out."

"She keeps the apartment for us," Morning explained. "We bought her."

"Like a vacuum cleaner?"

"No, man, like a maid." Morning said that TDY had been a *calesa*-girl, the lowest class whore, and Haddad had fucked her one night, realized what a gold mine she was, and convinced the Trick to buy her from the pimp she belonged to. Haddad provided the financing for half of his usual ten percent, persuaded TDY, then installed her a maid-of-all-tricks in the apartment which the Trick already rented in Town. The Trick kept her in food, clothes and money. She in turn kept the place clean and was available to any member without clap, when she wasn't at the movies. No one ever made her miss a movie. Cagle had tried once, and she cut him off for a month.

"Works out fine," Morning said. "You want in? Gives you a place to sleep, shower and shave on break. It's not fancy—six beds, a couch, a shower and a little bitty kitchen which is TDY's."

"How much?"

"Ten bucks a month to Haddad. He handles the arrangements and accounts, credits three-to-one, pesos to dollars, on your money, keeps the place up, pays the bills and gives the excess to the orphanage to outfit our basketball team and buy books."

"Come on," I scoffed.

"He's in love with one of the teachers, but she won't have anything to do with him because he's in the market. She thinks he's a threat to the economy, an arrogant Jew American Ugly. But she lets him coach the basketball team, and buys the books with the money he gives her. . . ."

"But that's by God all he gives her," Quinn shouted, then reared and roared again, his tooth flashing like the flint of cynicism in his laugh.

"We're a bunch of fucking philanthropists," Novotny said.

"A bunch of fucking nuts," I said, slapping Morning on the shoulder. "Move over and let another one in, mother."

"There's five guys from Trick Four who use the place," Morning added. "But they break when we're working, so we don't get in each other's way." He paused expectantly.

"So?"

"One of them is a Negro. . . ."

"So?"

"I just thought, if you minded, I should let you know."

"No sweat, Morning," I said.

"Just wanted to avoid trouble."

"You? Come on. You make trouble in gallon jugs, Morning."

"Sells well, anyway, man. Let's go have a drink."

"Take two—they're small."

"Goddamn, yours are," Quinn said, grinning slyly. "You a two or three beer man?"

As we walked away, laughing, Cagle remained leaning

against the wall. He hadn't moved during the whole time. Morning went back to wake him up.

"Little fart can crap out anyplace," Novotny said.

Just as Morning reached for his shoulder, Cagle jumped at him, screaming and brandishing a knotted cane like a saber. Morning leapt backwards, arms and legs spread like a spider's, shouted "Sonofabitch!", then hopped forward as if out of physical control. Cagle parried Morning's arms, slid into him like a fencer and stabbed him in the heart.

"Touché!" he smirked. "What sort of spy are you, Agent Monday Morning. Taken in by the sleeping-dog lie. Ha! I'm sending you back to the Sally League."

Morning was limp. "Someday I'm going to kill you, Cagle." He wasn't angry; but he had been scared. In spite of the calm and composure with which he carried himself, Morning was intensely nervous. He was forever on edge, but it never showed except when something like Cagle's attack caught him with his face down.

But never the same thing twice, Novotny explained as we caught a jeepny to go for a steak at the Esquire. Cagle had been scaring hell out of Morning since Basic, when he had crawled into Morning's tent one night on bivouac. Morning had torn up the tent pegs and run ten yards in his sleeping bag before Cagle calmed him down. Another time, after they had gotten to the Philippines, Cagle had hidden under Morning's bunk, waited until he was asleep, then reached up and grabbed his throat. Morning had gasped and stiffened, then didn't move for several minutes. Worried, Cagle crawled out, turned on the light and found Morning wide-eyed and white, his breathing so deep it shook the bunk, and his pulse so furious, his hands fluttered on his chest. Cagle had to pour cold water on him to bring him around.

I wondered what Morning had thought during that time, then realized that he had thought nothing. He had been turned off as completely as if he were dead. I reminded myself to ask him about it someday. He sat in the front seat of the jeepny, alone with the driver, apparently relaxed, smoking and watching the road as we hurried out of Town. Nipa huts flashed into walls, and Morning's smoke whipped around my head. He

seemed to have regained his calm by the time we reached the
Esquire, halfway between Base and Town, and laughed about
it over a bleeding steak and a beer.

Later that night, drunk again, Novotny and I were laughing
and stumbling our way down a street unfamiliar to me on our
way to the apartment, which I still hadn't seen. It was nearly
midnight, and people were moving: some home after work,
airmen back to the Base or into hiding until 0600 the next
morning, and those Filipinos who seemingly wandered the
streets at all hours. I was trying to tell Novotny something, I
don't remember what, when I looked around and he was gone.
His face, his brilliant teeth masked in a leathery grin, had
been assimilated into the random movement of the ill-lit night.
In turning to search for him, I forgot which way we had been
walking. I could see in the alcoholic fog around my head, but I
couldn't remember what I had seen. I pushed through the
crowds along the side of the street, forced there by the increased traffic of jeepnys and cabs heading for Base, but I
didn't see anything I recognized, then realized that I didn't
know where the fabled apartment was anyway. As I decided to
return to Base, and turned to hail a jeepny, they were all gone.
Zip. The rocking street was empty except for a few stragglers
hurrying underground and listless whores stretching their
backs after another night's labor. An old woman's cardboard
hand fluttered against my arm and her hesitant, fluting voice
said something. I thought her begging, and shook my head.
She was insistent with those stiff fingers on my elbow, and I
understood she was selling. Not me, old hag of a woman, I
thought, Not rich, creamy all-American me. But I let myself be
led into an alley, saying to myself that it would be at least a
safe place to sleep as she guided me over obstacled darkness,
over rough ground threatening to rise at me with each step,
into a small black cauldron of a room.
    (But no sleep is safe: it all echoes death.)
    I let her unresisting flesh ply its trade under me, added my
load to those long never-remembered other ones which filled
her crinkly skin. As I labored, I dimly heard rats gnawing at
the rafters, the sound of their teeth on the wood and their

squeaking voices a calliope above us. I asked why? and answered with abstractions like "responsibility to contracts made in good faith" and "be polite to old ladies and children" and the other rules by which I thought I lived. But I must have already known how the rules were failing me, the ordered forms gone in the rip that began with the rupture of my marriage and proposed career (how silly that word sounds now). Or perhaps with the rupture of my mother's maidenhead. Or, God knows, before. I hadn't learned about poetry and war yet. I still believed in salvation—and here I was seeking order and saving grace as my castle tumbled into the rising seas, searching with that funny finger in that aged dike below, that rebel finger which below me lived, aye, and even enjoyed. I mated with dark flesh that night, and she bore me dreams, magic, and hope, storm-festered dreams, magical revenge, and hope, and I never kissed her wrinkled face again and again.

Cagle was drunk. He walked straight down the sidewalk, but he half-faced the street, drifting like a Piper Cub in a high wind. Morning was in a foul mood, sulking about the fourteen ladies' drinks he had lost to Bubbles at the Hub. Three days in Town had flayed the skin from my body, and I was already making those familiar resolutions never to come back. We were walking up to the main street, looking for a jeepny to take us back to Base. As we passed the door of a foul den known as Mutt & Jeff's, three airmen burst out the door. The first and largest one was talking to the two behind him, and bumped into Cagle. Cagle rebounded two steps, then went forward again before the airman could move. He elbowed Cagle out of the way, and snorted something about 'Lookin' where the hell you're walkin' " and started back down the street in the direction from which we had come.

Morning, without a word, ran back to them, grabbed the airman's shoulders, spun him around and shoved him against his two buddies.

"You want to push somebody, mother-fucker, you push me," Morning said, anger quivering like a wind-tossed flame in his voice. "Don't push, man."

The airman had been openly attacked, was slightly larger

than Morning, and probably felt himself in the right. He and his two pals charged just as I ran back to make peace. I tried to say something about not needing to fight to the other two guys, but one was already throwing a roundhouse right at me. I covered up, ducked and pushed the first one back into the second. When he rushed again, I stepped back and kicked him in the chest. He staggered backwards into the street and sat down in a puddle to get his breath. I asked the other guy if he wanted any of me, and he agreed that he didn't.

"Let's break this up before the APs arrive." He agreed again.

Morning, for all his anger, was boxing. He had the guy against the wall, stepping in and out, ringing the airman's ears with combinations of body punches and open-handed slaps. Morning's body was turned, his chin tucked and his right protecting his face in a nearly classic stance. The slaps smacked loud and arrogant. Morning played with the guy, nearly letting him out, then driving him against the wall with the blinding, deafening slaps, but without hurting him badly enough so he could quit with some semblance of honor.

I stepped between them, peeled them apart, and held them off. Morning's chest was trembling so fast under my hand that I wondered if he was going to hit me. But the other guy did. It was only a blind slap from a dazed and confused kid trying to beat off a nest of hornets, but it glanced off my tender twice-broken nose. I shoved him against the wall, set him up with a poking jab to the head, layed two right hooks under his heart, then dropped him with a forearm slam to the face when he bounced off the wall. He slid to a squat at the base of the wall, head in hands. I whirled back—Morning was grinning. The airman who hadn't gotten in the fray was looking after his buddy in the street who was walking and breathing again.

"Boy, you really broke up the fight," he sneered at me. "A real fucking peace-maker."

"I'm sorry . . ." I started to say, but realized he neither understood nor cared to understand, and besides was right, I suppose. He had to say something to cover his guilt for not helping his friends.

"I'll . . . I'll remember your ugly fucking face," the other one shouted as Morning and I walked to where Cagle leaned patiently against the wall. "We'll catch your ass some night, son of a bitch. In a dark alley, by your-god-damned-self!" I walked back to them, thinking, What a long eighteen months it was going to be.

"Let's stay straight, buddy. You swung at me before I could say hello. You just made a mistake. You should have stayed out of it like your pal here. So shut your mouth before you make two mistakes in one night. Next time I see you all, I'll buy the beer. And tell the other guy to watch where the hell he's walking. Okay? Okay."

"Okay," they said in chorus.

I caught up with Morning and Cagle. Morning was chuckling quietly.

"You guys through yet," Cagle muttered.

"Set them straight?" Morning asked, grinning as we hailed a jeepny. He was loose now.

"Maybe they won't cut us off at the pass."

"Piss on 'em."

"You're pretty good for a passive resister, Morning."

"That's why I'm here. I took crap from rednecks as long as I could, then one spit in my face one hungover morning at a lunch counter in Birmingham. I dropped his peckerwood ass." He took a plate of four teeth out of the left side of his mouth and showed it to me. "But his gentlemen buddies got me. Damnit, I forgot to take this damned thing out," he mumbled, putting it back in. "Someday I'm going to take a shot in the gut and choke on my plastic teeth." He laughed. "How'd you like to try to swallow that monster of Quinn's?"

We were on the highway now and the quiet whiz of the tires, the cool wind and the receding lights of Town made the fight seem far away. As we swept past the Cloud 9, a wild burst of laughter shot out to meet us, mocking my thoughts.

"You're pretty salty yourself," he said.

"I'm out of practice, Morning, and intend to stay that way. The next time you tee-off on a guy just because you're pissed at a broad, count me out."

"Bullshit," he said, smiling again, stretching his arms and

popping his knuckles. "So I was pissed off. What's your excuse?"

"With you on the Trick, my stripes aren't worth a rusty razor blade."

"Not me, man. I don't rock the boat." He flipped his cigarette away and it flashed past me in a streaking red line, then sparkled the road like the fuse of a firecracker. He rubbed his hands greedily together, savoring the heat of violence. As I noticed him, I caught my own hand cradling my right fist, remembering the solid clunk it had made against the airman's ribs. My wrist would hurt the next morning, but not very much. No more than Morning's hands.

4

BARRACKS

Tetrick's admonition to step easily with Lt. Dottlinger commanding the Company proved all too correct. During the set of days after my lengthy initiation into the seminal rites of Town, a small incident, the breaking of four cases of bottles, touched off the events known as The Great Coke Bottle Mystery, or Slag Krummel Rides, Howsoever Badly, Again.

It was a Wednesday or Thursday morning—without the limits of an established weekend period of rest, we seldom knew the day of the week. Lt. Dottlinger always checked the Day Room first thing each morning. He counted the pool cues and balls, and the shuffleboard pucks, examined the felt of the pool tables for new nicks or tears, and made sure the Coke machine was full. These things were nominally his responsibility since the equipment had been purchased from the Company Fund and the Coke machine was a concession of the Fund. All seemed well until he felt a bit of glass crunch under his spit-shined shoe. He picked it up, and found it to be the lip ring off the rim of a bottle. He knew the trick: two rims hooked together, then jerk, and a neat little ring of glass pops off one or both. He didn't see any others at first, but when he examined the trash in the houseboy's dust bucket, he found dozens of rings. Also, he noted, there were hundreds of cigarette butts, in spite of his standing orders against extinguishing them on the Day Room floor. He checked the four cases of empties. All except for one had been broken. Dottlinger took the dust bucket and dumped its contents in a neat pile in front of the innocently humming Coke machine. He shooed the houseboy out, closed and locked the double doors opening to the outside passageway, unplugged the Coke machine, which burped twice like a drunken private in ranks, rolled shut the louvers on both walls, turned off the lights, then locked the entrance from the Orderly Room.

He took the pass box from the 1st Sgt's desk and placed it in his desk which he always kept locked. Then he called the Criminal Investigation Division.

The CID officer who came was a heavy Negro captain in a baggy suit and 1930s snap-brim hat which shouted "Copper!" He nodded his head when Lt. Dottlinger explained the situation and showed him the evidence, but said nothing. The CID man dusted part of one case of bottles at Lt. Dottlinger's insistence. There were over two hundred partial, smudged and clear prints on them. When Lt. Dottlinger demanded that he run a check on the prints, the CID officer shook his head and said, "Lieutenant, they are Coke bottles. For treason, perhaps even for a murder, I might be able to run the ten thousand or so prints on those bottles, but for Coke bottles . . . sorry about that." He shrugged and left. Tetrick heard Lt. Dottlinger mumble, "Damned nigger cops. Can't expect them to understand the value of property."

Shortly before noon a notice was posted on the bulletin board. There would be no passes pending confession of the bottle-breaker.

In theory mass punishment is against the Uniform Code of Military Justice but since a pass is a privilege rather than a right, it can be denied at any time for no reason.

Most of the men were extremely annoyed at first, but they quickly settled down, thinking, as did Lt. Dottlinger, that the guilty party would confess. During those first few days they found it almost refreshing not to be able to go to Town. They had the Airman's Club and the Silver Wing Service Club to pass the nights, or they could bowl or go to the gym or the

library. A new, exciting kind of party evolved in the large
storm ditches on the edge of the Company Area, called Champagne Ditch Parties. Mumm's was cheap at the Club and did
not count on the liquor ration. The ditches were concrete
lined, about five feet deep and shaped like an inverted trapezoid. A man could sit in the bottom, lean back and drink
Mumm's from a crystal glass, and hope it didn't rain if he
passed out. A kid from Trick One broke both arms trying to
broad jump a ditch one night, but took little of the fun out of
the parties.

So they did these things for one, two, then three weeks, but
no one ever came forward. I noticed that Morning who had
been the loudest and longest griper at first seemed to be
resigned to the lack of Town. By the end of the fourth week
the only hope was the return of Capt. Saunders. Tetrick had
given up trying to persuade Lt. Dottlinger, and had taken to
playing golf three afternoons a week, drunk before the tenth
tee. The men were quiet, but uneasily so. They, like Morning,
had stopped talking about it. They gathered shamelessly
around the older dependent girls at the pool; they who had
vowed to a man at one drunken time or another never to sully
their hands on a leech. Even Novotny shouted from the high
diving board, strutted his brown body before them and let
them pity his scarred leg. He had taken an eighteen-year-old
one to the movie one night, but Trick Two was waiting in
ambush and hooted him out of the theater. "There are some
things a man just doesn't do," Cagle snorted when Novotny
complained to him.

Every room had its personal copies of *Playboy*, and they
were closely guarded. Closed doors were respected with a
warning knock, and men took alternate cubicles in the latrine
out of deference to the *Playboy* readers. All the seed which
heretofore had been cast into the bellies of whores, now
flushed down larger, wetter holes, until it was a wonder that
the sewage system didn't clog or give birth.

I kept busy during this time, helping the sergeant from the
Agency outfit who was going to coach the football team draw
up plays and practice routines. He had asked me to coach the
line as well as play. Tetrick and I had tried to go to Town

twice. Both times we ended up at old movies and felt guilty for two days afterward. Oddly enough I had the best run of luck I had ever seen during this month. I won over seven hundred fifty dollars in four nights at the NCO Club playing poker, then went to Manila with Tetrick and took out three thousand pesos shooting craps at the Key Club while a quiet, fat Filipino dropped ten thousand on the back line against my string of thirteen straight passes. He looked as if he wanted to kill me when I quit after thirteen. But still I didn't have enough money to get passes for the men.

Then word came that Capt. Saunders was going to take a month's leave after the school. That meant another six weeks without Town, and that was unbearable for the men. It is one thing to be a soldier, to live in a world of close order drill, of Physical Training each morning, equipment maintenance, maneuvers, training lectures, and another thing to be a clerk, a changer of typewriter ribbons, a cleaner of keys. Being a soldier gives you the feeling of accomplishment no matter how stupid you think the whole idea is: you survive in spite of everything they can do to you. Being a clerk has all the stupidities, all the same injustices as being a soldier, but none of the pride: anyone can survive being a clerk. It is the same problem which attacks men on assembly lines and in paper-shuffling office jobs when they discover that their life is as senseless as their work. They take to the bottle, join lodges, coach little league teams, have an affair—anything to forget what they are. The men in the 721st had Town to cover all these areas of memory-killing. Oh, sure, some of them made their tours in the Philippines on library books, camera trips and butterfly collections, but most needed Town. That is why it was there. And Lt. Dottlinger had taken it away. So what happened had to happen. (Or at least I like to tell myself that it did.)

If Morning had come to me with his idea in the beginning, I would have, as he so aptly noted, stopped him, but he came near the end, when it was ready for enactment, and it was too late to stop him.

He came in my room the night before the mass confession, grinning and excited, popping his fingers and pushing his glasses back up on his nose. "We got him," he said, opening my door without knocking.

"Who?"

"Slutfuckingfinger, man. Lt. Big Butt Dottlinger. Pinned to the wall by his mangy cock. Betrayed by his own words."

"What? Who? . . ."

"I got every one of them, man, every last swinging dick." He danced around my room as if he needed to pee.

"Wait a minute. Slow down. Sit down and let me know who has got whom where."

He swung a chair in front of the bunk, straddled it, and said, "The man said, 'No passes until the guilty one confesses.' Right? Right! Tomorrow he is going to confess."

"You know who it is?"

"No, but it doesn't make any difference."

"You elected a savior to sacrifice?" I laughed. I wondered who.

"No." He smiled and rubbed his thighs as if he had a magnificent secret. "Tomorrow morning at 0700, beginning with the day-trick before it goes to work and ending with the mid-trick, every enlisted man in the Operations section will go see the commanding officer and confess. . . ."

"Don't tell me. Not another word."

"What do you mean? We got that son of a motherfucker dead. Dropped him down, man."

"Don't tell me. Jesus, Morning," I said, getting off the bunk. "This kind of crap is . . . damnit, it's mutiny or inciting to mutiny or conspiring to mutiny or something. I don't know the name, but I do know it is Leavenworth talk. Don't you know that? Goddamn don't tell me. I don't want to know. I can't know. Get the hell out of here. Now!"

"What's with you? He can't touch a hair on our heads. He hasn't got the guts to court martial the whole outfit, and he can't get me unless somebody breaks."

"Morning, don't you understand, somebody will shit out. Somebody will! Somebody always does. Even a single trick couldn't pull this off, much less forty men. They're going to send you to jail, babe, forever."

"Somebody shits, they get busted!" He popped his fingers

loudly, and I knew it would happen. There was no doubt in his voice. "Besides, it will never get that far. Dottlinger will blow his stack, hit an enlisted man or have a heart attack or something. I go in first, and you know how he hates me, and he hasn't got the brains to think that I've got the guts to organize this and still go in first. He thinks I'm crazy."

"What if he takes just you."

"So fucking what? I only have one stripe to lose for my country."

"But what about. . . ." I moaned, waving my arm in the general direction of heaven and hell. "Do any of the other trick chiefs know?"

"You're not even supposed to know. But I thought you'd want to."

"How sweet. I don't know! I don't know you! Get your ass out of here!" I took the cigarette he offered. "At Leavenworth, kid, they got even a literary magazine, but no women, no beer, but lots of walls. You won't like it there."

"It'll work. What are you afraid of? It will work."

"Don't tell me. I don't want it to work. I hope you guys never get your passes back. Never. You're all crazy. I hope they lock you up forever. Jesus, what a mess. Don't do it. Don't do it."

"What!" he shouted. "And let that half-assed Arkansas farmer do this to us. Man, we have to fight back, and now! What kind of men are we if we let him do this to us and we don't fight back."

"Write your congressman. Consult the chaplain. Shit in the air. But don't try to fight the Army. Don't."

"We tried that. A guy whose godfather is a senator wrote him. You know what he answered? 'Part of being a man, son, is learning that we all have to suffer for the misdeeds of a few misguided individuals. Why, I was in the Army, *the Old Army*, for two years before I even heard about passes, and then I didn't get one for another six months. Buck up, son, it will make you a better man.' How about that, huh? Great. And the chaplain told me to pray for strength. Me! Fuck they don't care. They're on the other side. They always will be." He stood up and started pacing around the room as I was. "You're not some old rummy sergeant who thinks the Army is his mother.

You can see we have to do this. Cagle's shaving the palm of his hand, Novotny's screaming about Dear Johns in his sleep, and Franklin is sneaking out the gate with a pass and ID card he bought from an airman. We have to do something. You don't want to know . . ."—he shrugged—". . . then you don't want to know. Okay. But don't tell me not to do it."

"Don't do it."

"Ah, shit, Krummel, there's more than just passes involved here. Damnit, there's principles, and dignity too. We're not animals. We have some rights. We're human beings, living, breathing, thinking people, and that dickhead needs to learn he can't get away with that nineteenth century Capt. Bligh shit. Who the hell does he think he is? And where's he going to stop? Gas chambers or. . . ."

"Joe, sit down again," I interrupted. "Joe, you don't have any civil rights. None. Not a single one. So settle down. It's your pass he's pulled, not your pecker. You're going to make too much out of this—like that senator said, twenty years ago you wouldn't be worried about a pass 'cause you'd only see one twice a year—and the whole works is going to explode right in your face. There's no dignity: privates aren't allowed any. There aren't any principles involved. You're in the Army, and you're wrong on top of that. You joined, you swore, you made a contract to remove yourself from the human race for three years, and just because it's getting uncomfortable doesn't mean you have any right to break the contract. If you want dignity, there's dignity in being responsible, in not taking oaths lightly. As long as you stay straight, Lt. Dottlinger is wrong. Do this tomorrow, and you're wrong. You're in the Army, and they have your permission to do anything except cut your balls off. They can demand your life for no other reason than the fact that some dumb bastard wants it. You don't have to like it, don't have to believe in it, or even try to understand that armies are this way because they have to be, but you have to do what they say. Or pay for it." I sighed. His face had closed against me almost before I started.

"It's cheap at the price. I'll pay. They may take my life someday, but I'm sure as hell not going to give it to them, nor my dignity. You think I'm going to fight if they send troops to

Vietnam? Fuck no. Maybe you can kiss that bastard's ass, but not me." He stood up again.

"Okay. You know what you're going to do—then get the hell out of here. You don't want my advice—then shove off." I had been afraid he wouldn't listen, but this was not just a case of not hearing. He believed, which I admired, but which was sad too. He came too late in time to be part of any of the great, violent revolutions, and now had to waste himself on a foolishness.

"I came because I thought you would understand, not to ask advice."

"And maybe brag a little bit? But I do understand. That's why I'm afraid. There's a good chance nothing will happen to anyone except you. I'd be sorry to see that, but it might as well happen now as later. You'll end up in jail or dead someday, anyway. Might as well be now. But what if other men who don't know what they really want, or are doing, follow you into the shit."

"You afraid of losing your stripes?" He looked for a moment as if he had found the answer, but then thought not.

"Maybe a little. I didn't come back to lose them over anything like this. Right now they're heavy on my arm, but I like the money, the things they buy. And they are on *my* arm." I sat in the chair he had vacated.

"What are you—for sale?" He flopped on the bunk.

"Until I get a better offer. I fight for the best price."

"Bullshit." He grinned. "You just think that."

"It's the same thing."

"Okay," he said, standing up. "Maybe they'll make me editor of the magazine in Leavenworth, and I can get my shitty poetry published."

"Bullshit. Not even you have such bad taste." It was my turn to smile.

"Wish me luck," he said, lazily strolling toward the door.

"Aren't you going to ask if I'm going to turn you in?"

"Of course not. You're a revolutionary too. I just haven't convinced you yet," he said, then smiled and left. His confidence in my silence, his trust, was quite a compliment, and no one's head can be turned any easier than mine, but it was also a burden I would just as soon not have.

Only Joe Morning had the personality, the voice and the gall to convince so many men to even agree to such madness, much less carry it out. But he did it. He talked in private to every enlisted man in the Operations section, and then hit them again with a band of converts. I learned from Novotny that Morning had first mentioned the idea during the wee hours of a ditch party, but only mentioned it. Then the next day, when everyone had forgotten, he spoke about it again in the back of the three-quarter going to work, and then again coming back. He convinced Novotny in a long talk that night. Quinn and Franklin wondered why they hadn't thought of such a great idea. Cagle was ready for anything. The rest of the Trick was easy to convince. Once he had the Trick, he had their close friends on the other tricks, then their buddies, then the whole damned Company. That they only had to use physical persuasion on two men is an indication of the mood of the Company. And keeping it quiet was even easier, since the men were already security conscious because of the work.

It was beautiful and funny and I loved and feared the whole idea, but stayed in my room, sleeping with the door locked, while it took place.

I was blasted out about midmorning by Lt. Dottlinger on the handle of a bull horn. It was so loud I didn't understand what had been screamed, and I charged out in my shorts, thinking partly of Pearl Harbor and partly of a public execution. Lt. Dottlinger stood at my end of the hall calmly announcing, "Company formation in fifteen minutes!" He had known what was up when he opened the door to Morning and saw the line, but he didn't say anything. He had already given a blanket permission for anyone knowing anything about the broken bottles to see him without going through the 1st Sgt. He let them all in, asked questions about the bottles, made notes, and took names. Outside Tetrick was racing up and down the line, bald, sweat-shining head in hands, pleading with them to

break it up and go away before they were all killed. He
remembered a pile of heads he had seen in Burma left by the
Japanese. But Lt. Dottlinger was calm and controlled through
it all, though his control must have been the absolute hold
which marks the final stage of hysteria. He quietly ordered
each man back to his quarters after the interview. The men in
the back of the line were frightened, as well they might have
been, by this quiet approach of the lieutenant's. Many might
have broken line, but Morning, intrepid, wily Joe Morning, had
placed men he could trust on either side of those he couldn't;
and he knew just exactly which were which. But he hadn't
counted on Lt. Dottlinger's anger taking this form. More than
men have hung on the nature of another man's mood in the
morning. When I saw Lt. Dottlinger in the hall, speaking
pleasantly into the electric megaphone like a daytime televi-
sion game-show announcer, I knew Morning's plans had
failed. I wondered what was going to happen, as I got into
uniform; I should have wondered who was going to pay. When
Lt. Dottlinger had first seen me in the hall, he had smiled,
nodded, and said, "Good morning, Sgt. Krummel." How little
he knew.

The Company had been assembled on the volleyball court
between the barracks and the drainage ditches for nearly an
hour before Lt. Dottlinger came out. He was walking from the
waist down, a smug, arrogant strut like Brando in *The Wild
One*. Ah, he was loose. I thought for a moment he might
mumble too, but he had added an English undertone to his
Southern accent to strut a bit more. He accepted Tetrick's
"Hall pre'nt an' 'counted for, sir," with a salute of languid
grace. I wanted to laugh. But it would have been a nervous
giggle. I, the whole Company too, was caught by that creepy
version of fear which only comes when you're faced with someone who is crazy. It isn't so much that you're frightened that
you might come to physical harm, but that you're faced with
something not human anymore. You don't know what it is,
and you don't care because you realize what it isn't, and you
can only run and run until you wipe the face of insanity from

the deepest regions of your memory; but as you run, you understand that some unsuspecting night you will dream that tormented, twisted face, and wake, oh my God, scream for the savior you had forgotten, and scream again, for the face is yours. Dottlinger scared us like that. If he had taken a rifle and shot the first rank of men or snatched a rose from his shirt and sniffed, none of us would have blinked.

"Well," he began, striding along the Company front, his hands clasped casually behind him. For once he didn't have his ball-point swagger stick. "It seems we have a small mutiny on our hands, troopers. Or at least a conspiracy to mutiny, troopers, which carries an equally harsh penalty. I would only guess, but I could probably put each and every one of you behind bars for the rest of your natural lives." He pivoted, paused and reflected. It wasn't a particularly hot day, but two large sweat stains were slowly creeping from under Lt. Dottlinger's arms like cancerous stigmata. He wasn't quite so frightening now. He was beginning to lose his edge, and was forced to begin to play himself. It had taken too long to write his speech. "But I'm not going to do that," he continued. "At least not right this minute. I'm sure most of you men didn't mean to cause this much trouble, or face such a stiff charge. Certainly your leaders lied to you about this—you're surprised I know there were leaders. Don't be, don't be. It was obvious. Yes, I'm sure there were leaders, perhaps even a single organizer." He paused, "And I would like to put him behind bars. I really want that. I want him!" He could barely control himself now.

"But I'll let that go. Let it go," he said, smiling suddenly, a forced, theatrical smile. "Yes, even that. Just to let you know I'm a fair and understanding officer. Yes, I'll forget this whole little affair ever took place, and I'll even lose the names of the men. Yes.

"But I want, I still want, and I will have the man whobroke-the . . . bottles." He took a deep breath before continuing. "I have an idea, mind you, just a hint of an idea, that he will be the same man who organized this childish little demonstration." Morning grunted with anger behind me. "This same whining disrespect for authority applies to property too and comes out of the same Godless overeducated under-spanked children.

"Until such time as the man who broke the four cases of Coke bottles, the ninety-six bottles, confesses, you are restricted to the Company and Operations Area, and to your quarters when not working, eating, or relieving yourself," he said, very businesslike now. A communal moan drifted up from the men. Morning grunted again, this time like a frustrated wart hog preparing to charge.

"At ease!" Tetrick growled.

"The day-trick will relieve the mid-trick after noon chow, and then make up the lost time by going to work at 0400 tomorrow morning." Nice move. The day-trick was going on Break, and my Trick would have to make up the time.

It wasn't good, but it wasn't disaster either. Then I heard another grunt from Morning, a furious exhalation, and he started to say, "Request permission. . . ." But I overruled him.

"Request permission to speak to the Company Commander, sir," I sang out. Dottlinger wouldn't hold to his word about forgetting about the mutiny charges if he got hold of Morning. Why he hadn't figured it out by this time was a wonder to me.

"Certainly, Sgt. Krummel."

I said dreadful things to myself as I walked toward him, but I wasn't afraid of him anymore. I just didn't know what I was going to say.

"Could I speak to you in private, sir?" I asked after saluting. The sweat blackened areas of his shirt had grown, and his face was pale, but his eyes still glittered with fire enough for one more encounter. He told Tetrick to have the men stand easy. I followed him a few steps toward the barracks.

"Yes, Sgt. Krummel?"

"Sir. Sir, I know I'm off base, but the events of this morning seem to call for unusual actions."

"They are unusual events."

"Yes, sir."

"Well, sergeant, what did you want?" he inquired when I hadn't spoken for several seconds.

"Well, sir, it's about the restriction to the Company Area."

"What about it?"

"Well, sir, ah, I'm worried about the quality of the work at Operations. It is already low due to the tension, and this, harsher restriction, sir, will probably lower it even further. The Filipino liaison officer has already threatened to go to the major if the work doesn't pick up." One lie. "And the men are terribly on edge, sir, already. Might even say they're horny as hell, sir." I giggled like a high school virgin. I was willing to be anything.

"I think the men can curb their physical appetites, sergeant. There's too much of that sort of thing happening in this Company anyway. And as for the quality of the work—send them to me if it doesn't pick up. This outfit is getting soft. It needs a little iron, and I intend to see that they get it."

"Yes, sir, I agree." Two lies. "But the men feel that if the man who broke the bottles. . . ." (God, I thought, is this really about some broken bottles.) ". . . is in the Company, sir, then he has confessed and, sir, no matter how silly this logic sounds, or how much a play on words it is, that's the way the men feel, sir, and. . . ."

"Well, if they think I'm going to be threatened. . . ."

"Excuse me, sir, but they don't mean that, I'm sure." Three lies. "They're just desperate, sir, and I'm afraid, sir, that we might have a real mutiny on our hands. I saw one in Korea, sir, and it was bad." Four lies. "Everyone's record took a permanent blemish, sir."

He nodded. He knew who was threatening whom, and he didn't like it. He thought for a bit, then smiled slowly as if he knew something. "You're perfectly correct, sergeant, a real mutiny would be quite disastrous. But I don't see how I can go back on my word, do you?"

"Sir?"

"Well, everyone hasn't confessed."

"Sir?"

"You haven't confessed, Sgt. Krummel. You might have done it, for all I know." He smiled again, a smile which said, "I've got you Mr. Master's Degree."

"Sir, I'd like to make a statement. I'm the one, sir, who broke your Coke bottles in the Day Room." Five lies. "I'll make restitution to the Company Fund, sir, and plead guilty to any charges you would like to make in connection with the actual destruction of the bottles, sir."

"Were you drunk, sergeant?" Oh, he was loving this.

"No, sir."

"Then why did you do it?" His best fatherly tone.

"Momentary loss of perspective, sir. The machine took my coin and refused me a Coke, and since the machine was unbreakable, I avenged myself on the innocent bottles, sir."

"Sounds as if you might be mentally unbalanced, sergeant." How he would like me to plead that.

"No, not at all, sir. Like all good soldiers, sir, I have a quick temper and a strong sense of right which, under the direction of competent officers, can be a formidable weapon in combat, sir."

For a second he had forgotten whom he was playing with. "Well . . . Well, this isn't combat. Return to your Trick, and report to me after this formation."

"Right, sir." I saluted sharply, whirled and marched back.

Lt. Dottlinger turned to Tetrick, told him to dismiss the Company after informing the men that all prior restrictions were lifted and the pass box would be open immediately. The Day Room would be reopened after proper cleaning. The men had already heard the lieutenant's words, and they cheered when Tetrick dismissed them. Most ran for the barracks to change for Town, but a few paused to ask unanswered questions of me.

I told Tetrick what I had done before I went in to see Dottlinger. He assured me that Dottlinger would not dare any more than an Article 15, Company Punishment. Tetrick seemed resigned that someone would be slaughtered for the greatest good, and seemed not to mind particularly that that someone was me. His attitude seemed to say, "It's for the best."

"To hell with it," I said. "Maybe I'll kiss the bastard and let him queer me out, or maybe bust his pussylick face for him and let him hang my stripes for teeth he ain't going to have."

"If you do, holler, so I can be a witness that he hit you first," Tetrick laughed.

But I had already thought of the worst thing he could do: ignore my confession, let me go, and then single out any enlisted man and bust him with evidence he would say I'd given; and if I didn't agree to this, then the Company would be back on restriction again. I was surprised how much I hated Dottlinger at that moment, but even more surprised to discover that I wasn't worried about my stripes and that I cared about the respect of my men. I had said, when I reenlisted back in Seattle, that God couldn't involve me with anything or anybody again; I wanted to be a happy, stupid, payday drunk. But what God couldn't do, Joe Morning managed.

Dottlinger did, as Tetrick had predicted, give me Company Punishment: two hours extra duty for fifteen days. One hour policing the Day Room and one hour marching in front of the barracks as an example with full field pack and blanket roll. "To begin immediately," he had said. He unlocked the Day Room, had me open the louvers, and gloated while I swept the floor with a short broom.

So for fifteen days no one spoke to me for fear I'd take their heads off. The whole thing was so public, marching in daylight, squatting in the Day Room like a recruit. Once at a particularly bleak moment Tetrick had said, "Tell him to fuck himself. He hasn't got a leg to stand on. He can't touch you within the regs."

"For a man with no legs, he's stepping on my toes pretty heavily," I answered—but thought about his suggestion more than I care to admit.

I had nearly decided that what I had done wasn't worth it when the only good thing of the time happened. This kid from Trick One came out of the barracks one day when the sun was pouring into my fatigues like lava, and at that dark, sun-blinded moment, had said, "Look at the little tin soldier. It walks, it talks, it's almost human." I don't suppose he intended that I hear him, but I had. Someone else had too. From the second floor above the door an invisible voice roared like the wrath of Jehovah. "Shut your wise mouth, fuckhead!" The kid

jumped, looked around, then dashed back in the barracks, perhaps wondering if God hadn't spoken to him.

I glowed. I sparkled. I felt heroic for a change, instead of
dumb. (I'm not ashamed: pride has turned better heads than
mine.) Someone understood.

"Ah 'tis a kind voice I hear above me," I said, but only a
deep laugh answered me.

But by the time my hour was over I had lost that quick lift
under the sun. The sun wasn't merely in the sky, it was the
sky. From horizon to zenith the heavens burned in my honor,
and in my chest and back and head. And in the shattering
light all clear things lost themselves. Colors faded into pale
imitations of themselves and became dust.

I had come back to be alone, to find simplicity, and had
found trouble, and in this trouble found I must fall back on
that which I was, that which I would be, that which I had
always tried not to be.

I am the eldest son of generations of eldest sons, the final
moment of a proud descent of professional killers, warriors,
men of strength whose only concern with virtue lay in personal
honor. But I still misunderstood a bit that day, I still confused
being a soldier with being a warrior. That small, mean part of
me which had wanted to care about rank and security and
privilege was dying, and with the death of order began the
birth of something in me monstrous, ah, but so beautiful. My
heritage called, and though it would be many long moons
before I answered, the song had burst my cold, ordered heart
and I hated in the ringing sweep of the sun, and I lived.

HISTORICAL
NOTE 1

There are days, whole, long, lovely days in the mountains which have nothing to do with the sun. A thick damp fog drifts in, draping the peaks and the high valleys in eternal mourning, gray, misty mourning. The fog limits my view but increases my perspective (that is, I suppose, what limits are for), and though I can only see the two dripping pines and an occasional bird, I can hear the world on such days. Not that I stop staring out the windows; perhaps I hope to see a sound. On my own, of course; you know how I hate drugs. But the sounds, clean, sharp tones . . . they pierce the blanket. I am convinced (sadly so, according to Abigail, or perhaps she said madly; she tends toward an insecure mumble when she speaks) that the only reason I can't hear watches ticking on golfers' wrists is because of the pounding of their pulses as they stride confidently past the windows. I still live out those windows. They have become my connection with life, except for Lt. Abigail Light, because Capt. Gallard hasn't spoken to me since the day of the incident with Lt. Hewitt.

But as much as I stare out those windows, I didn't see Gallard creep up while I was reading the Sunday *Stars and Stripes*.

"The present may be captured in those limp pages, my friend, but the past, and the future too, are out here, across this dim, gray, timeless mist," a voice tolled in the window. I started, but caught only a glimpse of a golf cap, and wondered who the hell was playing tricks on a sick man. I should have known: a doctor.

In a few minutes the voice came again, disembodied, from the hall. "Yes, the past, dim, bloody past, my poor, mad fellow." Gallard stepped in, wearing rumpled short pants, a knit shirt, crepe-soled canvas shoes, and a nifty new golfing cap. He looked half-pleased, as if he had just made a hole-in-one which no one saw, and a drowsy smile lifted the sagging skin along his jaw line. His face always seemed to me well-used: Whatever the expression, from grin to scowl, and whatever the extent of his emotion, his face had a wrinkle for it.

"Jesus shit. I thought I was having a visitation," I said.

"You are, you are," he chuckled, smiling still more. "May I come in?"

"Please do, kind spirit. I'd rather have you where I can keep an eye on you, than prowling around in the fog scaring hell out of me," I answered, folding the paper. The pages were limp at that.

"It's hell I'm scaring in, not out. Murder must pay."

"On the installment plan?"

"Don't read that crap," he said, gesturing with a large thermos bottle from behind his back. "Isn't it

enough that you give life, limb and dignity to the
Army? You don't have to wipe your mind with their
version of the news." He took the paper out of my
hands and tossed it into the trash can.

"Okay. What are you up to, besides collecting
newspapers for Great Britain?"

He explained that he wouldn't gather manure for
the English, claiming that they were too hesitant
about commiting their troops in World War II.

"Sorry," I interrupted. "But why are you creeping
about the clouds?"

"Well," he said, paused, then got up to shut the
door. "I was supposed to play golf with the Base
Commander but, as you can well see, we were fogged
out. So I've been at the Club, crying over a dozen
vodka martinis with the old man. And since he gave
me some good news about you, I thought you'd want
to know. So here I am. Hate golf anyway. I'll give
you a drink if you promise to stay sane." He poured
two small ones out of the thermos. "Cheers?"

"Cheers?"

"You should be happier than that." He seemed
almost angry, and sailed his new cap into the trash.

"Why tell?"

"Because our leaders have decided not to send you
to jail."

"Why not?"

"Why not? Well, mainly because I've managed, at
great expense, to convince everyone from Lt. Hewitt
to the Base Commander to an angry Air Police sergeant that you should be forgiven on the grounds of
post-combat reaction or some other bit of jargon.

"We haven't had so many Vietnam casualties that
we've gotten casual about them yet, and since one of
the ones we had died under rather suspicious circumstances—a drunken doctor and the wrong shot

and all that sort of stuff. So everybody has a tinge of
a guilty conscience right now which they will surely
soon get over quickly. . . ."

"Thanks. Who died?"

"Nobody you know. It's always nobody nobody
knows." Gallard paused, his shoulders and chest,
usually puffed in a knot of intense energy, seemed to
be caving in upon themselves, sucked down in the
wake of a sigh like a temple falling into the waves.
"He wasn't from your outfit. With the usual attempt
at security, they scattered your outfit's wounded like
illegitimate children all over the Pacific. There are
even, I hear, three guys in a British hospital in Singa-
pore or someplace. Security, yes."

"The bastards notified my old man that I was
injured in an aircraft accident."

"The security officer hasn't gotten to you yet to
swear you to silence; that's why you have a private
room. Less contact with uncleared personnel. Christ.
Now everyone in the Far East knows about it." He
sighed again. "I had to make a deal, though."

"What? What about?"

"Your court martial. As soon as you are marked fit
for duty, as if you ever were, you will. . . ."

"Get shipped back to Vietnam?" I interrupted.

"Don't be silly. Of course not. A medical discharge
will be drawn up, I'll sign it; you get out, plus a
twenty-five percent disability which you will lose at
your first reexamination. So you get away free; like
you always will, I suppose."

I laughed.

"What's so funny?" His face brightened for a moment.

"I'll tell you someday."

"Please don't."

I didn't quite know what to say; thank him or

curse him. I didn't even know what to think about him. His concern was obvious, even bordering on fascination. . . . What was Marlowe's line? "The fascination of the abomination—you know." I understood it, even welcomed it as far as I understood it. An odd relationship, doctor to patient, savior to warrior, officer to man. But I never said "Sir" to him, not because of the friendship, but because it was unthinkable. His innate kindness, his curiosity, his love gently thrust him outside the officer, the uniform and made him a man, a man to whom I could say, "How about another drink?", a man who would answer, "I'm sorry, I didn't notice that you were empty."

As he poured, I asked. "Why?"

"It's seldom men know why they do things," he said, then reflected a bit. How like him to know what I was asking. "Maybe because I hated to see anyone, even you, railroaded into Leavenworth."

"Not much of a reason."

"No, I guess not." He sat his drink down, then dug into his hair and continued with a nervous chuckle, "And not even the real one either."

I waited. I had time.

"You might say I did it because I used to dream about you when I was a child. Or have nightmares, I guess, would be more accurate." His face drifted through a series of frowns and half-smiles as he leaned back in the chair and clasped his hands behind his neck.

"I suppose I'm obligated to be flattered or something, but I don't really know what the hell you mean."

"Oh, not you really. It's a funny thing, a long story. You see, I've got this thing . . . ha! got . . . had this thing for World War I airplanes when I was a kid. I must have built thirty or forty models of them—it took ten tries to get one to fly; but it did finally fly. Perfectly. Nearly a quarter of a mile down the road to a neighbor's place and made this perfect landing. I ran all the way with it. God, I ran. But it landed, as I said, perfectly, but in a hog pen, of course, and the damned hogs trampled it and chewed it and ate it, rubber bands and all." He smiled to himself; he had forgotten about me. "God knows why. Maybe they liked the way the glue smelled or maybe they just didn't care for their pen to be used as a landing strip. Who the hell knows? They ate it though, every bit of it, and all the while I was crying and throwing clods at them, but they just bounced off their fat, complacent rumps. I ran home and cried to my mother that it wasn't fair, but she said that God didn't promise that life would be fair, but that He would have mercy. Well, I said so much for a guy who doesn't play fair, and that was the end of that.

"Where was I? Oh, yes. Anyway, in spite of God in heaven and pigs in the world, I kept building airplanes, tried some design modifications on the plans I got out of *Popular Mechanics,* even designed a few of my own," he said with pride. "And when I hurt my hand, the worst pain came from not being able to work on the airplanes. And then I became so wrapped up, so obsessed, that I began to dream about them. Every night. Every time I closed my eyes I was in the cold, blue air over France in a Camel. God, I was a gay, rake-hell dog, too. Theatrical smudges of grease here and there, a scuffed leather jacket. But no scarf. I had better taste even then." He laughed, then drank, perhaps dreamng of the thundering wind, the rainbow circling his biplane's shadow as it leaped and ran and leaped again over the hedges.

"I, of course, was an ace at thirteen; but there was always a single dark cloud in my dreaming sky. Perhaps I'd learned something from the hogs. The cloud didn't show up often, but often enough, and always so damned unexpectedly. I called him the Black Baron of Beirut, for reasons I've long since forgotten, but I think his name was Baron von Rumplested or something silly like that. He was always dropping out of the sun just after I had vanquished six Fokkers and wham! down I'd go in one of those awful falling dreams and then wake up in cold, heaving sweats. Not a dogfight, no contest, just wham! and down I'd go. He never bothered with finesse or fancy maneuvers or anything, he just swooped down and shot hell out of me. Once when my guns had jammed, he had the gall to pour sheepdip all over me, and while I was trying to get it out of my eyes, he dropped the five gallon can on my right wing and broke it off.

"God, how I hated him. How glad I was when I exchanged the airplanes for women and the dreams ended. But I never forgot that face, that beaklike nose and that evil moustache drooping past the corners of his mouth. He was a dark German, an Asiatic German, not at all a warm, sunburnt Nordic German. His face looked like the word 'Hun' sounds, and his eyes always made me think of the Black Forest, even after I learned that it was in West Germany. And later when I was older and had a real war to deal with, when I found out it wasn't anything except stupid and evil and cruel and without honor, his face became all that dark, primitive nature, that dark, throbbing blood, that fogged crossroads where evil meets beauty, and. . . ." He stopped; perhaps at the crossroads he paused once again, then went on because he thought he knew the way.

"Guess I got carried away. But I haven't talked about the dreams since the War, or even thought about them, and was glad to forget . . . until I saw your crazy, roaring eyes and mad face straining up at me as if I were the enemy, and I thought you were someone I knew. Then I realized you were the Baron's son—no, the Baron himself, and so I. . . . What the hell are you grinning about?" he asked, seeming half-angry. "What's so damned funny?"

I told him.

Once upon a time (yes, once upon a time, for this too is a fairy tale as all history is, and it, even more like history, makes its truth not from fact but from belief and, yes, I do believe) near where the present borders of East and West Germany and Czechoslovakia share a common point, where the old boundaries of Bavaria, Bohemia, and Saxony once merged in that indefinite way politics and religion and war joined in those days, there used to be a small village, called Krummel. The village served a small, nameless (as far as the journals of the first of us are concerned) monastery which brewed a tiny amount of a special heavy beer, described as being as good and as thick as black bread. The village, lying in a small valley served by a single road of sorts which ended at the village, or beyond, as you will, existed solely for the purpose of growing grain, hops and such for the brewery. The monastery and thus the village belonged, ostensibly, to an old abbot in Hof, but it had been many years since the abbot had made the rough, long trip through a range of rugged hills to Krummel, and by the period which most concerns me, the monastery regulations were quite lax. In fact the only difference between a monk and a villager was where the man worked, brewery or fields. As you might expect, Krummel suffered a peaceful isolation, nearly untroubled by visitors from the world.

Sometime during the early years of the seventeenth century, though, a visitor did appear; one Jacob Slagsted, driving a combined medicine-peddler's wagon, selling magic, feats of strength, stinking (thus potent) herbs, tinkering skills, and various domestic goods. This Slagsted seems to have been a giant of a man, but agile enough for his own wizardry. And even more impressive, he could read. He claimed to be a retired, reformed mercenary, and there may even be some truth in the village gossip which said, "Reformed into a highwayman." There were even those who claimed that Slagsted was hiding from both the authorities and his own merry band of cutpurses.

He took a several weeks' advantage of the hospitality of the monks, spending more for the beer than he took in for his goods and services, and in fact created a small economic boom in Krummel during his visit. There were many sad faces among monk, villager, and wife when Jacob finally left. He wasn't your run-of-the-mill peddler, though, and wasn't quickly forgotten, what with his breaking logs on his head and slipping pigeons and larks and finches out of the air and great, passionate readings from his Good Book in Latin, a large, leather copy which he kept in a carved camphor chest fit for at least a duke or a heathen Turk. No, he was not quickly forgotten. Nor, I suppose, did he forget the isolated village, the quiet valley, the fine beer, for he returned five years later.

The villagers found his wagon one winter morning; his horse hipshot, lather frozen on its flanks, still standing unharnessed. Slagsted was huddled in the wagon box, a great, red shield of blood frozen on his chest. The monks, as monks in spite of their religion will, were kind to him, carried him into the monastery, revived him with crude brandy and shook their heads at Jacob's tale of assault by highwaymen and attempted robbery and a gallant fight against overwhelming odds. Some may have doubted his story, but none doubted that he would die before morning, and the shelter and care they offered was to a dying man. But the old devil wouldn't give up the ghost, and once he had his hands firmly around it, he wouldn't leave the village. Through the long winter he stayed, helpful at small tasks, beer casks, and tales as he repaired crockery and tin for the village hausfrauen. Oh, the heathen wars he had lived over, the fighting, the looting. . . . But as spring came, Slagsted went more often for singular walks, roaming the stubbled, muddy fields or the small, irregular hills near the edge of the valley, and once even disappeared into the forest for several days. He returned, but when asked where he had been, he merely gave a deep, serene smile in answer. Somehow, however these things happen, the rumor started that Jacob Slagsted, man of uncertain origin, man of Low German, High German, Bohemian and other unknown tongues, had been seen conversing with the Virgin during his wanderings.

Then came the freshest day of spring, dawn in the sky like a blush, the air like spring water, and Jacob Slagsted standing on a nearby hill, silhouetted against a rosy horizon, standing still and black, his arms stretched for heaven.

The villagers noticed first, then called the monks, and they all gathered at the foot of the hill, awed and silent. Jacob stood as he was for what seemed hours as the villagers and the monks kept their watch. Then with a motion so swift as not to be seen, Jacob cast himself upon the earth, and above him rose a shadowy, wavering figure of white, a small cloud of fog on a fog-less morning, a translucence, a virginal white. Jacob remained against the hilltop until the figure dissolved in the breeze, then he knelt in prayer, his voice deep and echoing across the valley, his prayer in an unknown tongue. When he finished he strolled quietly down the hill and that same day, in an unusual, unheard of ceremony, took his vows as a monk, then embarked on a daily ritual of ordeal, fasting, hairshirts, prayer, and flagellation. Such piety had not been seen in many years; some of the older monks even cried. Ah, there were those, those who doubted, who claimed Jacob's miracle to be of his own doing, created out of a wisp of gauze, a bit of smoke, and a handful of wind; but there will always be those who doubt.

No one could deny, though, Jacob's devotion to duty, his piety, or his love for the prayer and the fast. If the truth be known, Jacob quickly embarrassed the other brothers—even those who had shed a tear or two—about their vows of poverty, chastity, and sobriety so loosely taken. Even worse, this Jacob-come-lately to the Church became a constant nuisance with his endless preaching against those brothers who kept wives of a sort which indeed included all those who had ever been young enough.

"Chastity, chastity fills the soul with purity, purity," he would chant at night in a low voice which invaded every polluted cell.

"Aye, he can speak of chastity, him who's had half the heathen bitches in this world and the next, already," one brother complained.

Brother Jacob so troubled the Father Superior about the laxity of the morals within and without the monastery walls that the old soul left his desk one morning, walked back to Hof to live with his married sister, and left the administrative chair in the spiritual hands of Brother Jacob.

And with this event began another period of quietude. The spiritual leader of the brewery again wandered the hills and forest, occasionally seen walking slowly, hands clasped devoutly before him, head bowed, followed by a one-eyed little man with a ring in his ear. The rumors ran again, except that now Brother Jacob had been talking with Satan instead of the Virgin and that the pious brother was negotiating for his (the devil's) salvation. But all remained quiet for the present, and the rumors died a worthy death. (It was during this time, I believe, that Jacob slipped into Hof with the yearly tithe for the old abbot, and released a dozen pigeons from the sleeve of his habit, and, during the confusion, nipped all the records of the monastery. Within the year the village was forgotten—few knew where it really was, anyway—forgotten, except for a few stout beer-drinkers who momentarily raised their watery eyes above their stomachs, belched and complained about their beer. Jacob somehow made arrangements to cart the beer north to Dresden for John George, Elector of Saxony.)

Things were easy now; Brother Jacob drank more and preached less and took a woman—more than his share, it was said. Then the Reformation came to Krummel one drunken, rainy night as Jacob Slagsted, Protestant spy and revolutionary, drove the good brothers out in the rain with a large sword he had hidden in his now rotting wagon. The brothers huddled in the rain, in the cold wind until they converted. Jacob dispensed with baptism, claiming God's own tears of joy water enough for any good follower of Luther. The brewery was seized in the name of good business; Jacob had laid his plans well, recruited some of the younger brothers and villagers secretly, and carried the coup with little bloodshed and less sweat.

The Reformation caused a slight ripple in the placid pond of Krummel; Jacob and the one-eyed man, who had silently appeared the next day, ran the brewery, the brothers became laborers, and the villagers farmed as always. Jacob married in a mass ceremony in which he married all the other brothers and their sinful women. Life was peaceful; living was good. Jacob's old wounds didn't ache so badly, and the beer sales to John George kept Jacob from drinking the village out of house and barrel. Oh, an occasional befuddled tax collector from the abbot's office blundered into the village; those unconverted by drink and fine living were buried with full rites by Jacob in the forest. But another came searching accompanied by five men-at-arms, and wasn't so easily disposed of. So Jacob, the one-eyed man, and several of Jacob's friends who had found shelter in the village began training the young men of the village in the varied pleasures of combat. The farmers and brewers took well to the excitement of pike and musket, and defeated, in ambush, several larger groups of tax men, some of whom came from the abbot's office and others from a duchy in Bohemia who unfortunately mistook Krummel for some other delinquent village. But all in all these were the quiet years, and during them Jacob produced four living sons, Johann, Georg, Bernard and Hugo.

But Europe wasn't quiet; the Holy Roman Empire was begetting wars as plentifully as soldiers bastard children in a foreign land. In 1618 the new Catholic deputy-governor and his secretary, appointed by

Archduke Ferdinand of Styria, King of Bohemia, Emperor of the Holy Roman Empire, had been attacked by a Protestant mob in Prague. The mob heaved the new deputy-governor and his secretary out of an upper-story window, exclaiming, "Now call on your Mary to save you!" When they looked out the window they saw, some sixty feet below, the two good Catholics running across the lawn.

Two years later when Jacob heard about the incident while on a trip to Dresden, he remarked in his journal, "She did, my God, She did." He began drinking heavily before breakfast and feeling badly about it. And once more he walked alone in the hills.

While Jacob brooded, Central Europe stumbled through the beginnings of the Thirty Years' War, and it wasn't long before this match between pestilence and war, with man as the loser, provided Jacob with more evidence of the Blessed Virgin's interference in worldly affairs. At the Battle of the Neiber River the Margrave of Baden led Protestant forces against the Catholics, Spanish under Cordoba and Bavarians under Tilly. The superior reformers had nearly carried the day when suddenly the figure of the Virgin was seen to rise over the Protestant lines. The Catholics, devout souls all, rallied, regrouped and re-charged, shattering the Protestant lines with the courage of their devotion. (An ammunition dump in the Protestant rear had exploded and the resultant pillar of fire and smoke had been so identified by some nameless, abstract soul—which I suppose only proves that, in spite of all the grand military academies and their graduates, battles, and perhaps wars, are as wonderfully absurd in execution as poetry.) When Jacob heard of the miracle he actually wept (his tears, as tears will, still stain the journal pages); he cried for days as he clambered about the wooded hills, crawling as often as he walked, followed by a small boy carrying a small keg of beer.

As Jacob fretted over his soul, his sons, knowing as sons always do that the war would come to them, increased the training program for the village militia. By the summer of 1625 Krummel possessed a tough, gristy band of forty fighting men which they assumed could hold the approaches to the valley against any foraging parties from either side—but, needless to say, they couldn't hold it against Jacob Slagsted. During that same summer, on a trip to Saxony with the second brewing, he heard that the Danes had entered the war. Jacob had been more or less drunk for seven years now, and although there is some indication that he didn't know who the Danes were, he hated them and decided to throw his strength and manpower on the other side, the Catholic side, the forces of the Virgin.

Off he marched with his small, merry band, provisioned with bread and beer, more frightened of Jacob than any Danes, whoever they might be, and ready for war. Thus the Lutheran conqueror of Krummel joined the Catholic armies of the emperor and, by mistakenly marching south in search of Danes, merged with the army of the mercenary, Wallenstein, Duke of Friedland.

The Duke must have been attracted to this mad, drunken giant because he personally signed the contract with Jacob for these forty men. Jacob and his sons prospered under Wallenstein and were all officers by April of 1626 when they fought Mansfeld at Dessau on the Elbe. In the fall of the same year Jacob commanded a company which returned from Wallenstein's pursuit of Mansfeld to reinforce Tilly against King Christian and his Danes. Jacob's hatred for the Danes hadn't been banked by a year of fight-

ing. In the battle at Lutten, Jacob led a charge on the
King's party, killed Christian's horse and, if his blade
hadn't stuck in a Danish adjutant's skull, would
have killed Christian too. For this Jacob was promoted to second-in-command under Wallenstein's
Lieutenant Hans George von Arvim, and with him
advanced into Brandenburg in 1627, wintered in
Jutland, then took part in the unsuccessful attack of
Stralsund on the Pomeranian coast. During the first
hour of the attack Bernard's horse was frightened by
a Catholic short-round, and it trampled Bernard to
death. Jacob somehow blamed the loss on the North
Sea, the Danes; he cried for the Virgin, but she
obviously preferred the warmer, greener pastures to
the south, and his prayers were lost on the gray,
northern wind.

But three sons remained. The fighting became
occasional; small, inconclusive engagements now
and again. In August of 1630 they went with Wallenstein, who had resigned, back to Friedland as part
of the Duke's personal staff guard. While resting at
Friedland, the Duke gave Jacob title to the lands in
the valley of Krummel and a title, Graf Jacob Slagsted of Krummel. But Jacob gave nothing: he lied
about the location of the valley. Because of the rest
Jacob thankfully missed the sack and burning of
Magdeburg, the Virgin City, and Tilly's defeat by the
Swedes at Breitenfeld in Saxony.

After two years of rest the Slagsteds marched to
join Maximilian of Bavaria. On the march Georg fell
to the plague and died in a muddy ditch filled with
swimming rats. Jacob seemed old after this; the only
joyful note in the journal after the death of Georg is
a remark about the death of King Gustavus Adol-
phus at the Battle of Lutzen: "*Ya, sehr gut.*" The
next entry is dated February 25, 1634, the day after

Wallenstein had been assassinated by English mercenaries at Eger: *"Schade, schade. Ich werde nach Hause weidergehen."* Then the long journey home, back to Krummel for the first time in nine years, across fields sown with barren seed, reaped with sorrow, through towns of vacant stares and constant corteges of the living dead, over a land tired, torn, wasted—and the war had come to Krummel too, so that the landscape of war didn't end, but continued beyond all human belief. Jacob closed the road into the valley, hoping to save something, and he closed his heart and locked himself in a room with his Bible, read till his eyes went out, then gave up that ghost he'd held so firmly, the spirit of war. He did his best to live a quiet life in the old monastery, brewing a little beer, having Johann read the Bible, and, if not pleased, at least satisfied to grow old in peace.

But war remained in the hearts of his sons and, with the strength of youth, they found farming too little of life for them. Jacob gave Johann the leather Bible, the journal, and the camphor box when he and Hugo went to France to fight against the Spanish in 1636. (Nothing more is known about Jacob or Krummel; the sons of his body and spirit never returned. The village ceased to exist so long ago, no records even remain, no trace, no knowledge, no sign, even though my father found several valleys where it might have been, could have been, on a six-week leave in '45. God forbid that Jacob's grave should lie wrapped in the red tape of another splintered Germany.)

As to the sons—by 1640 Johann led his own mercenary army of three hundred well-trained, hand-picked men. They were provisioned and not allowed to forage or pillage on friendly lands. They were well paid and, unlike other mercenary troops such as the

German lansquenet, uniformed for war instead of show: a tunic with a stiff, thick leather breastplate, boots of waterproof Russian leather, a tight fitting, unadorned helmet. The three hundred were cavalry unlike any other contemporary horsemen: they fought on the ground as often as on horse. In Spain the three hundred held the line against a thousand Spanish, beat them off three times, then attacked and chased them until dark. But the best aspect of the Slagsted of Krummel army was its reliability; contracts were signed for durations instead of months which meant that they wouldn't change sides in the middle of a battle, anyway.

This paid army, because of its compact size, survived the change from mercenary to national armies, and during the seventeenth and part of the eighteenth century fought and served as personal guards for every political organization which could afford them. Descendants of Jacob Slagsted controlled the army, maintained its size at three hundred, kept up the family literacy outside military academies, married fine horses of women, and by 1776 had spilled, in love and war, the bloods of Europe: Irish, Dutch, Polish, Magyar, Finn, Swede, Jewish, Alsatian, Prussian, and Greek, at least. But in 1781 the Slagsted-Krummel's, as they were known, came to the New World, and like all who came to America, lost everything in the coming.

They arrived in Boston only to discover the war was over. The ship with the men and arms was impounded by the authorites and guarded by a warship, a refitted cutter which had seen no duty. The brothers in charge, Johann and Otto, were obviously gentlemen because of the size of their bribes and were let ashore. Johann rode to Philadelphia to get the release order, and Otto gambled and drank away all the money in the waterfront pubs of Boston. When Johann returned with a release order, two slick colonialists had another for him, impounding his men as bond servants to fulfill Otto's debts. Johann traded his horse for the family chest, signed the papers, then he and Otto rode south on one horse, knowing, I suppose, what was going to happen. When the colonialists tried to collect their servants, the men—still armed because no one had the nerve to try to disarm them—killed the Americans, blew the cutter to hell, stole the ship, and sailed away into an untraceable sea, perhaps slipping ashore later to add themselves to the great number of scoundrels and cutthroats already in America. Otto managed a commission in the Virginia militia, but Johann, tired of Otto and armies, rode on south and west.

The Slagsted-Krummels were in a bad way by 1830, down to a single male survivor, one Joseph, who had a small ranch in South Texas along the Nueces River. He had come as a young man with a group of Irish settlers led by John Mullen, but left the settlement, San Patricio, to live some ten miles up the river, alone with Bible, bottle, and gun. He was able to trade with occasional roving bands of Lipan-Apaches because they thought he was crazy (primitives have always thought that madmen know too much truth to be killed). Joseph rejoined the Irish long enough during the Texas Revolution to attack Fort Lipantitlan—which guarded a ford on the Nueces—with Irish volunteers under Captain Ira Westover in 1835. In '42 he fought with the 192 men under General James Dix who defended the earthen fort aganst nearly a thousand Mexicans under General Antonio Canales, and successfully defended it. (It was a sort of reverse Alamo, except the drunks won this one.) Joseph lost an ear during the fighting and, the Irish of San Patricio said, the rest of his senses.

He returned to his cabin to live alone, un-visited, mainly because he shot at potential visitors for no apparent reason, until the day he came across a Comanche buck slaughtering one of his cows. The buck was short and stocky like all Comanches, and as he leaned his long body over the steer, Joseph shot him high behind the shoulder as he would a deer. As he took the scalp (a man living alone needed all the good medicine he could get), the buck's squaw ran out of a gully, waving a skinning knife. Joseph knocked her down with his rifle butt, then finished with the buck. Turning to the squaw, he noticed that she had fallen forward over a mesquite log and her buckskin skirt had flipped and her butt was showing. It was brown, dirty, large, but it was an ass, and Joseph, as I said, lived alone. (Like the scalp, he took what he could get.) He mounted in the quickest, most obvious way.

When Face-like-Horse awoke, a sputtering, one-eared wild man at her like a stallion, his teeth sliding off her greasy neck, she naturally assumed that the spirit of her man had entered the white man. No white-eye knew the secrets of Comanche love—and after battle, too, because before it, it steals the strength of a warrior. When the meeting was over, Face-like-Horse returned to her camp, which had been cut off and run south by Rangers, and gathered the People. The next night the People slept on a flood island in the Nueces, and Face-like-Horse became my great-great-great grandmother. Once again the Slagsted-Krummels were fated to ride.

No one has ever directly accused old Joseph of having been a Comanchero, but some people wondered why only three of eight able sons went to the

Civil War and why there was Comanche trouble in the south where there had never been any. Of the half-breed sons who went to fight for Jeff Davis, secession, cotton, slaves, and economics, one returned, Frederic, named Nose by the People. One was killed at Elkhorn Tavern (the Bluebellies called it Pea Ridge because they won) and the other deserted and went to Florida. When Nose, my great-great grandfather was buried, he was the richest man along the river. White sentiment necessitated that Nose be buried in the earth, but inside the coffin his hair was still braided and his hands, folded in Christian forms of peace, were crossed and held to his breast a secret blond scalp taken in Alabama on one of Forrest's railroad raids. Only the ranch, the family, and the Bible remained.

My grandfather joined the Canadian Army in 1915, and the only image he left me of that mad war in the mud was of creeping out of a trench on a night patrol and finding his arm sunk to the elbow in a rotted corpse. After only two months in the trenches, he said, he didn't even gag. (We had no one in the Spanish-American War: the Slagsted-Krummel who might have gone refused to join the Rough Riders in San Antone because the name sounded so damned silly.) My grandfather was also the one who changed the family name, leaving out the hyphen, and using Slagsted for a middle name for all male children. But except for my father, none of his children followed the tradition.

My father was thirty-one when the Second World War began, and he missed the draft. He enlisted anyway. The Army, of course, tried to make him a cook, but he cooked badly and became a private in a rifle company. He fought in Africa and France without distinction, but not without honor, I'm sure, and returned to say only that it had been bad. But I knew what he meant. I knew; in spite of his silence, I understood why he went, why he wouldn't talk, and how he came back.

I also knew all these things about the family because, as you've noticed, we Krummels are a verbose lot, and I joined the Army, the first time, in June of 1953. The truce was signed the next month. The old man had made me finish high school, and my education, as it will, cost me my war.

"And now we chose between tiny wars fought with booby traps and pamphlets and suicide . . . wars of attrition," I said to Gallard as I finished my tale, the history. "Perhaps there is even honor in these, though. But I am afraid. They are being fought for ideals and in the name of freedom and liberty and they are the dirtiest wars man has ever known. I trust greed and passion and lust, but God! never politics."

Gallard stood up to leave. A great sadness touched his face, shaded his eyes, etched his facial lines. "Why did you tell me this? I know you. I saw you murder women and children for fun, for stupid amusement. Why tell me?" He had begun to understand his use in my world, and wasn't so sure he liked it; but he had wanted to know. "Why me?" He turned away, his shoulders shaking. "You stink of death, Krummel, evil murder and death and. . . ."

"Don't overwrite, man. The story's just begun, doctor; only begun, not near finished."

He left quickly, without a word. I knew he would be back. Unfair, you say, to use him like that? Who else could I talk to? Who else would listen? Only those whose fear is deep enough and whose pride is great enough to conceive me in their souls; a hidden, hesitant conception, true, but a real birth.

(All is not darkness, though. A letter came today. Cagle and Novotny are alive, not dead as I had thought. Cagle lost an arm and Novotny is deaf, but they are alive and back in the States already, waiting for discharge to start a bar in Fresno with their disability money. Cagle writes, "Look, ma, one hand clapping [no pun intended: there is no clap in the U.S.A.]." Novotny writes, "Great not to have to listen to the little bastard anymore." God, I miss them.)

5

(NOTES FOR AN UNFINISHED NARRATIVE)

History, memory, or whatever you will call this foolish desire of mine to diddle the past, does present certain problems of relativity. It would be easier if I could, as authors of novels often pretend to do, be that objective, original, imaginative, righteous voice of God, but alas I am not. Nor am I able, as that other great multitude of confessors are, to act as if I have quietly moved, probably because of the deep understanding and perception I must have of my sins, to some distant point in the vacuum of space, disturbed only by occasional satellites, cosmic dust, and God, and there rest in peace as I recount my many and varied adventures. But again, alas, this is not so. For you see, I am still strapped to this bed in a traction cast, the sky over Baguio is still a sexual blue, the grass sensual green, Abigail Light lovely, lovely, and Doctor Gallard concerned. Life continually intrudes. I will neither deny this, as so many have, nor, though, will I make any other point about it than this intrusion. I see no reason why you should get off any lighter than me, for it was at this point in time—that is, the time of writing the narrative rather than the time of the narrative itself, different as it is from the time of the events being narrated—that Gallard brought me these sheets of yellow paper and this old typewriter, which so often seems to loom high over the bed like a great cathedral organ. Gallard brought them without explanation, but he and I both knew what he meant, what he wanted.

I found myself intrigued with the idea of a mechanical confession and began, as they say great writers must, to conceive my theory of aesthetics before I began to write. I quickly discovered that history was more interesting than art, and so instead developed the Blueberry Bush Theory of History, that is to say that Martin Luther King had as great a hand in causing the Reformation and the Thirty Years' War as Martin Luther. You may despair at this idea that no one and no thing is at the wheel of the ship of the cosmos, that there is neither wheel nor ship, but you would be smarter to laugh (and probably are if you did). Perhaps you may chide me for making elaborate jokes; point, if you will, your irritation elsewhere.

If, as they say, the writer's duty is to force order on the chaos, then the historian must force chaos wherever he finds order.

Perhaps this is all a personal reaction to the fact that I never did find out who broke all those damned Coke bottles, and I'm merely hesitating in my narrative because I hate to go on with that kind of loose thread bleeding behind me. If it bothers you, then say I did it because I was punished for it and must be guilty. Nothing worth having is easy to get.

So despair then because history is no thread to be cut, no chain to rattle, no string to be wrapped in a ball. Eat your blueberries; keep the toilet paper close at hand.

My ill-temper must have rubbed off on the men, particularly on Morning who acted as if I had stolen his thunder, his lightning and tears. I didn't find it easy in the weeks between the end of my tour of punishment and the beginning of football season to keep the self-disgust I felt out of my face. There were several bad scenes. Novotny finally received the long-feared Dear John from his girl back in Wyoming. He stayed sick and drunk for a long time—through a set of days, the Break, then a set of swings—then during the Break he and Morning nearly came to blows, as they regularly did, over the presence of Toni, Morning's queer friend, at the apartment. Morning felt sorry for him, as everyone did. Poor Toni, half in, half out of drag, short hair and make-up, high heels and levis, painted fingernails and a sport shirt, always waiting for a chance to seduce Novotny, Novotny always ready to kill him if he tried, and Morning, it seemed, also waiting for the explosion. I often felt that Morning wanted to see this double-humiliation so he could feel superior (not afraid?). He and I hassled when I told him this, for in my mood I bluntly told him, and we tangled another time when Quinn wanted to stay in town AWOL from work. Morning said it was only Quinn's business, but I made it mine. Then Dottlinger began his campaign to get Morning who, of course, was more than willing to be a martyr to this sort of injustice. And I . . . always with my crooked nose strained out of joint to get between the back and the whip. . . .

On the way to the beginning of a set of mids, I found Tetrick sitting in the chow hall waiting for me. As I ate, he told me that Dottlinger knew that Morning had organized the Great Coke Bottle Mutiny.

"How do you know?" I asked. This could be bad, I thought. Capt. Saunders still wasn't back from the States.

"I know, that's all. But the lieutenant ain't going to do anything right now. He's waiting. Make sure Morning don't get out of line, not even a little bit," Tetrick said.

"How?"

"You tell me," he said, shaking his head over a cup of coffee. "You tell me. These kids are driving me to drink. You know Hendricks, that little blond kid on Trick Four?"

"I think so. Why?"

"He's in the stockade—excuse me, confinement facility, that is," Tetrick snorted.

"How come?"

"How come? He's a lover. That's why. Girls in Town aren't good enough for him. No, he's got to have a captain's wife. He got caught, then she screamed rape like they always do when an enlisted man gets between their legs. She screams rape from the middle of her bed and Hendricks crashes out the window carrying his clothes. It's bad enough to run off, but then the Air Police catch him over behind the Kelly Theatre, and what's he do? Pulls a knife, yes, cuts two APs, which is bad enough, but now when he can get away, what's he do? Yeah, he climbs a telephone pole. They have to cut the pole down to get him. Smart kid. Now the least he'll get is five years and a DD. A real lover." Tetrick couldn't have looked more unhappy, he couldn't have had more wrinkles running back across his forehead up his tan scalp if he were the one on his way to Leavenworth.

I remembered Hendricks. A small, quiet boy from Kansas who worked part-time out at the riding stables, the kind of kid who preferred horses to people. "Damn, you wouldn't think he would be the type, do you? Can he beat any of the charges?"

Tetrick sneered at me, but then he paused, chuckled to himself, and said, "Speaking of people who don't look like it. Listen, keep this to yourself; don't make me more trouble. Guess who's shacking up with Sgt. Reid's wife?" Reid was chief of Trick One, a pale, thin, thirtyish guy who looked more like a shoe clerk than a soldier.

"Who," I said, "Dottlinger?" A joke.

"That's right, smart guy."

"You're shitting me."

"Wish I was. Reid doesn't know who yet, but he knows. She's always been that kind. His last CO shipped him out to get rid of her. I'll get her sent home when Saunders gets back, but can you see me going to the lieutenant and saying, 'I got this slut, see, for you to send home.'" Tetrick grinned, but I think in defense.

"Listen," I said, "next time you have some good news, be sure to tell me."

"You just tell Morning to stay straight." The grin was quickly gone. "If he makes waves, I'll bust his ass. He won't have to wait for the Lieutenant to think up something."

"Ain't it the truth."

I left Tetrick with his bad coffee and troubles; I had my own; he had given them to me my first day in the PI. On the way to work I was tempted to tell Morning that Dottlinger knew, but I was afraid that, in his mood, he would take the warning as excuse for action against the enemy, and I guess I was a little afraid, too, that in my mood I might egg him on.

Two nights later I had the OD and the Trick went to work a mid without me. Most of them were more than a little drunk at midnight chow, but Novotny was assistant trick chief and I trusted him to keep them working. At least they trooped out toward the motor pool on time, so I went back to the quiet Orderly Room and the novel Morning had forced on me, *The Wanderer,* which I managed to read until the phone rang about forty-five minutes after midnight. The CQ looked up at me and said, "Sgt. Reid." Now it was my turn to wander, lost again.

"What the hell's he want?"

"Didn't say."

"Reid?" I said into the receiver.

"Sgt. Krummel?" he said. He always called me "Sgt. Krummel" out of military courtesy. "Ah, where's the relief?"

No rest for the weary, I wanted to say, his voice was so tired. "Why? Aren't they there? Where are you? What?" My rush of questions silenced him. I heard a sigh slip over the wire.

"Ah, where's your Trick? They didn't, ah, show up, and it's, ah, an, ah, hour past relief now. Ah, my guys are, ah, complaining." He never would have complained, but would have stayed at the desk at Operations working on through eternity with an occasional guilty glance at the wall clock, knowing that if he complained *they* would only shove the dirty end of the stick at him again. The note of resignation in his voice seemed to say, *Yes, I know my wife is fucking around; don't all of them.*

I assured him that the Trick had left the mess hall on time, reassured him that ít was merely a broken down three-quarter or something so simple, and promised to check it out right away. I hung up in the middle of one of his "ah's"; there could be no relief for a man like Reid.

The night driver in the motor pool, a mongoloid from Alabama, had refused to let the Trick use two jeeps in place of a, yes, disabled three-quarter because motor-pool policy specified only one "vehickle purr trick." "They gave me some shit, man, but I tole 'em to hop their little ole Yankee asses in a cab or somethin'," he said to me.

"Thanks a lot."

"Motor-pool policy," he said, waving his arm at the dew-shining green metal and black asphalt, the dull canvas, the flood lights so quickly absorbed by the dank, dark air.

"Motor-pool policy," he said again, as if that explained the world.

"If there is any trouble out of this, soldier, I'm going to have your ass in a sling by noon tomorrow," I said, savoring for a moment the amazement lighting, as best anything could, that peckerwood face. "Shut up and get me a jeep real fast," I said as he started to answer, "Now." Rank does have its privileges, but only seldom do the privileged have the rank.

I found the Trick about a mile out the gate highway, walking in a shambling group, and I assumed they were looking for a cab until I saw the case of beer on Morning's shoulder, the bottles flashing in every hand. Franklin was taking a leak as he walked and the others were trying to stay out of range; Quinn had a beer in each hand, taking alternate drinks with military precision. I pulled up behind them and their faces and hands scrambled for a moment trying to hide the beer, then Quinn saw me getting out of the jeep and he smiled and shouted, "Hey, Morning, get old man Krummel a beer."

"Throw the beer in the ditch and fall in," I said.

They all smiled and walked toward me, Morning with an offered beer.

"Throw the beer in the ditch and fall in," I repeated. Smiles became perplexed. "Now!" They huddled back upon themselves. "Right now!" Collins bent over to try to set his beer down without spilling it. "Throw them in the ditch." He did. Morning threw the beer he had been offering me, flung it against the ground, and his eyes glared "what the shit" but he was too angry to say it. "Fall in!"

"What the fuck's with you, Krummel?"

"Sgt. Krummel to you, Pfc Morning," I said as I took the half-empty case off his shoulder and pitched it in the ditch.

Again his anger stifled his voice, and in his silence the others attempted a formation based on his unmoving figure.

"Attention," I ordered, and attention I got as they gathered old instincts and shuffled into straighter lines, stiffer stances. Morning still stood at an angle, half-crouched as if his anger curled his guts, his face scattered in wrath, mouth open, an eyebrow questioningly raised, a mad eye, the whole structure flushed in frustration, quilted in grief. I told him to straighten up. He did, and rage tightened his body into quivering stone, the first tentative nudge of an earthquake. He began to stammer, his lips jittering and a spray of spit flying out; but I told him to knock it off before his mouth could shape a word.

"Dress right, dress!" Again the training memories came back after a wondering moment. Morning had his mouth shut now, his face clenched like a fist; thumb screws, bamboo splinters, nor the rack could have made him say shit—but I did.

"I don't know what kind of little gathering this is, but I want you people to know, it's over."

"Shit."

"One more word, Morning," I hissed into his very face, "even a grunt, and you are through." Before he could test me, I shouted, "Right face. Forward march. Double-time march," and then he was trapped with the others, stumbling along the road. "Novotny, fall out and see if you can keep cadence for these girl scouts." I climbed back in the jeep and followed them as they ran the two miles on out to Operations. Everyone threw up at least once, and Haddad had to be half-carried half dragged between Quinn and Collins. All their backs reflected the shame which was on their faces; except Morning. They all knew something, except Morning; not so much their error, because that wasn't important, but the breaking of a trust, making me have to play the hard-ass (perhaps more ass than hard). A broken trust, a defiled faith, so we were all ashamed. Except Morning, and his anger spoke eloquently of the guilt he bore. We both knew whose idea the beer had been, and I wondered if this confrontation hadn't been what he had been after all this time. His rage blossomed so wonderfully when he was guilty; he indulged his anger, perhaps because with something outside to hate the vague phantom-demon he hated in himself let him alone, and together both halves hated not in an arithmetical progression of one plus one, but geometrically as dynamite adds to dynamite, so that he must explode. The others would be loosed from their shame by this run, and then a single joke, a laugh, and then we would be back in this thing together. But I wondered if Morning and I would have to fight to ease his guilt. I thought this might be the easy way (and I sometimes, when bed sores tickle *my* guilt, think it might have been the best way). His guilt, my shame eased in a blind flurry of fists, and afterwards battered faces, grins splitting bleeding lips, friendship cemented—but only if we fought to a draw, for neither of us could bear to lose in front of the other—his guilt, my shame eased. (Let me mention, lest you think I worried overlong about doing my job, that mine was perhaps the easier to endure. I *was* riding in the jeep, and he *was* struggling in the ditch. The twentieth century hasn't quite convinced me that physical pain is easier to bear than mental pain. Not quite. Keep that in mind.)

I hailed two taxis and sent them to Ops where they were waiting; the drivers laughing at the panting, puking rabble I herded into the compound. Reid met me at the gate with pale questions and whimpering objections, but I shut him up with a promise that we would make up twice the time the next two nights and told him that everything was all right. That's what he wanted to hear: that everything was all right. Had he for a moment suspected that his wife's lover had arranged this delay? His face answered, *Don't they always.*

I told him that I would appreciate it if that dick-head Dottlinger didn't hear about the incident. He hesitated before answering, and I wanted to scream the truth at him. But he was really worried about who was going to pay for the cabs. So I did. Then I went to get Morning and we went out back.

Turning from me, he walked over to the fence, anger still shaking his hands. "Well, what the hell you want?" he asked when I didn't say anything.

"What do I want? What do you want? A stunt like that—Jesus Christ, Morning."

"So I screwed up, man. So what? Didn't you ever make a

mistake? Didn't this shit ever get to you? Is it ever too much?"

"What?"

"I don't know," he said, turning as the beacon on the control tower turned. "Just too much."

"You make me sound like a sergeant: but that's no excuse. We're all in the same shit."

"It's not a fucking excuse, it's a reason. Can't. . . ." Silent for a moment, he turned back to the fence, hung his fingers in the mesh, staring out like a . . . like lost child? caged animal? . . . more like a man who didn't know if he wanted in or out, or even which side was in or out. "I'm just tired, man. I feel like I'm nine hundred years old. It's all too much, the army, Town, this stupid job; it's too much sometimes. Sometimes I wish I could go to sleep forever, then I wouldn't have to fuck with the world. I can't stay straight; I can't even go to hell right." He paused; I waited.

"That's funny. I was thinking about something today, you know. About problems. I used to be good at math, you know," he said, speaking as he had that first time I saw him talking to the mirror, detached, commenting on his soul as if it were a problem of formulas. "Really good at math. I should have majored in math or physics or engineering or something like that. At least that's what they always said, and I might have, if I hadn't tried to major in accounting to spite my old lady. God, you know, she used to put my old man down for being a bookkeeper. A cipher, she called him. Classic, huh? So classic it's a bore, you know.

"But there was another reason, too, why I didn't major in math. I didn't understand . . . I couldn't . . . I could work problems, could really work hell out of them. And not just plugging numbers into a formula either. When I started calculus, in high school, the teacher gave us a problem, something about getting a ladder around a corner in a hall, just to show us what one looked like. And I worked the damn thing without calculus. She couldn't believe it. She loved me because I was her best student, but for a moment I could tell that she thought I had done something wrong, and she never liked me after that for some reason. But I worked the damned problem, by God, I worked it, just like I solved all the other ones, but the thing is, the thing always was, I didn't know how I knew how to work it. I didn't understand why my mind worked that way. No one else could work it, but it was easy for me, but I didn't know why, or how. I could just do, you know, but I couldn't understand how, and that almost drove me bugs, man.

"Just like when I started school. I could read before I started the first grade, and I knew that no one else could, so when this old bitch starts off with flash cards and the alphabet crap, I raised my hand and asked, "Where are the books?" The class all laughed and giggled, and Miss Minder, who was old and hated kids, probably for good reason, threw a fourth-grade reader in my hands and told me to read and so I read, and when I finished a page, said, "Where are the hard books? This is only a fourth-grade reader." All the kids laughed and Miss Minder almost cried she was so mad, and I thought I was going to be the leader of the band. But I quickly discovered that nobody liked me because I could read and they couldn't, and then they didn't like me because I made good grades. So for the next eight years, until it became all right to be smart, I was the dirtiest, dumbest kid in school. On purpose." He paused as four jets roared over then settled like fat mallards against the runways.

"Always had trouble with my head, man. But in high school I let it go; it was enough to be able to do it. It was like football: when the coaches tried to teach me how to throw a pass, tried to change the way I threw a pass, I couldn't pass for shit, but my way, I could do it. Finally they left me alone, and I just threw the goddamned ball. But then that got to me too. Somehow I wasn't throwing the ball, somebody else was. Or maybe it was more like having a machine in my head that plotted trajectories and found ranges and figured windage and force vectors and triggered the muscles. I always felt left out of the process."

"No," I interrupted, taking the cigarette he offered, "you are the process."

"Aw, bullshit, that's no good. I'm not part, if I don't feel like I'm part, huh? No.

"Then," he said, pausing to light up, his face fired by the match, crimson like the hot exhausts of the jets coming over our heads, "Then at Carlton I found out something. The hard way." He laughed, but it sounded more like a snort. "I was making it with this chick, this good chick, down in Madison. A good kid but, Jesus, a bad scene. I was drunk most of the time, and mad at her most of the time for reasons I still don't understand. Maybe because she made me happy, maybe for no reason at all. But I'd get mad, madder than hell, then I'd tear her into little pieces. I made fun of her Church, her meatless Fridays—here's a piece of meat for this Friday, I'd say—her family, her friends, then I'd screw her and make her cry with passion, then laugh at her hypocritical tears, as I called them." He flicked his cigarette over the fence, then walked back into the shadows next to the building.

"But she loved me, man, and she hung on, though God knows why. All the way. Until one really bad night when I was drunk, blind, stupid, black-out drunk, laying on the floor of her apartment, beating my head on the tiles, keeping time to the music from the beer joint below. I busted my head all up and bled all over the place, broke furniture and all that kind of shit. And that was all right; but I wouldn't stop it with the head, beating away, and she couldn't stop me, and I wouldn't stop until I finally drank and battered myself into oblivion." He lit another cigarette. His face was as tired as his voice in the quick light.

"Then the next morning she said, very calmly, very plainly, that this was too much. 'Too much, Joe,' she said. 'You hate yourself too much. Either I'll get lost when you get your head and heart together, or else I'll get torn up in the fight. That's too much,' she said.

"I hated losing her," he said, looking up at me, "and I gave her all the horseshit about being afraid to live and too ignorant to die, which was just true enough to really hurt—I seem to know weak spots naturally, too—but I sort of understood something about myself, why I'd been beating my head on the floor. I hated it, pure and simple, and in spite of my new attempts at being an intellectual, I hated my head because it wasn't part of me. It has always felt like somebody's head besides mine, and I didn't understand, and I hated. She didn't understand either, but she knew enough to get the hell out of the way. Enough." He stopped talking again, and a jet engine being tested filled the silence with a steady, grating roar which seemed to rise out of the very night itself. Something was waiting in the darkness, an animal, a beast, all mouth and desire, growling, eating the very darkness, dissatisfied with the night.

"So what the hell did you want?" he said suddenly, shaking his head.

"I thought I wanted to beat your damned head in. But I guess I . . . I guess not. Let's go in before that noise makes idiots of us all. Stay cool. Lt. Dottlinger is after your ass; he knows that you were the organizer of the mutiny."

Morning started to say something, stopped, then said, "Don't sweat it. I can take my own licks. If he wants me so much I may let him have all of me." A rice bug, a pale cockroach-looking, flying beast as big as your thumb, crawled along the sidewalk, stunned from dashing into the wall under the floodlights. Morning stomped him into a brown spot.

"He's smarter than you think, and he's drowning, Joe, and he'll hurt you. He knows how to do that, if nothing else," I said, pausing at the door.

"You should know," he said, grinning like Novotny. "They can't hurt me, man. Not any more."

"Not if you keep setting me up for the kill," I said, smiling too.

Inside I shouted something about the Trick calling me if they needed to go to the latrine because after tonight it was obvious that they couldn't pee without it running down their legs. They laughed, shot me the finger, assaulted my mother's virtue, and we were all okay again. I told Novotny to police up the beer bottles on the way in.

"Hey, I'm ah . . . I'm . . ." he tried to say.

"Next time you want to get in some close order drill, tell me. I'll arrange it."

"Don't do us any favors," Morning said as I left.

It was over for now, and I enjoyed the cool peace of the night on my way back.

But, God, it's never over. The finger of God is never satisfied, always moving, always rewriting life, always making a scene go on and on until even He must cry, "God, will it never end," even as His finger moves on.

"Where are they at?" Tetrick shouted at me as he came in the Orderly Room the next morning. Red splotches of frustration interrupted the yellow of his face. "You've got to be kidding me? Say it ain't so. Get 'em in here, Krummel, now. Every one of them." I managed between flying arms and screams to get him into Saunders' office. "Whatever you're gonna say, no! already. I want those idiots in here."

"No," I said.

"What do you mean, no?" he shouted.

"They're my trick. You said so. I took care of it. You hang them, you hang me."

"I should hang myself. How could they do a thing like that? The Lieutenant will kill us all," he said.

"He'll never know."

"He knows everything. He has a spy system better than the CIA. God," he groaned, rubbing his shining head, "what's next? No, don't tell me. I couldn't stand it."

"Football season is next. Three weeks, then all the anger can go somewhere else." I felt as if I should comfort him, maybe pat his shoulder, because he really did care about his troops. I'd never seen anybody like Tetrick before.

"Football, huh? Maybe you will all get killed." He shuffled out as fast as his feet would let him. I followed. Dottlinger was standing in the middle of the door waiting for someone to call "Attention." Dottlinger gave "At ease" his usual arrogant inflection, which made it mean exactly the opposite: "Don't relax a second," it said. He raised an eyebrow as if to ask what we had been doing in Saunders' office, but he didn't ask; he had other things on his mind; he was next.

No one ever quite figured how Dottlinger came up with the idea, but he did, and that same day he called a Pfc from the motor pool, a repairman from Trick Four, and Morning into his office to inform them that a board of officers would be assembled to decide if they should be undesirably discharged for immoral conduct. The other two were real trouble-makers —the Pfc got his kicks by beating up whores, and the repairman had gotten written up by the APs every time he went to Town—but Morning's only sin was reporting three cases of the clap to the hospital.

Nearly everyone caught the clap in the PI; I think the official rate is about sixty percent, but that doesn't take into account the married men with wives and without who were faithful, nor unreported cased treated by doctors in Town, which would probably put the rate for single enlisted men around eighty percent. Everyone on the trick except Collins and myself had fallen prey to the sly gonococci. Collins was reasonably faithful to his wife and extraordinarily careful about not catching the clap, wearing two condoms, only fucking on Wednesday afternoons when the whores received the results of their Tuesday morning smears, always carrying a bar of antiseptic soap in his pocket, and other such precautions which seemed to take the fun out of it, which may have been exactly what he was trying to do. I had already had my punishment from a sixteen-year-old high school girl in Atlanta, Georgia, on a three-day pass in 1953, and so I was somewhat more cautious than the others. Franklin had had six doses; he claimed one more notch than Quinn with five. But like everyone else, they went to the doctors in Town for their penicillin, so the hospital never knew. But Morning always said that he wasn't going to take any chances with such a fun thing as his privates; no hypos of Wildroot Cream Oil masquerading as pencillin for him. So he went to the hospital all three times, the last time about a month before. The hospital always made a routine report of the third case to the unit commanders, but usually a bit of fatherly advice was all that happened. Service policy had changed from the days when a dose was an automatic bust; in fact thousands of posters pleaded with the troops to report to the hospital and promised no disciplinary measures. But an undesirable discharge is an administrative action, technically, so Dottlinger had his way to Morning.

Perhaps Dottlinger understood that, being a good (really), middle-class Southern boy, Morning probably felt guilty as hell about the doses anyway and that he probably bought the usual nonsense paraded everywhere in America—schools, colleges, corporations—that achievement is measured by collecting pieces of paper, and that a bad piece of paper, a bad discharge, like a criminal record, would haunt a man right into the grave (when in reality, no one ever asks to see your goddamned discharge anyway).

At first Morning seemed unconcerned, as if he understood the game and could care less about playing it. He drank the ritual fifth of VO, then tied the yellow and black ribbon from the neck of the bottle into his button hole, identifying him as a short-timer. He strutted around laughing and quipping, "I'm so short I can sleep in a matchbox, so short that when I fart, I blow sand in my eyes, so short." But I saw, perhaps, a truer picture of how he was taking it one night during the next Break in the weight room.

(I lift weights, barbells, you understand; it's been a secret long enough. I like it, in fact, I'm very snobbish about it. I dislike people with skinny arms who call it boring; I dislike pretty boys with their definition bulging and rippling like snakes coiling in a sack; I dislike hulks who think a 400-pound miliary press is the highest man can reach; but at the same time I've held each of these attitudes once, and am now quite sure that mine is unique, far superior, perhaps the only worthy attitude. I think weight lifting is beautiful, an art of circles, curves and graceful arcs, a delicate symmetry, an hypnotic calm in the repetition, a powerful contentment when the skin seems too small for the muscle.)

I was nearly finished with the workout, pleased with my body, really pleased that I had finally kept one resolution to spend a peaceful Break away from Town, when, through the louvers, I saw Morning get out of a cab. The light in the weight room was the only light on the second floor so his eyes rose naturally to it, but because of the artful deception of the screen, he couldn't see me. But he shouted, anyway, "Lift and toil, Krummelkeg, you virtuous, muscle-bound, ant-brained idiot."

"Ah, 'tis Daemon Rum his-self," I answered.

Shortly, he came in, more tired than drunk, face sunburnt and drawn, but his eyes glittered like glass ornaments. The bow of his short-timer's ribbon, untied, drooped like a pennant in the rain.

I asked why he was back, suspecting the worst.

"Just tired," he said, fooling me again, rubbing the stubble of beard. "I been sweatin' . . . sitting in a swing all day. Talkin', talkin' to a sweet little girl."

"You found a new way," I grunted, doing my first set of squats.

"No, man, really, a little girl. Bow-legged Dottie's little girl. Went over with Quinn to fence some records for . . . so Dottie could. Anyway, he had to screw her first, and they made me take the kid out to the swing, you know, one of those old-fashioned bench swings." He sat heavily on the edge of the mat, then flopped back, an arm covering his eyes. "So, man, I spent all morning popping bennies and drinking beer while Quinn was farting around. Then he and Dottie went off to sell the stuff and made me stay with the kid, but by then I wouldn't have left for anything. Great kid, lotsa bennies, and the kid would run to the sari-sari store for beer. She fixed us lunch, like a party. Beautiful lunch. First time I ever noticed how pretty food is. Tomatoes about the size of your thumb, tiny little red things; white rice, as white as the sun; little bitty raw fish, churds, or chaps or something, little gray devils; and those great little bananas sort of hovering between green and yellow. Hey, man, one of the bananas was a twin, you know, two bananas in one skin. Dottie's kid said that's the best kinda luck, twin bananas. She said if we ate them, the two of us, we would get married, and I said she didn't want to marry me 'cause I was no good, and she said she did want to marry me 'cause I was so sad. Ain't that great, man. So sad. Jesus Christ, what a kid. Nine years old, man, and she knows more about life than Aristotle, Plato, St. Augustine, and your fucking Edmund Burke all thrown together in Archimedes' bathtub." He laughed and sat up. "Hey, man, you ever see how silly you look doing squats. You look like the most constipated man in the world." He laughed again.

I finished the squats and put the weights up. "So go on. You got Aristotle, Plato, St. Augustine and my fucking Edmund Burke in Archimedes' tub singing 'I'm Forever Blowing Stinky Bubbles in the Tub.' "

"No, man, Plato don't allow no singing. Aristotle ain't sing-

ing, it ain't in the plan; he's just sitting there farting and bitin'
the bubbles when they come up and calling it a catharsis.
Ca-fucking-tharsis! Augustine is trying to hide a hard-on, and
Edmund Burke is casting a baleful eye on the whole proceed-
ings, wishing he had a hard-on," he crowed, "and Archimedes
run off with a belly-dancer from Bayonne, New Jersey, who
promised to teach him about spirals and specific gravity and
the Archimedean screw."

"Maybe you shouldn't drink so much," I said.

"Maybe I should drink more," he answered. "Particularly
with lovely, sweet little girls. 'Joe Morning,' she said when I
left, 'How come you GIs all-a-time drunk?' I think I love her."

"Yes, Pfc Morning, we've noted your interest in the younger
members of opposite sex," I said, mocking Dottlinger's dry
whine. In my own voice, I asked, "How many packages of gum
did she sell you?" Dottie's kid was one of the better con artists
among the horde of gum and flower girls with bare feet and
scraggly hair who were constantly in bars, day in day out,
constant reminders of poverty and want, a constant whine at
your sleeve, "You buy gum, joe?"

Morning was silent for a second, then said, "You don't
believe in shit do you? Well, fuck you, golden-hearted cynic."

"Don't sweat me, jack; I won't be sitting on the board. They
can't make me tell about that twelve-year-old girl in Chew
Chi's hotel—at least she said she was twelve, didn't she?" The
night I had shared that black, rat-ridden room with the old
woman, my first night in Town, digging, as it were, into the
past, Morning had asked Dominic for something young and
tender, and received, he discovered the next morning, a
twelve-year-old girl in a red crepe-paper party dress with
clumsy white valentine hearts stitched around the skirt.

"I was drunk."

"You're drunk now. Don't snarl at me just because Dottlinger is after your ass. You made your own bed," I said. (God, he
could make me angry, and I, him.) "You didn't tell me how
much gum she stuck you with."

A sleepy grin wavered about his eyes as he emptied the
pockets of the baggy light-blue pants he wore to Town. "I ain't
counted 'em, yet." He smiled. Twenty-six shiny green packages

of Doublemint. "It was worth it; I love her. I think I love her."

"I think you ought to go to bed."

"No, sir. Benzedrine and sex don't mix."

"To sleep."

"I can't sleep; I'm too tired." He paused, fingered his ribbon. "I'm too short to sleep; might miss my plane."

"Don't sweat that. You can beat this thing," I said. "Easy."

"Shit, man, you ought to read Slutfinger's instructions to the board. 'Subjects may show superficial intelligence and verbal ability, and attempt to make philosophical justification for immorality, but the board must keep the good of the service in mind rather than some vague good-of-man ideal that allows certain types of immorality, usually sexual, as long as the higher principles are followed. The board must remember that immorality is immorality.' God, he loved reading it to me. I think he wrote it for me. Jesus, he's crazy. It's not me he's putting out of the army 'for the good of the service,' it's the whole twentieth century. Morning, Joseph J., unsuitable, sir, for duty in the service of God and Country because of a lewd and lascivious character established by the prima-facie evidence of three contractions of the vile disease of gonorrhea, an article fifteen company punishment for being caught off-limits in one of the most notorious dens of prostitution in the whole Philippines, if not the whole world, naked and, we can assume, having had subjected himself to carnal intercourse with these low women, and keeping constant company with a reputed pander and black-marketeer and an admitted homosexual, etcetera, etcetera, etcetera."

"Did he say all that."

"No, but he will. He wants to, but he can't spell all the words." He stood up, walked to the screen, leaving a trail of dirty footprints across the canvas mat. "He's gonna have my ass, like you said, one way or the other. Who gives a shit, really? They can't hurt me."

"You can beat it. I'll testify, Tetrick will, maybe even Capt. Harry if we push him."

"I'm not going to try. I'm tired, man. I told you that. I want to get out of this fucking, stupid, dirty country and the dumb goddamned army. I'm going back to the States." He leaned his forehead against the screen. "Home for a while, then maybe back to Phoenix, maybe back to school. . . ."

"Not this way, for Christ's sake." I picked up a dumbbell and began doing one-handed curls. "We can beat it."

". . . maybe Mississippi. I've got a friend with SNCC there." He mumbled on, but I wasn't listening.

"Ellen's in Mississippi," I said absently. Mississippi looked as if it were going to once again take its toll on me. First Ellen and Ron Fowlers, now Joe Morning, I thought. Then an odd picture intruded, Joe and Ellen in bed. Somehow I knew if they met, and in Mississippi they must, she would fuck him with all that wonderful, religious, rebellious ardor she once spread for me. After long nights of talk, she had to have me, as if the words caressed her, a long flickering tongue of talk, and have me she did, a mount and a sudden charge. Even now the stale cigarette breath ripened by cheap beer, the dry lips, the sticky tongue, the hot, hot breath of a woman talking close and intense in your face. . . . I was suddenly sorry I hadn't gone with her to Mississippi that summer; but no—she had said, love me, love my cause—no, I said. But that pale hot face, pale mouth cuddling like a sleepy kitten against mine. . . .

"Huh?" I said as Morning poked me. My arm still curled absent mindedly, the muscles tight and hard and bitter now. "What?"

"Go take a shower," he muttered, turning back to the night. "You stink."

As I showered, he came down and we talked, but he seemed resigned, and refused to fight Dottlinger. (I recognize it now: The victim by falling may rise; one vanquished without a fight isn't vanquished at all.) Afterwards we strolled to the Flight Line for a sandwich. Lightning skittered across the clouded face of Mount Arayat, silent flashes, then distant afterthoughts of quiet thunder. The walks and the streets and the grass gleamed wetly in the mist, the mist like tiny balls of light suspended in the cool night, the heart and coming of the rainy season delicately foretold. In spite of the threatening rain, the hesitant thunder, we walked quite slowly, speaking of home, of girls once touched, once known, of friends half-forgotten, drunken rides and football games. Once again Morning spoke of the girl from Madison. His face, drawn in fatigue, echoed the longing in his voice:

"God, man, I miss her sometimes. Nights like this, sometimes in my rack just at dawn when the light is soft and the air . . . so much I don't think I can stand it." He shook his head. "But, Christ, I'd probably just treat her the same way again. Shit. You know what I did once. I was drunk again, always, and we'd fought, always, but had half made-up and were making love on her couch, covered with tears and recriminations, but then she whispered something desperate about love—we'd prom . . . I'd made her promise never to say "love" —then all the anger came back, and I jerked out, then sat on the side of the couch, jacking off. She started crying again, moaning, and asking me "why? why?" in this goddamned sad little whimper. So I told her why, good old Joe Morning told her why: 'Less complicated than fucking you, bitch.' Isn't that lovely. You know, I wonder why she took so long to leave me." He looked up, waiting, it seemed, for me to speak. When I didn't, he seemed embarrassed by the confidence, and quickly walked on.

"Some of my best friends are bastards," I said as I caught up to him.

He smiled, then poked me on the arm, and said, "Yeah. Mine, too."

After eating sawdust hamburgers, we went back to the barracks and drank a fifth of Dewar's he had been saving for the market, sipping straight from the bottle, then dashing to the water fountain for a chaser, but by the time a sullen grey daylight floated like fog out of the dawn, we were chasing Scotch with Scotch, dreams with whiskey, laughter with tears.

At noon Novotny found Morning sleeping under my table, his head on the Lattimore translation of the *Iliad* that Ellen had given me for Christmas the third year we were married. It might have been a more suitable pillow for me, but I was on guard, crouched in the corner, asleep but not dreaming, the empty bottle cradled in my arms, a dead soldier.

I stayed abed and nursed my hangover the next day, but Morning was up before three and back in Town. Novotny,

Quinn and Cagle brought him back just before curfew. He had passed out in Lenny's, and when they tried to move him upstairs, he woke up insane. With the arms draped around Novotny's and Quinn's shoulders he banged their heads together, then turned and ran out over Cagle. By the time they had collected themselves and gotten outside, Morning had disappeared, but they heard screams from the Keyhole, and raced there. Morning had ripped the door from its hinges as he ran in and had shouted, "I'm gonna kill me an airman." When the others came in, Morning was chasing the smallest airman in the world around and around a table. They wrestled him outside just as the Air Police jeep drove up. Luckily, Novotny knew one of the APs and persuaded him to let them take Morning back to base.

He woke me screaming and shouting as they tried to tug him out of the taxi. Novotny and Quinn finally sat on his back while Cagle tied his hands behind him; Cagle was gagging him with a dirty handkerchief when I got downstairs. A steady rain began to slant across the bands of light as we picked Morning up. Perhaps the rain, perhaps the drink, something had washed the mask from his face. As I leaned over to grasp his shoulders, the hate blazed from his eyes, stunning, savage, blood-lined eyes directing malevolence, loathing, and God-forbidden hate; the mad, mad eyes of St. John the Divine casting God's wrath and bitterness against the fruit of man, great, blood-lust hate to cleanse the world in blood and fire. ". . . And the angel thrust in his sickle into the earth, and gathered the vine of the earth, and cast it into the great wine press of the wrath of God. . . ." How many times had I heard Morning shouting that mad verse in a drunken and surely, half-serious vein. His anger condemned the earth, and I nearly dropped him when his hate flamed up at my face. I might have dropped him, but the eyes suddenly clouded and the mask returned like the closing of a great portal, a thick iron door trundled across the opening in the earth, sealing the rift in the crust which sank deep into the night, into the fire of eternal night.

Upstairs we threw him into the center of the stall and turned all the showers cold, turned them on him. He lay very still, his eyes closed. His previous noise had drawn a crowd, but Morning remained motionless, bathed in the rushing water, silent, until even the group of curious began to leave. By then the leather belt stretched enough, so he slipped his hands out. He sat up, untied his feet, but left the gag. Sitting there, his eyes clouded by streams of water, he very methodically removed his shoes, his fingers operating so exactly on the laces, denying their wet, wrinkled infirmity. Quickly, he threw his shoes at us. One, wet, slipped out of his hand and hit the ceiling; the other speared Cagle in the shin. While Cagle danced on one leg, we laughed, then were silent as we realized the silence, the waterfall silence, that we had broken for the first time. Before this, not a single word had been spoken.

Morning responded to the laughter. He scrabbled to his feet and began a damp, slippery stripper's parody of sloshy bumps and clammy grinds. He went on for long minutes, dancing, stripping, until he wore only the jockey shorts he wore to Town and the gag binding his face as tightly as wire imbedded around a live tree trunk. He did much more, stuffed his shorts down the drain, fell down, ripped the gag from his mouth and began screaming "Mother-fucker! Mother-fucker!" until finally we carried him to his bunk, tied him with web belts and shoe laces, gagged him once more, then left him to his struggles and dreams.

On the way to our rooms, Novotny said, "Just crazy. Sometimes he's just crazy. One time he's drunk okay, then he's crazier than a poisoned coyote. I saw him run through a wall in his girl's apartment in Madison one night just 'cause she had the rag on and wouldn't put out for him. Crazy. Don't know." He turned into his room, his broad back wrinkling in perplexity, a discomfort I also shared. Who knew Joe Morning? Surely not I.

From my bunk I could hear his teeth gritting, grinding through the gag, his cot rattling against the cold concrete floor, his bonds aching against the flesh, his voice, muted, silent, persuasive in the night.

I woke, wondered why because it was still dark, but then realized the silence. More out of sleepy habit than purpose, I

got up to glance toward Morning's room and saw him wrapped
in a blanket, walking slowly toward the stairwell. I dressed
and followed, half-cursing, twice-intrigued (God, it seems as if
I spent my whole life trailing after Morning, following him;
two vaudeville acts, he the magician, me the strong man with
a magic of my own, forever on the same endless circuit). I
found him in one of the drainage ditches at the edge of the
company area. The rain had changed to drizzle gently floating
from gray, clotted clouds drifting ten feet above the barracks.

"You take me to raise?" he asked as I stood above and
behind him.

"You came so I would follow," I said. "You all right?" I
asked, climbing into the ditch with him.

"I'm always all right. Or I would be if you'd stop following
me around like a maiden aunt worried about my virtue."

"I'm a member of the Dottlinger spy organization." I sat
down, but he said nothing and his silence hung as close as the
clouds about us. Out of the American tradition of male com-
radeship I offered him a cigarette as I might have a wounded
soldier, but the rain killed my match and he threw it away. We
sat for a long time in the stolid mists before he spoke.

"You know," he said, "I've done this about once every six
months for the last five or so years. Stupid, crazy drunk. And I
never know what starts it, never know why.

"It wasn't always like that. I remember the first time I got
drunk. It was down in Georgia. At a lake. You know, one of
those sad places high school boys go because there are supposed to be, everybody says there are, millions of chicks, and
there usually are, but they are as scared and stupid as you are,
so nobody gets a tumble. But this trip I did. Girl named Diane,
blond, sweet, lovely girl named Diane. I remember we danced
and danced to two pop songs that summer, ah, 'Love is a Many
Splendored Thing,' and something called, let's see, yeah, 'Gum-
drop.' Danced like we were made for each other and all that
shit. My first taste of summer love and, man, I was dizzy and
stupid with it. I got such a hard-on just dancing with her,
nuzzling her cheek, that I thought I'd blow up or something.
Long, thick, curly blond hair. . . ."

"Back in the days when broads had curly hair?"

". . . Yeah, a thousand years ago. It was kind of like custard, I guess. You know, thick and creamy and looped and it shook when she moved her head. I was in love, man.

"But then it was time to go home. I stayed over when the guys I was with left. I slept in the bushes, bathed in the lake, collected pop bottles, and mooched meals off everybody I met, and all this time I had a pint of Four Roses burning a hole in my AWOL bag, saving it for my last night, the ace up my sleeve. And all this time I never heard her talking about this guy Smokey from home. Then he showed up, a big guy, home from the service, driving a '32 Ford rod and wearing combat boots with his Levi's. There went old Joe Morning, shot out of the saddle before he gets his foot in the stirrup. Jesus Christ, you know, she even introduced me to him. Told him I was the nice kid that had been dancing with her—she didn't say anything about wrestling in the bushes though, and he was so damned big, I didn't really mind. So he thanked me, said I was a good kid, then they cut out for a beer joint outside the park, The Rendezvous, a den of lust and drunkenness where they did the dirty bop.

"So much for Diane. But I still had the pint and was still as horny as an old goat. So I began a new campaign, fought a single skirmish—saw a girl who looked vaguely familiar, asked her to dance, she said no; I remembered, she had said no the year before too—then I dashed down to where I had the bag stashed and sat down by the lake in some goddamned Doris Day moonlight, drinking, feeling sorry for myself, listening to the music and laughter from up at the pavilion. I got half a pint down, more than enough, lit a cigarette, stumbled, giggled, and walked—walked hell, strode, man—back up that hill. Ten fucking feet tall, man, fulla piss and vinegar. Boy, it was great. I can't forget it. Somehow I could feel the whole earth through my loafers. You know how you always feel sort of apart from the works, sort of a piece of a puzzle packed in the wrong box, like maybe the whole world is playing a joke on you, laughing at you? Well, I didn't feel that way any more. I wasn't just me any more, I was part of the lake and the moon and the grass growing under my feet, part of the hill tilting up toward the stars, and most of all part of that dancing and lights and music up above; and the lights were brighter, the music louder and wilder, and me itching to be scratched all over. I guess you might say I was cool for the first time in my life.

"Shit, I went back to that chickie who had turned me off two years in a row and I didn't ask this time, I told her, and grabbed her and danced off before she could say no. She couldn't say no all night; 'course I lied a lot, told her I was bumming around the States on my way to Mexico where I played the guitar in a whorehouse. The pint worked; I just didn't understand that you were supposed to drink it; I thought the girl was supposed to drink it. Love struck again. She followed me around for days, buying my meals, pestering me with hungry hands until I finally had to sneak off from her to hitch home.

"That's the way it usually is. Being drunk is good for me. Give me a pinball machine sober and I'll tilt every time, but drunk I'm lights and cold steel balls and action. A car, the same thing. Conversation: I talk better, know more what I'm saying. I'm all together, I belong. Like now. . . ." He paused. ". . . Yeah, like now." He remained still for a while, holding his tongue like a man who has just realized what he has said. I tried another cigarette that lit, and we cupped it in our hands like a jewel till it was a butt, then lit another from it. Leaden swirls of smoke surrounded us, cold and damp as the air. Morning hunched over the cigarette, wrapped in his blanket like a Comanch' medicine man, his face in the flow a gaunt amulet worn by his soul, portentously warding off vague evil, clear virtue. I lay back against the sallow cement, my face swathed in gray mist and smoke.

"Yeah, it's wonderful to be drunk that way. Great," he said. "But then there is the other kind, like tonight. Just like a storm or something.

"The first one came in high school. My senior year, I think. Yeah, the Sunday after we had lost the state football championship. One of my more brilliant games; I ran seventy-five yards in the last minute of the game, then dropped the damned ball on the three-yard line, nobody around, I just dropped the damned ball, so we lost 10–7. The football team was drowning our sorrow, those of us who drank, in a wood outside town. Somebody had brought two kegs—more beer than we could drink in a year—in back of a pickup, and by dark I was really wiped out. I'd puked all over my clothes, had a fist fight with my best friend, and passed out twice. Before dark, mind you. A social drunk, you know.

"Then some little white-trash girls showed up. Two fat ones who were the local punches, gang-bang Southern belles, and a little skinny one who wanted to be. They got the fat ones drunk, then they got the skinny one drunk and naked in the back of the pickup where she was going to make her social debut on some old mattress ticking while everybody watched. But, you know, she drew the line there; no watching, she said. That's about the last thing I remember: her sitting in the back of that pickup, both hands up tight against her crotch, little-bitty-bird titties pinched between bony arms, crooning, 'un-uh, un-uh, un-uh,' like a little kid who's fixing to get whipped.

"After that I sort of lost things, blacked out I guess, but didn't pass out. But the others told me about it, told me what I did, what happened. Like tonight. I won't find out till you tell me. Anyway everybody argued with her about watching. You know how drunks get one thing in mind and the rest of the world can go to hell. We argued with her till dark and somebody built a bonfire, but she kept shaking her head, hiding her face in her stringy hair. Finally they gave up, and everybody except the guy who was first walked off down the road, then ran back and hid in the bushes next to the pickup. The first guy, a real cockhound lover boy, couldn't get a hard-on. He just stood there in the firelight, banging on his pecker and cussing and—by God, I just remembered her name, Rita Whitehead—Rita kept saying 'what's wrong, what's wrong' and he kept saying 'shut up, shut up.' You couldn't see Rita except for one naked foot up over the side of the pickup bed with one of those dime-store ankle chains and a little green track underneath it where the plate had come off and tiny, chipped, painted toenails. We laughed lover boy out of the scene. What the hell was his name? Dick something, Wilber, Willard, something like that. Then two big cherry farm boys, brothers, were next, but they both blew their rocks before they even got in, and remained cherries.

"The next guy said he didn't have time because his mother expected him to go to Training Union down at the Baptist Church with her. So it looked like that little ole gal wasn't ever going to get screwed. Then up steps old Joseph Savior Morning, screaming drunk, ripping off his pants out of turn, promising that poor white-trash girl some real welfare meat and potatoes. I, also somewhat of a lover, tried to warm her up with my hand, warm her up for a gang-bang, shit, but she was so drunk it didn't matter, so I went ahead without her. Till she started puking. I'd poke her, and she'd puke, like poking a sack of chicken feed with a hole in the other end. She wouldn't quit, so I got mad, they told me, and got off. Then I saw the blood. It covered me from belly to knees, all over my hands. Everybody was laughing and I thought they had played a joke on me, but then I tore the rest of my clothes off, and started washing off the blood with beer and throwing handfuls on her and shouting verses from Leviticus that I just happened to know, 'And if a woman have an issue, and her issue in her flesh be blood, she shall be put apart seven days: and whosoever toucheth her shall be unclean until the even. And everything that she lieth upon in her separation shall be unclean: everything also that she sitteth upon shall be unclean. And whosoever toucheth her bed shall wash his clothes, and bathe himself in water, and be unclean until the even.' And then, they said, I shouted the last verse and held her head under the spout, 'And if any man lie with her at all, and her flowers be upon him, he shall be unclean seven days; and the bed whereon he lieth shall be unclean!' Well, dad, I was well-flowered, to say the least, twice drunk, and everybody else sort of went insane with me, throwing beer on each other and everything." He paused—to think? to remember?

In the short quiet I noticed that the rain had stopped. Morning sat now arms about his knees, the blanket draped over his head, light from a cigarette hanging from the corner of his mouth exposing half a face perhaps as thin and tired in the shadow as Rita's must have been, trapped in the back of a pickup with a madman. Darkness hid the other half of his face, as if he were a leper hiding his sores from the Lord thy God. He went on in a slow, measured voice.

"We tied Rita naked to a sour persimmon tree next to the fire and danced and screamed and laughed—everyone joined me, no one tried to stop me—and washed away her blood with beer and rough hands. But I didn't stop there, they tell me, but grabbed the fat girls and had them stripped, shouting like a nigger preacher because they were wearing slacks, 'The man shall not wear that which pertaineth unto a woman, neither shall a woman put on a man's clothes: for all that do so are abomination unto the Lord thy God!'

"Deuteronomy 22:5," he said to me with a sad smile. "I always remember the good parts.

"Then somehow all of us were naked and washing the girls and slapping the fat girls' titties and rubbing them until they cried. Then my best friend, the one I'd already fought with, tried to screw one of the fat girls standing up. Somehow in the back of my mind I must have remembered that he had lost a nut when he was a baby. He had told me not to tell anybody; he was afraid we would laugh at him. Yes, count on me, I probably said to him. We tied him to the tree with the other sinners to the tune of Deuteronomy 23:1, 'He that is wounded in his stones, or hath his privy member cut off, shall not enter into the congregation of the Lord.' A photographic memory, a miracle my teachers called it. He wasn't as easy to hog-tie as the girls, but nine of us managed.

"I woke a couple of hours later when it started to rain, and in the flickering firelight saw—well, let me say, real abominations. Seven kinds of sodomy at once. The scene made my stereo cabinet look like a Victorian play by comparison. The farm brothers had finally lost their cherry, in a way, and my best friend also lost any illusions he might have had about clean, healthy American farm boys. I untied him from the back of the pickup where they had carried him, and he and I fought again, and I let him whip me. But it didn't help. He always acted as if I'd done it instead of the farmers. Anyway, he never spoke to me again.

"It might make a good story to say that he killed himself or ran away or something, but right now he's selling insurance in Charleston, and if you asked him about that night, he wouldn't remember, either.

"Somehow we all got home without permanent damage, but it took a long time for me to believe what they said I'd done. I tried to ask Rita for a date, as a way of apology, but she told me to go fuck myself, '. . . or maybe your best buddy, huh?' God, what a night. Too much. And half a dozen times just like that since then." He stopped, shook his head, then rested it on his arms.

"You never remember anything?"

He looked up at me quickly, almost as if he were disgusted with even the idea, but then laid his forehead back down, mumbling something.

"What?"

"I said, 'Of course, I remember,' you asshole."

"Yeah," I said.

"Everytime. Shit, I remember even better drunk than sober. Remember everything. I just can't stop myself, at all. Just like that night. I remember those delicious fat titties, wet and stinking of beer. I wallowed in flesh, then whetted myself on bone, bony thin Rita, and I saw what those dumb farmers were doing to Jack. And I cheered them on. I knew what I was doing, but I just couldn't stop. I guess I didn't even want to stop. And then I always lied that I didn't remember. Ashamed, I guess. Like tonight. Shit," he said, "I don't know what's wrong with me." He seemed near tears. I didn't want to see him cry.

"Don't you know that's what being drunk is, Joe?" I said. "Don't you know?"

"What?" he said, half angry, perhaps at the simple answer.

"To be drunk is to be out of control. Sometimes the good part of a man gets out of the cage, sometimes the bad, man. Didn't you know that?" I tried to explain, to sooth, but he was too long convinced of his guilt, irrevocable guilt. Though we talked till daylight, gray morning, mist, and fog; I could still see the sadness deep in his dull, red-cracked eyes. Understanding, slow yet as sure as the sun slaying the mist, crept heavily into me . . . and I resolved, in spite of himself, in spite of myself, to save him.

I fell to conniving that morning. First I tried Tetrick.

"No," he said, when I asked him to speak to Dottlinger again about Morning's discharge. "No. And don't you. After that stunt the other night, after last night—yeah, I heard about last night—he's hanging himself."

"Maybe that's why we should help?"

"I've got seventy-five other men to help, men who don't give me trouble all the time. You got nine other men, and Morning is going to get his shit on them one of these times. I'm sorry that he has to go this way, but I'm not sorry to see him go. He's been trouble from the beginning. The first night he's in the Company, I go to Town and find him in Esting's, and he smiles at me and says 'Hi, sarge,' as if I hadn't told him that same morning that he couldn't go to Town for fifteen days. I still haven't found out how he got off base. Even I spent fifteen days on base before I got a pass. But not him. Rules are for other guys, not him. I won't miss him. Neither will you. He's already got you in crap once. He'll do it again. He's not worth the effort; he'll turn on you. He's not." Tetrick punctuated his "he's not's" by slapping his bald head and stomping his feet under the desk. "Ahh," he groaned. "This damned rain is killing my feet."

"Maybe I'll just walk in and kick Dottlinger's head in."

"Don't make troubles for me. I don't need them. Sgt. Reid didn't show up for work again this morning. Twice this week already. Once more and I'll have the Operations officers down here bitching at me again."

"I can't let it sit. I've got to do something. It's all wrong."

"Now you're talking like him. Leave it alone. Don't make waves for yourself. He's not worth it."

"Maybe not."

"What?"

"Nothing. Nothing. See you."

I left with, as the saying goes, a germ of an idea, though it turned out to be a disease, a plague on both our houses.

It cost me thirty dollars (because I didn't have ten cartons of Salems, fastest moving menthol cigarette on the black market) and a whole tired afternoon listening to Dominic stomp his peg leg against the Plaza bar to make points about his experiences in the Spanish Civil War. He told a fair account of the coming of the revolution to his small town: *guardia civil* executed kneeling against a wall, Fascists clubbed and beaten over a cliff by a mob of drunks, a priest reaped with sickles. But I'd heard it before. I paid the price and in return received a solemn beery pledge from Dominic, on his honor and faith as a stout member of the *revolución,* on the soul of his leg buried in a nameless Spanish grave, that he would take prompt, decisive action, and send the evidence by way of my houseboy.

I heard nothing for a week. Morning stayed away from me, and when work forced us together, he avoided talk, feeling, I assume, that he had talked too much already. He was odd that way. He had a compulsive need to confess, and often expounded on the need for complete honesty in human relations, love, friendship, etc., but after the kind of confidence which he claimed drew people closer, he always drew away again. But finally the manila envelope appeared crinkling under my pillow, and I quickly spilled the 8x10s on my bunk, half in fear, half in excitement.

There they were: Sgt. Reid and his skinny wife in their bed. Damn Dominic's fumbling one-legged idiot soul. Reid looked as he always looked, as if he didn't exactly know what was happening. His wife seemed to know precisely what was going on, but she was looking at her husband, her head cocked like a setter bitch, as if wondering, trying to remember who she had climbed into bed with this time, or perhaps wondering what her husband was doing in her bed. She had a sullen, sly face in the glossy print. A thin, pouting face probably a great deal like the face of Morning's Rita Whitehead. A thin Scotch-Irish build, a bony small frame so common in the South (as if poverty had its own special gene), hair tangled in rats' nests, small breasts with long, almost stringy nipples—I didn't see what Dottlinger quite saw in her but, of course, nor did I understand what she saw in that bastard; except perhaps a congenital attraction to bastards.

The three other pictures exhibited a bit more diligence and imagination on Dominic's part. It made me sick. Dottlinger and Reid's wife were chemically locked in that most compromising of love's positions, known in the idiom as 69. I'd seen blue movies, stag films, before, but always drunk, and now I knew why. Love is private, and whatever its motives or methods, it deserves that privacy. The thought of how confused and dazed Reid must have been, caught in his own bed by blackmailers, was bad enough, but Dottlinger's exposure somehow touched a more tender wound. I marveled that he had both the imagination and guts to love a woman that way (for it does take imagination and guts for a Southern boy: the term "cocksucker," certainly a vile implication across America, in the South refers not to fellatio, but cunnilingus, linguistically). Then the terrible thought came: what if they really were in love, star-crossed lovers? and Dominic intruding with a dirty foot, my man against love? Party myself to accidental evil, I almost threw the photographs away. I did tear Reid's candid shot and the negative into bits, but I was a blackmailer with a mission and, saying "The greatest good for the greatest number," I was on my way, telling myself, as one must in this sort of affair, "Don't force the rat into a corner; leave him room to negotiate." I thought I might begin by asking for his resignation in exchange for the negatives, and work from there. . . . But then I laughed, a smothered giggle, a belch, then a roar. I stumbled back to my room and, laughing harder than I had in months, burned the prints and the negatives and the manila envelope. (I must admit that I took another look at the pictures which, as I remember, I laughed at tenderly, delightedly.) Fire and laughter and a bit of madness saved me from being both fool and martyr (and Morning).

I went to the Provost Marshal's Office and found a smart Dartmouth lawyer serving his time with a wry smile and a wonderful ability to beat courts-martial. I explained, with some slight exaggeration, Morning's plight, and within the hour he had called Dottlinger, quoted some legal, Latin nonsense to him (I think I overheard *Illegitimi Non Carborundum;* I hope so), and Dottlinger dropped the whole idea the same day. (Morning I saved, but incidentally loosed two more idiots on the world. One later made it to Leavenworth anyway, but the other went straight. Two out of three will get a fellow out of the Sally League any season.) Morning acted his part with mock sadness, I with mock humility; but he spoke to me again.

Football practice began the next week, Capt. Saunders came back the next, and we slogged on through the tail end of the rainy season, crazy about down-field blocks, gang-tackling, and mud.

It all seems important now, and there was so much more . . . a great football season, an undefeated team with Morning at quarterback and me running the defense, backing the line. A really fine season, a wonderful time, but I'm not sure what it might mean to you. Our last game—we had won the base championship the game before—we were quite drunk. Morning's passes faltered and tumbled like wounded ducks, and my defensive signals were at best unintelligible and more often confusing. During the last quarter we alternated between an eleven-man line and an eleven-man secondary. When first presented with an eleven-man secondary, the opposing quarterback left the field in disgust. But none of it mattered. Receivers—stretcher-bearers, I assume—appeared under Morning's sick passes; there was little need for defense since the other team not only couldn't hold the ball, they couldn't walk. The disgusted quarterback tripped on his way off the field; his receivers dropped seven passes in the end zone in the first half. And we couldn't do a thing wrong. Even I scored a touchdown on a two-yard plunge that Morning arranged for me. It was my first and really a thrill, except that I plunged through the end zone into the goal posts which shattered my shoulder pads and fractured my collar bone.

So I spent New Year's Eve 1962 in Baguio in a cast. I should have never let Morning call that play. I had to drink left-handed. Morning found a bar, The New Hollywood Star Bar. It was a *real* place because there was no icebox for the beer, no one put money in the jukebox but lifted the face and punched the songs they wanted, and the other patrons were Communists, students, and gold-miners, representing the labor and radical wings of the party. Morning played Trotsky to their Stalin and Mao, and they loved it. No one spoke to me because Morning told them I was a major when I was gone to the latrine the first night. Morning also fell in love at The New Hollywood Star Bar. The girl was *real* too, a short, stocky Benguet girl; young, pleasantly plump, with a square face and square hands and fingers, and best of all (as Morning told me seventy-two times that night) dirty fingernails. He had visions of sleeping with her in a tiny nipa hut, surrounded by jungle, washed by rain, devoured by her muscular body. But she wouldn't go the first night, and on the second she had cleaned her fingernails and wanted lady's drinks and a trip to the Club on John Hay. The first night she drank beer from heavy glasses, drank like a man with dirty fingernails. The second night he argued louder and longer with the Communists, and I had visions of fighting our way out, but nothing came of it. Later, in our room at the Club over a bottle of Dewar's he insisted that I tell him about my wife. Insisted in that drunken, persistent, arrogant way he had; his fist clenched except for the forefinger, which he held up with his thumb. "You need to talk about it, Krummel. You need to." He kept it up until I threatened to bust him even with one arm tied around me. He believed me, though, and let it go. But the next day he blew up at Cagle (who was a hell-and-back-again better golfer) on the golf course, and Cagle took after him with a four wood. Morning was stunned for a second, but then leapt down the fairway, Cagle two steps behind, and Novotny two steps behind him, leaving me collapsed in laughter on the tee and three very amazed caddies watching it all. Novotny caught Cagle and disarmed him, and while he sat on him, Morning apologized so contritely, so humbly that Cagle began to laugh, and when they came back up the fairway we were together again. They finished the eighteen holes in the rain as I tried to keep my cast from getting wet, all of us convinced that we were the four greatest guys alive. Then we feasted on two-inch thick sirloins, and drank cognac in our room until we were disgustingly maudlin, stupidly drunk, and God-ever-so happy; blind drunk and lost. We stood at the edge of the bluff in front of the Club in a windy, wet night, staring at the lights far down in the valley, looking up at the clouds so close. Wet and in the wind we were almost cold, chilled for the first time in months, and we savored it, warmed ourselves with cognac; but already in the wind, in the waning rain, came word of the long, hot dry season, a hint of dust, a touch of fear.

There is so much to tell, so much. . . .

6

RAID

The morning the Huk bandits tried to rob the Central Exchange, my trick was on the last of a set of mids. The six mids had seemed like six months to me. It had been too hot too long. The work had long lost any magic for me. Even Town was too dreary to bear. Hot and dusty and dry. The manure dropping from *calesa* ponies raised small dust storms in the street, and the wet cakes dried before they could stink. It had been five months since Lt. Dottlinger had tried to take Town away from us, but we would have given it to him now.

At 0200 I telephoned the Flight Line, hoping that we had received courier mail on the 0100 flight from Travis, but there was nothing. I crossed a flying trip to the Flight Line with Cagle bulling the three-quarter all over the road from my list of possibilities to make the rest of the trick bearable. I wandered around the room several times, checking copy sheets, half-hoping Morning would start an argument or a word game or anything to pass the time. All the men were jabbering about the Trick's Break trip to the beach at Dagupan planned for the next three days, but I had heard about nothing else for the past week, and didn't want to hear any more. Back at my desk I wrote the 0300 entry in the log—something nonsensical, hoping for a laugh when it was read, but knowing no one ever read the damned thing anyway. The room and all its contents seemed to be turning gray. All the equipment, desks, chairs and consoles were already gray, and the faded green fatigues could have been gray in another light, and the cream walls were surely a shade of ashes. The same talk, the same faces. Without windows who could know if it was day or night outside? I might have been trapped in that square one-room building for months, even years, and not know it. The same work, the same non-work.

I sat down and allowed myself to enjoy the idea of soldiering again—usually I didn't think about it. I could have almost been excited about spit-shining my footgear, or laying out a full field inspection for myself. But I had my houseboy for those things, and no real reason to do them anyway. No more were the three fingers of my right hand stained soft and brown like those of the Negro shineboy in my home town. (Boy? Old Luke was sixty when I was ten. Morning must strain in his grave when I say that.) No longer the pleasant order of a perfect bunk, or me in khaki stiff armor and standing tall. But like most men, I fell easily into the easy life. Luxury is like a Sunday afternoon nap: "Oh, I meant to, ah . . ." but you are already dead for an hour or two, and you always wake with a filthy taste in your mouth. But you, and I, will sleep again next Sunday. If they took your houseboy away, Krummel, you'd cry like a baby. Besides, soldiering is for brutes and animals who don't understand, and you, Krummel, are an educated, sensitive and intelligent man, and. . . .

A face appeared before me. Distraction, I shout! But who would it be but Peterson with a tale about a new girl at the Skylight, a real honest-to-God blond named Gloria who was an ex-movie star from Manila. He thought he might shack steady with her since she was the best thing eighteen years of life had found him. Or was it nineteen?

"Sure, Pete, I fucked her once. Her hair's bleached, she uses too much make-up to cover small-pox scars, and she gave a guy a blow-job in a blue movie once. Lovely girl," I shouted above the electronic whispering and the grinding of the damned malfunctioning air conditioner. Voices stopped, heads turned. Peterson, poorest son of Peter, frowned slightly and spoke to his friendly trick chief, "Geez. I thought she was a nice girl, Sarge," then quietly dissolved into a film of ashes. I swung out of my chair and up the ladder to the roof before I got soot in my eye. "Geez," he said behind me.

On the roof I slammed the trap door on the noisy square of light. Novotny turned from his post at the edge of the roof. I waved at him, and he turned around to lean on the waist-high wall which outlined the roof. The compound was as bright as a supermarket, vastly illuminated by new floodlights on poles around the fence and on the corners of the building. It seemed very sheltered in the dark square of the roof, a safe place to stroll, to watch the world without being seen; the only sounds a scattering of gravel across the tarred roof from your feet or a gentle thump as a rice bug discovered its fate against the brick wall below the beckoning lights. A pleasant and roomy crow's nest but with very little to spy upon—the spying went on below. The fences, the gate, the parked three-quarter, and fifty yards of *cogon* grass. Occasionally a small pig might be glimpsed racing across the thirty-yard swath cut around the fence, but where the grass wasn't cut, it waved higher than a man's hopes and anything you chose to see out there was a ghost of your own construction. A patch of darkness in a square of light in an eternity of darkness in a hole in the bottom of the sea. To the right in the distance were the lights of the Main Gate, to the left those of the Central Exchange, and behind were the dancing colored lights of the runways, dipping to the swinging baton of the endless beacon. But these were only lights, distant cold dots without the warmth of stars. The sullen night was no more pleasing than the eternal daylight below. Even the silence held a gritty whisper, and I walked around to hear the track of my boots and spoke for the sound of my voice, "Got a cigarette, Novotny?"

He shook his pack at me, scattering several across the roof. "Have some," he said. I could see the light gleaming off his cheeks and knew they were clenched in a grin.

"Thanks."

"You got a bug up your ass tonight?" he asked as we searched for the lost cigarettes. "Heard you holler all the way up here."

"Maybe I'm going Asiatic like the rest of you bastards. Who knows?"

"Told you this place wasn't home."

"You did, didn't you? Pete thinks it is."

"Huh."

"Pete's fallen in love with a new broad at the Skyview. Do you know who she is? He said she had blond hair."

"Yeah," he snorted, "she's got blond hair, but she ain't got pink nipples. She's okay in the dark, but in the daylight she's bad news." We stood up and leaned over the wall.

"He says he may steady shack with it," I said, flipping my cigarette among the pile of rice bugs on the sidewalk below. "Hope he doesn't bite off. . . ."

An explosion and a clatter of automatic fire at the Main Gate interrupted me. We could see bouncing headlights and splashing bursts of automatic fire followed by their rattle.

"Jesus. What's happening?" Novotny asked quietly, grabbing my arm.

"I don't know, but load your weapon, anyway," I answered on my way to the trap door.

Later I learned that six jeeps of Huk bandits had hit the Main Gate with everything from a 20mm cannon stolen from a jet to a .25 caliber Nambu light machine left by the Japanese, and lots of swivel-mounted .50s and .30s. And they knew how to use them. They came through the gate without changing gears, knocked down six Air Policemen, two Filipino guards and a KP coming to work early; blew up the guard shack, a jeep and a three-quarter, and kept on moving. But we did not know any of this until later.

I hit the floor shouting, "Shut her down! Shut her down! Levenson! get on the phone to PMO and find out what's happening at the Main Gate!" I fielded seventy questions by not answering, then caught seventy more when I unlocked the weapons rack and the ammo locker. "Everybody get a weapon and ammo and get on the roof!" They stared at me with a single question furrowing every face: War? Then the same sadness touched every pair of eyes when the next thought followed, as had been promised since they were born: The Bomb? *Oh, my God,* the faces said, *Oh my God! Nobody told us. We're not ready. There's too much left undone.* We all stood very still for a long, long second, very quiet in the metallic hum and beep of our useless equipment, as if wondering why it hadn't warned us, listening again for a clue from the silent, glowing and smug tubes. I thought they would be all right. They were just stunned by the opening of the ammunition locker. None of them had ever seen the green footlocker opened. The weapons' rack was okay, even familiar, an ordinary thing of day to day inspections or alerts, but live ammunition was only for the range or standing roof guard and being very careful not to accidently fire a round because old Johnson had caught a Special Court for firing one round. But this was different. Frightening, exciting, but mainly different, and it grabbed them and held them silent and still. But like all captured moments, this one was as short as it was long, and it ended as I shoved several bandoleers of M-1 clips into Morning's stomach, and shouted, "On the roof! Move! Move! Move! Cagle, get the outside lights. Move!"

They moved.

I grabbed a rifle, some ammo and swung up the ladder, shouting once more for Levenson to call PMO. "Busy! Busy! Busy!" he screamed back, his voice as high and irritated as the signal he was getting.

On the roof madness was unleashed as everyone tried to load, look, and run around knocking each other off the roof. A line of headlights had already turned off the main highway on the side road coming toward us. I could barely keep my mind on the men: the rifle in my hands kept begging to be fired. Another jeep followed the line at a distance which I later judged to be the effective range plus one hundred of a .50 caliber at night from the back of a speeding vehicle. Two sets of headlights were coming across the grass from the runways behind us, and more along the fence next to the Exchange. It looked as if we were being attacked from all sides, and since I had forgotten about the money in the Exchange half a mile east of us, this attacking fear did more than I could with all my pushing and shouting to make the men stay in one place. Peterson still stood in the center of the roof, lost, holding an M-1 in one hand, a carbine in the other, and he looked doubly helpless because it was obvious he was not about to turn loose of either rifle long enough to get both hands on one. Novotny led him to the wall, and sat him down behind it. Collins, Quinn and Morning were kneeling behind the wall and at least had their weapons pointed in the general direction of the lights stringing swiftly closer. Levenson popped through the trap door and screamed, "A holdup! A holdup! A Huk holdup!" He giggled and ran to the wall loading a carbine. One of the jeeps from the runaway patrol swept through our lights, an AP hanging out of either side, shouting and shooting, one with a .38 revolver, the other with a shotgun, at the jeeps over a thousand yards away. They were having a grand time. Once more my rifle pleaded to be fired.

Suddenly the floodlights went out, fading quickly away, and the headlights and muzzle flashes leapt closer out of the blinking darkness. "Where was Moses when the lights went out?" Morning said. I could not see him now, but I remembered how he looked a moment before, cold in his poise and readiness. "Down in the cellar with his shirttail out," he answered himself. He sounded drunk, but I knew he wasn't. Until I saw him at the wall, a faint question had been tickling the back of my neck. But now I knew he would fight as the lights and firing came on us like a squall line:

Cagle came up, shut away the last bit of light, and said, "Hey, Slag-baby, you boys didn't leave me a gun."

"Little fart don't need one," Novotny said beside me.

"Pete's got two."

Cagle shuffled to the wall. "Gimme one, you stingy bastard."

"What now?" everyone asked in one way or another—except Morning.

What could I answer? Me with my trembling fingers knocking on the hard wood stock and me with a fine quiver in my guts and the blood in my ears like thunder. . . .

"Shit. Shoot the bastards."

No one cheered, but they listened quietly as I did all that Hollywood crap about firing on my signal and short bursts, and made a Jimmy Cagney joke about not shooting any AP dirty rats by mistake. I didn't get any laughs either. A snort from Quinn, a few nervous shuffles, a slap or two at bugs, a muffled cough or prayer, then everyone was quiet, watching the racing lights.

I waited until the line was what seemed close enough, and slid my rifle over the wall. Then I wondered how Pete had climbed the ladder with two weapons, then I worried about not mentioning setting battle sights at three hundred yards. The lights of the first jeep were fuzzy in my peep sight, and I waited, and then I screamed.

The crash of my shot seemed like an explosion in my hands, loud, too loud, and the recoil knocked me back like an unexpected blow. The whole complexion of the night changed. The walled roof, secure and safe as it had seemed earlier, became a naked, frightened place, as if some unnamed part of me had been launched into the distant battle, leaping across the border between a safe here and an unbelievably dangerous there. It wasn't like I thought it would be. It wasn't easy to shoot at men, or a grinding noise and light which betrays where men are. I had never thought that it would be otherwise—but it was so frightening, as if I had to cross that time and space and stand stupid and scared and shooting at myself. I was numb, but all the nerves of my body were on fire, fire.

The others must have felt the shock too. Novotny and Quinn had fired only one or two rounds, Collins a couple more, and Cagle had split the night with a clip-long burst which had jammed his carbine. But Morning fired steadily, rocking with the recoil, then back into firing position, his rhythm broken only by the ping of his clip as the last round ejected and the click and snap as he loaded another.

I whipped back to the jeeps, sorry they must be gone, and found they had barely moved. I fired again, and again, and the more times I pulled the trigger, the easier it was, the more numb my nerves became. Quickly the rifle was as light as a wand and magically waved, cleanly leading the first jeep, the recoil gone, and I knew, knew, knew I was hitting the jeep, and fired again. Then we were firing and screaming and laughing and lost.

The beams of many vehicles now splashed everywhere, up and down and around, swinging and bouncing over the grass as if hundreds of hunting giants were running with flashlights. But some jeeps had stopped, and burned like jubilant bonfires. As the Huks passed the gravel road which led to Ops, the first jeep skidded and the second hit it, turning it over in the road, and it rode its passengers for awhile. The third clipped the left rear of the second, trying to swing around it, so both stalled in opposite ditches near where the first burned. The remaining three whipped off the road in a tight, dusty circle, then came back going in the other direction. They caught an AP three-quarter which was following with its lights out, and knocked it off the road. Other vehicles behind it scattered like frightened quail, flying faster the further away they got from the hunters.

One down, two stopped, three away, and our side stood up to cheer, to shout and fire off-hand at the cluster of wrecked jeeps. We had drawn only a casual answering fire: once or twice a bass string had been plucked over our heads but who knew where it had been aimed, or even come from. The Huks were busy with the Air Police who now had eight or ten jeeps and three-quarters and two small armored riot cars, but they still had a moment for my bunch. Just a moment, but they hit the front of the building with six .50 caliber rounds. The building rocked as the slugs snipped through the cinder blocks as if they were gingerbread. A brick chip or a ricochet kicked Quinn's M-1 out of his hands, but nothing else was hit on the roof. Quinn cursed and crawled after the weapon. There was noticeably less cheering and absolutely no standing any more. A grunt and gurgle came from the other side of Novotny, followed by Cagle's surprised voice, "I didn't know I was scared. I didn't know."

Fewer bursts seared away from the two fallen jeeps, then they stopped completely after the two riot cars fired tear gas grenades with their cannon. Gradually all the firing stopped as three men ran out of the gas cloud. Two had their hands in their faces, but one held a rifle. Single rounds and short, concise bursts rattled again until the one with the rifle and one without did flip-flop dances across the road into the ditches. Morning still rocked and fired until he finished the clip. The

ping, as his last round ejected, seemed too small a punctuation
to end so much noise.

But of course the night was not over yet. A grinding crash
came from the fence behind us. I ran to the back wall. A jeep
had hit the corner of the fence and now sat with its right rear
wheel hanging three feet up in the wire like a little dog
cocking its leg to pee.

"Who is it?" I shouted down.

"Why don't ya'll turn your goddamn lights on?" a tired voice
drawled.

"Didn't want any you dumb-ass airmen shooting us," Cagle
sneered.

"Doesn't matter," I said. "It's all over now."

"She-it," the voice said from behind the tilted headlights,
"She-it." Two APs climbed out the driver's side, then walked
toward the road. "Fuckin' ground-pounders hidin' in the dark
like a bunch a fuckin' niggers."

"Might jes be a might careful callin' a man that when he got
a gun pointed right at ya'll's lily white ass," Morning sang out.
" 'Member ya'll can't see my ass in th' dark." The airmen
hurried on.

I stopped the laughter and chatter before it could start.
"Cagle, downstairs and turn on the floodlights. Novotny,
Quinn, stay up here. You spot anyone in the grass, don't fire,
but sing out so I'll know. Collins, Levenson, Haddad, take the
inside of the compound, one by the jeep, one at the gate, and
one walking." The lights came on; most of the fires around the
wrecks were being extinguished, and headlights were bounding down our road. Things were trying to reach normal, when
the jeep slid up behind our three-quarter, and Lt. Dottlinger
leaped out and ran for the gate and shouted, "Open up!" as if
he were under fire.

"Of all the bastards in the world . . ." Morning mused.

"You didn't show your badge, sir," I answered, agreeing with
Morning. I had forgotten that Dottlinger was the OD, but I
should have known.

"I haven't got it. Is that you Krummel? What are you doing
on the roof? Sightseeing?"

"No sir. The Trick is up here." Jesus, I thought, here we go
again, around the chickenshitberry bush.

"What for?" He peered harder into the lights, a muddled, myopic chicken. "Are those weapons loaded, sergeant?"

"Yes, sir."

"Did you fire? Did you? I want to know. I'll have to report this."

"Yes, sir."

"Who authorized you to open the ammunition locker? Who ordered you to open fire? Just who, Sgt. Krummel?"

"Good question," I muttered. Levenson giggled.

"What's that, sergeant? Damn those lights, anyway," he said, shielding his eyes.

"He must really be pissed," Morning whispered. "He cursed."

"We were fired upon, sir. I assumed in an emergency that I was authorized to answer. I couldn't reach the major, Capt. Saunders, or you, so I assumed responsibility myself."

"Oh," he said, tugging at his ear to let us know he was thinking. "All right," he said, obviously disappointed. "I suppose we can find a regulation to cover the situation for our report. Open the gate."

"Sir, I can't unlock the gate from here unless you put your badge in the key-box."

"I told you, I didn't have it. I didn't have time to get it."

"Then I'll have to come down to let you in." It curdled my blood to lie to the bastard about being fired upon first, changed me from a man to a kid with his fly open. And I didn't really have to. I had said that I was not worrying about my stripes any more. There must have been guilt on that Apple Tree instead of knowledge—or maybe they are the same. Take two men, stick them in uniforms, tack bars on one, and the other one will find himself guilty. To hell with this man's army, I thought, Just to hell with it.

"Okay, the guards I posted, move out. All the rest of you shitheads, downstairs. Clear your weapons before you try to climb down. I don't want you shooting your own tender asses off."

"We'll back you up, Slag," Haddad said, slapping me on the shoulder. He could smell trouble for all of them if I got stuck. "All the way."

"Just move out, shopkeeper. Just move out."

Downstairs was a mess. Six three-thousand-dollar radios had taken slugs through their respective consoles, and now were bits of wire, plastic, and glass. A couple of typewriters had been hit; type scattered like broken twigs. A swivel chair had been blown over a desk, and the desk's drawers were hanging out. A sixty-thousand-dollar piece of equipment, our message encoder, had gained a new eye but lost a rectum the size of a basketball.

"Fourteen chickens and a hand grenade," Cagle chanted. Levenson hammered at a typewriter with a clenched fist and a wide grin, but the mill answered with only a tilted "E." Haddad was clucking through the radios like an old woman at a fruit stand looking for a rotten tomato she might get for free. I pushed the three guards out, took the weapons from the rest, and started them unplugging equipment before a fire started, and policing up the junk.

"Hey, Cagle," I said casually on my way to the door, "If Dottlinger asks—we were fired on first, okay?"

"Fuck you, Slag-baby. I ain't lying to save no lifer's stripes," he answered without stopping his broom.

Where would a man be without friends, I wondered on my way out. They keep us from taking ourselves too seriously, keep silly little things from becoming big. . . .

But then there are the Lt. Dottlingers whose worlds are constructed of mountainous molehills. He complained about my slowness, then wouldn't come in. He wanted a look at these Huks, and also thought I'd best fetch a couple of weapons and another man. I went back, got Morning and two carbines.

"Is Slutfinger very pissed?" Morning asked.

"Who cares."

"You do. All you fucking lifers do." He had a deadly stillness to his face.

"Not so much as you think. Besides, he's too curious to be pissed now. Wants to observe the disaster firsthand, get an eyeful and claim it for a bellyful. . . ."

"And we have to guard him against dead little fuckers. Where was he, when the lights went out?"

"I don't know. He doesn't go to the Officer's Club."

"I hear he has the thing going again with Reid's wife, the turd."

"Just be glad Saunders wasn't here. Trick Two would have charged those jeeps."

"I thought you might." He wasn't smiling.

"Huh?"

"How long have you been waiting for a chance like this."

"No longer than you, Morning."

"Fuck," he muttered, his voice tired, as we followed Dottlinger toward the clustered headlights.

But Morning's mood couldn't stop the grin on my face. The carbine seemed very small in my hand, like a toy outgrown. My body was tight, hard, as it was after a workout with the weights, solid. Dottlinger's nose, Morning's mood, the lie before—these no longer clouded the night. Not them, nor the sick, greasy nudge of fear. The enemy had risen out of darkness, had stood erect and dared me, and if he paid a price, it seemed only what he owed for the honor of standing. I had been afraid but had acted, and the action transcended, as ever, the emotion. Morality did not matter, nor mortality, only the act, the duty, simple and clear. I could not have chosen otherwise. Hundreds of lines through the space of time had converged in that fire-seared, light-spitted night, and one of the lines was me. Some stopped, some dodged the impact, and others could not have crashed if they wanted to; but mine endured. I too stood and dared, then, now, and forever. The cool night air blessed my face, and whatever throats gagged on the odors of the night, mine didn't. I breathed only victory as I strode over the gravel into the smoky circle of light.

People moved in all directions: hospital orderlies tended the wounded, gathered the dead; photographers recorded the scene from all angles; a priest with a pale, yearning face blessed friend and foe alike. A tall Air Force captain came over to Dottlinger, smiling, and extended a congratulatory hand.

"Lieutenant! I was just on my way down to thank you and your men for their timely help. Understand your men knocked off the first jeep, the one with the cannon on it," he said,

shaking Dottlinger's surprised hand. I might have been crazy,
but this captain was a fool. What had been, however per-
versely, salvation for me, became a golf match in his mouth.
His voice, prideful voice, sullied the world.

"Sorry, sir, but all the credit goes to Sgt. Krummel here,"
Dottlinger answered. I was surprised he didn't lie. Then he
lied. "I was making the courier-run."

"Well, I guess I owe you a great big 'thanks,' sergeant," he
gleamed.

"Don't forget God," Morning whispered in my ear.

"No telling how many lives you saved."

"Or took," came the whisper.

"We really broke their backs this time," the captain continued. "Three jeeps and ten men here, and another jeep and
four men at the gate." He smiled. "We were waiting for them,
all right."

"Sir?" I asked.

"Trap," he answered, quickly, proudly. "But they pulled a
fast one on us." He frowned slightly. "Came through the gate
instead of busting the fence as we expected. But we broke
their back, all right."

Morning whispered again. "Who the fuck trapped whom?" I
heard him walk away. Looking around the field, I couldn't
answer him.

The captain discussed the Communist problem in Asia, and
Dottlinger agreed, but before they resolved it, Tetrick and
Capt. Saunders, just back from the States, came wandering
across the crowd in civilian clothes. They looked like Town.
Capt. Harry smiled as if he loved the entire concept of human-
ity, and Tetrick frowned as if he were worried about it.

"Any of our men hurt?" he asked as soon as he saw me. I
shook my head but he kept frowning.

"Everyone all right?" Capt. Harry asked. "Looks like the
men got a little action tonight." He rocked his large body,
smiled and slapped me on the shoulder as if I were his brother.

"Yes, sir."

"Well, goddamnit, that's all right. Trick Two's a good bunch,
and I knew they would do all right." Dottlinger stopped trying

to get his attention, and huffed off. "But wish to hell I'd been here. We'd have run right out and knocked the bastards right off the road. Yes, sir, by God."

"Sgt. Rummel did a fine job, Harry. One hell of a fine job," the airman captain said. Morning was gone, but I heard him whisper, "Yeah, yeah."

"Sir," I asked while he still remembered me, "You don't need my men for anything tomorrow, do you?"

"Why?" He and I were no longer comrades-at-arms, but were returned to suspicious officer and crafty sergeant.

"Well, sir, they've had a trip planned for over a month, and I'd hate to see them miss it, after doing such a good job tonight, and they planned to leave tomorrow morning."

"Oh. Well, I don't know. . . ."

"Come on, Fred," Capt. Harry interrupted the captain, "Ease up. You know you slice the ball when you tighten up." He laughed and slapped the captain on the back.

"Oh, all right. Take off. We can get statements from you later. You've earned a break," he said. "And thanks again, sergeant."

"And thank you, sir." I excused myself, thanked Capt. Harry, reassured Tetrick, and went to find Morning. The kiss was off the flesh now, and I wanted very much to get to the beach tomorrow and forget . . . or remember.

I found Morning squatting in the ditch, watching some debris, a gutted jeep and a half-naked body lying on its face. Exit wounds covered the back like black roses with an occasional gristle petal. But for all the poetry of death, he looked no different than the charred jeep. Morning was alone. The crowd hadn't found this body yet.

"Maybe that's why man invented God," he said as I walked up behind him. "They saw dead men and understood that dead men weren't men any more. They had to have something in man they couldn't kill, something holy in man alive, some-place for man dead to go, something that couldn't die. Couldn't die." He had been waiting for me.

"Don't eat on it, Joe."

"A man needs to know what the hell he's done."

"You won't find out eating his liver. Or yours."

"You smug son of a bitch. You've got all the answers, don't you?" He stood up. He was crying. No sobs, just tears. We both remembered who had had the last shots.

"I only know what questions not to ask," I said.

"Slick, smooth counter-puncher, aren't you? You take all the shots on your shoulders. But you never miss, do you? You fucking bastard." His voice was quiet and grim. I could only wait.

"Come on let's go back to Ops."

"Shit," he sighed. "Shit."

Neither of us spoke as he followed me through the high thick grass toward the lights of our building. The air hung warm and heavy in the grass, and the insects swarmed up about our legs, circling and rising to our faces. The tough roots clutched at our feet, and we stumbled and cursed the heat, the bugs, the grass scratching at our eyes, and the darkness. And later we cursed the light when it blinded us.

7

DAGUPAN

Trick Two packed itself into the Air Force bus with the rented Filipino driver before seven-thirty the next morning. As I came out of the barracks, they greeted me with hoots and jeers for being so foolish as to want breakfast, then booed when I sent half of them back to the Orderly Room to sign out. When they came back, I climbed aboard behind them, swung down the aisle over the stacked K-rations, the garbage can of iced beer, the four cases of beer and six cases of Chianti and Rhine wine, and finally dropped into the rear seat between Morning and Novotny.

"What are you? an ape?" Cagle sneered, puffing on a huge cigar.

"Naw. What are you? a forest fart?"

"Ah, all you fucking Jews are the same," he answered, blowing smoke my way. "Have a gas attack, you. . . ."

"Oh, no we're not," Levenson simpered at him, waving a limp wrist over the seat as the bus pulled out of the drive.

"Vhy, there hasn't been a single Jew in de same house mit a Slagsted-Krummel in twenty-five venerations."

"Nazi," Morning said. "Gary Cooper's queer."

"Genet isn't."

Et cetera.

It was a good morning. The air still held a trace of dew and a cool wind eased the fatigue left over from the night before. All faces bloomed, brown, bright, and happy, all voices bubbled. Even Franklin's acne was better. No one mentioned the raid, until Pete came out of his perpetual daze long enough to remark in a surprised voice, "Geez, somebody might have got killed last night. If we hadn't been on the roof. Geez."

No one spoke for several minutes, and then the bus was at the Main Gate. Filipino carpenters were already cleaning up the two piles of lumber which had been the sentry box and guard shack. Several gaping black circles marked where vehicles had burned. The Air Policemen who came aboard to check passes and search for black-market goods were quiet and methodical about their work, without any of the usual GI-airman banter, nor did they check as closely. Their faces showed the loss of friends, and ours the guilt of going out to play.

Every man on the Trick had a legal quart of Dewar's Scotch and one legal carton of Chesterfields in his AWOL bag. Twenty new classical records were stacked on a new portable record player. Everyone understood that these things were going to the market, but nothing could be done. The APs had to let the goods out the gate, since it only became criminal when you sold them, and no one, except fools and children, ever got caught in the act of selling. The big operators like Haddad paid certain Air Policemen a high tariff, so they weren't usually caught either. As the APs left the bus, one knocked over a K-ration carton. Morning jumped slightly, but let the AP pick it up. The gate routine was always unpleasant, and everyone was glad to get down the highway toward Tarlac.

Just past the nearby barrio of Dau, the driver turned on a dirt track which led behind a clump of banana trees.

"Where's he going?" I asked.

"Meet the man," Novotny answered.

"What man?"

"Breadman."

The bus halted beside a jeepny with two men in it. Packs of cigarettes suddenly appeared from socks and shirts. The top four K-rations were opened to reveal tobacco instead of food. Cartons were collected from under seats and hood and behind a false fire wall. It was a black-market Merry Christmas, and everyone streamed off the bus to barter with the breadman except Haddad and me. After the sale Morning collected expenses for the bus, driver and beer, then waving the pesos, shouted "Hallelujah" and passed out the beer.

North of Tarlac the bus swung left toward the Lingayan Gulf, sweeping past small barefoot boys attending lethargic water buffalo sprawled in the ditches like forgotten mounds of tar. The sun had burned all memory of the morning from the air, and we raced toward a glassy, shimmering haze as it in turn ran from us. The metal edge of the windows burned your arm when you propped it up to catch the hot breeze, and sweat ran in crazy rivers down your ribs. In a second the fatigue and beer would make you forget the hot window and your arm would slip back up, then be cursed and jerked back again. The beer was cold and biting in your throat, but not cold enough. Novotny's drunken voice buzzed in the heat; near, then far away in the drowsy haze.

"That was all right last night. After you got over being scared, it was all right." He sat easily in the bumping seat, his body loose and fluid with the swaying, jolting bus, while a perfect gyroscope balanced him. The beer in his bottle stirred, but the rest of us were busy wiping beer out of our faces. "Maybe we all need a couple of good wars for Christmas."

"Yeah, but what if somebody had gotten their ass shot off," Morning growled from across the aisle. "Wouldn't be quite so much fun then, would it?"

"Oh hell, there aren't any more good wars," I said. "Not since the cannon was invented and airplanes started firing on ground troops. No more. Now there's the bomb. How can a man enjoy a good war, if he knows there's a chance that some silly bastard who believes in things will push the funny button and wipe up the whole works. There's no sense in it any more."

"Fuck. There never was any sense in it. War is stupid. The most terrible thing man can do to himself," Morning said, leaning up.

ditional surrender. Man's supposedly—and people like you
have done all you can to convince him of it—only a higher
animal, so maybe his sensitivity to encroachment is more
highly developed and he kills for other kinds of assumed
offenses. I don't know . . . there are a lot of things I don't
know that maybe I'd learn in a war. How many novelists find
war to be the most perfectly defined moment in their lives?
How . . ."

"How many find it the last moment of their lives?"

"People die in car wrecks."

"I'm against them too."

"Christ, Morning, man has always been obsessed with murder. Maybe it answers questions. Maybe the killing gives you
something holy. Maybe you find out about God then."

"It seems to me," he said, shaking that pedantic finger and
thumb again, "that *you're* obsessed with murder. You got
killing mixed up with screwing in that Puritan middle-class
mind of yours." He laughed harshly. "Man, it is wrong for one
man to kill another man. Don't you understand that."

"Of course I don't understand that. Everyone tells me its
wrong, but they don't tell me why."

"Shit, it's self-evident."

"Bullshit, it's self-evident. All my life I've read about the
glories of killing. What about the millions of comic books and
B-movies I ate up? Like every kid. Like every one of us. I
learned that killing the enemy was a good and beautiful
thing. . . ."

"But those were. . . ."

"You goddamned right they were lies. So three goddamned
cheers. All men lie out of their ignorance, so how am I to
choose between lies?"

"Like I was saying," I eased out, "I learned that killing the
bad guys was all right, even noble when it was done with
honor and dignity. And then you people taught me that there
are no bad guys, no black or white hats, just misguided gray
ones. But you did it the wrong way—you made fun of the good
guys instead of trying to make me understand the bad ones.
You made fun of them, and since the Western idea of morality
is totally without a sense of humor, you made me care more

"I don't know about that. A little war every now and again seems to put a bit of backbone in a people. They can't function as a people except during a war, and even if it's only a little bit more than usual, it is more."

"Man," Franklin laughed, "that's all you lifers do—wait for a war." A general chuckle followed.

"So what's a soldier for? To paint shitcans and file reports? All of you know how you hate being that kind of menial. . . ."

"Maybe we'd hate being murderers too," Morning interrupted. "Anything is better than being a hired killer, anything, and that's all a soldier is. It seems to me," he continued, pinching air between his forefinger and thumb and shaking it at me, "that soldiers are nothing but dumb shits who don't know how to enjoy life so all they can dream of is a glorious Viking death. Whatever they've done or not done in their whole damned lives is okay if they die fighting. My God, Krummel, you've seen them; unhappy turds, either drunks or religious fanatics, waiting for a war. And if they had the chance and the power, they'd have one too. And someday when America goes Fascist, they'll have their war, and burn 70 million American Negroes when they start losing. Soldiers, ha, frustrated boy scouts and latent homosexuals."

"If they are, Morning, it's only because guys like you have made them that way with your believing in things, in thinking that men should fight not for power or money or lust but for ideas or gods which are the same thing. War is the human condition. It's natural for a man to want more than is his, and when he wants it badly enough, he'll kill to get it. That seems to me to be more sensible than fighting for ideas. People once recognized the warrior as the leader of his race, but now you think he must be a fool or a brute, and since it is you guys with your mouths open all the time, you even convince him that he is. . . ."

"What other animal kills his own kind, but a foolish and brutal one?" Morning interrupted. Franklin started to make a joke, but stopped when he saw the anger in Morning's face.

"Any one that finds his kind, even his brother, in his way, encroaching on his territory or trying to steal his food or mate. Except that animals don't believe in right or wrong or uncon-

for the bad guys. You peddled the crap that a gangster was better than a snappy, wheeler-dealer preacher because the gangster was more honest. Okay, so tell me it's wrong to kill another man?"

"Okay, mother-duck, I'll tell you: It's wrong for one man to kill another, and war is an evil fucking horrible thing!" He ended with a shout.

"Would you have killed Germans in the war?"

"Sure. . . ."

"Because they believed evil things?" I asked.

"Sure . . . but I would have realized it was. . . ."

"But now it's America which believes the evil things?"

"That's right."

"But we believed in evil in the forties just as much as now, perhaps even more, but you would have killed the Germans rather than the Americans, then. . . ."

"All right," he shouted, "but I would have realized that it was wrong and done it like a painful duty, an awful but necessary job."

"Jesus Christ, Morning, now it's you who doesn't care about man. You can't kill men like it was a job. What an insult to the whole human race that would be. It has got to have romance, it has to be the completion of a love affair, and an act of love, not a duty." I opened my arms and lowered my voice. "It isn't just 'Wine, Women and Song' men lust after, it's war too, by God! And until you damned moral Christian Romans came along, men had sense enough to have gods which enjoyed wine, war, women, and song along with us frail mortals. But now we're civilized, Roman and Christian—even you atheists are Christian—a nation of shopkeepers, carpenters and librarians; slaves in the name of individual freedom. Shit! Death defines life. . . ."

"Can't you get it through your thick damned skull that war isn't like you think it is going to be. It isn't beautiful; it's ugly, awful and ugly, and painful and cold and hungry. Man is for life not death!"

"How do you know?"

"I know."

"Okay, and I know it is the best thing in this miserable

damned civilized world. It is a clean and simple thing, a fire
that brands a man, and if it hurts it should, damnit, and men
love it deep in their sinful hearts! Love it! And so do you, Joe
Morning. You whine now, but you loved shooting at those poor
little bastards last night."

He stopped, took a hasty drink of beer. I'd stepped on his toes
too hard, too hard. "You mean you love it," he said, shaking
that clutched finger and thumb again. "Mean, sick bastards
like you."

"I don't know yet . . . but I'm going to find out. I've got to
find out."

"Oh, you poor crazy son of a bitch," he said, then paused,
sighed, and continued, "you really are crazy."

"Don't be silly," I said, ready to smile and forget.

"You bastards talk too much," Novotny drawled.

"Don't patronize me, you son of a bitch!" He stood up and
flung his arms away from his body as if casting off a heavy
cloak.

"Come on, forget it."

"Fuck you!"

"That's a pretty intolerant attitude for the great white Left,"
I said.

"Boy, you play the big educated soldier, ancient tradition of
intelligent warriors ready to defend man against his enemies,
man, but when it comes right down to it, you're nothing but a
half-assed impotent brute looking for your balls on a battle
field!"

"No, baby! My balls are right here, for better or worse," I
shouted, standing. "So why don't you try to take a bite out of
them, or shut your mouth before you piss me off!"

"That's the way your kind of guy operates. If you can't fight
it or fuck it or drink it, it don't make sense," he said to my
back as I walked up the aisle. "All you fucking madmen."

"Whatever I am, I'm not a mental masturbator," I tossed
over my shoulder as I swayed on to the front of the bus, opening my beer.

The anger burned tight and hard in my stomach, pure and
hot as it was before a fight. Morning would have fought me

but would I have him? Telling myself that it was in the name of friendship but, as always, thinking myself a coward for backing away from the fight for whatever good reasons. If you ever worry about being a coward, you can never convince yourself that good reasons aren't rationalizations to save inner face. A poker game started in the back of the bus like an embarrassed cough, and I guzzled my beer and ate my guts. Fear is the act of running away and bravery, that of running forward: they are not abstractions. Yes.

The bus passed through an area of jungle, dark, limitless foliage which marked our passage with a few stirred leaves like the splash of a castaway's bottled message on some distant sea. Only a few villages huddled against the flicker of the highway in the vast wilderness, breaking the solid wall of trees.

I knew this country. Both the American and Japanese invasions had followed this route from the beaches on the Lingayen Gulf. The dense mass of green had long since consumed any sign of the invasions with its mad twirling vines. Even on the beach only the code name, Blue Beach, and an occasional rusted piece of unidentified metal hinted of the past violence. So time and the dumb growth healed the scars with the slightest of efforts, but that day, that burning day, the ghosts forever uncured spoke to me, summoned me to their bleeding sides. Did I hear a monkey's cry, frail in the rushing wind? Or the endless scream of a man trapped under mortars exploding in the trees above—a shriek which echoed through the cave of time? The bus crashed over a bridge, and something flashed above the brown water. A bottle curving toward the creek? or a hand sucked down for the last time, the millionth last time, fingers arched not in a plea but in defiance still? I knew, I knew. The past, history, memory, had always waited for me like a specter. My memory never knew the chains of time. I had walked the peaceful grounds of Pittsburg's Landing while ragged men fell at every step. I wandered under the shaded sun on Elkhorn Tavern as cannon spoke and cannon answered and men cried into stained faces. I stood motionless on the Upper Brazos as six Comanches took the hair of a farmer and his

wife and child, then climbed calmly on their horses—all
drunk, three bleeding, one dying from the farmer's stand—riding back to the Staked Plains. Yes, I saw, and forever will see,
the ghosts of men dying, and as I saw I understood, despite
the protests of the fallen themselves, that it was heroic, was
perhaps the last noble thing.

I wanted to shout it to an indifferent, cowardly world which
had, in the name of Utopia, forgotten Valhalla. Or perhaps I
only wanted to say it once to myself to be sure I still believed.
But I remained silent in the clatter of the bus, thinking myself
a fool, a dreamer whose visions were the nightmares of mankind; a fighter not for peace but for eternal war. But I could
not stop: I had seen things I could not forget, and remembered things I had never seen. For me the two Siberian armies
still stumbled across the snow as they encircled the Germans
outside of Stalingrad. There had been no sound track on that
film clip, but I had heard them cheer. Flat-faced Siberians ten
thousand miles from home, fighting for Russians they didn't
like against Germans they didn't know, because it was right
for a man to die well, to stand and not run, to fight and
perhaps die. But victory is not the only face of war. I also
remembered the sad German faces—starving for weeks and
freezing for longer—numb with capture, waiting to march
further than they had meant to with 107,800 going, and
waiting still longer for only six thousand to march back. But
the losers did not really look that different from the victors as
they marched away to more freezing and fighting and stinking
and enduring. I saw and remembered, and God forgive me,
thought it noblest of all.

But that was then, riding toward the sea, when I was
ashamed of being a warrior.

I dozed fitfully into the city of Dagupan, thankful not to
dream, but the bus stopped in the city so we could buy more
beer and ice and fresh bread from a little bakery Morning
knew. I had no need to leave the bus, so I waited in the heat,
watching the town, the corrugated iron roofed, wooden buildings decked with soft drink signs; the people scuffing about in

Jesus boots or wooden clogs, seemingly never entering the buildings. Almost all of the buildings were unpainted, but the wood—perhaps because of its own sturdy nature or the heavy, washing rains—refused to look untended. The skin of the people seemed to be the result of some inner brownness, as if their flesh might be earth colored and their bones as delicately hued as ancient ivory keys. There was the brown dust of dirt you find wherever men sweep it out of their houses, but it wasn't filth. That came when the twentieth century god of progress managed to sell itself to the have-not's as salvation, and as a result killed the best of the old society with its worst. If I had asked the teen-aged Filipino outside the bus window, the one with a transistor radio plugged to his head, "Is this progress? These things steal your dignity at the price of your pride." He probably would have answered, "Yeah, man, yeah!" I didn't ask him; and no one asked me.

The others came back from their errands, and we drove the five or six miles to the beach. The bus stopped in front of a large pavilion marked by a neat, freshly painted "JOHN'S," surrounded by the graceful bows of coconut palms, and sitting on a slight rise above the beach and the estuary. Morning greeted the fat Filipino, obviously John, with a true lover-of-real-places familiarity. John, who I'm sure misread Hemingway too, returned the salutations like a true good fellow. John was a fat man who looked very uncomfortable being obese, as if remembering thinness and mourning its passing. He was also queer, and stocked the pavilion not only with a small café, sari-sari store, and a score of weathered tables, but seven or eight Billy Boys in partial drag. Morning introduced me as Sgt. Krummel, Trick Chief, so for the rest of our stay John called me Chief. But he was not nearly as bad as he sounds. His eyes did join his thin smile with some warmth, and refused to shake hands in deference to his sex, as if to say, "I have my boys!" He introduced his boys, Violet, Rose, Magnolia, etc. His place wasn't as out of the way as Morning had led me to believe.

The Trick rented the largest of the nipa huts on the beach and I, childishly, took a smaller hut near it. I wanted to stay away from Morning. The bus drove the couple hundred yards to the hut, but most of the guys walked. I stayed behind to have one of the boiled crabs Morning had talked so much about.

The pavilion overlooked a tidal slough fed through an ankle-deep cut to the estuary. Across the tepid water ten nipa huts dotted the scrub grass at the edge of the beach. The largest hut was the last one on the right, and mine next to it, separated from the water by one hundred yards of the loveliest beach in the world. Its shining white arms stretched open in an embrace of the flat, shimmering sea from the mountains distant and hazy on the right, then left across the estuary to that wavering point where sea, sky and sand fused into invisibility. The pale hot colors, the faintest whisper of a breeze on my face—surely it must be a miracle, I thought. Voices came, faint and silly in the heat, playground sounds lilting from some past.

Quinn, child of bricks and alleys, had taken off his shoes and danced about the hot, packed sand, chasing a small gaggle of domestic geese at the edge of the slough. Pete, remembering his grandfather's farm over in Michigan, shouted a belated warning to him. The gander had already snaked out his long gray neck along the sand, spread his wings high and wide behind his head, and was racing toward a laughing Quinn. Quinn jumped and grabbed one leg as the hard red bill whacked against his ankle bone. While he tottered, rubbing his ankle, the gander retreated slightly, regrouped, and charged again. Quinn tried to lift the other foot and, in drunken amazement, fell down, his open mouth lost for the sound of laughter not his own. Pete shooed the gander away with a stick which he then had to take away from Quinn who was shouting something about killing that goddamned bird.

The gander, noble fellow that he must have been, ignored his fallen enemy with a champion's poise, puffed out his magnificent breast as if to receive a medal, and with a measured, heroic step herded his maidens in the opposite direction.

The next day Quinn loudly claimed that those bruised lumps on his ankles were from the bus ride and that he hadn't been looking for brickbats at all but for his cigarettes. But his protests served him not at all; he quickly became "Goose-killer, son of Goose-egg." The name would fade into the night of half-remembered much-embellished war stories told to the folks back home, when it would be revived as anything from "Father Goose" to "The Great Gray Goose." The spirit of the nickname would survive even that distant future when graying heads would be scratched in search of "that crazy guy's name that got bit by a goose."

Watching Quinn and Pete walk away, I constructed the legend while waiting for my crab, rolling the cold beer bottle across my forehead, watching the small fishing dugouts slide over the glassy sea.

John brought my crab shortly after the field had cleared. I explained that I had never eaten crab before, and asked if he would show me how to break it open. He seemed oddly pleased. I supposed it was good as crabs go, but like a man it carried its skeleton on the outside, and resisted my prying attempts beyond death. I finished clawing, paid a sullen Billy Boy whose mascara had run in the heat, and sauntered to the bus. I picked up my gear, the book Morning had recommended, and a basket of beer. Then, as I said to myself, I, lord of the manor, retired to my chambers peacefully content to dream of past victories and future conquests, not at all sorry I hadn't bunked with the others.

Morning woke me at the very hottest part of the afternoon.

"Hey, animal, you want to take a swim?"

My neck and shoulders were slimey with sweat and the bed was wet underneath them. I poured the half-finished beer through the gaps in the bamboo-strip floor, shut the novel without marking the three pages I had read, stretched slightly, and started sweating again.

"Too hot, jack."

He waved two coolie hats and two wine bottles with the straw bases cut off and explained that we were going swimming because it was too hot. After a bit I realized that he was trying to apologize, so I rolled off the lumpy mattress and swapped my shorts for a swimsuit while Morning hummed "Meadowlands." I followed him into the sun which filled the

sky like a malevolent overcast above the pristine reflector of
the sand. The water, a pale even blue, seemed flattened by the
heat, compressed into a level sheet of glare marked only by
slight irregular swells which died half-noticed against the
baked finger of sand like faint pulses. Morning and I joined
the others and sat neck deep in the water, cooled in it, shaded
by our hats and anchored by the wine bottles tied to our wrists.
As the heat of the day continued and the wine expired we
drifted around the point into the estuary as the panting tide
came in like a tired runner. In spite of our elaborate defenses,
within the hour our bodies resembled water-logged bread
crusts dipped in wine. Novotny, Morning and I sought the
mottled shade of a fishing village up the river.

We found a bit of shade under the village pavilion where a
wedding reception was in progress. The Filipinos had seen us
walking past, called to us and, laughing and patting our
sun-tendered shoulders, invited us in for a beer. We should
have felt foolish attending a wedding reception in swim
trunks, but their greeting was so warm, so unpatronizing, we
felt truly welcome. It has been a long time since any stranger
had a friendly word for us, and these short, happy people
embarrassed us with their warmth. Beer and sweet greasy
roast pig and purple rice and fried chicken were pressed upon
us with champagne smiles. They were humbly polite, turning
down the rented jukebox to introduce us to the milling crowd,
but also shared their laughter with us, even at us in that fine
way old friends have. An old withered man kidded me about
my beer belly which had grown like a tumor since football
season, and I returned the favor with a motion at his egg-bald
head. His face disappeared into a mask of wrinkles, and a
happy cackle flew from his toothless mouth. I shook hands
with the now joined families, then with the slight, handsome
groom and his shy bride who hid her smile with a dip of her
head. I sailed once more into the tumbling maze of people.
Each way I turned, smiles bloomed like flowers photographed
in time-lapse; brown buds of faces burst into blossoms under
the sun. I spoke with a man who claimed to know all about
Texas, about cowboys and Indians, and when I told him that I
was both a cowboy and an Indian, he laughed and laughed

until tears rimmed his eyes. I didn't know what was so funny but I too laughed, even harder than he, so hard I abruptly sat down, and he wailed off again into breathless mirth. We ended both sitting and giggling and holding each others shoulders until the last seizure passed, then smiled and parted.

I rested at a table, sitting next to a white-headed Filipino. He looked to be fifty or so, but his hair was full and bushy, his face firm and his body held in a vigorous, controlled strength. He wore a starched light-blue pin-striped shirt like I remembered my father wearing before the war, and a dark-blue pair of trousers which obviously belonged to a double-breasted suit; but his shoes were brand new, a stiff almost metallic brown, and he had sat them on the bench next to him as if displayed for sale or trade. His dusty calloused feet, broadened and toughened by too many barefoot years to count, splayed across the packed dirt under the table. He nodded politely, but neither smiled nor spoke. He mixed a drink: one part Black Dog Gin, one part orange soda-water and one part beer poured into a thick water tumbler. He drank hunched over the glass, slowly, like a man on a long road between drinks. I watched him and his ugly feet which clawed the earth like stubborn toads, then finished my beer and walked away.

In ten minutes I was back, sitting across from him, smiling and inquiring, "How are you today, sir?" He had moved his shoes on to the table.

"Fine, thank you," he said, looking up. The voice was as worn and rough as the skin of his feet. "You are in the Army?" he asked. His tone was soft and deep and weary, his English exact.

"Yes, sir."

"That is good. I, too, was once in the army," he said, staring back into his glass as if time were telescoped there. "A very long time ago, during the war. The Japanese took my sawmill and I went to the hills to fight with Colonel Fergit on Mindanao. I was a major."

I wasn't surprised: I hadn't yet met a Filipino male born before the war who did not claim to be a guerrilla. (But no one had even heard of the Hukbalahap rebellion of the fifties.) A restaurant owner in Angeles, a woman, had told me, "They all lie. They hide in the hills and call it fighting. They should be a woman and learn about fighting."

The old man pulled a battered wallet from his pocket and showed me a picture of himself, three other Filipino officers, and General Douglas MacArthur. Other bits of tattered paper were taken from the leather sheath: his college diploma, folded and faded, showing his degree in civil engineering; pictures of the wife and children killed by the Japanese in '43, and his sawmill, and part of his outfit; his commission and various citations; a membership in an engineering society, dated June 2, 1936; a smudged dollar bill with the fuzzy red ink signatures of all the Americans in the band; a barely recognizable snapshot of Betty Grable's ass. He laid his very life out before me, faded, flaked at the edges, torn in the creases, scattered like wasted time around his new shoes. In a voice as ragged as the edge of a shell-ripped jungle, quiet from too much whispering, he explained how he had been cheated of his pay for the five years of fighting, shorn by crooked politicians and apathetic Americans. He told me, an American, but the blame and bitterness held a very dull, chipped edge in his voice.

"Ah," he sighed. "So long ago. So very long ago."

We both understood that he had just told me that he was a Huk, a member of one of the few remaining small bands of roving bandits who operated with little or no pretense of any political means or end to their banditry. I wondered if he had been on the raid the night before, wondered if those were his comrades we had killed.

He stowed the captured fragments of time in the wallet, then exposed his right calf. A mottled stitching of a machine gun wound scarred the leg. An old, smooth scar reflecting the unforgotten pain, pain compounded in nearly twenty years of running and fighting and dying after it was supposed to be (it had to be!) over. I remembered the blasted body of the night before, thought of wounds never healed to scar.

He and I talked until dusk, even smiled twice more together, then gravely shook hands as if over the coffin of a common friend. He tucked his gleaming shoes under his arm and walked toward the mountains in the sunset, his white hair waving like a flag of a forgotten truce in the strengthening breeze off the sea, and tiny mushrooms of dust puffed between his misshapen toes.

That night and the next day swept past like the waters of a rapids; our pleasure and peace leaping and laughing over any discontented rocks we might have brought to the beach. Once a fierce yellow sunset drifted into a delicate green, lime-aired dusk. The gentle surf crested in the quick darkness with swirling phosphorous fringes of tiny animals like liquid silver. Under the black water the shining protozoa loomed like little lights into our eyes, then curved away like speeding cars. Long careless daylight hours were spent watching the chameleon in the thatch of my roof, and he observing me with the same lazy indifference. I slept once in the window-box at the large hut, too drunk to walk, peaceful among the deep sleeping noises, the shimmering ribbons of light reflected on the slough. From the pavilion across the way laughter and the ingratiating whine of the jukebox wound over the dead water as Quinn, Morning, Haddad and some of the others danced drunkenly with the Billy Boys until fat John turned out the lights. A mosquito buzzed me, but a breeze off the gulf chased him inland. I must have slept through a shower, for when morning came my clothes were damp. I swam in the sunrise, disturbing for a second the still, perfect sleep of the sea, then washed from a sand well, and breakfasted on coconut and raw fish, and watched the sun creep like a sly snail up the early morning blue. I wondered aloud why anyone would ever leave this place.

That night we took the bus into town and went to a whore house.

It was a tall, nearly three-story shell of mud and straw bricks. The whitewash had peeled away like scabs to expose older and more flaky coats. The ground floor was open and cluttered with the usual assortment of cracked tables, bamboo chairs, bar, and bubbling jukebox. Over the back half of the room a jumbled maze of bamboo rooms climbed all over each other toward the roof. The small cubicles were stacked in a

random association, each seeming to have no relation to any
other, nor as a whole any connection with the outside walls.
Halls and stairs and landings went off at every angle as if an
abstract expressionist had decided to become a carpenter. A
drunk might wander up there until he was sober and still be
lost, passed from giggling whore to giggling whore forever.

The girls who stood up when we arrived were of a very
provincial sort, either indecently young moving up in the
bonded hierarchy of whoredom, or absurdly old, having fallen
to the last layer. The Trick, except for Morning and I (he
because of his peculiar brand of romantic puritanism or puri-
tanical romanticism, and I because of my . . . rank?), didn't
seem to mind and fell to seducing them in wholesale lots.
Cagle sat on the lap of the largest professional in the whole
PI, and acted like a ventriloquist's dummy to her great pleasure. Morning and I drifted to the rear where a solitary woman
was shuffling a deck of cards under a bare light bulb. It
was still early and there were no Filipino customers in the
place.

"Okay, man," Morning said, "that's for this one."

"Don't be in such a rush. Your old sarge may have something to say about that, young trooper. That's your problem,
kid, too big a hurry." He laughed and walked up to the table.

She had the delicate features—the thin, well-bridged nose,
small curved lips—which spoke of some Spanish blood, but her
body was squat, full and still firmly stacked in spite of the
twenty-nine or thirty years of use. She would be shorter when
she stood up than we had thought her to be. She wore no
make-up and dressed in a simple black jersey and slacks and
no shoes.

"Do you mind if we join you, young lady. Perhaps buy you a
drink or something?" Morning asked, his cool, confident self
as always with the women.

"I am not so young as I was but, yes, please sit if you wish,"
she answered, her voice as soft and heavy as her breasts. As
we sat, she laid out a game of solitaire, placing each card as
carefully and deliberately as if it were a piece in a puzzle. She
moved with a patience, a sad dignity, but jolly wrinkles
pinched the corners of her eyes and the suggestion of an ironic
smile rippled about her face like a breeze on a pond.

"I'm Lt. Morning," Joe said, "And this is. . . ."

"Sgt. Krummel," I interrupted before he made me a major again.

"Hello," she answered politely, not pausing in her game. She gave no name. Morning asked her. "My name is what you wish it to be," she replied. "That is my job, to be whatever and whoever men wish. Their girl friend, their wife, their mother, their battle, and I've even once been a sister. But it will cost you a lot of money, my young friend, to find out my name, because I'm a fine player. Yes, very much money." She did not glance up from the cards.

"Do, do you work here?" Morning asked.

"No." She answered as if that were the end of it, but after a short pause, added, "I work in Manila at the Golden Cave, but I also own this place. I come here to rest. . . ." She paused again. "But for a profit, an unusual profit, or for even an unusual excitement, I might tell you my name. For say as much money as a lieutenant makes in, let us say, a week." She raised her head to stare into Morning's eyes, her long loose hair swaying back from her face. I saw mountain showers crossing the horizon at dusk, night rain swinging in the wind, and shimmering black strands coiled on a pillow. Her breasts bobbed shyly like a child's first curtsy.

"Is it worth it?" he asked.

"Is it ever? Isn't it always? I know a captain who says it's better, something like—my accent is different from his—'Ya pays ya money, an' ya takes ya chance.' "

Morning laughed, then stood up to go for beer.

"Yes, I would very much like a beer, thank you," she answered when he asked. "You don't talk very much," she said, looking up at me as Joe walked away.

"Keeps me out of trouble."

"Your friend, he talks very much?"

"Very much. And lies a little, too."

She laughed, soft and mocking like a muted trumpet. "All men lie to us. It doesn't matter. I think I prefer the lies to the truth. Once a sailor told me the truth, that he loved men instead of women because he couldn't help himself. After that, when he couldn't make it, he cut his arms with a broken beer bottle. Yes, I better like lies, I think."

"Did he die?"

"Who? Oh, the sailor. No, he was lying about that. But he did ruin four of my dresses and nearly lost my job."

"The Golden Cave is a very famous place. I've heard about it, but I've never been there."

"You must come sometime. During the week. Never on weekend. But this is a famous place, too. It isn't as . . . what would you say?"

"Elegant?"

"Elegant, yes. But it is haunted." She stopped her game, took the beer Morning brought and continued, "It has been here—the house, I mean—since before the war. It was the only building left standing when the Japs shelled the city. An officer, a colonel I think, used it as his civil headquarters or something like that, and he ran the city. He was big for a Jap, even as big as you, and very mean. He killed many of my people in here. He shot them against that wall, in the stomach, and watched and laughed and drank as they bled to death. Some people say you can still hear the laughter and screams on certain dark nights. They say his evil is still in the walls." She drank from the bottle. "For three, four years the blood soaked the floor. Then once a young girl, a virgin he stole from the church altar, was brought here, and when he tried to screw her, she vomited on him. They said he beat and beat her, then cut a breast off and ate it before her as she bled to death. But he was upstairs drunk when the Americans came and was left behind.

"My people came and took him and many wanted to torture him, and they tore one finger off and made him chew it a little bit before the leader stopped them. Then they chopped his head off with an axe. They said his mouth was still laughing when it hit the floor." She rose and motioned us to the bar, showed us the three deep gashes in the wood and then made us put our fingers in the bullet scars in the wall.

"An evil devil," she said as we sat down, "and evil never dies. You know that. My people tried to burn this place, but a storm came and put the fire out.

"Then one night about three months later a wind blew out all the candles upstairs and down. Before they could be lit again, a girl ran downstairs screaming, half-naked, with one breast cut off. She died of fright, and though they searched and searched the house for the breast, it was not found. Never. "And so the lights are never turned off," she said, waving her delicate hand. "Never. And when a monsoon wind breaks the electricity, something bad happens. Always very bad." She smiled as she finished the story as if it had rubbed her tired back. "So this is called The Haunted Whorehouse."

"A fine tale," I said. "Beautiful."

"Oh, but it is not a tale. Go ask any of the girls."

I walked over to the giggling mingle of whores and asked the one with Novotny. The girl on Novotny's lap flung her head up at me, quickly covered her breasts with her arms and in a child's voice said, "Oh, but you must not talk of it for bad luck."

The world continued around me, the talk, the music, the dancing, Cagle squealing on the fat whore's lap, but inside the needle-iced shell of my body, time stumbled long enough for the girl's fear to be mine. The ghost was real.

"I think I need a beer," I said when back at our table.

"I told you," she said.

"Joe, that kid was scared out of her mind. It was as bad as seeing the ghost myself." I had always kept a silent fear of seeing a ghost. Not that I expected the spirits to harm me, but that fatal knowledge of seeing one would be fright enough. I looked too hard not to see one someday.

"And now you're scared shitless, too," Morning sneered. "Man, you kill me, Krummel. A mystic reactionary frustrated hero. Man, you have to stop it with this ghost bit," he said.

"But that's what makes history, ghosts," I said.

"Come off it. Forget about dead bastards and worry about live ones. You can't help the dead ones, but you can sure as kill the living trying to satisfy all those ghosts of yours. Look at Germany. Man, there must be at least thirty thousand ghosts per square mile left over from just the Thirty Years' War alone. . . ."

And as easily as that he and I began arguing again, fretting all ranges of human knowledge; both, I'm sure, doing our best to impress the nameless lady in black. But she didn't play that way. Morning was expressing the usual liberal line that better environments make better people.

"People make shit," she said, "not the other way around." She stepped right in, disparaging our philosophies, matching our educations with her life. Morning and I might have eight years of college between us and all sorts of misquoted quotes to use, but she had started life as a twelve-year-old whore and had not only gone up instead of down, but still could laugh about it. She was a tight, mercenary little thing: there were no, so to speak, "for love" pieces in her collection of girls, and the only gold she covered with her toughness was deposited in the bank in Manila. But she wasn't too hard to laugh, to be capricious when the mood suited her, or even to be foolish if she wished. She had paid for this liberty, and as long as she could keep up the payments on her luxuries, she intended to enjoy the freedom. If Morning and I had lusted for her body at first, we ended loving her husky, mocking laughter. A new warmth rosed Morning's face and I knew he, too, was enjoying the wonderful ache of having a woman to talk to. A piece of ass, even a good piece, was reasonably cheap in the Philippines but, ah, a man couldn't buy conversation with an intelligent woman for love or money. (But why did she talk to us? Later she was to say because we acted as if we knew everything and she wanted to teach us better, and also because she had never seen two such good friends who hated each other so much.) She talked even more than Morning and I, which was going some. She shouted and slapped the table and gulped lustily at her beer, dismissed a long involved argument with a wave of her hand, and laughed with us and at us. Once she touched Morning's cheek and the bastard blushed. Then he laughed at me when she tugged at one end of my moustache and said, "You're not so mean. I could take you." She made me remember the good things and I suppose it was my happiest night in a long while, wonderfully happy without violence—until David came.

He called himself David and he wanted more than anything to have Teresita (she had slipped us her name for free during the laughter earlier). He had slept with her, but always for money, and never as often as he wished. David was twenty-four or five, tall for a Filipino, over six feet, slim and well built. Managing to forsake the slick-haired thin-moustached look of a petty Latin gangster, he kept his hair in a bushy crew cut, and except for the *barong tagolog* he wore, he might have been an airman from L.A. or San Antonio.

"Hey, man, you cats cooling my chick for me?" he quipped as he swung up to the table. Teresita introduced us, explaining that David owned, or rather ran when his father was out of town, the only other respectable whorehouse in Dagupan.

"Sure, man," he laughed. "Just lay around and watch the bread make."

"You giving any free samples tonight?" Morning asked. "Or maybe it's Happy Hour and I can get two for one, huh?"

"Man, you're putting me on. Like you have to keep ahead in this racket. Right, T-baby? And a little free tail can sure put a man behind, and though I'll admit to like a little behind now and then, most the time I take my stuff straight." David told us about all the Americans he knew and loved, and how he had worked as a yardboy at Subic Bay Navy Base a while after high school to get his English perfect, and how he was not like those ungrateful Filipino cats because he really loved Americans, and how that was the trouble with the PI, not being enough like the U.S. of A. where he was going someday. Morning stopped him right there to explain what a shithole America was, and how David would be treated like a Negro in many places, and how awful it was to live under the dictatorship of the bourgeoisie. Teresita fell out of the conversation and began another game of solitaire while I watched.

Morning and David dug all the manure in American life, then collaborated on a mythical black-market deal which would make them both rich (and ruin the Philippine economy), and then chatted about burning some grass if David could score. Teresita lost three games, and I drank two nearly uninterrupted beers. I understood by David's quick dismissal of me and his patronizing references to my size that he thought me stupid and slow. I answered his questions in confused mumbles to help him think so even more. I didn't like him; he was too cool, too friendly, too much. David thought that Morning was his competition. Not that he wasn't, for at that point in the evening Teresita might have gone to bed with any one of the three of us purely out of bored exasperation, like an old bitch hounded into a corner by a pack of yapping, horny, squirting puppies will sometimes squat just a bit for one just to get shut of the pack.

When the conversation died for lack of an easy connection, David suggested that we, good-natured, intelligent group of friends that we were, should run the pasteboards together. He wanted to play poker, but Teresita absolutely refused. The only game we all knew was Go Fishing, but no one could remember how to play it, so we settled on Hearts even though we had to teach Morning of all people as the game went along. Teresita had learned the game from another girl at the Cave; David had been taught, yes, by a Navy lieutenant's wife at Subic; and I had learned the game at my father's hairy knee.

Not to brag, mainly because it isn't worth boasting about, but I was and am a tough Hearts player, and I pinned David's ears to his short-haired head. Oh, I played sloppily, acted the fool, spilling my hand about, and being so amazed each time I dropped the queen of spades and thirteen bad points on David's trick. "Har har har there Davey-boy. Guess ya caught the old bitch again, har har." He caught on quick, but it didn't help, and he lost his cool, stopped his incessant man-man-man routine, and started sweating. Twice he whispered to Teresita in Tagalog, but she answered with a shrug as if to say, "Maybe so. Maybe not." The single time he managed to drop the queen on me, I said, "Well, ya got my butt that time, Davey-boy," and then ran the rest of the tricks and put twenty-six bad ones on him. "Sons of bitches" he shouted, slapping the table; then whipping on his too-swift smile, said, "Oh, not you. These damned cards." Teresita was completely indifferent to the whole game, and played as if it were just a game, though she knew that in some dead-end alley of the masculine mystique we were playing for her. Morning lost his love for David and sat on him a few times too. Teresita soon tired of both games, but not too quickly for David to think that he had been humiliated.

She walked away to see to the bar or some other unnecessary thing, displaying her wares for the bidders one more time.

The price rose right away. David said, "You're a big guy. Want to arm wrestle? I'm just a little guy, but I'll take you on." I put him off longer than I really wanted to, but he kept pushing and Morning kept prodding, so I finally said okay.

David was wiry and not lacking in flesh and muscle, and had probably beaten all the kids in town the same day he saw his first arm-wrestling match in a movie; but he was giving away forty or fifty pounds to me. I was fair enough at the game to be able to quietly, humbly boast that I had only been beaten once, and then by a professional football player, as long as I didn't add that he was a halfback in the Canadian League. I had been held or nearly beaten several times by medium-sized wiry guys, and I understood how David beat Goliath: not only God, but the whole damned Christian world is always on the side of the little guy. It's like never getting to play on your home field. So I worried. Everytime I happened into one of these things I would reassure myself that the world wouldn't end, nor my life become meaningless, nor my pecker fall off, if I were beaten. I always told myself such and, of course, never believed it, but I should have realized that night in Dugupan that my instincts had been correct all along.

I was ready, I thought, but not for the knife in David's hand, a *balisong,* a blade with a split handle which folded over the two cutting edges, a sort of primitive switchblade. David opened his slowly as if it were an old friend in his hand, laid it edge-up on the table, and motioned to his two buddies sitting behind him who no one had noticed coming in. They looked like something out of an L.A. rat pack, and one was slipping another *balisong* from his pocket.

"To make losing more fun, man," David said with a sly grin on his face.

"Not me, man," I said. "I only play for marbles and match sticks."

"Sure, man," he said, closing his blade and waving his troops away. I noticed that my troops had gathered, and wondered at all this fuss for a fuck. "Just putting you on, man." Like hell.

The knife had chilled me, had scared me in a way I didn't like to admit, but it made me madder than hell, too. It was back in his pocket, but the challenge still gleamed in his arrogant smile, and his shadow lay flat and stark against the tabletop like an echoing slap. He reared his forearm on the table, strong and supple and slightly weaving in a hypnotic dance. I matched him to the murmur of a muffled "Get 'em, Slag-baby," to Haddad's voice wailing like a street vendor as he took bets. I placed the brown of my arm, white against the brown of his, in the circle.

"Let's put a little bread on it, man," he said, snapping his fingers. I shook my head, knowing as he knew: whoever lost, left.

Our hands clasped, separate fingers carefully placed, molding a primeval bond. Morning held the hands as David and I eased into the clasp, then stepped back and shouted "Go!" No fancy stuff, no waiting, no more playing around, I leaned into his arm as if trying to shove him out of the universe.

I should have known. What match was primitive cunning and arrogance against the enlightened rage of a civilized man? I should have known. White, paunchy middle-class American that I was, I was also the boy who had dug ten-thousand post holes before I was eighteen, milked twice that many cows, and lifted how many countless pounds in how many curious ways for the past ten years to retain that initial strength. Fed on eggs, fattened on steaks, nourished in the land of milk and oatmeal, was it any wonder I slammed a skinny Filipino's hand to the table, ending with the same motion I began?

Before the echoes of David's hand on the wood stopped, I already felt silly, even guilty in the sudden quiet. He slowly flexed his hand, staring at the sliver of blood which split the middle knuckle. He grinned wildly and said, his bop-talk gone, his accent heavy, "We play your game, motherfucker, now we play mine."

He stood up, kicked his chair away, flipped the table from between us, and opened his *balisong* in a flickering, sickening twirl. The instance charged into my mind, clear and stark as if time tripped again. I saw everything with an incredible vision: the writhing crowd making room; Novotny's aghast face; Teresita waving frantically at the bartender; an old whore already crying; Morning's perplexity. All the figures as clear and dis-

tinct as if I had sculptured them, molded and cast the pano-
rama of the stricken crowd. A crystal drop of sweat paused in
its race down the side of David's face. If I could have held that
cleft in time, God knows what flaming stars, what nights of
space I might have seen—but for fear. But I couldn't have seen
those things at all, for even as David moved, I stood as swiftly
as he, and as his blade held the light, my chair already flew
toward him.

Ah, poor David. He might have sliced me into slivers, but he
had no luck. The chair leg, four pieces of wrapped bamboo,
slipped past his raised arm and slammed into his mouth. He
staggered back with a surprised pinch around his eyes, as if he
remembered all the movie chairs broken on virtuous backs,
then he stumbled to the side as if the world were spinning too
fast for his legs. He fell, then propped on his elbow, lay on his
side still amazed. When he moved his hand from his face, he
exposed a bloody gap where several teeth had been broken off
at the gum line. The stubby root of one still gleamed optimisti-
cally in the cavity.

This too was a clear picture out of the corner of my eye as I
ran away, but I didn't realize what it meant until I bumped
into Morning standing like stone next to me. I turned back,
no more thinking now than when I had run, and leapt toward
David as he tried to get up. His blade scraped in his struggles
like a rattler on the cement floor. I kicked him in the ribs,
then stomped his hand, and scooted the knife away. Behind
me I heard a crash as Morning and Novotny tore the legs off
the table and cornered David's rats without a fight. David was
up now, and I caught his staggering rush, blocked his right,
then grabbed his arm and spun him toward the bar. A clot of
spectators kept him from hitting the bar, and he was quickly
up. But in the short spin I had heard the singing and knew
where my blood beat. When he came, I was ready.

Did I cry? shout? suffer? I triumphed.

I panted over David and had an unbidden impulse from my
boyhood to mount my foot on the bowed neck and wake the
jungle with my call, and as the thought came and went
unacted upon, I laughed away.

Back I came at the touch of Teresita's hand and the whisper

of her voice, and found, on the far side of violence, desire coiled tight and hard about me. *It's violent we leave that place,* I thought, grabbing her arm and pushing through the crowd, *and fitting and proper violent go back.* She did not struggle under my hand, then valiant hand.

Once she slipped from my grasp in the scrambling people, but before I could reach back, she thrust up to me and I felt her swelling breast nibble at my arm. Across the floor and up the steps into the shadowed helter-skelter of rooms, our breaths breaking the air before us, we ran. At the first door I slapped the bamboo curtains aside and crashed into the room only to find the bed already occupied. Cagle rode like a monkey on an elephant's back among the acres of his bloated lover, humping away as if mere friction might consume the indifferent tons. Gripped in his saddle meant for no earthly horse, he rode, his hairy arms each wrapping a huge flabby breast, his tiny white ass flickering in the slitted light like that casual muscle it drove, while the unprotesting hulk calmly flipped the limp pages of a comic book above his burrowed head.

Teresita and I laughed and laughed, but hurried to the room at the end of the slanting hall, our impatient hands flying at each other's flesh like mad birds. She was naked and blood from a clumsy kiss ran sweet in our mouths before I could get my pants off; so I took her, damp and quivering, hobbled by my britches. She arched, bucked and achingly arched against me, reared like a mare in the chute, and the curve of her back embraced a void I must fill. And again she came from the bed, lunging up as if it were afire, and again she fell to earth, to earth and into the void beyond where our frail members hesitate to go; but I went with the proven strength of my back, swinging myself like a club, and I went like a child lost in a dark echoless cavern, and I went.

And then we were easy and slow and rolling but not over, and her breasts quivered hot as tears on my face as we began the effortless lope through the foothills toward the snow on the mountains, blistering white snow in our sun. And as we ran, time fled past us like a startled bird, a beating, hurrying flutter, and the beard grew on my face and the drying mud of the jungle stiffened my clothes and the stench of the battle mingled with the steady slow suck of boots in muck. A web belt encircled my waist and a canteen thumped at my back and I knew my weapon lay under the bed, my rifle in frightened reach as I paused this moment from the fighting, this moment so precious between the fear, so perfect and beautiful because it might never be again, for I too must someday play the vanquished. . . . But I had the smoothness of now, and clutched it as I felt the first bite of the snow as the cold, cold heat gathered to burst pure white re-creation, white and hot as the snows we trampled.

But a shadowed voice, then a cackle of laughter intruded from the unfamiliar darkness, and in the pale candlelight, a hunched, headless shape fumbled at the curtain. I raced, oh I raced from the snow, down, down across the hills to the rotting, mucking jungle again, and a bitter scream escaped the aching teeth of my mouth, and I launched myself at the shape of my enemy, fell, jerked up my pants, then lunged again.

The door ripped away, and I clubbed at the figure. We grappled and rolled, bumping down the slanted hall, the blood thick in my ears, then rolled down the steps to the darkened floor. The whack of my fist in his chest (I never thought he had a head I might hit) threw him back, and in the light from Novotny's candle I saw Joe Morning sprawled like a bug squashed on the wall.

As Novotny explained that David had slipped away and cut off the lights, I clutched my crotch, moaning a thousand times. The pulsating mountain I reached for wasn't even a slightly quivering molehill, but a bag of ashes in my hand. The snows had melted, running into mysterious underground rivers, and however cold they might flood, they would not be the snow again for a long weary cycle of time.

Then Teresita was there, her slacks on backwards, a convexo-convex bit of pale brown flesh winking from the hastily clutched zipper, explaining to the police who promised to lock up David until his father returned. It seemed they had to do this every time his father went away.

So wan and tipsy and aching I gathered Trick Two, herded them to the bus, then said goodbye to Teresita.

"I'm sorry. Jesus Christ, I'm sorry."

"Yes. I too," she said, "as much as you. I will come to the beach tomorrow and we will look again." She touched my face with a gentle hand; her lips were fleshless skin under mine.

As the bus bounced away from the haunted whorehouse, Morning shouted up to me, "Jesus-shit, Krummel, you nearly broke my back. What did you think I was, that Jap ghost?" He laughed.

"That's okay, Morning. You only fucked up a wet dream."

She did come the next day, and it was good walking in the still dawn far down the beach to make love beside the easy swells breaking like whispers. She rubbed my bruises and kissed them. We swam naked, our laughter bright across the sun-sparkled water as we frolicked like silly children. Her heavy breasts scrambled in the water like puppies, their soft, wet noses nuzzling my chest. Once she lay on the beach as I swam far out, and when I came back, I almost cried at the beauty: the black gleaming span of her hair against the glare of the sand, the sweet melting brown of her body, the waiting blue of the sea, a rippled shower draping the mountains in a shimmering veil. I was naked man first flung from the sea, crouched humble over the sleeping paradise of woman. But pride, not of possessing her or the world but of simply and foolishly being a man, made me rise and look to the green mountains and across the faraway sweep of the sea . . . what for, my God, for what?

Later we watched the chameleon in my hut, then had a sweaty slide at love, and afterwards strolled the cooling sand as great rolling clouds piled up the horizon. When we said goodbye, we knew it was. (Though, of course, it wasn't at all.)

During the trip back to Clark, Morning inquired as to where I had been going when I bumped into him the night before.

"Looking for running room, mother," I answered. His face was hidden in the rattling darkness, but he was smiling.

8

MANILA

Oh, if the comedy were only divine.

I, of course, select things to leave you with, but I must try to tell the truth, too. How nice if you retained, say, a picture of Slag Krummel swinging like a pagan, rioting, raping, lusting all over the place, or perhaps even Jacob Krummel, naked above nakedness, on a primeval beach, contemplating original sin as his woman beautifully sleeps. But, no, you'll remember the way Morning made my voice vulgar in the darkness: You only fucked up a wet dream.

I have so few illusions; he robs me even of those.

But, by god, I'm having the last word here (which may be why I'm having any word at all), and if you are going to persist, and you will persist, you bastard, you will even endure, in remembering me stumbling across that darkened room, torn from the greatest fuck of the decade, my pants heaped around my ankles like a burlesque comedian, then I will also joggle your memory, aptly, of course. Whatever sort of harmless fool I played, it wasn't me courting madness across that drunken lagoon, dancing with sweaty, sad Billy Boys, their make-up running off their eyes like cheap dolls left in the rain, it was that devil-may-care Morning. In his case the devil does care; Morning had an awful attraction to self-destruction, moral, physical, sexual.

I say this so you will remember that he did interrupt me. How odd, how odd the sexual connections we make. We all sleep in a circle.

Abigail kissed me this morning and I cupped a tiny breast fluttering like a baby chick in my hand. I strain in my bonds. Morning interrupts me again. I interrupt myself. Time is the interruption of space, or is it space, the interruption of time.

How silly I'm getting in my old age. How silly.

After Dagupan a strange uneasiness captured me. So much, so fast. The raid, then touching Teresita, and quickly now snips of rumor that the 721st might go to Vietnam, a persistent and persistently ignored rumor for the past months. I was ready to believe it, ready to go, ready for anything, I thought. I began staying apart from the Trick, spending my breaks and all my money in Manila. I soon squandered my savings. Teresita was lovely, long, and sweet, her body strong under placid skin, her pubic hair silken and straight, her love satisfying, and expensive. Moving once again away from commitments, as I had when I reenlisted, I made her take money for her love, made her eat the bitter grass. And when the money was gone, I wouldn't go to Manila. This is not counting the seven hundred or so I'd won on the long restriction. Not a penny of it had been spent or even touched, but it abided in the form of figures in my savings book. A reserve, but for what I wasn't sure. Morning had been after me since the restriction to let him use the money to ease us into the black market. My capital, his contacts, and he guaranteed to double it within the month, but I wouldn't turn it loose. Not saying anything derogatory about Haddad, mind you, I just didn't fancy myself as a black market czar. Enough money for my woman, my beer gut, and me.

Haddad had really done well on the market. He was well-suited to the business of business, generally no better or no worse than the average American businessman, and probably better educated than most. He wouldn't cheat his friends; he was at least a political liberal, though economically he was of the buyer-beware school; and he was the only person I'd ever known who had read all of Proust. I think that may be the secret to his soul. He would work hard, and he saw the making of money the art one prepares his life for. God, he loved to make money, not for what it would buy, nor for power, but just for money. Plus he had imagination; and he never cheated me. If I could have convinced him to play the profit game, keep enough to live on and play again, and give the rest away, he would have been a better sort. But he said, very seriously, that the tax structure was such that . . . well, you know. But he was free with his money and when success laid half-ownership of a bar in Town in his hands, he planned an opening night party for the Trick. It was really a fine bar, an old Spanish home, two stories, set on half an acre of grounds, and it would have been a fine party . . . but it was Good Friday, April 12, 1963.

Good Friday, *Karfreitag*. Day of suffering, prelude to resurrection, day of judgment, epilogue of life. Good Friday?

We were on Break off a set of mids, in Town by 0730, drunk before 1000 and off to see the flagellants. Blood has always sickened me slightly, but I felt it was something I should see, or Morning convinced me it was something I should see.

They were at the edge of Town in a small and, as far as we knew, nameless barrio. Those flagellants who, during ordinary years, made their homes in Angeles made a point of arriving back home on Good Friday; they were joined by a few weekend worshippers. A year spent dragging a heavy ironwood cross around, across Luzon, had built a scum-brown callous on their shoulders, down across the blades. Pain, spiritual anguish, and living on the charity of their brothers had seeped away the flesh of their faces, swelled the bones of their bodies, mottled their eyes. And here they lay their crosses down, not on a significant, bald hill, but among scattered nipa huts, on a dry, dusty street thick with stray dogs, rooting pigs, occasional chickens, and watched by the vaguely religious, the curious, and the sick. The Lord, their Father, refused them even the relief of a single cloud to intercede with the dry, parched heat of the sun, refused a single drop of rain, even the tiniest

breeze. But the sky was split asunder all the day by passing
jets tearing their angry tails of thunder behind them. The
three, for this year there were only three though Morning said
there had been twice as many as the year before, arrived
slowly, singly, denied even the friendship of suffering, stopped
at the end of the snaking path marking their trail. The path, if
followed backwards, would lead you across the plain, through
the heat, into the jungles thick with steam where the sun
sucked the very moisture from the leaves, and through the
jungle to the mountains thrust up in the earth's time of agony,
up trails which hung to the steep slopes with the uneasiness of
mists. Up and across the highlands, past men with filed and
betal-stained teeth who buried their dead sitting in clay bee-
hive huts, past the missionaries who were telling these same
men about Jesus' suffering, but these same men laughed at
those foolish devils carrying about wood not even good for
fires, laughed, and sometimes killed them, and the missionaries too, but always with a laugh. But these had made it, and
except where the monsoon or the casual passing of other men
erased their marks, you could follow them backwards. As they
came and eased their burdens to the ground, their backs bent
in habit, they took up branches and whips and, with the same
patience and calm with which they lugged their crosses, began
to beat themselves without pause for food or drink; striking
the sinful flesh until welts, then blood, rose from their skin.
An occasional onlooker would join the devotion, until his sins
were washed away too.

And above, jets tolled the sky.

"Such peace, man, on their faces," Morning said as we
watched, a basket of beer at our feet, shame in our eyes.
"Wonder if it's the pain, something in the pain?"

"Inflicting or enduring?" I asked, but he didn't answer.

We watched and drank ourselves into a bright haze;
watched until blood splattered in the dust at our feet. A single
bright drop, as small as a tick, nestled in the sun-blond hairs
on my arm. Almost without a word, we left. The word: Jesus
Christ.

Before Haddad's party, we attended the middle-class Good
Friday: all the suffering endured by statues. A long march of

wax and wooden and plastic Christs, wooden pain, plastic blood, and little boys in white robes. Though the streets were thick with bodies, the only sound was breath, shuffle of feet, click of beads, a silence of shame more than reverence. Those other three, fools, yes, still out in the darkness, still bent under their own blows, wailing sinful flesh with enfeebled arms and enhanced determination, the blood syrupy and thick with flies against their wounds.

Haddad's party, had it been the end, would have been the perfect climax to this odd day. We ate a good dinner prepared by Toni the sad queer, good filets and beer in the old master bedroom on the second floor, but Haddad had hired sad, naked whores to serve in high heels and long white gloves. He expected the last course to be love among greasy plates patched with parsley, but the girls were so ashamed of their nakedness—for what he paid them to do this, we could have fucked them in the dark ten times, and had enough change to get back to Base—that they lost any appeal they might have had. What he'd meant to be old-fashioned revelry became a quiet mean drunk. Not all his fault, though, I'm sure. The religious violence twisted all our faces like a cheap mirror.

Toni had to flitter about the table seeking compliments, snatching feels, his soft hands patting shoulders, his tired voice pleading for good opinion. Surly as we were, we weren't even polite. "Okay, if you like shit," Quinn said. "You should love it," Morning said, and Quinn answered, "I'd rather eat shit than cocks," then they both stood up. But I, with my love for the dramatic moment, hurled a beer bottle between them and it exploded on the wall behind. I told them to sit, and they did. God knows why; ordinarily I couldn't get either one of them to do anything. Maybe they thought I was going to kill them; they might have been right. But the winds blew again, quickly.

Toni squeezed Novotny's arm once too often, too lovingly. He stood up and hit Toni full in the face with such a painfully happy smile, I had to answer it. But Morning came around the table swinging, and there was a brief moment of fists glancing from hard faces and skulls, bouncing off shoulders and tensed arms; but only a brief moment, then I plunged between them like a fullback making his own hole. Morning fell against the table, scrambled, then the table collapsed. He fell among broken dishes and spilled drinks on the floor. Novotny had stumbled over Toni's inert body, and fallen also. As I turned, I grabbed a heavy oak chair from under Peterson, and said with a smile:

"You boys stay down, or I'll bust you wide open. Either one, or both. No matter."

Novotny was willing; he was already ashamed. Morning was less willing, but no less ashamed, so he stood up, shook his head, made a vague gesture with his arms, then walked quickly out. He had a glob of mustard hanging from one haunch, beer sloshing in one shoe, and baked potato in his hair. A ruined exit.

I held the chair cocked, and felt for an instant the crushing need to demolish something, but paused in soldierly soberness, and lowered the chair. "Fuck it," Haddad said. I threw the chair through the French doors which led to the small balcony. A great lovely crash as doors and glass and chair plunged to the ground outside. Haddad was smiling when I looked at him.

"Is it deductible?" I asked.

"The fucking world is deductible, Krummel," he answered, then threw his chair toward the open windows. It hung in the drapes, but he ran over, grinning as if he had just cut costs ten percent, rubbing his hands like a Jewish pawnbroker, and tore down the drapes, wadded them in the chair, then heaved the mess away from him. The troops were right behind him.

In a mad flurry of laughter, everything in the room flew out the window in less than a minute: table, chairs, table cloth filled with stale food and dishes, a brocaded settee, a rattan couch. It made no sense, but it was great fun. Collins grabbed what steak knives he could, then tried to stick them into the papaya tree. Quinn tried to throw a still inert Toni out, but reason prevailed, for a moment. Later we discovered that he had rolled Toni up in the carpet and heaved him into the papaya tree. Only his feelings were hurt. He never came around us after Good Friday.

When the room was bare, absolutely bare except for the whores huddled against a bare wall, hoping we wouldn't throw them out, someone, Quinn I think, began tearing his clothes off and throwing them out the window, sailing them into the night wind. The troops followed. (I tell this as if I were not there out of a natural sense of modesty.) In a moment, nine mad soldiers sat their bare cold butts on the tile floor and drank beer with six much more at ease whores. Laughter and drinking and one thing led to another. The only moment of any note to anyone but ourselves came as drunk Cagle fucked a small middle-aged whore on the floor. He would poke her, she would slide, he would crawl after her and poke her again, and she would slide away again. Around the floor they went, two complete circuits before he cornered her, lodged her head against a baseboard and, in finishing her off, nearly knocked her brains out. Everyone in action took a smoke break to watch this new pornographic position. We called it the Cagle Crawling Fuck, or How to Get Scraped Knees While Falling in Love.

The destruction of the room had cleansed us of hate and fear and pretense, had left us only laughter and our bare skins, more than enough for salvation. We died in violence, but were resurrected in laughter.

Downstairs, after the party was over, we found Morning slumped against a plaster column, one arm around the chipping evidence of more ornate days, one hand clutching an empty bottle of TDY rum. Infirm, blind, perhaps even dead, someone suggested. We sacked his slack body behind a couch, out of Air Police sight, then settled in, since it was still quite early, for, as Quinn said, more and more serious drinking. Not that we were sullen, but that we just drank all the time anyway. We understood it was an evil poison, causing madness more often than not, but it was our way through the mask, and nothing else seemed as appropriate.

But other winds were blowing. . . .

Over in the 9th ASA the mood must have been just about the same as ours. The troops had planned a company roll call for the Saturday night after Good Friday. Not a Trick Roll Call, which was bad enough (bird colonels had strokes etc.), but a Company Roll Call with over three hundred men signed up, solemnly pledged to take part in the Roll Call, Riot, and

General Disorder. The company officers, sly as officers often manage to be, had broken wind of the event and planned, secretly, to close the pass box Saturday morning. But the foxes smelled the dogs' shit, and moved the roll call to Friday night. Thus, in a very direct way, the Good Friday Night Riot was caused by the officers, sly devils, of the 9th ASA, and in an indirect way by Joe Morning, professional innocent.

You see, still other plots were brewing. . . .

Cagle, only an EM but silent and devious, had chanced upon a funeral procession the week before, a silent line of pallbearers, candle carriers, road guards, and the corpse laid out in a fine white lace shrouded coffin looking for all the world like a big giant birthday cake. He inquired of a professional candle carrier and discovered that the coffin had been rented from the local undertaker for a very small fee, considering the immoral beauty of the frilly pine box. This night he rented this lovely coffin without a word to a soul, and returned to the steps of Haddad's place, ten holy candles in hand but no smile on his face, solemnly saying, "We must bury Joe Morning before morning; we must bury our dead before they stink." We tittered, but he silenced us with a frown stolen from an assistant undertaker in Kansas City. And as the coffin was filled with the body, then shouldered in the dim light, we became as silent as mourners.

And so we formed: pallbearers six, Quinn, Franklin, Levenson, Collins, Haddad, Peterson; road guards two, Novotny, Cagle; and one to count cadence, Krummel; the corpse we carried, Morning; tears in our eyes, pride on our drunken faces; fuck all the rest.

We marched to the measured beat of a dirge, pagans bearing the fallen to his pyre, the coffin level with the pallbearers' shoulders, candlelight and lace flickering in the night. It seemed for an instant, or longer perhaps, as we marched that we were as sad as if Joe Morning were really dead, as if we understood that he had been the best of us all, the most damned of us all, the most damned and the best. Step, pause, mourn Joe Morning, and move, solemn, silent, drunk, our homage paid. With each slow step the earth sank beneath us, tears plied our distant faces, and we knew no hope of resurrection, and tears plowed the dust of our faces. Lord knows where we might have ended that night, our sadness was that great. I headed us where I might, Cagle and Novotny stopping taxis and jeepnys and *calesas* at every corner, leading down dark rutted off-limits streets, past cribs where blankets separated the struggling pairs, past bars where card games stopped and beers paused between hand and mouth; into, into and through, the labyrinths of the market, among slabs of meat nailed by rusty hooks, where this morning's fish became tonight's garbage, through the darkness, and finally out at the blazing light of Chew Chi's kiosk, jammed as it was to the walls with the 9th ASA, mourning things of their own.

They poured out behind us, two hundred fifty strong. I picked up the beat to the usual 120, and the dirge became a roar, anger, mirth, carnival, death. My men sang, their grief gone:

> We are Krummel's raiders.
> We're rapers of the night.
> We're dirty sons a bitches.
> An' we'd rather fuck than fight.

And the ASA was singing, to the tune of the old Western, "She Wore a Yellow Ribbon":

> Behind the door her father kept a shotgun,
> He kept it in the summer and the merry month of May.
> And when I asked her father why the shotgun,
> He said, "It's for her lover, who's in the ASA.
>
> ASA!—Suck! suck!
> ASA!—Suck! suck!
> He said, "It's for her lover,
> Who's in the ASA!"
> Suck! Suck!

As you might remember, about fifty thousand Filipinos also called Town their home, though we often forgot. On Saturday night they would have expected it, on an ordinary night they would have been unhappy, but not too angry; on Good Friday, man, they went insane. The police switchboard, the Town switchboard, and the Base switchboard all jammed at once with irate calls and threats of international incidents and war. With the telephones down, the Air Police, using radios and intelligence, formed up with the Town fuzz, and came to do harm to us, racing toward the market with about forty jeeps and six hundred sirens. It came to me that I was slightly out of place at the head of this mob, but it also came to me that I belonged here more than with the law, I was more my Trick's man than the Army's. So I gave the only order, they tell one in basic, which will stop a marching company in less than two steps: GAS!

The troops dispersed, rats down holes of darkness, and when the law arrived, they found only innocent Joe Morning asleep in his coffin. The jeeps circled once like a band of raiding Comanch', then sped after the shadows, but they were only shadows fleeing from their headlights. I, as an eyewitness, can categorically state that any damage, except to religious sensibilities or to shinbones fleeing through the night, was done by this marauding band of jeeps. There were four accidents within my hearing. A lone late arrival flying around a corner in the edge of the market clipped the side of the sari-sari store under which Novotny and I were hiding. The whole corner came off, the small building tilted, and Cagle rolled off the roof. He hit the ground running, and by the time the jeep turned around Cagle was singing, "Ho, ho, ho. You can't catch me. I'm the Gingerbread Man!" and in a flash, he vaulted a fence and disappeared, leaving a bewildered AP behind him, shouting to an empty street, "Stop or I'll shoot—I guess he got away."

Morning fared as well as any of us. The APs woke him in the coffin, asked him what the hell he was doing in a coffin, to which Morning answered, "I'm dead, you dumb fuck." They wrote him up for conduct unbecoming a member of the armed forces. "For being dead and kidnapped by vandals, they give me an IR?" Morning said to a harried Dottlinger the next day. (Capt. Saunders had gone back to the States again.) Dottlinger took his pass for seven days, saying, "Lord, I don't know what's happening in this world. I just don't know." For the seven days without pass, Morning became a national hero.

All over Base: "Hey, that guy there. He was the one in the coffin!"

No one else was caught or connected with the march. Hardcore Townies *just* were not caught by Air Policemen, and we were all professional Townies. There was a period, shortly before the Huk raid, which I haven't spoken about partly because it wasn't really important and partly because I'm somewhat ashamed of my conduct during these few weeks. Cagle, Novotny, Morning, Quinn, Franklin, and I would sit in the market after curfew, drinking beer, daring the APs to come in and get us. They never touched us. In fact, I'm the original Gingerbread Man. I had to relax sometimes. Dottlinger gave me foul looks, and Tetrick commented, "You guys are all going to get killed someday, and I'm gonna laugh like hell," but I'd learned from Morning how to play innocent too, so I did. The United States Government picked up the damage tab, as it should have: foreign affairs are strange and expensive adventures.

Okay, so we desecrated a holy day, insulted the people's religion, tore up the American image abroad, but what the hell; everyone already hated us when we got there. We ran with pimps and whores because nice Filipino families and their daughters spat at us on the street. Since we were not officers, we were scum, so we said to the world in general: suck. Suck to the good folks of Fayetteville, North Carolina, Kileen, Texas, Ayer, Massachusetts, Columbus, Georgia, Columbia, South Carolina, Norfolk, Virginia, etc. You name it, baby, I've been there, and it ain't good. Maybe soldiers in general, and Americans abroad, deserve the treatment they get. Maybe they've earned it. But soldiers in general, and Americans abroad, aren't any worse than the people they have to deal with, and most of the time they have to deal with bastards. Morning, Novotny, Cagle, none of my guys, not even Quinn, were Ugly Americans. When they were told that they had to pay the price of all the bastards before them, they said, Shove it up your ass, jack; we didn't make the world, baby, and we ain't paying for no mistakes but our own. I know I'm sounding like Morning (what an admission), but there are a lot of people in the world who should be dead. Morning said Hitler had the right idea, but the wrong criteria. My hate isn't as deep as his was, probably for good reason, but I almost agree with him.

And, too, what we had done that night—and I say this without apology—affirmed, said, shouted that men, even the most ordinary of men, will sometimes, in whatever way they can, refuse to be part of the system. In the defiance of that night, we bought back a bit of our individuality; shouted, as Quinn had shouted that night, "They can kill you, mother, but they can't eat you!" Goddamn, Morning never learned that. He knew THEY were always going to eat him alive. I know they'll never take me alive. Goddamn, goddamn, sometimes I miss him. Sometimes I do.

But relief is never a moment away.

It was all downhill after Easter, we said, not knowing quite how we meant it. I grew fat, fatter, slimy and oily in the heat, sucking beer after beer, crying, it didn't matter. And the money, too, down, down. In desperation I gathered a week's leave to spend with Teresita in Dagupan on the beach, but we both caught colds the second day and squandered most of my leave in fever sweats, sneezes, halfhearted love, and stale, gamy sheets. To recover, we fled back to Manila on an air-conditioned train to spend two days and nights in a luxury hotel. That helped, but on the second afternoon I refused to give any of my quickly vanishing money to a ragged beggarboy. Terri and I stupidly fought, and the whole leave was lost in anger.

Back to work. Air conditioning goes blink; major goes mad; repairman short circuits the whole Det, leaving the Head Moles to rage in sticky darkness, rage at me until I actually beat my head against a wall. At 1645 I left it in the hands of the next unfortunate, Sgt. Reid. He'd shucked his wife but hadn't found happiness, and his face killed me each time he relieved me. Then evening chow was ham. We had ham, frozen ham just this side of rotten, eighteen times a week. That could be endured. But the nineteenth time busted it. "You must have miscounted," the mess sergeant says. "Don't make mistakes," say I, handing him my plate. I sat in my quarters, the buttons on my khaki shirt straining to hold back the flood of beer gut jammed behind them. Sweat covered me, not running, but drifting like an oil slick. A Coke, I thought, I would have a Coke. Change in my pocket? No, only keys to doors behind me. Surely I had ten centavos somewhere. Less than a nickel. After fifteen minutes I came up with an old one, green with mis- and dis-use, lodged in the watch pocket of a pair of Town pants which stank like sin. Down to the Day Room like a kid after the ice-cream wagon in August. The damned machine (oh, foul machine, I ran astray of you before) took my last ten centavos silently, made no acknowledgment, gave me no cold Coke, made no apology, refused categorically to return my money. I hit the son of a bitch in the mouth. Bull-assed bastard of a machine. I shook the damned thing until Tetrick raced in from the Orderly Room to pull me off.

"What's wrong?" he asked. I don't believe I'd ever seen him concerned about me before.

"Lay twenty on me till payday," I said, and without a word he handed me two tens.

The Trick carried me back from Town that night. The next noon I took the seven hundred out of the bank.

Morning and I moved into the black market in high style, capital behind us, untold riches ahead. We bought cigarettes in the barracks for seven pesos a carton from the troops, made a run each break to Manila, carrying the cartons in the back of an AP's 1948 Dodge, and sold the cartons of Chesterfields and Salems for eleven pesos. One hundred cartons, four hundred pesos, between $135 and $150 U.S. depending on how you changed it. We also carried twenty new stereo albums, which paid well too. We had several people on our payroll, buyers in other outfits, two APs, a Manila drop man, but we still cleared about one hundred dollars a break. I usually spent my fifty in Manila, as did Morning, but the seven hundred stayed in reserve. Ah, we lived well . . . but it didn't help a thing.

Krummel, fatter, meaner, more sullen each week. Morning, more anxious for violence, for change, for something. The Army, far from being the peaceful sanctuary I had sought, had become more complicated than civilian life. Black markets and beer, and love once again, of a sort, and the Vietnam rumors flying again. I began to hope, then chided myself for being a dumb drunken lifer just waiting for a war, but still I hoped.

One Break after a set of mids, Morning and I were half asleep after the beers we'd had on the drive down. It wasn't quite noon, but it was hot as hell outside the hotel. I was waiting for him to go make the drop, deliver the two large suitcases sitting between the twin beds.

"You going to make the drop, Joe?" I asked, feeling like a bad movie gangster.

"You do it, man. It's too hot outside," he answered. We had been through this scene the last trip. I didn't know what was bugging him, and he wouldn't tell me.

"I don't know where to go. You know that," I said, my eyes closed in the cool conditioned air.

"Yeah, I know," he mumbled. "I'll tell you."

"That's your part of the deal," I said. "Remember."

"Well, why the fuck don't you do something, you fat lazy bastard," he said, only half in jest. "Swill beer like a pig all day."

I opened my eyes. He had sat up and now faced the windows, his sweat-stained back toward me. "What's up?"

"I'm just tired of doing all the work. Taking all the risks."

"I'm tired of you bitching all the time. I put up the money; you run the operation; that was our deal." I sat up to open the last beer.

"Krummel, you and your . . ." he said as he turned, ". . . commitment shit.

"Well, fuck, take the last fucking beer, too, why don't you?" he spat at me.

"Eat shit," I said, and left.

The Golden Cave, in spite of its name and reputation, was a rather ordinary looking place, a two-story house hidden behind a stucco wall in a residential section. The grounds were nice, and the large banyan trees kept the noise from disturbing the neighbors; best of all, though, were the girls and the central air conditioning; they commanded a price. It was run by a small sad man, an ex-priest, a homosexual who was writing a book which, he said, would give the homosexual a place in heaven, if not next to God, at least near the more compassionate Jesus Christ. I often drank with him while waiting for Terri to finish with a customer upstairs. He was good company, never pushy, and he ran a good, tight bar and whorehouse. But he was still unhappy about being disrobed by the Church. It seems he often used the confessional for more than a place to talk. He had knocked all the walls out of the lower floor. The low ceiling gave the place the intimacy of a home, the big room, the freedom of a house.

Terri was having a drink at the tables back near the bar with a fat, somehow familiar man when I finally drank my way to the Cave that long afternoon. She saw that I was more than a bit drunk, and her eyes tried to wave me past the table, but I was in no mood to be waved off. I walked past, then peeled back behind her to put my hand on her neck. She smiled, frightened; her partner frowned, disturbed, and I answered both. She introduced him as a Mr. Alfrado Garcia, the owner of several bars and houses down by the stockyards in Pasay City, a section where a night on the town usually included waking up naked and half dead in one of the blood gutters the next morning. A big, fat man, his eyes almost in the back of his head, a greasy smile like a dimple in his face. Was I that fat already? I asked myself. Of course not.

"Garcia," I said. "A Spanish name, huh? You don't look Spanish."

"I know we haven't been introduced yet," he said, ignoring my insult, "but I do know you." His voice sounded like a sulphur bubble rising in a mud pit, or like cow shit falling on a hot rock, and his face contorted in a jolly fake of a smile.

"Yeah," I said, walking behind the bar for a beer, "I know you, too. Next time don't bet against winners." He was the guy who had dropped several thousand pesos against my thirteen straight passes at the Key Club back during the long Coke bottle restriction. Terri followed me, got two beers for them, and when her back was to Mr. Garcia, her mouth formed "No, Jake, baby." I acted as if I hadn't heard.

"I usually don't," he said. "That's why I'm rich today. I usually don't. But perhaps if you had made one more pass . . . perhaps."

"But I didn't. The wise man knows when to quit. It's better to be wise than rich," I said, sitting.

"Exactly as I would have said," he chuckled. "The wise know when they are beat." He reached across the table to pat Terri's right breast. "Yes."

I should have killed him then, but I said, "That's not what I said."

"How is it that a sergeant can live so high?" he asked, the sick dimple sinking again between his fat cheeks. "Perhaps the black market? Now, I have some connections. One could eliminate the middle man. Chesterfields might bring twelve-fifty, perhaps thirteen pesos a carton. Something to think about."

"You can buy her, if you can, jack, but I'm not for sale," I sneered. Terri flinched, but said nothing.

"I didn't mean . . ." he started.

"We both know what you meant. What you pay for, fat man, I get for love." Which wasn't quite true, but it could have been.

"He who loves a whore would sleep with his mother," he said, calmly.

I assumed he had a pistol in his back pocket under the baggy *barong tagalog* he wore.

Heat forced its way from my guts to my neck, but I only said, "At least one who sleeps with his mother has one. One can't sleep with a monkey, then call the offspring Garcia."

He tried to stand, but I pushed the table into him, then rolled it over him, and when he got his hands free from table and chairs tumbling on him and reached for his back, I kicked him in the stomach. His hands came back, but he tried to kick at me lying on his side. I kicked him on the inside of his thigh, then, when he moved his hands, kicked him in the stomach twice more, then leaned over to get the pistol. He waved a feeble punch at my head, but I chopped the inside of his arm, and he quit. I took the gun, an old pearl-handled .38

automatic, threw the bolt, chambering a round and cocking it. Terri stood out of the way, crying, saying, "No, Jake," over and over. Holding the gun in my left hand, I stood over him until he tried to sit up, mumbling curses and threats. I chopped him above the ear. His jaw fell open on that side, and he stopped even trying to talk, but lay back down again.

"Get up, you fat mother-fucker," I said. "You lay there, I'm gonna shoot you in the guts, then drop you in the bay. Right there," I said, and kicked him again. A line of spittle and puke crept out the side of his mouth. He was finally afraid now. "Okay, fat boy, I'm going to let you go now. But I want you to remember something." I had learned enough about Manila minor gangster operations from the ex-priest to carry this off. "Remember Mr. Taruc at the Yellow Bar. Remember how he liked to knock soldiers in the head, then drop them in the blood gutters. Remember. You will also remember that last month someone shot Mr. Taruc's legs off with a Thompson as he stepped out his bar door. Remember that. But he wasn't dead. Two Molotov cocktails did that. Did you hear how he burned, did they tell you what color the flames were, did they tell you how he smelled? I know, fat boy—he was fat too wasn't he—I know because I did it. Mr. Taruc doesn't knock American soldiers in the head any more, does he? My sergeant and I stopped that. Remember you're fat, you'd burn well too." I went on, mixing up a story Tetrick had told me about a real incident in India after the war with the late lamented demise of Mr. Taruc. I think he finally believed me. Worst of all, I think Terri started to believe me. Mr. Garcia left, wobbling like a man after a bad accident, leaving me to clean up my own mess behind him.

"Why you do that?" Terri asked, as I got a beer. "Why?"

Everything spilled out at once. "Why? You want to know why? The weather, the Army, my screwed up life. You want to know something worth knowing, ask me why I didn't kill him. I wanted to kill him. I wanted to blow his fat, ugly guts all over the bar. But I didn't. Sometimes I get unhappy. Sometimes life is too much. Why? Why? I don't know why." I spoke mostly to my beer bottle, then took a long cool drink from it.

"You sound like Joe Morning," she said, seemingly far behind me. "Most time you are gentle man, Jake, but today you have kill in your heart. I sorry for you." She was crying; I could tell without looking around. I'd heard the sound before. "He offer me one thousand pesos a month to live with him," she said. "I am. Goodbye." She walked out after Mr. Garcia, but stopped at the door. "Maybe I keep him from having you killed," she said.

"You've been seeing to many American movies," I said without looking up.

She went on into the afternoon sunlight wearing the same black pants, the same black jersey, the same lovely bare feet soft in the grass. And I knew exactly how her breasts rippled under the jersey, knew exactly the animal smell of her body, satin skin over a cat's muscles, the way her legs climbed my body when she really wanted me, the night rain of kisses after she came. *She was right,* I thought, but I couldn't help thinking, *What if I'd let him kick the shit out of me? Would she have stayed?* No matter. It died aborning, conceived in violence, buried in hate, how could it be love? Once more Krummel loses to a loser. How fucking quaint.

I finished my beer and left. There was no rain as I walked back to the hotel down the stinking bay front. No rain. Nothing so conclusive as that.

Morning was still in the room, but drunk now, and the two large suitcases still sat heavily in the center of the room, not treasure now, but a sad burden.

"Off your ass, trooper. Let's sell some cigarettes."

" 'Bout time you did some work around this place, fella," he said, rolling off the bed to call the drop man.

The drop man came for us in an old Chevrolet. He was small, nervous, and in a hurry. Usually the transaction took place in the moving car, but he said it was too late and he needed to pick up the money at another place, so he drove us to Pasay City and parked in front of a wood and thatch house on a narrow dirt lane. Morning and I carried the suitcases in the house as the drop man hurried off down the street, explaining that he had to pick up the money. A tall, busty broad in a red dress met us at the door, laughed huskily at the weight of the suitcases, asked us to sit, then, in the same voice, the voice an American mother might use to ask a child if he would like cookies and milk, asked us if we wanted a quick blow-job. I said, thank you, no, but Morning asked, How much. Nothing, she said, A customer service, and laughed again. "Isthey inkstay," I said, "Let's cut," but Morning said "Onay," then followed the chick into the bedroom, her big legs rustling against the red satin of her dress.

Inside, he later told me, she stripped him quickly, laid his clothes on a chest at the foot of the bed, then undressed except for her bra, and went to work. With her body hiding his pants, the floor opened, or something, and one hundred sixty pesos disappeared from his wallet, leaving him, as Filipino thieves usually did, enough money to get back to Base. Morning asked her to remove her bra, but she just laughed, and spat against the wall, he said.

After ten minutes or so two men in loud baggy sport shirts walked in the front door. I stood, expecting anything. Neither of them were the drop man, but both looked like cheap hoods. My first thought was that Mr. Garcia was about to have his revenge (which may or may not have been true; if true, he revenged himself on Joe Morning, not me; a refreshing change, if true).

"You are off limits, you know, GI Joe," the younger of the two said. "You could get in bad trouble, GI Joe." His voice dripped threat.

"I'm in a private home, Jack, and my name isn't GI Joe, and just who the hell are you?" I said, the fire of fear and anger blooming again.

The older man looked on in disgust, then took out a battered card in a plastic case from his hip pocket, slowly, though, so I might mistake it for a gun.

"Pasay City Secret Service," the younger said, meaning, as I knew, a fancy New World name for the vice squad. Once more, slowly for effect, "Pasay City Secret Service."

"Spartanburg Mickey Mouse Club," Morning said in the doorway, tucking in his shirt. "What the fuck's up?"

"Talk nice, GI Joe," the younger said, flashing his card, too, which was only in slightly better shape than the other's. "We

have report that two crazy stupid American GIs down here in
off limits place. Bad place. Very bad. American GIs come here
by mistake, sometimes have bad trouble. Sometimes fall down
die. Sometimes," the threat now clear in his tone, then doing a
silent movie double take, he saw the suitcases, "Those belong
you, GI Joe?"

"Maybe. What about it, fuzz?" Morning said, his voice cool
with anger now. "You boys fixin' to stir up a hornet's nest," he
said in his best Ku Klux Klan voice, but they didn't understand.

"If not yours, then must be mine," the younger cop said, a
fat grin on his thin face. This was getting silly. The older one
was stocky, looking a little like a cop, but he was still small,
maybe 5'7", 155, and the younger one was even smaller. And
they wanted to take on the pride of the 721st. I didn't know if
they had pistols or guys outside. One or the other though.

"They're mine, bud. All mine," Morning said, quietly, turning his left side to the two cops.

"Then captain must see," the younger said, smiling still
wider, playing the game to the hilt. "We will take to captain,
yes?" but not a question at all.

"How?" Morning said. "Just how?"

I looked for something to swing, but the room was furnished
with a single rickety wooden table and chair, a cheap vinyl
couch, and a whore's altar, plastic saints, nickel candles, and a
slant-eyed Christ. Nothing a dissatisfied customer might get a
purchase on.

The younger cop, smiling like a Buddha now, slowly raised
the bottom of his gaily printed shirt, revealing the butt of a
nickel-plated .45 stuck in his waistband. "Take it off, honey,"
he said, then did a bump and grind.

"Ease off, Joe," I said. "They'd love to shoot us in the backs
and say we were resisting arrest. Keep your face to them, and
your mouth shut, and we'll be all right."

"You shut your mouth, joe," the younger said, dropping his
shirt back over the pistol as if he meant it to be a dramatic
gesture. "This not California. You not mess with Beni Boys
now," he sneered.

While Morning was looking puzzled, I got mad again that

day. "You're not too smart, are you?" I said. "That gun's in a bad place. A good fast man could break your neck while you're reaching for it. Your partner might get him. But that ain't going to put your head back on."

"Hey, man," Morning said, smiling, too, now. "Don't scare the little man; he'll blow his balls off going for that cannon."

The younger cop suddenly looked afraid, then bent into a slight crouch, but the older one said to him in Spanish, "That's enough. Go to the car, now. I will talk now." The younger one didn't look happy, but he moved. As he reached the door, I said, "*Si muchacho. Tu padre lo dice* get out." Tex-Mex, but he understood and started back, but the old one waved him off again.

"You speak Spanish?" he said, turning to me.

"No, man," I said.

He turned to Morning and said, "You boys shouldn't talk to him like that. He's really a nice kid. He's just got a quick temper. He really likes Americans." His English was very good, his voice quite naturally kind. "Now, if you. . . ."

"Don't pull that buddy-buddy shit with us, man," Morning said. "We've seen as many movies as you."

"Your friend is quite a wise ass," the older cop said to me, no longer even faking kindness. "You should teach him to keep his mouth shut."

"Nobody likes a cop," I said. "Particularly a crooked one."

"Let's go," he said, motioning us out the door. "Bring the cigarettes."

"Oh, the little shit told you they were cigarettes, huh?" Morning said as he picked up one suitcase. "Tell him hello from me, will you, when you pay him off. Tell him I'll have another drop next Break, huh? A big one. A cement overcoat in the bay."

We followed the silent cop out the front and into an old jeep, gray and rusted, touched with a thousand dents. The younger cop sat behind the wheel, smoking a hastily lit cigarette, posing tough. He drove us through more crooked lanes for about ten minutes, stopped once at a call box to prepare the station for us, then took the longest way round to the station house. Morning and I carried in the suitcases and set them on a desk in an office shut away from the rest of the large wooden room by glass, then the cops took our names and our valuables, our belts, and Morning's shoe laces, and afterward locked us in a wooden cage in the center of the room, across from the glass office. No place to sit, the floor, smeared with shit and vomit, too filthy to sit on, so we stood, waiting, saying nothing, watching the other occupant of the cage, a ragged drunk curled in a corner who never moved the whole time we were in the room, so still he might have been dead waiting to stink. We might have smoked, but the cops, the two who had brought us in and five or six others, were quickly demolishing our cigarettes in front of the booking desk at the other end of the room. The booking desk, like the one in the office, still bore the marks of whatever American military unit had used them before they were released for surplus. I shouted about the cigarettes, but one of the cops told me to smoke my toe, whatever that meant. If it was an insult, it didn't work because it gave us a terrible case of nervous giggles, which relaxed us more than any cigarette. Morning shouted back to ask if it was okay if he smoked his thumb because his toe was empty, but the cops missed the joke.

In about an hour a tall neat man in a *barong tagalog* came in the room, neatly combed hair, neat nails, and a dapper line of moustache. He nodded as he passed, as if we were casual acquaintances, spoke to the man at the desk, then walked in the straightest line into the glass office. Two different cops came, handcuffed Morning, then led him to the office. For five minutes there was a quiet businesslike talk, calm motions, thoughtful head movements, but Morning began, it looked like, saying no, no, no, in more fiery language. He stood up, and though I couldn't hear him I could tell he said Bullshit in his best voice, allowing no argument. He was handcuffed again, not roughly, but forcefully, and taken outside. Then they came for me.

"Sgt. Krummel, I believe it is," he said, reaching out a hand as they removed the cuffs. "Capt. Mendoza, second in command of the Pasay City Secret Service."

I didn't shake his hand. "Where did they take my friend?"

"Just to an outside cell. He will be all right. I didn't want him making any more, how should I say, bad blood with the two sergeants who brought you here." His English was very neat too, but he sounded like an insurance man making a pitch for increased coverage, or a Bible salesman.

"Just talk straight, huh? What's your price? What's it going to cost us to get out of this fairy tale?"

"Oh, everyone is in such a hurry today. But it is late, and I, ah, shall we say, have a lady waiting. So to the point. If you had not made my two worthy sergeants quite so angry, we could arrange some sort of deal where I, ah, would purchase your cigarettes at a very small loss to you. You pay seven for them on Base, I would pay you seven. You would be out nothing but your profit and expenses, and be much the richer, as they say, for the experience. A very small loss, indeed," he said, pausing to offer me a cigarette, which I didn't take.

"A small loss?" I asked, "or a shakedown?"

"Oh, such a crude term. I would have expected more from an educated man," he said, lighting his Chesterfield.

"Educated?" I said.

"Oh, yes, I know about you, Sgt. Krummel. I've known Teresita for many years. A lovely woman, as they say, yes, indeed. I've known about your business for some time. I also heard about your unfortunate encounter with Mr. Garcia this afternoon. He is a pig, but he could be dangerous, yes, indeed. As they say, I have my ear to many walls, yes, and you might call this a tax, a luxury tax. And the small loss you speak of so heavily would indeed be small compared to the price you would pay if you force me to call the U.S. Military Adjutant. You will surely face charges, be, as they say, busted, and perhaps spend some time in the stockade," he said, finishing with a perfect smoke ring.

"But, as I said," he quickly continued, "that was before you two boys made my men so unhappy, so damned unhappy. Now, unfortunately, it will take only a gesture for you and your friend. You must walk out, forgetting you ever saw these cigarettes. You have reserve, surely, and it will take all of this to, as they say, grease the angry palms around here." There wasn't a trace of irony or of threat in his voice, but a slight note of sadness; the director of one company hearing about the director of another falling into a bad but not disastrous deal.

"My friend said no deal, didn't he?" I said.

"Unfortunately, yes. He's such an emotional creature." Another perfect smoky circle.

"Then no deal."

"Don't be foolish. You made a mistake dealing with such a, as you might say, small tomatoes for a drop." He rustled in his desk for a moment, then handed me a card, and offered me another cigarette. I took this one. "My address and telephone number. I also deal slightly in the market. When you make a run after now, call me. If you can boost your load to three hundred cartons a week, guaranteed, I can raise the price to eleven and a half. You will get rich; I will get richer. But you have to take this small loss. The younger man has, as you might say, political connections. A small loss. You'll make it up in a month."

"Did you tell my friend this?" I asked, blowing a ragged ring of smoke between us.

"Yes," he said, standing. As he walked around the desk the crease in his trousers lay as precise as a ruler edge, the shine on his expensive shoes, hard and brilliant. "And other things. Other things."

"And he still said no?"

"Yes."

"Then, no."

He sighed, then said, "You must be very good friends, indeed. Money can't buy friendship, as they say." He made out a receipt for the cigarettes. "But I think this is going to be an expensive friendship for you." He reached for the phone. "Good luck. Think about what they say, Money can't buy friendship."

"I guess not," I said as I left, cuffed again. They walked me out and lodged me in the cell with Morning.

"He give you that get-rich-quick shit, too?" he asked out of the dark corner where he perched on a bamboo cot.

"Sure," I said, sitting on the other after the two cops removed the cuffs. "I told him it was a great idea. Told him to go ahead."

"Don't try to shit me, Krummel. You told him to shove it right back up his crooked ass. Just like me." His words seemed very close to my ear, but I still couldn't see him; my eyes hadn't adjusted to the darkness. "Crooked mother."

"Where do you get off being so damned moral?" I asked.

"What we're doing is okay; what that bastard is doing is crooked. He's supposed to be a cop. And so what if we do have to deal with shit, at least it knows it's shit, like our lovely drop man, but that mother up there thinks he don't stink. Where do I get off being so moral? Shit, man, where does he get off being so crooked. So I told him to shove it," he said quickly, something, not fear, nor excitement, making his voice high and tired, almost a whine.

"And why? Why not take the loss?" I asked.

"Why? Because, man, I've been lied to, stolen from, and shit on for the last time. It's too much. Nobody pushes me around any more, man," he said.

"And how do you know I didn't take the loss?" I asked.

"Nobody pushes you around either," he said.

"No, I guess not," I said. "Guess not."

The adjutant had us out in an hour. In another half hour we sat with a bottle of black-market Dewar's—bought with my money because Morning discovered his loss—in the hotel. I was very numb, but tired too, and the Scotch seemed to run to my legs and weaken them, divide the very cells holding the muscles together. It seemed I should feel more, something more, anger, rage, shame, something about the loss of Teresita and my stripes in the same day, but for now I was just tired. The rage mounted behind Morning's unfocused eyes, but I was just tired.

(The night Ell left with Ron Flowers to go to his apartment, after Ron and I had argued about going to Mississippi for the summer project, and he had drawn the switchblade he had carried without using since he was ten, and I called him a nigger, then broke his arm, saying, "I will not be pushed"; after Ell left, saying, "You don't need me. You always win. You just never lose. I can't stand that," and I crying to her back fleeing through the door, "But I thought that was what a man was for," and my voice echoing in the empty hallway, "was for," and the past tense striking me like a boot in the face, and the loneliness clawing in on quick feet, not just Ell gone, but the world gone from me, and I screamed into the empty hall again, "But, baby, I'm losing now. Goddamn, I'm losing, and the losers are winning, and goddamn, baby, I don't know why," and I cried for a bit while curious fools peeked through cracked and darkened doorways, then I sat in the living room all night, drinking; I was just too damned tired to move.)

I left the table once to pry open the window, to flee the conditioned air, but found only the stink of the sea's dumb expanse, the growl of the streets, and a hot breath on my face as some tired mad hound raced toward me through the night.

"Money can't buy friendship," I said to the sweating dog.

After the first quart, we ordered another even though Morning was already as drunk as one man should be. He hadn't stirred from the table, except to take a leak, and he drank straight from the bottle. I had been as still as he, after trying the window, and may even have been as drunk, but I was silent, counting the blossoms on the flowered wallpaper, while he constantly mumbled to himself, his whispers like bees in the room, his hands flying about his face. And when I wasn't counting, I was just there. Sad and numb, the way it is when you catch a good one on the jaw and in that time between the fist and the darkness you float away from the world, consciousness unconnected, unanchored by pleasure or pain, just ether dissipating in the vacuum, tumbling through fire-streaked skies. But Morning's voice, now loud, grasped me from the whirling peace, sat me back on earth:

"Hey, man, you know what that mother said?"

"Who? What? No," I said, moving over to the bed, perhaps to feign sleep. I didn't care what any mother said.

"That crooked fucker," he grunted, "that head Dick Tracy."

"No," I said, my eyes closed, drifting.

"No, what?"

"No, I don't know what he said, and I don't much give a damn."

"Oh, yeah. Well, he said that broad was a Billy Boy, the one at the house. What a bunch of shit." He slapped the table.

"Huh?"

"The broad. The mother said she was a Billy Boy queer chomping on my root, man." He hit the table top again.

"So what. Who gives a shit. Queer, smear. Go away."

"I give a shit, that's who," he said, now hitting the table with his fist. "I give a shit. But it wasn't."

She had been a big broad, and could have been. I'd seen Billy Boys who looked more like women than men, and I wanted to go to sleep, so I said, "Could have been."

I thought he was coming for me, which woke me up, but he just sat at the table, pounding it until I made him quit, shouting KILL THE MOTHER-FUCKER until I quieted him with a weak drink from the second bottle, which the bellhop showed up with in the nick of time. He blubbered until I asked him what was wrong.

I asked; he took the rest of the night to tell me; I shouldn't have asked.

HISTORICAL NOTE 2

I can only tell the story that Joe Morning told me.
There might be some advantage in trying to re-create
his voice, except that he was so drunk that night he
seemed to have lost his voice, the voice I knew, the
intelligent, articulate voice which he could usually
maintain, which he had maintained on other nights
even as he fell drunk to the floor. But not this night.
He mumbled, coughed, laughed, perhaps even lied.
His words ran in confused flight from his mouth, the
truth pouring out of his head like wine from a broken pitcher. He told the story without any sort of
order, repeating himself, skipping about in time,
across place. Unless you knew him as I did, his
story, told in his words, would only confuse you, so
I've taken the historian's liberty of retelling it as I
know it. There are some disadvantages to this
method, agreed; it would be easy to twist this method
to my own purposes and, of course, there is some
twisting always going on, but please accept it, as one
accepts Gibbon on Rome, Carr on the Soviet Union,

Prescott on the conquest of Mexico. Krummel on Joe Morning. As this is my truth, not *the* truth; take it with a grain of bitter salt in your beer.

He called himself Linda Charles, and Joe Morning first saw him (her?) in a nightclub in San Francisco. The other men performing in the show were professionally good, but obviously men, betrayed by a walk too exaggerated, a hand too strong, a wig as stiff as frosting on a mannequin's head. But when Linda Charles walked out to sing, long blond hair, real hair instead of a wig, sweeping down and back across her white shoulders, slim, firm legs swinging beneath a simple green silk sheath, a voice in the club, dim behind Morning, said in drunken awe, "My God, that's no man." Linda Charles smiled a woman's smile, enchanted with flattery, at the voice. Then she clapped her hands, stomped a delicate foot, and roared into a blues arrangement of "Saint James Infirmary" in a fine husky contralto. The green high heel behind her, her hands clasped in front, then a passionate shake of the head would send the blond hair out of her face in a shining ripple down across her round shoulders.

Morning felt a vague, guilty excitement heat the drinks in his belly, as probably did most of the men in the audience. The forbidden thing: taking on the trappings of woman, imitating the beauty of woman. And with the beauty, the forbidden wisdom, the possibility of being a receptacle for the seed, being the gift rather than the giver, possessing a firm lovely breast for your own, a slim silken leg which must ache with pleasure as it moves against its mate. Morning started to rise, but smart enough not to betray his fright, fearing the fear the fright might betray, he stayed through to the end.

But when he left, the perfume of fear followed him, and he took his already generalized guilt, too, and perhaps mistook the one for the other. He had been punished so much, he must be guilty of something. Perhaps this? Who knew?

During his junior year of college, Joe Morning had been sitting on a car fender in front of his fraternity house, drunk, watching, but not taking part in, a springtime panty raid on a nearby girls' dorm. He could act the part of the amused observer because in his basement room in the frat house lay a drunk coed from the very dorm being raided, naked but for her loafers. Earlier in the evening he had, with his silver tongue and a pint of Southern Comfort, persuaded the girl to climb into his ground level window. And now, fresh fucked and smiling, he had come out to investigate the noise.

But when the police came to stop the raiders, which a single dorm mother with a Coke bottle had already done, and to stop the girls hanging out the second-story windows who were waving lace-fringed encouragement, they arrested everyone in sight, including the irate dorm mother who had assaulted an officer of the law on his way upstairs to stop those silly girls, and including innocent bystander, Joe Morning.

"Man, I'm not doing anything," he said to the cop who tried to pull him off the car. "I been sitting here all the time."

"Oh, sorry, boy; thought you was a girl-child, sitting there with all that hair," the cop drawled as he stepped back. "Let's go."

"Fuck off, peckerwood. I haven't done a thing."

"You just did," the cop said as Morning tried to jerk away. He skillfully stabbed him in the stomach with his billy, slid him off the hood, twisted an arm behind, and guided him to the wagon. At the steps Morning struggled slightly, more to get his breath than to resist, and in the scuffle was jabbed again, but managed to vomit in the cop's red fat face. The cop laid Morning out with the billy against his neck, then stood over him, thumping his ribs until another cop stopped him.

Morning awoke face down on a thin mattress on a cement floor, his hands painfully cuffed behind him, his feet shackled and tied to an iron ring in the wall, and his ribs blue, bruised, and aching. The tiny cell was hardly wider than the mattress, and a solid steel door with a small sliding plate over a barred window protected the world from this innocent bystander. Morning shouted until a jailer came to tell him to shut up or be gagged or worse, and Morning complained that he needed to pee, the Southern Comfort no comfort now, but the cop explained that there would be a time in the morning for toilet, and that the prisoner best not piss in the cell 'cause that would be defacing city property, which carried a minimum fine of one hundred dollars. As the cop spoke, which seemed to take hours, Morning noticed that his head felt bald against the mattress, and realized that his hair was gone. He asked why. It was explained that no dirty beatnik pinko was bringing fleas or lice into this jail which had been awarded a plaque from the governor for being the cleanest jail in the state. Morning said that he was honored to stay there, but he sure would like to pee. The cop slammed the plate back over the barred window, saying, piss in one a your books.

Morning, of course, couldn't hold his bladder, though he tried, so spent the rest of the night laying in his own waste and stink, cursing the world for that waste and stink. Damn, it had always been this way. Expelled from school for someone else's smoke in the john; whipped by his mother for the kid next door's lies; punished at random for the sins of others, he took to sins of his own, smoking, lying to his mother, and he was never caught.

The next day he found himself charged with disturbing the peace, resisting arrest and, yes, defacing city property. Morning pleaded not guilty and asked for a lawyer, but the justice of the peace said guilty without looking up, dismissed the resisting charge, sentenced him to two hundred dollars or two months in jail. Morning shouted appeal, but the justice of the peace told him no appeal was allowed for misdemeanors in that state.

Morning settled himself for two months, though he had the money in the bank, but the city called his mother. It seemed they'd rather have the money than Mrs. Morning's son. She paid the fine that afternoon, and as she walked out to the street with him, she asked, "Joe, Joe, what *are* you going to do next? What are you going to do?" He walked away without speaking.

Back in his room he found a note from the assistant dean of men, asking him to leave school. Morning ran still stinking and dirty to the dean's office up the quiet, pleasant, shaded hill, but the dean refused to see him, saying, in a precise Tidewater voice, You're not one of our students; our students are Southern gentlemen; please leave my office.

"Southern gentlemen suck cock," he said, and left the office.

He drank the rest of the afternoon in the cool basement. The chapter president sent a pledge to tell Mr. Morning to please move out of the room, but Mr. Morning sent the pledge back up to tell Mr. President to come down to try to make him do anything. Mr. President didn't come, but the vice-president did: Jack, Morning's high school buddy buggered by the two farmers that night after they had lost the state championship. He stood in the open door, his face composed, ready for the pitch, acting as if he had forgotten the hate of that night, acting as if he were big enough, as he had said, to forgive and forget, stood there in loafers, gray slacks, a crew-neck sweater, for the winter chill still clung in Morning's basement though spring had come two weeks before.

"Joe, boy, what's the matter with you? Where did you go wrong?" He had been taking business psychology. "You came down here a football star, a stable, straight, clean guy. Then you quit football, the thing you do best of all, calling it stupid, throwing away all those hours of intense preparation. Boy, you better believe, if I could have played as well as you, I would have never quit. But you quit, threw all that God-given talent away. Then you moved down in this dirty basement, down to this damp dirty room with all your fine library of books stinking with mold, and this place stinks like a . . . a . . . a nigger whorehouse," he said as Morning tossed a pair of stained panties at his feet. "You bring girls down here, and to the parties, you wouldn't want your mother to meet. And you haven't had a hair cut, till now, since God knows when. And you sit down in Mickey's with those damned pinkos. Joe, I don't know, I just don't know. I know you're good inside, but the things the brothers say about you. Sometimes it hurts me real bad to hear them." While he talked, Jack had been carefully removing mildewed books and dirty clothes from a chair. He sat down, clasped his hands in front of a knee, and said, "And this hurts me most of all, Joe. The chapter voted you out this morning. Mind you, we can't vote you out of the national body. I mean once you are a member of this fraternity, you are a member for life, just like when you joined the church. But they can vote you out of the house. I talked for you, but in a case like this an officer just has one vote, too. It really hurts me, Joe. We been together a long time. I just don't know."

"Morning out in the morning," he chanted. "Tell my brethren I'll be come 'fore daylight charms their ruddy cheeks. You're gonna make a wonderful junior executive, Jack, you know that?"

"Joe, boy, what's gone wrong?" Jack asked again, his voice and face soft in professional concern. He fooled a drunk Morning.

So Morning tried to answer him as he lay back among the twisted, dirty sheets, looking vacantly up at the poster of an intent Lenin pasted on the low ceiling, but after a moment when he looked over at Jack's bored, dumb face, he snorted, then said with a smile, "Jack, baby, let's talk about you. I mean what's wrong with you, son? I know how you acted when them farm boys corn-holed you, I remember that, but they told me you loved it, and wouldn't let them stop. And your roommate been looking kinda peaked lately. . . ."

"You son of a bitch," Jack said, standing up. "You bastard, I should have killed you that night."

"That's right, bugger, 'cause you sure as hell can't do it now. They fucked the guts out of you that night."

Jack sought the dirtiest curse he could think of: "You damned Communist."

Morning laughed and laughed, wild, happy roars that drove Jack from the room, across the basement, and up the stairs, and might still drive him wherever he may be. "Better Commie than queer, Jackshit." He laughed until in that quickly, for him, vanishing point between pleasure and pain, he found tears falling on his dirty hands, sobs raw in his throat, and a great lonely hole growing inside, the hole he drank into all the night long.

The next morning he felt, as he always did when chance laid him open to the world's fateful arrows and errors, that not only his civil, but even more his moral rights had been played with fast and loose by the minor officials of the various legalities he was subject to, fraternal, academic, municipal. In his drunken way he was going to demand redress, even if that redress would cost him in the same careless way: he was born to be a loser. Loser or not, though, he presented himself before the steps of the college administration building at eight o'clock in the morning, neatly dressed, shaved, clean, wearing the slacks, sweater, loafer uniform of his fellow men, and carrying a neatly lettered sign which said simply, as Morning said all his days, I PROTEST, meaning merely that he was protesting the world's treatment of him.

The administration had learned from other protests the best defense: they quietly, calmly ignored him in the way a father ignores his errant infant son. The administration was also in the process of ignoring four young Negroes who came each day with signs to protest the segregation rules of the college. The administration, adept at ignorance, also paid no mind to the eight or ten football players who appeared each morning at ten o'clock to formally spit on the Negroes who, if they blinked at this, were left curled in silent pain on the clean sidewalk, or dropped on the carefully clipped grass, or stretched over a neat hedge. But this was to be a different morning.

Just as the first Negro fell, the tall lean hungry end from north Alabama who had hit him found himself falling as Joe Morning landed square with both feet in the middle of his back. Morning became all feet and elbows, his frenzy the madness of right-eousness, his strength that of surprise and holy anger, and the infidels fell about him in waves, and if he could have them away from his ribs, he might have stood them off until sweet darkness. As it was, he made them forfeit such an unholy price for his defeat that they left the other three Negroes alone that day, and from that day let the Negroes protest in peace.

So for the second time in three days, Morning woke beaten and bleeding slightly on that thin mat-tress, which still held the stink of his waste, bound and chained again, though on his back this time. Ah, even the fuzz is wearing thin, growing soft, he thought as he woke, and smiled, then touched his tongue to the stiff stitches in his split lip. Holy rage had eased the bitterness. He felt as clean as the lamb, washed in his own blood, but clean nonethe-less, and he sang happy songs until he was released at five.

A civil-rights organization had bailed him out, and a sweet-faced, collegiate-looking cat from Cornell thanked him for his zeal and love, but chided him for resorting to violence, then bought him a beer. Partly because he wanted to throw it at his mother, partly because he needed a place to rest, but mostly because he was enchanted by this soft-spoken choco-late cat with a touch of a Yankee twang, Morning moved with the Negro into a small room off the war room in the basement of a Negro church. "Basements again," Morning said, "Always the lower depths for me," with laughter. He refused at first to even allow that non-violence had any positive possibilities; his plan was to bring the bluebellies back down the Mississippi, then let them march dreadfully to the sea, burning crops of white men in their wake. But Richard, the Negro, refused even to allow Morning to sing with them until he at least intellectually acknowledged that non-violence was the way, for now. So Morning did, mentally preparing himself for being spat upon and called niggerlover, but Richard sent him to a man in East St. Louis who then sent Morning and his guitar and his discontent off with a fund-raising group around Mid-Western and Western college campuses. So Morning sang with a Southern accent, and worked, and lived off checks sent secretly by his father instead of taking expenses from the organization, and he worked well except for a few lost weekends, or week days, depending on his moods. It was on one of these dark times, wandering about hilly San Francisco in the fog, that he stepped into the nightclub where sang the man called Linda Charles, and first acknowledged his fear.

But he forgot, as best as Joe Morning ever forgot anything, during the heat of the next summer. He marched in Birmingham, sat-in in Tampa, sang all over the Southland, sang about freedom, and all the while bound by his love for violence, and every step closely watched by Richard. He had to grab Morning in Tampa when a skinny deputy spit his chaw on them, but he couldn't have held Morning alone. Morning held part of himself, and he made it through the summer.

In the fall he drifted to Phoenix with a chick he had worked with, and he lived off her and his guitar until January, then went back to the fund-raising scene. In San Francisco he stayed away from the club where he had seen the shimmering vision of Linda Charles, stayed away until he became conscious of his absence, then he went, sober, sweating, but she wasn't playing there. Relieved, he went in to exorcise her (him), and found himself enjoying the show. It *was* funny, and did *poke* at the hypocrisy of middle-class America. And professional too, said the guy at the next table who said, and who looked the part, that he had just retired as a 49er defensive lineman. "These guys aren't queer. They're just actors trying to make a living. That one guy there," he said, pointing to a slim stripper, "has got six kids out in San Mateo." After the show he and Morning went down to Chinatown, drinking together until the ham-handed bear of a bastard made a clumsy pass at him. Morning swung on him, but the guy lowered his head, and Morning broke his hand. He ran like the wind, pulling over barstools behind him, and escaped with his life and virtue intact.

The old doctor who set the bones that night gave Morning a long lecture on the vices of the world. "The devil wears many faces, son, many masks. Be forever on guard. Tempt him not for his strength is the strength of ten men," he said, forming the cast with white hands connected to thin arms on which all the veins had collapsed from shooting. "Tempt him not. That will be twenty-seven fifty," he said, but Morning ran out of the emergency room, shouting, "The devil wears many masks, old man," diabolical laughter falling behind him as he ran. (Six months later he mailed a check to the old doctor, but the old doctor mailed it right back with a short note, "Son, I know what the devil costs. You'll need this more than I.")

"Why do things always happen to me?" Morning

asked Richard the next summer. "Why me?" and Richard answered, "They happen to all of us, man, so just stay cool." But coolness wasn't Morning's long suit, so Richard refused to let him demonstrate. Morning, in anger, moved to a more militant organization, and on the first sit-in of the summer at a dime-store lunch counter in Birmingham, he laid low a nineteen-year-old kid who only said Pass the salt, niggerlover. Then the kid's buddies moved in, and Morning left the civil-rights movement the same way he entered, swinging and kicking for holy hell.

Charged with felonious assault, Morning faced one to three years, but his mother, faithful Southern mother, had a cousin (in the South one has cousins everywhere) who shot pool with the judge. So instead of three years, he was exiled from Alabama, in effect. The charges were indefinitely postponed, but the case would be reopened if he crossed into Alabama to demonstrate for anything ever.

The anger he held for the judge's sentencing, he held until he was outside. Once again he walked away from his mother without a word, stopped long enough for his guitar and a flight bag, then, anger still his only impulse, he walked from downtown, out 3rd, all the way to the city limits before he stuck out his thumb pointed toward Phoenix. But anger doesn't lend itself to hitching rides: the action is too slow, the long waits while asphalt puffs in the sun and the sparse shade of a jackpine protects neither man nor angry beast against the hot, dusty winds trailing semi's. The time after midnight, which may be the witching hour but ain't the hitching hour, he stood at lonely crossroads, stood for hours that never end, then ran from side to side from road to road at the call of the headlights booming up through East Texas piney woods, hoping only for a ride to anywhere, and again the semi's roaring past like fast freights. Then the afternoon sun like lava on rocky West Texas hills and a man makes the only shade there is, fatigue and dust and sunburn like a mask eating his face, until finally he hasn't even a damn for the arrogant cars hissing past, slinging gravel at his hot feet. Then Phoenix rising in the heat waves as he watched from the back of a cotton-picker truck filled with Mexicans, and he was ready to lay his burden down.

Four cold beers at his old girl's place, then he fell into his first long sleep. He slept for days, thirteen to be exact, in her bed, rising only to relieve himself or swill a glass of tepid water. But not so much sleeping, he said, but dreaming of sleep and dreams. He ran dreams like movies with intermissions for a leak, then right back to the film—war, honor, love, the past, the future—running until it seemed his brain could contain no more images, yet still going on like a bad Italian movie. Frightened, the girl called a doctor who merely sedated Morning into real sleep for another twelve hours, then told the girl to throw a glass of cold water into his face the next morning. He came up angry again, and was all right.

Back to the guitar and the bottle for a couple of months, then the music became enough. He sang professionally now, four thirty-minute sets six nights a week in a small sometimes coffee house sometimes bar, Harps on the Willows. He had never been better. More faithful to the box he played than the one he slept with, he barely noticed when she drove her small sports car back to Boston. But people were noticing him, and Morning never denied liking that. He played student gatherings on off-nights, then an occasional party at an English professor's house. He grew a beard to go with his long hair, and was soon a minor rage among new rich, pseudo liberal, culture vultures in Phoenix, even out in simple, suburban Scottsdale, and there he met his fear face to mask, Linda Charles.

The party was at a large, rambling house on three acres of clipped, watered grass. It was an engineer's house, filled with electrical gadgets, a button to flush, a button to roll off a neat amount of paper, ice makers, drink makers, and wired from asshole to elbow with sweet stereo. The floors were laid in rugs as thick as bear skin, and peopled with people fighting the way they made their money, the hesitantly liberal, the casual un-Godly who occasionally would quietly say "fuck" for special emphasis and quietly slap a fist into the other hand, and the women very careful not to blush. Morning came here, his credentials not much better than these who received him, came in a buckskin shirt stained with someone else's sweat, scuffed cowboy boots, and faded, frayed Levi's. He sang the soft protests, a few old English ballads (he could make me cry with even old hat "Barbara Allen"), then some wild bawdy Scotch songs, some popular comic snatches, then the dirtiest Irish roar he knew, and came on in the finale leading the group in "We Shall Overcome" like an intellectual cheerleader. He knew his audience. After him came the Twist as the crew-cuts and drizzleheads paired off. He worked two sets, then a little mixing with the crowd, a few casual references to the Movement, and a crisp fifty from the hostess whom he had screwed in the English professor's bathroom four times before she hired him. Out here, though, he made gentle verbal passes at all the

pretty women, flowers caught in plastic paper-
weights, but he never followed them through. He
knew his audience.

But this particular night the Movement was
moved out by a wonderful bit of risqué humor and
singing by the hostess' personal friend, the famous
female impersonator, one Linda Charles.

He remembered her (he couldn't keep himself
from thinking her instead of him) and saw her
across the room, prim in a high-collared sleeveless
black dress, sitting on a white sofa, alone because
the men were afraid; and the women, either envious
or unconcerned, stayed away too. The hostess led
Morning across to her, introduced them, then fled.
Morning shook her hand, trying not to examine it for
any trace of male hardness, but finding none in spite
of his failure. She said hello very softly, offered the
seat next to her with a slim white arm. Morning
hesitated, but she said, "Oh, hell, sit down. I may
have balls but I don't bite." She laughed with such a
sense of her own vanity and foolishness, such an
ease, that Morning did sit, feeling it would be square
not to, sat in the seat next to her, and all that was to
come, with open innocent eyes.

"You're pretty good," she said, "a professional,
shall we say, phony. You didn't get those hands as a
passive resister, jack."

"I beg your pardon," he answered, stupidly, not
knowing what to say.

"I beg your pardon," she mocked, tilting her head
with a musical lilt to her voice. "You are a straight
arrow square, aren't you?"

"I just didn't know what you meant."

"You're as much a fake as I am. Those old clothes,
sweat stains, scuffs, and holes. I'll bet you bathe
every day and would rather die than wear dirty

shorts. Your beard's too neatly trimmed, too," she said, but smiled quietly as if they were conspirators in the same plot. "You're obviously as hip as Richard Nixon, but you're good enough to fool these johns out here. Your father is probably an accountant and your mother sings in a church choir, and that's where you learned to sing, in a damned church choir."

"Yeah," he answered, "you're right, but you've been talking to old bumble butt about me," he said, pointing a thumb at the hostess.

"Need to know what my competition is up to."

"You, too?" Morning said, amazement clear on his face.

"She's the kind of broad who says, 'I want to experience everything in this world at least once before I die,' never knowing she was stillborn. Of course me too. What do you think I'm doing here? Don't be square forever."

"Well, I'm learning every minute," Morning said, lighting her cigarette.

"Really," she said, leaning back on the couch and raising a delicate eyebrow behind a stream of smoke. "Then be a good boy and run get me a drink."

Morning started to rise, then slouched back and said, "Screw you, jack," but said it with a grin.

"Save your strength for bumble butt," Linda said, smiling too. "I guess you are learning. Let's go back to Phoenix and I'll buy you a real drink to kill the taste of this cheap punch bumble butt calls booze."

Morning had just noticed fifteen or twenty heads turned in his direction, heads which turned back when he faced them, trying to conceal looks and smirks puckered in oatmeal faces. "What?" he said, turning back to Linda.

"Don't sweat it. If you read your Kinsey, or Ellis,

or whoever, you know that true transvestites aren't queer. I got problems, but not that one, man." She spoke without hardness, without pushing, and a small verticle line pinched between her wide green eyes made her look discriminated against, told of being mistaken by narrow minds. "Besides," she continued, a sad touch of a grin at her mouth, "it will be good paper for you. Raise your fee from what, fifty, to one bill for sure."

"For sure," he said. "Let's split."

"I know I'm lovely, but I'm not built that way, really," she said, white teeth holding her lower lip off a smile.

Morning laughed, then as he stood, he involuntarily offered his hand. She looked at it, her head cocked to the side like a puzzled puppy, he looked at it, then they chuckled together.

"That's all right," she said. "Sometimes I forget too." She rose without his help, then walked toward the door, movements neat, trim, fluid, hip motion not exaggerated but terribly feminine.

The son of a bitch practices, Morning thought, Jesus.

Outside she offered to let him drive her XK-E. When he whistled at the metallic blue car gleaming under the desert moon, she said, "There are lots of burly chaps who are quite happy to pay a ten buck minimum to see some crazy cat in drag. Plus my mother left me about two hundred fifty thousand dollars, bless her drunken hide."

As he drove, Morning told her about his fight with the huge queer in San Francisco.

"What a flaming queen he is, honey. He makes Mardi Gras every year so he can go in drag. What a riot. Smokey the Bear in hose and heels. Too much," she said.

They stopped at a quiet expensive lounge and drank at the leather covered bar for several hours, sipping slow Scotches, each seeming to wait for the other to get drunk. They discovered a mutual affection for Faulkner, then Sartre and Gide, particularly *The Counterfeiters,* then with wild laughter discovered that they were members in bad standing of the same national fraternity.

"I've got this friend," Morning said, thinking of Jack, "who'd love to meet you." He laughed, then told her the long story about Jack.

When Linda drove him home, they were laughing together like old buddies who had forgiven each other in advance, and when she drove away, her exhausts hammering the pavement as exhausts will, Morning chuckled with great relief. He had braved the darkness in its most attractive shape, for if she was nothing else, Linda Charles was a lovely woman with a wide handsome mouth and a clean laugh and the carriage and poise a woman needs, plus that touch of sad melodrama women break hearts with. And Morning had braved it, conquered it, and tonight he owned the world. He slept without dreams, woke without guilt, then in the middle of a yawn, remembered that he had left his guitar in Scottsdale.

He didn't see Linda again for nearly a week, and then he didn't talk to her. She came in the Harps with a group of white waving hands and flitting voices. Morning was in the middle of a set, and she nodded to him, then turned up her nose at her friends, laughing. Another time she came in alone, seemingly depressed, so Morning had a drink with her between sets. He made a few bad jokes which seemed to cheer her up, not from mirth, but from the effort. Then she came by his apartment one afternoon, her hair up, wearing a flashy red dress, looking like an expensive whore, and asked him to have a drink or two with her before he went to work. They went to the same lounge as the first night, sat at the back of the bar, and swilled Scotches like sailors. Within the hour they were quite drunk.

"You know," Morning said, grinning, "That's the only thing you do like a man."

"What's that?" She didn't seem worried that she did anything like a man.

"Drink. That's all. You even move like a woman. Christ. Sometimes I wonder if you're not a chick with a strange hang-up who likes to say she's a man."

"No, man," she said. "You ought to pay one month's hormone bill, then you'd know I'm a man. But I know what you mean. Maybe I should've been a woman. Shit, I even had a breast tumor removed. They cut my little bitty nipple right out. But this way . . . Crap, I can't lift anything heavier than a beer glass, I can't go out in the sunlight, can't even get drunk more than once or twice a month or my face starts getting hard." She paused, circling the water ring on the bar with a perfectly done fingernail, then looked up and smiled a smile which, if it had come from a woman, would have broken a man's heart. "Drag is a drag, man, more often than not."

Morning, a drunk man, an indiscriminate man, a man more frightened than he knew, let his heart be touched. "Jesus Christ, man, what is a guy like you doing in a bag like this."

"Good as any other in this stupid fucking world," she answered, smiling slightly. "Good as any."

"Yeah, guess so," he said, then laughed. "Shit, yes."

They drank silently for a few minutes, acknowl-

edging each other's sadness, but soon were scolding
the darkened air with words again.

Later she began talking about herself, saying,
"And as long as I'm careful about choosing my
friends, neither too straight, nor too gay, I live the
good life. The only thing," she said, pausing, then
looking directly into Morning's eyes, "The only thing
is that this is a dead-end bag. I've found a couple of
chicks who thought they could make the permanent
scene with me, but both of them finally asked me to
drop out of drag, and I wouldn't. Sometimes I even
think about a family, oddly enough, but then I wonder what would happen if a kid of mine found out
about me. I'm foul enough; no need to pass it on. I
get enough ass off latent dikes; I'm beautiful; I'm
happy." She smiled, happiness professionally touched
with sad eyes.

"That's what counts, man," Morning said.

They drank, talked some more, then Morning realized that it was past time for his first set. Too drunk
to sing, he called his boss, who said, I know your ass
is downtown drunk with that flaming queen of a
bastard, and Morning said, My ass is here, yours is
there, shove my guitar up it and smile. Thus went
his job.

When he went back to his stool, he found a slick
middle-aged man who fancied himself a swinger
sitting there, putting a big play out for Linda. Morning sat on the other side of her.

"Kansas City, Kansas," the traveling man was saying. "Sales. Regional director. Electronic bookkeep-
ing equipment." He then thrust out a hand at Morning, an aggressive hand, saying, "Howard Tingle.
Electricity in that hand, boy," then laughed, and
squeezed Morning's hand.

Morning winced in mock pain, saying, "Hey, cat, lay off the hand, huh?"

"Young fella like you ought to keep in shape, boy," he said, slapping his gut. "Hard as a rock, all the way down," he smirked. "Handball twice a week at home. Swim in motels on the road, but not always in the pool." He laughed again. "You young kids shouldn't let yourselves go like that."

"Yeah, man, I'll take up toilet tilting tomorrow," Morning said, but the salesman had already turned to Linda, whispering in her ear.

She laughed, half-turned her head to wink at Morning, then seductively poked the john in the ribs. She led him on for nearly an hour, matching Morning drink to drink. The three of them moved to another bar, a place where Linda and the salesman could dance and cuddle in a booth. The salesman tried to kiss her on the dance floor, but Linda leaned back, coy as a high school girl, and shook a finger at him. Morning had to grin drunkenly at himself. After one song, she swept by the table for her purse, then pranced, hips thumping under the tight red satin, to the rest room, whispering over her shoulder to the salesman, "Now don't you be a bad boy and try to peek."

"Boy, oh boy, that is some woman," he said, sitting across from Morning. Sweat beaded his forehead and he wiped at it with a cheap handkerchief, his face slack with whiskey. "Say, I'm not messing anything up for you, huh? Hate to do that," he chortled, unbuttoning the blue collegiate blazer he affected.

"Not a thing, man."

"God, she's some broad."

"She'll show you things you never dreamed of, man."

"I'll show her something she's always dreamed of," he said, patting the lump in his crotch.

"Go, baby, go."

Even in the dim light from the jukebox Morning could see the heavy coat of fresh lipstick gleaming like a wound on Linda's mouth as she walked back to the table, a smile of anticipation curving across her face.

"Let's dance," she commanded.

They swayed close, slowly, and Morning saw Linda place a perfect lip print on the salesman's rolled oxford collar, then the salesman was trying for her mouth again. She avoided him, laughing, teasing, until the end of the song when she turned away then quickly spun back, grabbed the salesman's face, and kissed him long and hard, the muscles of her neck rippling like her tongue in his mouth, but she pulled away before he could raise his startled arms, and ran giggling back to the table. Morning didn't answer her grin; he turned his face, then ashamed, turned back with a slight smile.

The salesman stayed on the dance floor, stunned as if the red on his mouth came from a fist, but then he came at the table, lust ugly on his face. He cornered Linda like a dog after a bitch, clung to her mouth as if receiving life itself from her, his hands clutching at her arms, then running like crabs at her legs, up the smooth sand-colored hose, toward the the dark crevice. Morning saw what was coming, so he ran to the rest room.

The water gushing in the sink as he washed his face didn't cover the angry gasp, the curse, the mocking laughter, the knifing "what did you catch hold of there, john," the quick stumbling across the dance floor, the hand stabbing at the door knob.

But the salesman's face wasn't angry, just sadly confused, when he said to Morning, "She's a goddamned man. Did you know that? A fucking man." His shaking fingers gripped Morning's denim jacket. "A man. Did you know that?"

"That's okay, man," Morning said, pity twisting to contempt on his face, "I'm a woman."

The anger needed a second to travel from the salesman's tired, drunk brain to his face, and then another to transfer to his arm. But the room was narrow, and his wild swing ended against the metal towel container, but his words got through:

"You fucking queer bastard."

Morning's knee and fist moved at the same instant; the knee, faster, found soft purchase first; the knuckles swept a red trail across the salesman's blanched forehead. He fell back on the white toilet, his face framed by the pure white wall: his smeared, benumbed, moaning mouth; his eyes clenched as tight as his fist had been; the lip print perfect on his white shirt, gleaming like a deliberate clue left by a clever, romantic cat burglar at the scene of his crimes. Vomit bubbled at his shamed mouth as he hiccupped, then reeling to the side, he retched into the cavern of the urinal.

Blind madness and rage hit Morning, and without thought, he slammed his fist against the side of the salesman's face and neck, five, six, maybe seven times. His head rattled against the inside of the urinal like a marble in a cup, but wouldn't bounce out, and when Morning left, he still moaned into the blood, piss, and whiskey; a small moan, no louder than the trickle of water dripping down the drain of the urinal, but it had the same determined futile patience of the trickle, determined to wash the waste of man away, and the same futility too.

Linda had the Jag running when Morning walked
outside. She had scrubbed the smeared make-up
from her face and let her hair down. She had good
clear skin under the cosmetic mask, and under the
street lights she could have passed for a sixteen-
year-old virgin.

"Bad?" she asked.

"Bad," he said.

"Then maybe we should take a quick run up to
Tahoe. I've got a place where we can lay up for a
while. You have anything you can't leave?" Without
seeming to drive fast, she took the car quickly down
to Indian School Road, then up on the Black Canyon
Highway, north toward Flagstaff. "You have anything you can't leave?" she asked again as she laid
the car out up the expressway.

A guitar, some records, a few books, but the land-
lord would hold them for back rent. "I don't have
anything anywhere that I can't leave." He paused,
then said, "Hey, don't pull, don't pull that kind of
shit around me again."

She turned her face, clean, fresh, soft in the
muted glow from the dash, and from her scrubbed
pink mouth: "Why the fuck not?" The exhaust followed them in the silence, a trailing echo chasing its
source.

"I don't know. It was a bad scene. That cat was a
turd, but I didn't like beating up on him." He refused
to look at her, but her hair brushed past his face as
she tossed her head.

"Baby, remember that each time you laid one on
him, you laid on a blow for freedom. When all the
dumb shits like him are pounded into the sewers,
then people like us can start to live, then everybody
can live. . . ." She went on for several miles, listing

the sins of the American middle-class businessman, saying all the things Joe Morning had said so many times in the past two years. She found a bottle of Scotch under the seat and a stack of bennies in her purse, and she let him take the wheel at New River when they stopped for gas. By Flagstaff they were popped up and tight both, singing protests and laughing and crying. They shouted The Revolution is Coming to drunk Indians and sleepless Mexicans wandering the highway's edge. On a lark they detoured through Grand Canyon, whipping past complacent, sleeping campers. They stopped to stand in the moonlight over the South Rim, feeling on their high the smallness of this tiny scratch in the earth. Linda softly sang Joan Baez ballads, and an occasional echo would drift back up on the wind out of the heart of the canyon. As they walked back to the car, she stopped; stuck out her hand, and said, "Joe Morning, you are a good cat."

Morning took the hand, saying, "You too," but the thought *whoever and whatever you are* stuck in his throat.

They raced on across the desert, that night, the next day, across rock and brown earth, through receding heat mirages to the green shade and cool, cool blue of Tahoe.

Morning spent the first three or four days worrying about living in the cabin near Meeks Bay with Linda, but she showed little interest in his sex life; he relaxed. The days were easy, cool from the first cold dip in the lake until the last brandy after dinner. They both read and slept most of the time or lay in the mountain sun until the salesman's face faded from Morning's dreams. There was a party down the beach one night the second week, and Morning found himself quickly smothered in Scotch and women. He drank, he fucked, he kissed, it seemed, a thousand women that night, and the next day, sleeping off the drunk, he dreamed that one of the women had been Linda, and then it was the salesman, kissing him, and then Linda and the salesman were clawing at each others crotches, and Morning was angry, until they began tearing at his clothes . . . and he woke.

As he lifted his head off the bed, a sledge hammer crashed into his forehead. He reeled back, rolled off the bed, his eyes crossing and giggles tickling up his throat. Sitting on the floor, he giggled again, groaned, stood, then made a circling lunge toward the bathroom door, the bathroom between their bedrooms, the door he had always been so careful to lock, so careful to knock on, but this morning he slammed into it, thinking only of cold water splashing his hot, painful face.

Linda stood, unstartled, before the mirror, obviously carefully preparing her face for something. "Hello, baby," she said, smiling. "Come on in," she said.

But now it wasn't easy to think of her as Linda. She had tied her hair back with a blue velvet ribbon, and she had almost finished with her face, except for one small false eyelash which she still held expectantly in her hand. This made her face seem slightly unbalanced, but it was still a lovely woman's face, but only the face. Below ran a bare, somewhat thin, white hairless chest without even a budding titty to break the line. There was one male retarded mockery of a nipple, but a stretched diagonal scar supplanted the other. Linda's chest seemed to be winking conspiratorily at him, and Morning giggled again. And then his eyes dropped below the bare chest and the naked waist, and he laughed out loud. A huge throbbing erection cast its vote for some kind of masculinity, raised a one-armed salute to the world, as if to say, Whatever *he* is up there, I'm by God a man. Morning doubled with laughter.

"You mother-fucking straight son of a bitch, don't you laugh," Linda screamed, her voice more like a woman's than ever before. And Morning didn't pause. "Stop it!" she screamed again. "Stop it!" But Morning couldn't stop.

He laughed as if he hadn't for years. There was, no more than there naturally is, no malice in his mirth. He even expected Linda to join him, but she stomped her foot, shook her head as if it were weighted with a heavy witch doctor's mask, and screamed, "Stop it! I'll kill you! Stop it!" Then she slapped him. She slapped him with both hands, flying at him like a little dog, her fine mouth curled in hate. Morning stumbled out of the bathroom and fell back across his bed, still roaring, rolled off, and felt his head bounce off the night table, then heard the sea-like roar of oncoming unconsciousness. The last thing he remembered was a rather bony white foot with tiny red toenails swinging at his head, but he couldn't get his hand up to stop it.

Morning felt, though he couldn't think why, that he had been asleep for a long, long time, leaving his brain groggy and stupid with sleep, a troubled sleep too, a heavy bond holding him, sticky, smelling as sweet as taffy. Waking took time. More unconscious than alert, he rolled to his stomach, pushed up to his knees, then stood, and for the second time in two days, though he thought it the same day, he fell toward that bathroom door. Leaning heavily on the sink, he threw up a dribble of clear liquid, then he rinsed his mouth, drank, then immediately threw the cold water from stomach to sink. He rinsed his mouth again. Then he raised his head, not to look in the mirror, but merely to hold his head up for a change, and in the silvered glass was reflected the ghost, the face which haunted him into the Army, across the sea, his own face.

(We all see things we can't face at one time or another; even I once ran as Joe Morning ran from that image. Picture, if you can, a gargantuan draft horse ripped in half by lightning from a summer shower, then a boy that afternoon racing on a bareback pony to see the destruction and finding the front quarters and head moving and jerking and grunting, and his horse shying away in the mud, then the boy advancing with a thick live oak branch, afraid to run, for he had never known running, his code allowed no running room, stepping up to the heaving carcass and swinging his cudgel against the withers with that mad terror named courage. The carcass convulsed. A three-hundred pound sow backed out of the cavern she had gnawed into the rank flesh, entrails and lights draped from her shoulders, congealed blood and flesh dripping from her grunting mouth. A jaded sneer wrinkled her nose and she was ready to fight for her pounds of flesh. I ran; she followed me in spirit. My grandfather spoke of pigs rooting among the corpses between the trenches; I couldn't stand that.)

The visage in the mirror wasn't exactly Morning's. His neatly clipped beard was gone, and his face, it seemed, with it. Pancake foundation lay thick on his cheeks. An angry red slash gaped open in mockery of his mouth. Dark, blue-shadowed, lined, amazed eyes glared under drooping mink lashes. A long blond wig, sensuously mussed, hung to his shoulders. The hand that touched his face sported tear-drop nails of blood red. His body became aware of the rustle of a white nylon nightgown, a cotton stuffed bra pinching his chest, his crotch feeling naked in panties, and stockings encasing his legs. Even the hair on his chest and legs had been shaved.

He dried his face carefully, then walked about the cabin looking for Linda. Her things were still there, but she was gone. He did find seven color Polaroid pictures of himself in various stages of being dressed, but the eighth picture wasn't there. He looked among the empty sacks and boxes on the bedroom floor, but the picture wasn't there either. Price tags and cash receipts were though, and he calmly marveled at the price of perversion. Then he went to the kitchen and fixed breakfast.

After breakfast, he noticed that his lipstick was faded. He went to Linda's room and fixed it, then turned on the TV, opened a bottle of champagne, and drank a toast to himself: "Why not? Why the fuck not?"

"Well, why not?" I asked as dawn fled in the windows of the hotel, then I laughed.

"What are you laughing about?" he said. "It wasn't funny."

"Why not? You were drunk; drunks play games. Laugh and it ain't so serious; don't laugh and it's trouble," I said.

"I can't laugh about it. I'm still scared." He hung his head, all the way down to the table.

"Of being queer?"

"What else?"

"Oh, hell, come off it. You were used, taken, then you played a child's game coming down from trouble. That's all," I said.

"Three days ain't a game," he said. "Three days in drag."

"Three days, three months. It's all the same. If you were queer, or any queerer than the rest of us are naturally, you would have already fallen."

"You think I subconsciously knew that broad tonight was a Billy Boy, don't you?" he said into his folded arms.

"Christ, get off that shit. You want to be queer, jack, be queer. You want to be straight, be straight. But quit bugging the world about it." I stood up, rubbing my face.

"Always Krummel with the easy answer."

"It is easy. Just say what you want to do, then make yourself do it." I walked to the window. Manila Bay seemed filled with mud that morning.

"Maybe easy for you, but not easy for people with feeling, sensitive people."

"That's cute, boy. You're just too sensitive to live. Well, jump out the goddamn window. If you will excuse the metaphor, Morning, you are a pain in the ass sometimes."

"That's because that's the only place you got any feeling, fucker," he said, looking up. "You're the one who might as well be dead."

"Yeah, it's tough all over." I walked to the bathroom to shower, and when I came out, he was gone. "May God watch out for the innocents," I said to the empty room. I caught the next bus back to Angeles, knowing that the next time I saw Morning, he would be hating me again. I knew too much about him. But then I always had.

9

PREPARATION

Let me warn you now. Three days, then out of this damnable traction rigging. The warrior's necessity: Mobility, in the form of a wheel chair.

Gallard said: A wheel chair, fool, not a chariot, not a tank, not a war horse, but a wheel chair.

We do with what we can.

"No drinking," he said, "no fighting with the nurses. Understand."

"I always understand."

"You never understand," he said. "Don't drive it off the bluff."

"Don't drive what off the bluff," Abigail said, walking into the already crowded room, a childish grin bright on her face, her hands clasped behind her.

"Watch him," Gallard greeted her.

"Yes, watch me, wench. I get wheels."

"Rolling to hell," he said.

"My home," I said.

"Man's fate?" he asked.

"Destiny is a kinder word."

"Fate is death. Destiny is life. You've got them confused," he replied.

"God confused them, not me."

"What are you two talking about?" Abigail asked.

"Nothing," Gallard said, "Krummel's fly is down again, and his death wish is exposed." He smiled, but he couldn't meet my eyes.

"Impossible. You've got it in traction."

"I wish I could," he said, walking out. "I've got more idiots to repair, more fodder to rearm."

Abigail turned back to me, a question cocking one blond eyebrow, a question she was afraid to ask. She slipped a pale pink rose from behind her. "An offering, sire," she said, then curtsied.

"Thorny," I said. "A warning."

"A promise."

"Thank you," I said reaching for her hand.

"Three days, my liege, then I wheel you away to my flower castle." She kissed my hand. "Three days. But now I must hurry to prepare another room for another knight back from the crusades, a crippled knight from the Holy Land." She kissed my hand again, then bit the base of my thumb. "Three days. . . ."

"Hey," I said, stopping her at the door. "You're as silly as I am."

"Yes," she said. "Don't you just love it." And then she was gone.

In three days, free, free of bed and burden, for then my confession will be over, the tale concluded, and the judgment will begin. I will be glad, I think, to be finished. To think about it makes me smile. . . .

But even as I write these lines, a scream spears down the hall, holding my hands from the machine. Then words, slurred with pain and drugs: "Please, God, let me die." Then a closing door muffles the cries.

My guilt seems so petty next to that cry. I bear only the guilt of Joe Morning, but that voice bears the world.

As I write these pages, I find that I love him both more and less as I begin to see behind the masks he troubled to wear. And now my hands are heavy, and his voice whispers to me, ". . . too much, too much, . . ." Then another echo. "Now I come down at night to make sure I'm not making a face, just to be sure." The task of masks, never knowing whose face will meet your own in the mirror, then for Morning to find a woman's face where his used to shine. How did you stand it, Joe, how? Why did you let it happen, and once done, why did you let it matter? Evil is in the world, Joe Morning, and man isn't meant to play with it. You touched it so often, sinned against and sinner, true innocent because you thought the world innocent and you guilty. You asked me, Do you see evil everywhere, or reflect it? And I answer your ghost now, Both, like all men, even you. And now I remember something I had forgotten. You said that the most terrible, frightening thing about that woman's face in the mirror was that it was still you. You were right, but you misunderstood why. You were scared inside because you realized that everyone had always seen through all your masks. All your trouble in vain. Why wish yourself grief? And in a world where so many are so ready to give it. And, God, sometimes I think I gave the most, and sometimes I think I saved you from the worst grief of all, and sometimes I just don't know.

And again the echo: "Too much, too much." But it seems to be my voice I hear. Yes, I'll admit to it. Too much, too much. I said that, me, Jacob Slagsted Krummel, sometimes warrior, ofttimes clown. Too, too much.

But I have my duty . . . And damned little else, I hear you say, And damned little else. I'll even say it with you: AND DAMNED LITTLE ELSE! But your voice was bitter, and I just laughed, laughed like hell, and now I'm ready to go again. So screw you. My duty makes me free; what chains of delusion do you wear?

Back at Base after the abortive Break in Manila, four bits of news awaited me. Capt. Saunders was back, from the second unexplained trip to the States. Novotny had made Spec/5 (Specialist 5th Class; same pay as a buck sergeant, but without the rank), and I had been promoted to Acting S/Sgt (Staff Sergeant, Acting; the rank without the pay, of course). The fourth piece of news had to wait until the next day.

I talked Novotny, rather Cagle did, into going to the NCO Club for a steak in celebration, and a few drinks in preparation. Cagle convinced him by saying, "Sure, Specialist 5th Class, run on to the fucking lifer's club, you fucking lifer." Novotny said, "Who's a fucking lifer? Screw you, I go where I want to." Thus we went, and there Capt. Saunders found us.

He made Novotny buy a round, then he bought two. He spoke about my beer gut, Novotny's Dear John and such, then asked, as we spoke about the Coke bottle crisis, "Why did you volunteer to be the goat?" But he didn't specify sacrificial or Judas.

"To keep Morning out of Leavenworth," Novotny answered for me, surprising me with his knowledge.

"Must be a good friend," Saunders said.

I answered his accusation with silence and a round of drinks, then I went on in silence as he asked about the cigarettes and the note from the adjutant in Manila waiting on his desk. He supposed he might work out Article 15s, Company Punishment, instead of courts-martial, purely because he didn't have time nor energy enough to draw the courts up. I kept my mouth shut again. Novotny asked why no time, but Saunders refused to answer. He asked me to bring Morning in after the company formation at 1300.

"Why are we having a formation?" I asked.

"What formation?" he said.

We soon managed to get drunk enough to forget about rank, privilege, and pay grades. Saunders was a strange officer, part buffoon, part drunk, and yet (with appropriate apologies to all concerned, particularly Joe Morning) he was the sort of man who would have had told of him in Georgia, "He runs his niggers so damn good 'cause he's part nigger himself." He treated Novotny like a son and me like a younger brother, with that familial respect and trust we couldn't resist. We would have, as they say, followed him into hell that night, but not necessarily the next day. He did give us a ride back to the barracks in his MGB. As he screamed away, Novotny said, "Might follow him to hell and back, cowboy, but I ain't ever riding with him again. Ain't ever."

The next morning at work I told Morning that Capt. Saunders wanted to see us. He said nothing, acting as if he were involved in copying. I added that we would probably get Article

15s because something was up. He, I, everyone had seen the four shiny new radio vans parked in the motor pool, had seen, and understood they meant Vietnam.

He turned to me, removed his cans and said, sneering like a phony villain, "It's so nice to know important people, Sgt. Krummel, to have friends in high places, friends who really care."

"Just show up in Capt. Saunders' office at 1430."

As I walked away, Novotny said, "Nice to have friends, huh?" Morning heard, but acted as if he didn't; I could do no less.

The company formation at 1300, for reasons of national security, was held in the mess hall. The Filipino KPs had been herded out to the volley-ball court, the louvers closed, and armed guards posted at every exit. The blackboard set up behind Saunders announced in small but clear letters: TOP SECRET. We were verbally reminded of the classification of the forthcoming talk, then it began.

It amounted, simply, to Vietnam for the 721st Communication Security Detachment, except that we became, in name only, the 1945th Communication Training Detachment (Provisional). Our assignment in the Republic of the Philippines was over, and our duties would be handled by Filipino operators now, ops that we would train as training for the time when we would begin training South Vietnamese ops. That time would come after we had set up a mobile det in Vietnam. But still things weren't simple.

Because of the political implications of snooping on one's own army in a country where the army is in almost constant stages of revolt against the government, Diem had demanded the highest sort of security for our operation. "We will not," Saunders said, "be used as an arm of the political police," but no one had suggested that we would. For reasons of national security, Vietnamese, South, our Det would have to be located, not in Saigon where lovely chicks paraded in *au dais,* but the south of the central highlands, west by southwest of Nha Trang in the foothills of the Lang Bian mountains, hopefully out of the way of both the Vietcong and the bulk of the South

Vietnamese generals. We would also travel to Vietnam in civilian clothes, but our old uniforms would be waiting for us at the new Det.

The major burden of perimeter defense would fall on three reinforced companies of provincial militia (and their families), but due to lack of training and weapons, etc. (the "etc.," patriotism, I assumed), we would have to be ready to be responsible for our own defense. We were going to soldier as well as clerk, for a change.

Our present operations closed as of this day, and one month of intensive training would begin immediately. Basic combat infantryman training in the mornings, working in the new vans, training Filipino ops, listening to tapes of South Vietnamese army tapes, and learning new net operations in the afternoons.

"Remember," Saunders said at the end, "that even though we are advisers in this no-war war, we have the right to fight back if attacked, and if we aren't mentally and physically ready to fight back, a bunch of you are going to find yourselves dead. If you want to stay alive: get ready." If he expected a Hollywood cheer, his face didn't show any disappointment when he didn't get it. "And I'll be kicking asses and taking names to be sure you do get ready." He smiled at the Head Moles, out of their holes for today, but they didn't smile back. They didn't go to Vietnam either, or to Hill 527, which was all I saw of Vietnam.

Comments as we left:

Novotny: Sorry, man, I'm too short to go.

Cagle: Reenlist, stupid.

Quinn: Big rumble tonight. Kick some ass, huh, Frankie?

Franklin: I'm a lover, not a fighter. I got a purple heart for the clap to prove it.

Haddad: My God, it'll cost me a fortune to go, a fortune, my God.

Peterson: Geez. . . .

Levenson and Collins: . . . (Nothing, because they both, like Novotny, had less than a month to go before their discharges.)

Morning: Fucking America off again to make the world safe

for General Motors and AT&T. Tattletales to political spies in one easy step.

Quinn: I got lighter fluid and a lighter, mother, if you want to file your stinking protest right here in the hall.

Peterson: Geez. . . .

Krummel: Knock it off, you idiots.

Morning: You're sick, Quinn, sick.

Haddad: Wonder if the chaplain would understand my situation.

Krummel: Knock it off.

Quinn: I ain't a coward, and I ain't a Commie, and I ain't so sick I can't bust you up in the middle, Morning.

Cagle: Save your verbal enemas for the enemy, you guys.

Someone: Ah, shit, who gives a good goddamn?

Krummel: (whispering) I do.

Morning: (shouting) Me, mother-fucker. I fucking won't go.

Someone: Ah, shit.

In his office, fired by the war lecture, Capt. Saunders was less friendly than the night before. He gave us a long lecture on the dangers of the black market. One might damage the Philippine economy; one might fall in with evil companions, be beaten, robbed, or even killed; one might also get his butt sacked in this man's army. But we were lucky this time, and we could accept company punishment under Article 15. I quickly answered yes, but Morning, as quickly, said no.

Rattled for a moment, then angry, Saunders shook his head, then said "Shit, Morning, go to your quarters. Confined till further orders." As Morning left, Saunders turned to me. "What's wrong with that kid, Krummel? I don't want to convene a court for him. Not now. Damn. What is wrong with him?"

"I understand his mother used to ask the same question, sir."

He smiled. "Can you get him to change his mind? Talk to him?" he asked, turning his chair around so he could stretch his legs.

"No, sir."

"You can't, or you won't?"

"Same thing, isn't it?"

The back of his neck wrinkled, then reddened. "The major will throw the book, the desk, and the chair at him, and there is no one else to sit," he mumbled without moving.

"Yes, sir."

We stayed that way, a sweat stain bleeding across his back, I standing at that mockery of ease, At ease!, sharing a common burden, unable to name it, only at ease to acknowledge its mutuality with silence. He turned, blushed, said, "Get the hell out of here, Krummel. I've got a court-martial to draw up. Tell Sgt. Tetrick to come in on your way out."

I did as he said.

Tetrick said to me later, "You best let that kid fall back in his own shit. Here, he can only get you trouble; over there, he can get you killed."

"Nope."

"Why?" I asked him in his room. "For Christ's sake, why?"

"They can't hurt me, man."

"They're not trying." I shut the door behind me.

(I wanted to say, so many things . . . *True, they can't hurt you; they don't need to. The world isn't unjust, it just doesn't care. You walk around expecting injustice, baby, you get it. Just because a man is on the other side doesn't mean he is your enemy. You already understand that about the Communists, but you won't give your friends the same understanding. You can't make the world fit you, you have to fit the world, and it'll crush you if you don't. You already know that, too. I don't ask you to stop fighting; just be sensible about the way you fight.* But I don't suppose I've any right to ask him to be sensible; I never was either. I should have said: *Okay, man, you're wrong, wrong, wrong, but I'm with you 'cause you got no one else.* But I couldn't say that; I could only do it, and keep doing it, and keep doing it, until the end of time. Don't knock the artful cliché.)

In seven days he walked into his summary court-martial, charged with possession of more cigarettes than allowed under

Clark Air Base Regulation 295–13. His face was as calm and reposed as only anger could make it, a smooth furious mask. I remembered the night he backed the airman against the wall and slapped him insensible. In the room (artfully enough, Lt. Dottlinger's office), he found our cigarettes, the younger of the two cops from Pasay City, and a very (and I've never quite figured this out), very frightened major. Confronted with the major's fright, and the cop's lack of cockiness and lack of ease, Morning became twice as calm. Though he claimed that he had a plan from the beginning, I believe he didn't know what he was going to do until he saw the major's flushed face, shaking hands, and a pulse that bounded even into the tiny whiskey-busted veins snaking across his pitted nose. I believe that as strongly as I've ever believed anything about him. This is important because I learned my greatest lesson about guerrilla warfare from this: attack establishments with absurdity.

The major read the charges and specifications in a halting voice, then asked Morning how he pleaded. Morning paused for a moment—I know this because I, like an idiot, was listening with a water glass against the office wall from the Day Room—then, in the voice he seemed to reserve for such occasions, blissfully, peacefully, arrogantly, innocently said, "Oh, not guilty, sir. Not guilty at all."

(I could barely contain my laughter, sure that he had discovered what I had about our arrest.)

The major went on, somehow, placing the damning evidence before Morning and his cocky smile.

"What are you grinning about, soldier?" the major asked. "What's so funny?"

"Isn't smiling permitted when at ease, sir?"

"Attention," the major hissed.

When he finished his presentation, the major then asked Morning what evidence he had of his innocence.

"Oh, no evidence, sir. I'm just not guilty, not guilty at all."

(I swear, I swear I heard the major's jaw hit the desk.)

"You don't . . . have . . . any evidence?" he asked, his words muffled as if his hands covered his face.

"Innocent men need no evidence, sir, none at all."

After a long silent minute, the major went on as if he hadn't heard, reading very quickly what he had already written on the back of the charge sheet: guilty, etc.; reduced in rank to private E-1; fined fifty dollars; and to be confined at hard labor for fifteen days; to be confined to quarters immediately pending approval of sentencing by approving authority.

Morning said, in a wonderfully bored way, "Oh, thank you, sir, very much."

As Morning left the Orderly Room, I came in from the Day Room. The major still sat at the desk. I asked to speak to him, and before he could say no, told him that I possessed evidence concerning Pfc Morning's court-martial, legal evidence, really, a statement from the Dartmouth lawyer suggesting that evidence against Pfc Morning had been obtained by illegal methods.

"Get out of here, Sgt. whoever you are," he said, dazed as if he had been sentenced, "Just get away from me."

"It's pertinent, sir," I said. "The approving authority will. . . ."

But he cut me off. "Get out!"

I left, but I put the statement in the same mail to Okinawa, where it did prove to be pertinent. I dug the bird colonel's reply out of the files later. The findings of the summary court were, as I already knew, reversed. A handwritten personal note had been added at the bottom, addressed directly to the major, stating in effect that the bird colonel didn't know what the hell was going on down there, but if another screwed up court-martial like this one came through, he would fly down to find out. The major took a month's leave, for reasons of health, immediately afterward.

(Ah, Joe Morning, Joe Morning, what a team we were, what a team we could have been. I could have saved you from yourself, with a little help from you, but you never gave an inch. When the reversal came down you had to roar into my room, screaming about me getting off your back, then ran drunkenly back to your bed for another big sleep. I gave you two days, then a bucket of water in your face, and ran you all that day, till your tongue hung down like a dog's and you didn't have another word to say, ran you till blood dripped into your boots from scraped knees where you'd fallen rather than quit. I told you, "My name is Sgt. Krummel. My great-great grandfather was half Comanch', and they buried him with a blond scalp in his hands, and trooper I'm gonna have yours. You think I been on your back, son, well this child is gonna show what that means. I'm gonna give you something to cry about." But he, of course, wouldn't. He was like that. But I did make him sweat.)

We began to get ready. It wasn't bad. I found out why, in spite of my trouble in Manila, I had been promoted. Tetrick had made me Training NCOIC, which meant that I would also be in charge of perimeter defense when we set up the new Det. When asked why, he said, "I can trust you to fight. They didn't educate the guts out of you yet. Sometimes you're stupid, but you'll fight." How do you know? "Because I been there," he said. Will we have to fight? "You know how secret this move is. The girls at the Keyhole are talking about putting in 1040s for Saigon. If they know here, they'll know there. The Vietcong are good. They'll make these kids look like old ladies the first time. All we can hope is to out firepower them the first time, or there won't be a second time. Make them understand. They don't listen to me any more. Make them get ready. Make them. For my sake." He seemed already in mourning; he looked old for the first time I could remember. I believed him; I tried to get them ready.

The same sort of sadness, which had tinted Tetrick's voice, appeared in the troops. Morning called me Sgt. Krummel now, and was surly every chance he had, but his heart wasn't in the game. Novotny reenlisted, saying, one night drunk in the Keyhole, "Can't let the little fart go over by himself," and Cagle cried where no one could see him, whispering, "Dumb fucking cowboy." Collins and Levenson climbed on their flight home with sadness pinching their faces as if they would never forgive themselves for missing their war, but we were sad too and forgave them and sent our hopes home with them.

(Southern Wyoming in the spring, green hills rolling away, and the smell of the new grass as sharp as the winter cold still hiding in the wind, and new colts awkward as teen-age girls

under a cobalt sky. Rain on the summer bricks in Brooklyn
and thirty-five cent shots of raw whiskey in a sad old bar
across from the Navy yard and Jersey girls smelling of Juicy
Fruit and Johnson's baby powder. Pale blond faces and hands
catching blond hair, girls whose faces glowed with politics
equated with love, their breath laced by ripe beer and stale
cigarettes, their eyes smiling at the sound of his guitar. Live
oak trees gnarled along the Nueces bottoms, and my mother's
cherry cobbler, my crazy brothers as innocent as puppies.
Levi's, white cowboy shirts, handmade boots, and forty-dollar
Stetsons jammed in the pickup, off for a VFW dance on
Saturday night, Lone Star beer, long-legged girls named Regan
Bell, Marybeth, and Jackie . . . all our hopes flying home on a
silver C-124. There was mourning.)

But with the sadness came a wild elation, too. It may have
been only the physical conditioning, or the release from the
tedium of rotating trick, or merely the idea of a change of
scenery, but there were nearly one hundred brown, happy
faces looking up at me each morning at 0600 as I climbed on
the platform to lead the exercises.

PT, then a five-mile run, and the rest of the morning whiled
away learning about new ways to die. Tetrick lectured and
lectured about booby traps, tried to teach us to make our own
in the hope that we might understand the psychology behind
Malayan Gates, Punji spikes, foot traps, and the ever-mined
corpses. Two Special Forces sergeants came down from Okinawa to teach us a bit of the combination karate, judo, and
barroom brawling they had learned. It wouldn't, as a few of
the troops quickly learned, make a superman out of the average guy, but it did serve to remind us, John Wayne aside, that
elbows, knees, feet, and teeth are more formidable weapons
than the right cross.

A new shipment of M-14s had to be cleaned and fired again,
since our usual armory consisted of old M-1s and .30 carbines,
and even a few old grease guns. For sentimental reasons,
Tetrick would not part with his grease gun, and a few of the
officers preferred to keep the light carbine. We also picked up
four M-60 machine guns, a supply of Claymore mines, five
81mm and two 60mm mortars, but we weren't able to find

even one of the new M-79 grenade launchers. Someone in Okinawa kept promising them, but they never came. With the new equipment came new men to flesh out the tricks to fifteen men each, kids whose names I barely learned. Novotny had my old Trick now, and I was left with clichés about the loneliness of command. You can't have everything, Krummel.

At the range one afternoon, my old Trick was firing the M-14 on semi-automatic at pop-up silhouette targets at thirty to seventy yards. The targets stayed up for two seconds or less. Morning was on the line, and I was at the control panel, letting him fire until he missed. He had hit thirteen in a row when Tetrick came up. Morning hit five more in a row; like a cocky young gunfighter out of a bad western his movements were consciously slow and arrogant until the targets came up, and then arms and feet and rifle were slick and smooth and snake-quick. Tetrick told me to give him two at once, one thirty yards to the right, the other fifty to the left. Morning didn't even jump, but took the right one first, then hit in front of the second, but the ricochet took it down.

"Pretty good," Tetrick shouted to him. "But when it's for real, take the close one first."

Morning said sure, but with such sarcasm that I knew he would get killed, now, rather than do as Tetrick asked.

Tetrick took off his fatigue cap, then rubbed the fringe of hair, mumbling, "Kids like that took all my hair, Krummel. Now I'm bald. Shit, I'm getting old." He said that we had received a shipment of the new AR-15s that the Special Forces had been using in Vietnam and half a dozen shotguns. "Which do you want?" he asked as Morning walked up.

"Get one for each foot, Sgt. Krummel," Morning said. "Shit, that little old AR-15 bullet is better than a dum-dum. Shit, when it comes out of a man, it takes about fifty percent of the blood, bone, and flesh—no, that's semi-liquid gelatin I believe the Army calls it—right out the other side. And you know what shotguns do at twenty yards, don't you, Sarge? Shit, one for each hand."

"Morning, Morning, Morning," I said. "What am I going to do with you." I called him to attention. "What am I going to do with you."

"Push ups?" Tetrick inquired with a professional interest.

"He's already done about two hundred today," I said.

"Run him?"

"Another five miles?"

Tetrick laughed. "He is sure gonna be in some shape by the time we get over there. Well, do something with him. *You* do something; I don't want to see him." He shuffled away.

I turned back to Morning's face, which showed as little as did mine. "Pfc Morning, I want a hole, six feet long, six feet wide, and most of all six feet deep. You'll find an entrenching tool in the three-quarter and lots of dirt right where you're standing. Move." He moved with clean hate like a halo around him.

I went back out to the range at 2200. Morning sat on the pile of dirt, smoking a cigarette, looking up at the stars as if he were on a cruise ship.

"Lovely night, Sgt. Krummel," he said, but his body sagged in the harsh light from my jeep headlights.

"Did you dig me a beautiful hole, trooper?"

"Aw, cut that role-playing shit out, Krummel, you're driving me nuts." Sudden anger curled up with the smoke from the cigarette, and there was almost a plea in his fatigued voice.

"Fill it up."

"Fuck you."

"Fill it up. Right now."

"You're not going to break me. You can't even bend me." He waved the small shovel like a club. "You can't touch me."

"I already know that. Either fill up the hole, or get ready for a year in the stockade."

"You're joking."

"Try me, boy. I'll bust you wide open. Fill it up."

He hesitated, then began flinging dirt into the hole. I stood over him the whole time.

"There," he sighed, throwing a last shovelful onto the pile of loose dirt.

"There what?"

"There, sergeant."

"Fine. Would you like a ride back to the barracks, Pfc?"

"Not with you, sergeant. Not with you."

I double-timed him back to the barracks. He kept his mouth shut this time, but he couldn't close his face.

"You can hate me all you want to, trooper, but keep your mouth shut. You're going to die for being stupidly stubborn, but I don't want you rubbing off on anyone else. As long as you keep your mouth shut, only you are hurt. But what about Franklin and Peterson and those new kids? You want them dead because they won't obey orders on principle? Answer me, trooper."

"I'm sure I don't know, sergeant."

"Yeah, I'm sure you don't. Dismissed."

What could I do with him? Would he have been different if we exchanged places? Does power corrupt, not just morally, but mentally too? Not just the powerful, but the weak also? I didn't feel corruption creeping in my soul. All I could feel was responsibility, fatigue, and hopeless desire to fight for money and let the governments go to hell.

But then it was time to go.

We flew to Saigon at night, then were hustled into an empty hangar with all our equipment, including the four vans. For twenty-four hours we lounged in our cheap civilian suits provided by the government, ate cold C-rations, slept on piles of barracks bags, and used five-gallon buckets for latrines while Saunders tried to find the trucks which were to carry us to the new Det. Our tribulations were just beginning.

When the trucks came, they were driven in one end of the hangar, loaded, then driven out the other end. The vans were to go next, but two of them wouldn't start, so we spent another six hours without barracks bags to lie on, without cold C-rations to gag on, but we still had the clammy cans to shit in, and one Lister bag of tepid water which seemed to have absorbed the stink from our bodies and the bitterness of the constant bitching from the men.

But then it was time to go, again.

We were loaded in trucks whose beds were covered with sandbags, then laced tightly shut, locked in our own stink. I assigned myself to my old Trick's truck, since I was in charge of assigning NCOs to keep the men from getting out of the trucks. While doing this, I noticed that the lead truck in the convoy pushed a heavy trailer arrangement in front of it like a cowcatcher in front of a train. A mine-catcher, I supposed, but I kept my suppositions to myself. The sandbagged floors and the company of ARVN troops riding shotgun in armored personnel carriers had already started talk, thought about death. But, as usual, dying was going to seem the easy part.

Sixteen men secured in the course, heavy heat, the constant sift of the sand, and the stench of each other and the tarstink of the canvas isn't a Sunday afternoon drive. Piss calls were infrequent, and we ate more cold C-rations and drank more water tasting of tin and dirt and last week's wash. Uncomfortable trip but uneventful, we drove through the first night, the next day, and that evening. Men slept, but a rough, fitful sleep as they tried to rest on the sandbags, or lean against the ribs, or each other. When the feeble light creeping through the canvas belied the raging sun above, some of them tried to play cards, but sandy dust and sweaty fingers chewed all the spots from the deck. Others tried to read, but raw-rimmed eyes couldn't follow the leaping, bounding words. Most sat silent in the grime of their bodies and in the blackness of their thoughts, wondering about the sandbags and wishing for the heft of a weapon in their hands. We all cursed—bitterly, without jokes —at everything, until the curses became as much a sound of the trip as the random rattling of the truck. Even asleep, each bump, each rut, each chuck hole drew forth epithets from sleepy mouths which never noted words passing.

But when the cowcatcher caught a mine and the convoy slammed to a halt, no one said a word. A single drawn breath robbed the truck of air, and we gasped like dying men. One man farted, another belched. Stomachs grumbled, guts contracted and growled in protest.

A few rounds were fired in front, then steady chatter and little pops as if from toy guns, then silence again. The Trick tried to climb out of the truck over me, Franklin leading the way, shouting that he had to pee. I pushed him back into the crowd, kept pushing until they all were down, faces hugging the sandbags. Fear rose like a visible cloud from the huddled bodies, but I made them stay, while I dropped out the back and crouched under the truck. Inside, Franklin groaned, trying to hold his bladder, and Quinn shouted not to pee on him, but no one laughed, not even Quinn.

The road, a track through a jungled forest, was gray in the light from a moon as big and bright as a searchlight. *No one ambushes by moonlight*, I thought, never thinking that those who would would do it in a way I wasn't ready for yet. Murmurs, shrouded by canvas, seemed to fill the space between the darkened trucks. Bodyless voices swept on a ghostly wind, turned, then turned back, till they seemed my voice drifting away from me. For an instant I was drunk with fear, and I knew the only way I could control it was to do something, but there was nothing to do but hold my bladder, keep my peace, and wait. Someone ran down the road toward me, stopping at each truck, then angry, frightened whispers sawed the night like the alarm cries of huge insects. Tetrick ran flatfooted like an old cop chasing a young pickpocket, but an old cop who firmly intended to catch that pickpocket. I stood, whispered an order to stay down inside the truck, then stepped out to meet him, already feeling better.

"What's up?" I asked, my tone calmer than I expected.

"Nothing," he said. "Just a mine. No real damage, but it will take about half an hour to get the truck going again."

"Who fired?"

"Nervous fingers. One ARVN squad ran into another. One dead, four wounded, and lucky at that. Idiots," he said. "Let the troops out for piss call or they will be pissing all over themselves. Tell 'em, for God's sake, stay on the road; the ditches may be mined." But as he said this, two squads of ARVN troops ran past in both ditches heading toward the rear of the convoy.

"Guess not," I said. As I looked, I saw a white track disappearing quickly in the forest, a trail. "But I guess we're lucky."

"Keep 'em on the road anyway. Then get down to the weapons truck—first one in front of the vans—and get yours. Okay?" he asked, then ran off without an answer, his feet slapping against the dry road.

"Okay, you old ladies," I said, unlacing the canvas, "pull

down your bloomers, and come out to pee-pee. Trouble's all over, but stay on the road. Novotny, keep them on the road." As I trotted away, I heard Franklin's voice, high and loud with relief, "Sgt. Krummel, Quinn tried to rape me while I was laying down," and Quinn's answer, "And I woulda, if you hadn't been shaking like a twelve-year-old virgin," and then his raw laughter. "Knock it off," I shouted over my shoulder, not even hoping that they would.

Coming back, I tried to be casual, carrying the Armalite by its handle like a suitcase, four grenades bagging the thin pockets of the civilian suit, two full clips sticking out of my back pockets like fifths of cheap whiskey. Morning commented, of course, "Mamma Krummel back to protect his little brood," but I laughed at him. He expected push-ups and an ass-chewing, and grumbled, "It wasn't a joke," and I said, "Yes, I don't think so either." We smoked and talked quietly, our talk like the chatter from behind the other trucks, relaxed, confident, safe, but this cool babble couldn't cover the raw grunt and moan which slipped out of the forest to the right. No one spoke, then everyone, but the metallic clang of a round snapping into the Armalite stopped the noise. I sent Cagle for Tetrick, Morning to the truck cab for a flashlight, and the men into the opposite ditch, then gave Novotny two of the grenades.

Quinn's tooth flashed in the moonlight as he said, "Frankie. Frankie? Where you at, you ugly bastard."

One of the new men mumbled that he had been seen drifting down the moonlit trail. I gave Quinn the third grenade, then Morning the last when he came back with the flashlight.

"Five yards apart on me," I said. "Quinn last. No light yet. Morning behind me. Let's go," I said, then stepped off down the trail.

The trail seemed twice as white as I moved between the dark walls of foliage, following the faint trail of sharp prints made by new shoes in the dust, then the wavering serpentine track where he had peed as he strolled. The trail bent to the left, and as I cautiously slipped around the corner, I didn't need Morning's flash to see.

Malayan Gates, they call them, a bamboo pole tied to a tree beside the trail, a bamboo pole with three or four twelve-inch bamboo stakes lashed to its end, then bent away from the trail and tied to another tree and a trip wire. Franklin hadn't finished, and urine still dripped into the black pool at his feet where he knelt, his grey face turned back toward me, one arm pegged to his stomach where he had been holding himself, and the points of the stakes gleamed out of his back two inches above his belt. His eyes were wide and alive when I first saw him, but before I could move, they were wide, white and dead in his face. A muscle spasm gripped his mouth, and a rumbling, sputtering release from the large bowel mocked the prayer his mouth seemed to form, but his eyes were dead in his face. Morning quietly said "Jesus Christ" behind me. Novotny, stricken, mumbled "Told him to stay on the road. Told him . . . Told him . . . Told . . . ." Quinn dropped his grenade and started to run. I laid the butt of the rifle into his stomach as he reached my side, laid it harder than I should have, but a rage clutched at my muscles, and I wouldn't have been surprised if I had started firing into Franklin's offending body. Quinn dropped to his knees and gagged.

"Take him back," I said, my voice colder than I could remember it ever being. "Take the son of a bitch back." I slapped Morning's shoulder and pushed Novotny. Their eyes came back to me from Franklin, then they started to stumble toward him. "No, you bastards, no! Quinn! Quinn! Take him back. Take the son of a bitch back."

Like two owls dazed by sudden lightning, they asked, "Who?"

"Quinn," I said once more. "Take him back. Have someone sit on him. Bring me a poncho and a roll of field wire. Now, goddamn you, now! Move!" I shoved at them until they moved, cursed them in various tongues, then they moved back down the trail, Quinn between them.

I waited with Franklin's body. God, he stunk. He offended me with his rankness, his malodorous halo clinging to the trees. He stunk worse than any animal I've ever gutted. If I hadn't been sure that he lay on a pressure release mine, I would have kicked him until he stopped emitting that fetid, slimy, smell. I might have anyway, but Tetrick ran up, two sergeants behind him.

He stopped, clicked on the safety of his grease gun, then said, softly, "The bastard."

We stood there, looking and feeling guilty for looking, until Novotny came back with the roll of wire and Morning with the poncho. I made a loop, then tossed it over Franklin's head, around his neck.

"Not his neck," Morning said, but nothing more.

We rolled the wire back to the road and made the troops lie back down in the ditch. Then I tried to pull the wire, flinching like a nine-year-old kid firing his first shotgun, flinching as he does until he learns that it is the flinch not the shotgun which hurts him. The second time I didn't flinch.

Nothing happened. The wire jumped toward me like a slim black snake. Each of us, in our own way, jerked away from it.

"It came untied," Tetrick said. "Or broke. I'll get it."

"I will."

Once more down that white trail dividing the darkness, the moon still bright in the sky, still searching, stars twinkling ordinarily, even the small sounds of the jungled forest peeping out once more. I tied a knot that would not slip, then walked back.

I pulled again, huddled with the others in the ditch. The explosion was lost, soft among limbs and leaves, but a naked flash climbed the sky, and the earth trembled under us. Novotny and I went for the body, but there was none: A charred log, not hard like wood, but soft and rubbery as we rolled it on the poncho, and it squeaked, rubber against rubber. Warm rain fell on my hands as I bent over the body, and it would be the next day before I remembered crying.

"Told him, told him to stay, stay on the road," Novotny gasped as we carried the surprising load, too light for man, too heavy for whatever it was.

"You told him; he didn't; forget it."

"Don't know how," was all he answered.

The troops, officers, non-coms and all, here is the first loss, forgot the standing orders against bunching up, bunched like cattle in the rain, lowing, and chewing their fearful lips.

"You?" Capt. Saunders said to Tetrick. Saunders stood
among the troops, but they moved away when he spoke. He
moved back among them.

Tetrick's head gleamed in the moonlight and his words were
half lost under a dropped face. "Too tired," he said. "Krummel, Krummel will."

Sure, sure, Krummel will. Yes, Krummel, savior of his
brood, mother-hen to the world and that miscarriage in the
poncho. Fuck yes, Krummel will!

I stripped back the poncho, and waited until the sight stuck
in every mind, then said, not too loud but loud enough:

"Not much to send home to Mamma, is it?"

No one misunderstood. Now we were ready.

10

VIETNAM

For the next ten hours, until the convoy reached Hill 527, I sat in the stifling darkness of the truck, glad of the darkness, pleased with the heat of my own body. None of the ordinary things, none of the expected emotions came to me; no vomiting, only those few warm tears no more real than the glycerin dripped on an actor's cheeks. First there had been cold anger, then calculated madness, and now nothing, so much nothing that I was glad when Morning noted my silence and said, remembering that I knew his secrets, hoping that I would now have a secret guilt too, "What's the matter, Krummel? War not to your taste? The intellectual warrior get sick to his dilettante stomach? Don't be sick, man, that's your war back there, your lovely war incarnate in that sliver of flesh. People die in wars, you idiot. . . ."

Even then I couldn't raise an answer, a spark of feeling.

Oh, I had things to say: No, Morning, not my war, baby, but yours; he wasn't killed in a war, he was murdered.

But these were thoughts without feeling.

Of course it must rain our first two days at Hill 527, air mattresses and shelter halves must leak, and men sweat and stink in ponchos, or stand naked in hard, cold rain, or fall prey to malaria and cat fever and fungus. Boots must mildew, and meals be cold, and mud ball at our feet and creep up our legs and stick to our fingers and clog in our eyes. Sleep must come in nightmare snatches, and guard be stood, and waiting drift in long cross hours, and of course it must rain without pause for two days and two nights square in the middle of the dry season. And of course the sun must shine, eventually. And it all must be endured.

Hill 527 and its twin, 538, were not really big hills, but tall rises in the middle of a large clearing where a jungled forest encroached on a grassy plain. Five hundred and thirty-eight was a gentle rise, an easy slope up and down from all sides, and 527 was the same except for a flat triangular peak like a surrealistic nipple smack in the middle of it. The sides of the nearly equilateral triangle were approximately one hundred yards long. A forty degree slope separated the flat nipple-top from the more gentle slopes below it. On the first two muddy days we laid wire around the steeper slope, dividing us from the two companies of provincial militia already entrenched in a rough circle about fifty yards further out and down. Outside of their wire and their mud and sandbag parapets, the grass and the occasional patches of brush had been cut down for about one hundred yards. The jungle was on three sides of the clearing, east, west, and north, but on the open side the land sloped away in rolling, grassy hills. The jungled forest came to within four or five hundred yards of the compound on the north and east, but because of Hill 538, it was between nine hundred and one thousand yards away on the west. Our antenna field was to be built on 538, and then the whole hill mined.

All in all, it wasn't a bad position. The peak was high enough so that we, if we had to, could fire on the lower slopes without chewing up the protective coating of Vietnamese militia. The militia had good wire out, and we had wire ten yards wide, two fences and four rows of concertina on the slope off the peak. (The harried American major who advised the Vietnamese major commanding the militia said he wished that we hadn't strung the wire between our two forces. The Vietnamese major thought it an insult to both the patriotism and the fighting ability of his men. Capt. Saunders showed them his orders signed by the admiral in charge of American forces in the Pacific, the area military commander, and the major's commanding officer, so the wire stayed, and we stayed alive.) We dug a four-foot deep trench along the inner edge of the wire with twenty rifle positions on each side of the triangular peak, then put machine gun bunkers at each point of the triangle, a communication trench midway across the triangle, north to south, connecting to the ammo and gas bunkers, then dug mortar pits at the four corners of the trapezoid formed by the communication trench and one behind the eastern point. A spotting tower was erected over the mid-point of the communication trench, and a CP and guard mount bunker dug under it. All the trenches were dug in a regular wavering curve so that a man could step around half a curve and be away from a grenade explosion. After this was done, we began slit trenches all over the compound, laid Claymore mines to protect the western side and gate, and constructed a concrete landing pad for choppers, south and west of the gate, inside of the outside wire.

All this work, which was not nearly the total work we would do, took the first week, a hard week of digging and filling sandbags, of sleeping on the ground under shelter halves, of cold rations, and lots of heavy guard duty. Thirteen men had left on med-evac choppers, ten with fevers and/or malaria, two with infected shovel cuts, and one who couldn't stand the waiting; but we were beginning to feel secure, as if hard work could keep death away, as if dying could be endured like manual labor, but Capt. Saunders set us straight.

"We have no intention," he said, "of being impregnable, because the intention would be foolish. The VC could take this Det any time they wanted to pay the price. The trick is not to be impregnable but expensive."

Some trick, but we were dug in, dug out, and halfway ready.

On the third day of the second week, the troops were still busy, raising squad tents with wooden floors, a four-foot protective wall of mud between two rows of logs on the three

open sides of the lower half of the triangle, and digging
bunkers for ammo, gasoline, and a guardshack command post
radio room. Four rhombic antennae were being erected on Hill
538, now known, of course, as the Other Tit. A log cutting detail had gone off to the edge of the forest on the north to cut
trees for the wall and the bunker roofs. I had mounted guard
details for the log cutters and the antenna builders, then finished drawing up the guard roster for perimeter duty, two men
in each M-60 position, two men at the west gate, a walking
guard on each of the three sides, and a man in the spotting
tower, day and night.

The paperwork had bored me, so I left my tent to check
guard posts, then climbed up the steel spotting tower in the
center of the compound. I stayed there a bit, bumming a
cigarette from the kid on duty. I was trying to quit for physical
and professional reasons. Morning had tried to give me a bad
time about it, and about wearing my watch with the face
against my wrist, and carrying a .45 automatic, and the tiger-
striped camouflage coveralls I used as a uniform of the day,
and the razor-sharp bayonet slung in the scabbard sewn on my
right boot, and the combat harness, etc. He couldn't piss me
off, though. Quite frankly, I felt above such minor emotions,
minor griefs, even above the constant irritant of dysentery
which I, like the rest of the Det, seemed to have caught out
of the air. Like a Trojan on the walls, or a Kamikaze pilot,
I felt anointed, and afraid.

As I smoked, the day became perceptibly hotter, but a
fragment of morning air drifted under the hot steel roof and I
stayed a moment longer. Inside the outer perimeter, children
played, wives gossiped, and their soldier husbands and fathers
sat in shaded places and cleaned their old Springfields. Smoke
from cooking fires ascended stiff columns straight into the
ashen blue sky, but sounds wafted about the compound like
the odor of burning charcoal: a soft curse and a grunt of pick
into dry, rigid earth as the bunker diggers toiled; a metal
squeak streaking from the Other Tit as nut and bolt strained
metal to fit tightly; the clunk of an axe late after the swing or
the sweeping fall of a tree from the cutters on the northern
edge of the clearing. In spite of the activity, the compound, the

scene, seemed essentially peaceful; perhaps because work is a peaceful occupation, whatever you're building. I was reminded of the American West, of building a fort against the hostile land, of peaceful treaty Indians camped about the stockade walls; out-riders, wood-cutters, and scouts moving out and back across the parched grass hills. And over all this, controlling each contraction of muscle in this new land, the confident, foolish idea that because man piddles in the earth with pointed sticks, because he shits in holes and covers it like a serene tomcat, because he cuts trees and replants them where he wishes, that because of these things man shall inherit the earth. That we shall be masters, inheritors with the tried and true strength of our brown arms and calloused hands and with great boldness and strength, never fearing for a moment the violent winds which might cast us like chaff across the land; nor afraid that the land itself might buckle and rip beneath our very feet and suck us into its soft hot core; nor afraid, least of all, that the aborigines who came before us can stand against us, feathers and paint and leather shields no hope against a Sharpes or a Henry. It seems our only fear might be of those who come behind us, the wave pushing behind us just as the Huns and the Vandals pushed the Visigoths into the Romans and the Romans into the sea. But we know there are none behind us, know we are the last, the best and the last of the barbarians, the conquerors, the long knives, the jolly green giants of history who move at first across the land with fire and sword, then with transistor radios and toothpaste, seeking not even greener grass, nor even movement itself, but merely senseless turds in the large bowel of history. . . .

But I stayed too long in the tower; I revealed my position to the enemy. As I climbed down, Morning looked up from where he dug in the ammo bunker, saying, "Looking for them pesky redskins, Sarge?"

"And the angel of the Lord shall sink his scythe into the great winepress of the earth," I said, "and bring peace to the heathen."

"Stop stealing my lines, Sarge," he said, raising the pick, then plunging it deep into the ground.

"Stop stealing mine," I said, walking away.

I collected the Armalite and two clips from my tent, hooked two fragmentation grenades on my combat harness, and then walked down to where the log detail was stripping limbs from the felled trees. I watched, chatted with the guards, and had the second cigarette of the morning. The forest, though not as thick as it had looked from the compound, blocked out the sun fifty feet inside, so the men had cut their logs at the very edge. After splitting them, they cut them into five-foot lengths and, two men to a log, started carrying them back toward the compound along a trail beaten through the hip-high elephant-grass by previous details. I followed, last man behind one of the new guys, a kid from southern Ohio who hated the Army with remarkable passion because the dentists had pulled all his teeth during Basic. He thought nineteen premature for false teeth, and he let the world know it, bitching a while, then clacking his choppers, then bitching again. His buddy in front told him that the girls back in the ZI would just love it if he took out his plates and gummed their titties. Like all Army discussions, politics, religion, war, or false teeth, this one moved quickly to the terminal point of all of them: fucking. The kid laughed, only partly convinced, but in a way that promised he would try it with the first girl who showed him a bare breast.

I was still chuckling when the sniper shot. Before my mind recorded the sound of the rifle behind me or the snap as the round whipped past my ear, a hole magically winked two inches to the right of the base of his spine, blood and dust clouded before him, and his legs buckled. But even as my mind wasn't recording, it was working. I dove and rolled into the high grass at the right of the trail. Another shot skimmed the grass tops up the slope, and the ricochet scattered chickens and children in the outer compound.

"Stay down!" I shouted, but everyone had already burrowed into the grass roots. The snipers held their fire now. Either cutting out or waiting without revealing their position, I thought. Two shots from different rifles: no automatic weapons. One shot down, one up: one man in a tree, one on the ground, and probably a third covering who hadn't fired yet. Thank God for the grass. The protection of the outer perimeter was two-fifty or three-hundred yards uphill. I had twenty-five men, counting myself, but only five weapons. "Smoke!" I shouted. "Holler it up!"

As the cry for smoke drifted back up the hidden line, I crawled as close to the trail as I could. The kid's body slowly stretched out, easily, carefully, as if he carried eggs on his back. Once flat, he lay as still as the dropped log, his hands out in front of his head. He began to moan, to whisper please, but the moan seemed almost conversational, detached as if he might be having a discussion with an ant crawling below him. A rivulet of blood, black in the dust, beaded red hanging on the trampled grass, crept sedately back down the trail.

"Hey," I whispered. "Roll over here. Roll over, kid."

Another face appeared between two clumps of grass on the other side of the path. It was the kid from the front of the log, and he was crawling out into the path.

"Stay put," I said, but he came on.

"Harvey," he said. "Harvey, you bastard, I told you to take the front, you fuck head, I told you, I told you."

"Stay put, soldier," I said. "Goddammit, stay put, and shut up."

"Digs, Digs," Harvey said calmly, "Digs, I think they done shot my balls off. I sure believe they did." As he talked, he sounded calmer, but his body shook in quick tremors.

"Oh, Harvey, goddamn you, Harvey," the other one said, reaching out along the ground for Harvey's hand. His thumb disappeared in a burst of dust, and while he was throwing himself back into the grass, three quick but spaced shots searched the grass around him. Harvey shook harder, as if by vibration he would sink into the earth.

"Roll over here," I told him again. "Please roll over."

"Sarge? Sarge, is that you?" he muttered into the ground. "Sarge, can you find my teeth. I lost my teeth."

His buddy appeared once more at the edge of the path, closer to the ground this time, holding out his hand so I could see the thumb missing above the second joint. "Sarge, they shot my thumb off. My fucking thumb, right off. What can I do, huh, Sarge?"

"You bastards, shut up or I'll shoot your heads off. Shut up."

I slipped the Armalite on automatic fire, threw a long burst downslope, then leaped across the trail. I landed on Harvey's teeth, laughed, kicked the other kid away from the edge, and as he rolled one way, I went the other. The sniper followed me, rounds stinging my face with dirt, burning at me as I rolled and crawled, until I thought that the automatic fire I heard was directed at me. The rolling and crawling went on after the sniper stopped firing, and when I stopped, my hands, with their own will and concern, flew about my body seeking wounds, blood, bone, gristle, searching until they found me intact, then nodding yes to my stupid face as the first of the smoke rounds dropped twenty yards downslope.

I went back to the two wounded, wrapped the bleeding hand and stuffed a T-shirt into the bleeding crotch, and sent them back through the lovely smoke with two men to help each. I screamed at them to tell Tetrick to give me mortar and automatic fire at random intervals; made them scream it back with angry faces at me. The two M-60s had stopped ranging and were beginning to traverse in short bursts cutting up the edge of the woods. I crossed the trail again, waited for more smoke and rifle fire, then shouted for the men to go.

The two VC rifles opened up, one right and high, the other left and low on the ground, two rounds apiece, my rational mind confirming what my instinct had already known, and I migh have spotted the snipers but for some low rounds from behind me that sent me to earth again. The smoke, thick now, and the M-60s coming in hard at the edge of the trees kept the snipers down while the men moved uphill.

I slipped back into the thickest smoke, then ran back to my left, jumped the path again, the log and the bloody mark, then crawled another twenty-five yards to a brush-choked depression which ran down from the saddle between our two hills. Brush we had meant to clear the next day. The slight dip offered cover only because of thick growth, but the dip quickly became a dry wash as I moved downhill, and the brush was too tangled to move through. But at the bottom, just like the mesquite and cat-claw thick arroyos back home, I found eighteen inches of clear space under the growth, and I crawled down that until the smoke rounds and the covering fire ceased.

I assumed that the men had make it back, so I waited for them to give my instructions to Tetrick.

I caught my breath in the pause, dropped the web belt with canteen and first-aid pack, changed clips, had a quick drink, then poured some water on the wash bottom and scrubbed the mud on my face, ears, neck, and hands, and waited. I assumed patience, in this case, to be a major virtue.

When the fire started again, I moved down the wash with the bursts and the echoes following mortar rounds, looking. The wash turned to the left, then sharply back to the right, as I had remembered, and I moved down it on my belly, looking. If the two men had been deer instead of men, and this happening in a South Texas arroyo in the afternoon heat, one slow step then a long look and watch your shadow and don't turn your head quickly, I would have seen the men much sooner. But they were men with guns, not deer, and I was belly-flopped under the brush, each breath raising tiny dust-devils below my chin, and they were men with guns, hunting too, and not deer.

You don't look for bedded deer, but for an ear, a horn, a folded leg, a black nose, or a quick eye turning to see you. When my father taught me to still-hunt, he wouldn't let me shoot until I saw the buck before he did. He would stop, try to show me while I blinked and tried to see a whitetail where there were only gray shadows, then let the buck go. It's like those funny pictures that have a cow or a face hidden among blurred lines and shadows: once you see it, you wonder how you ever missed it. I shot my first buck through the neck where he lay, and he never got up. But I had never looked for men. This was a different game, but I always was a fast learner.

At the bottom of the slope, thirty yards from the trees, the wash broadened into a small sandy flat. I crept into the shadow of a bush and against a ten-inch bank, and lay on my back, feet downhill. Patience again. Let them make the first move to escape. Tetrick would send a patrol soon, and they would have to move. But while waiting, I saw them: the guy in the tree, easy, a foot, small, brown and dirty in a clump of leaves. The leaves moved in the wind, the foot didn't; fifty yards directly to my right. The one on the ground was harder, but after locating the one high, I knew just about where to look for the lower one. The grimy cloth wrapped around his head to keep sweat out of his eyes drooped a gray tag where it was knotted; I found that, then the dark eye beside it. The clump of brush where he sat, his legs crossed, was about thirty yards out from the trees and twenty yards left and above me. Two of them, one of me. They would kill two men on the patrol, then vanish into the thick forest. There should have been a third to cover the other two, but cockiness is not just an American fault.

During an automatic burst from above, I slipped a grenade from my harness, straightened the pin and pulled it. In the next mortar explosion, I flipped the Armalite from auto to single fire, and in the next explosion, I released the handle, waited, then threw the grenade in a high arc toward the clump of bushes, firing two quick rounds along the ground toward the VC while the grenade was in the air. On my side before the explosion, I laid four carefully aimed rounds two feet above the hanging foot. His single round was faster, but wide to the left and high, but mine were like axe blows in his chest, and bounced him off the tree trunk. He flipped out of the tree like a Hollywood stunt man.

The grenade had exploded and the bits of shrapnel sung past while I was turned. I rolled, then fired toward the bushes, twice, but there was no answer. The grenade had cut the brush in front of him, and he lay on his back, his rifle blown away from him. I ran to him, circling to the left, but there was no need for the caution. The grenade must have caught him as he tried to stand and to duck my two rounds at the same time. The left leg was completely severed at the hip, the genitalia, a bloody stump, and the stomach wall split from hip to navel. The black pajamas had been blow off, and he was naked in his death. Warm gray intestines looped out of his torn belly, loops furrowed with gashes dripping decomposed rice. The stink sputtering out as the guts kept contracting as if the business of life went on as usual. The eyes turned back as I walked up, and the breath came as fast as the flutter of a bird's wing. I shot him in the ear, then went to check the other.

He was dead, four bruise-ringed pin holes in a line up the chest; almost no blood in front; almost no flesh in back. An old rifle with wire holding the broken stock together lay beside the body. I shot him in the ear, then walked back up the slope to meet Tetrick and ten men coming at a dead flatfooted run.

(I know you'd rather hear about the fear, about my lungs seeming to lunge up my throat after air, about the infinitesimal but now eternal tremor clutching my hands, or about the dizzy reels of my brain, or the watery shit running down my leg. But you know that part by heart now. I did what I did. Two men died, two others lived, perhaps. It's not supposed to make sense. Fear and trembling is no excuse; action is no reason; dead is dead.)

"You shoulda let them go," Tetrick huffed as he arrived, grease gun swinging and fear in his face. "But you did good, kid."

"Yeah," I said, "Fine. How are the wounded?"

"Should be okay. Med-evac chopper's coming quick." He pointed over the hill where a black dot buzzed closer.

"Fine," I said again, then walked on up the hill, the men behind me carrying the two bodies.

They laid the bodies in front of the spotting tower, and everyone had to come see them, to gape at the guts hanging out of the one like an atrophied papier-mâché leg, to slap me on the shoulder, to point out my brilliant shooting. It wasn't unlike a successful hunt, back in camp with the drunk card players who only hunted peace from their pinched-faced Texas wives, middle-aged men with fawning mouths and bitter, envious eyes, and hands that grasped at your youth.

"Cover them up," I said to Tetrick. "Jesus Christ, cover them up."

"Let 'em get used to it," he answered.

And Morning answered too from behind: "Too late to be sensitive now. Not much to send home to Mamma, huh?"

I walked to my tent and lay down and let the fear wash out of me. When Morning walked into my tent, the shaking had just began to get bad, violent, like a fever convulsion, and the legs of my cot were rattling against the plank floor. A shaft of white hot sunlight plunged through the open flap into the blackness of my tent, and Morning's face was black and his head outlined in fire-haze white.

"They say the first one does that to you. But you'll get used to it," he said as he stepped in.

I raged off the bunk without thought. One hand filled with his shirt, the other with the bayonet off my boot, I shoved him back toward the door, tripped him, then kneeled on his chest, the bayonet against his throat.

"You keep your mouth shut now. You let me alone now. I liked killing those stinking little animals. I pretended they were you and all your stupid bleeding heart kind." I screamed, spittle flaying at his face like the dust motes suspended in the brilliant stab of sunlight. I lifted him off the floor, then shoved him out of the tent, followed him, pushed him again. He fell, rose angry, and started to come, but I had the bayonet low against my hip, and he stopped.

"You gutless mother-fucker," he said. "You got guts enough to drop that nigger blade, I'll bust your head for you."

"When it happens, son," I said, "You're going to die. But I want you to kill first. I want things to be even; then there can be hair and brains all over the place, then, yours."

He stepped back, his face twisted as if I'd hurt him. "No worry about that," he muttered. "No worry." He turned and wandered off, shaking his head, saying to Novotny, who had run up with some others, "What's with him?"

Though the question hadn't been meant to be answered, Novotny said, "Fuck with the bull, Morning, you get the horn."

I walked back in the tent. Morning's cigarettes were scattered across the muddy floor. He'd come to offer me one, yes, and his hand too, and his face had been twisted in pain as he walked away. *Joe, Joe, you can't push and pull and fart around with life, then just say quits when you get ready.* I hadn't given him time to say "sorry" and now he wouldn't listen to mine. Hard-headed bastard. I would have killed him now, if he had come back to the tent. The game was over between us. Shit, shit, shit. I lay down in the darkness, alone now, calm, resigned, anger gone, fear gone. I slept.

Then came the idiot Lt. Dottlinger fast on the wings of a jet. The first, cracking over the compound like thunder, rolled me out of the bunk without waking me fully. Outside, still dazed, the second drove me to the ground where the rest of the men already were, including the third casualty of the day, the guard from the tower who had jumped and broken a leg when the first jet came over. Just as I stood up, asking "What the hell?" the first came again too fast to be real, wing cannons hammering at the earth, explosions of dust through the grass. The jungle never acknowledged any hits; the rounds might as well have never been fired. Then the second jet was back, firing in the same senseless way. Then the first again, laying napalm eggs at the edge of the trees, then the second, then both in a quick pass and dive at the hilltop, a waggle of wings and two brown faces and white smiles, and zip the South Vietnamese Air Force was gone, leaving behind one American casualty and one hell of a grass fire and one Lt. Dottlinger running out of the CP Bunker, shouting, "That'll teach the commie little bastards. That'll teach them."

Capt. Saunders was heard to mutter, "Three weeks, you dumb son of a bitch." Three weeks being the time left until the promotion list came out with Dottlinger passed over a third time and reduced to S/Sgt and transferred to another outfit. "Three weeks."

The grass burned from the outer perimeter to the edge of the jungle trees, and the jungle itself might have burned except that it was still too green from the rains which had plagued our first week in Vietnam. When we tried to fight the fire with wet blankets, we lost two more men to smoke inhalation, so we could do nothing but stand and choke on smoke and grassy cinders and try to keep the tents from burning for four hours until the fire burned itself down and away toward the rolling hills below us, smoke plumes above it like the banners of a victorious army moving on to other, more significant engagements.

That night sparks winked all around us, and the canvas of our tents, soaked with water and smoke, seemed to breathe the heat directly at us. Most of the troops spent the night out of their tents, and there was much talking and laughter about the day. But I went where I could be almost alone, the cot in the guard section of the CP Bunker, underground, sitting with the sleeping supernumerary, the silent radioman, the humming tubes, the small lights, and myself.

You might wonder that I, experientially green as I was, could take on two men belonging to perhaps the best insurgent guerrilla force in the world, take them on, kill them, and walk away physically untouched. You might wonder, but I don't. The deer I killed, the first one I told you about: I was nine. Deer are easier than men, but not easy. They hear with their feet and have eyes evolved for catching motion and noses bred for smelling the enemy. I was already a hunter; I only needed to find my game.

I know that hunting is out now, and all that, and I will be the first to admit that I never hunted out of a need for food nor, I hope, for sport, nor for the blood since that warm sticky smell has always slightly sickened me, but for the ritual, the remembering of the time when men needed to be both smart and strong, crafty and swift and silent of foot, the remembering. And I remembered well, and I was good. . . .

All the things pressing. . . .

Remember: I came from a working ranch, grew up digging fence post holes, driving a tractor, herding cattle more often with a Jeep than a horse but sometimes with a horse, riding in pickups with a rifle and shotgun racked behind me and a .38 in the glove box, cutting cattle and a few hogs while they protested the loss of their maleness. Remember I won my first fist fight when a kid laughed at the book of fairy tales I was reading on the school bus home, and I won a few and lost a few after that but never quit, and the first time I put on football equipment it felt right, and I did it well, and my high school time was spent learning to maim, to make the other guy quit, and I did it well, but other things too. Remember: I went away to be a college professor after Korea, to be educated, and in the process educated the girl down the road and lost her. I had killed and fought and drunk in Mexican whorehouses, but to those who would say—then, not now—to me, "beast, monster, killer," I would answer, "See my degrees, examine my transcripts, my As and Bs." And to those who would accuse "intellectual," I could point to my trophies, the bear-skin rug from a honeymoon trip to Canada, the elk head and rack so large my father had to knock down a wall to put it in the living room across from the wall of books above the Krummel Journal when I shipped it from Washington. And if that wasn't enough, I could show them the back of my hand with their blood on it. But that is the past past; for now I can say nothing. That's not to say I've learned nothing, but that I know little.

Don't be surprised that I had a troubled youth. I learned about masks long before Joe Morning.

But there are other things: Gut a bear, slice the thick belly skin with a keen knife, ease the blade through the membrane, cut around the anus and the genitals, split the diaphragm, reach up the chest cavity, grasp the esophagus and the larynx, cut them through, then pull from the top, pull the guts out with your hand, the pink lungs, the muscular heart smashed by a mushrooming lead-nosed bullet, the still-moving intestines, wash the clotted black blood off the ribs with an old cloth. But don't stop there, skin the manlike carcass hanging from a barn rafter, pepper him to keep the flies away, let it cool as the weather decrees, then butcher, slice the flesh, saw the bones, and wrap the meat in freezer paper, eat the backstrap chicken-fried and roast the forelegs and smoke the rear, and eat your bear, knowing as you chew, as you digest, his mortality is yours, and this is what he would do to you, though with more animal reason and less waste, and even then what you've learned is only the beginning. It is not as simple as this, not at all, but this is a beginning.

If politicians, revolutionaries, reformers, preachers and priests, generals, Gold Star Mothers and the Daughters of the American Revolution, Veterans of Foreign Wars and Sons of the Republic, if they had to field dress and butcher and eat all the useless dead they contract with warriors to produce, then . . . God, how the beef market would fall.

You will excuse the digression. Looking back, it seems I'm saying that I butcher game with more love and understanding than I have when I butcher men. Don't believe it. But don't pity me, either. I may be down but I ain't dead.

You *will* excuse the digression. As I told you, the smell of blood makes me slightly sick.

The rest of that week and the next were tense but busy. The antenna field was finished then mined, and that night two VC were killed trying to cut the cables. The bunkers were roofed with logs and sandbagged, and small concrete ammo bunkers were built into the sides of the mortar pits. An arrangement of pits and earthen walls protected all but the top half of the radio vans and the roofs were sandbagged against mortars. The generators and gasoline came, and a field kitchen too with cooks, stoves, and hot meals. The troops began to feel at home. They were brown and healthy, the last drop of San Miquel had been sweated out, and those who didn't have cat fever looked as if they could go hunting bears with a willow switch, between trips to the latrine, that is. The Det had already dug eight and filled six latrines, and used enough toilet paper to raise wood pulp stocks 3⅗ points on the big board.

On the morning before we were to begin operations at 1600 the next day, a Caribou chopper appeared filled with tons of warm beer. Saunders had saved our beer rations for one big bust. Everyone in the Det, except me, spent the whole day drinking warm Schlitz, puking, and getting totally wiped. I broke up seven different fights, none of which drew a bit of blood from either fighter, and pulled at least twenty men out of tangles with the wire, which drew a great deal of blood. They went on after sundown, as long as they could keep enough beer down to keep their buzz up, and I spent the night poking Benzedrine down sick, sleepy guards, praying they didn't shoot each other, worried until I finally took the live rounds away from them, deciding that if the VC came this night we could hold them off just as well with empty beer cans. Once, on my rounds, I heard Saunders and Morning in one of the latrines talking about their football past, recounting every single football game they played in, saw, or even heard about. They really pissed me off. Who was I that I shouldn't be drunk? Why was I always responsible? I stormed the latrine, shouted to Saunders that he could take care of his own goddamned Det because I was going to rack out, by God. As I walked away, I heard him say to Morning, "That Krummel is sure a mean drunk, huh?" The bastard, I thought, but I had to smile. And the next morning at 0600, he was up, showered, shaved, and handing me a fifth of Dewar's, and the young men were up, out of their tents, as ready as they were ever going to be for what was to come. I had two pulls on the bottle, and when I lay down on my bunk, I was as peaceful as I had ever been.

At 1600 that afternoon, I mounted the night guard, Trick One climbed into the vans for the first swing trick, and the 721st Det was back in operation. At 0315, approximately, the first mortar round fell in the outer circle among the sleeping militia troops, a woman began screaming, the attack started, and the 721st went out of operation.

At almost the same moment as the first mortar explosion, two Bangalore torpedoes blew the inner and outer wire, one at the east gate of the outer circle, the other to the side of the M-60 bunker at the eastern point of the inner triangle. The inner wire had been blown by VC members and sympathizers among the provincial militia, about thirty of them. The mortar rounds kept coming in, walking across the compound, and a quick flurry of small-arms fire and three or four automatic weapons lashed at the hill from the edge of the clearing, east and north. The M-60s answered quickly, but the one at the eastern point just as quickly stopped as it was overrun.

I had been checking the guard at the western inner gate, and as I ran back to the CP Bunker, circling around the mess tent, a fragmentation round landed ten feet to my right. The concussion lifted then casually tossed me through the back door of the mess tent. As I tumbled, I thought only one thing: Jesus, not so soon. I fell among pots and pans and the sleeping mess cook, but I couldn't hear the noise. I got up, kicked pots one way, the cook the other, and ran back outside, and I couldn't hear the sound of my laughter. The ringing in my ears was pleasure compared to the storm of noise assaulting them when the ringing stopped. I seemed intact, though, but my shirt had disappeared. I ran on without it.

Men milled everywhere, like cattle in a lightning storm, two
and three men throwing themselves at one slit trench, men
slitting the sides of burning squad tents to get their footlock-
ers out, men running still clutched in mosquito netting, and
mortars falling steadily now, throwing men in long looping
dives along the ground. Rifle rounds snapped past, usually
overhead, but an occasional red explosion or black hole stung
among us; sparks trailed above our mortar pits, now, answering, and the rifle fire slowed. I hit and pushed my way
through the flying naked arms and legs, screaming Alert
Positions! but it seemed that no one heard me, no one felt my
blows, not one returned them. I stopped by my tent for the
shotgun and two bandoliers of ammo, slung them, then ran
for the CP Bunker. Fifteen feet from the bunker, our M-60
began to wink at me from the mortar pit behind the eastern
emplacement. I dove and rolled into the communication
trench, falling among five or six crouched troops holding
smoke grenades. I shook them, shouted at them, then kicked
them, but they refused to move. I threw the grenades for
them, so we had a bit of smoke cover about thirty-five yards
out, and the M-60 slowed its rate of fire. As I turned to go back
to the CP, the troops were beginning to throw grenades on
their own, smoke and fragmentation, but they were mostly
short, and the M-60 began to answer with waspish vehemence.
Two troops were hit with a single burst directly in front of me.
One's right arm came back mangled from a throw, forearm
hanging at an oblique angle; another's brains and bits of skull
rained upon my back. I threw the dead one out of the trench
before he stopped kicking, and dragged the other to the CP. An
aid station had been set up in the guard section, so I left him
with the white-faced medic.

Saunders, wearing fatigues he had obviously slept in, was
on the other side, screaming on the wire to the mortar pits,
"Illumination, goddammit! Illumination! Alternate! Illumination!" Then he would shout at the guard in the spotting tower
to get off his ass and direct fire, goddammit. Tetrick ran in
behind me, dressed in underwear and combat boots. He
rubbed the side of my face, my shoulder, and my ribs, then
drew back a bloody hand.

"Just scrapes," he said. "You're all right."

I had been, as long as I didn't know I was bleeding, but the sight of his red hand hit me behind the knees, and they shook so badly, I staggered as I followed Tetrick over to Saunders.

"Get some men in the com trench," Saunders said. "Need cover so the men in the vans can get over here."

"Already done," Tetrick said. "I got Barnes and Garcia kicking 'em outta the slit trenches," he continued, but Saunders was listening to the phones.

"Coming down the trenches. Both sides," he yelled. "Stop them. Spotter says demo teams."

Tetrick waved me toward the right, then pushed me as he went to the left. Behind us, Saunders screamed for illumination, the radioman screamed for a flare ship and an air strike, and the wounded screamed for mercy. Saunders was getting some illumination, but no one else got anything.

In the trench, by the pale ghostly light from drifting flares, I could see men leaping and running out of the vans, trying to get to the trench. My old Trick had been working mids. Cagle and Novotny flew directly at me, but a mortar explosion threw Cagle ten feet to the right. He landed still running, but now as if he were being pushed from behind, three or four quick shoves, and bursts of black blood exploding across his chest, and I knew he must be dead, but I didn't think about it. Novotny slid into the trench like a man stealing second, his rifle held high, but I grabbed him before he hit bottom, jerked him down the trench behind me, then up to the wall around the nearest van where we crouched, trembling, mouths sucking for air, until three VC in jockstraps carrying satchel charges crept down the trench below us. As they passed us, I elbowed Novotny, set the Armalite down in favor of the shotgun, then stepped behind. Three quick rounds of 00 buckshot smashed them to the ground. Two more, directed at the two that still had heads, saved me the trouble of checking them out. When I turned, Novotny still sat there, looking up at me like a whipped pup. With a double handful of fatigue jacket, I pulled him to the trench.

"Shoot, you bastard, shoot."

He fired a tentative round into the trench. I slapped him. He turned, angry, then back, and he fired into the bodies until I slapped him again. He followed when I turned and ran, leaped the trench, and rolled over the protective wall into the mortar pit.

Novotny fell directly on top of me, and what little wind I had left fled into the stream of incredible noise wailing about my head. Vaguely, I wondered if he had broken any of my ribs. It felt as if the right ribs were sticking into my lung, and when I vomited up my supper, I ran my fingers through it to see if there was any blood. I didn't find any. I wasn't quite tired enough yet to sleep in my own vomit, so I got to hands and knees, and as I did, the sergeant in charge of the mortar pit stepped on my hand. I stood up quickly, knocking him down.

"Get off my fucking hand," I screamed.

"Get out of my fucking pit," he shouted.

"I'm trying to get some cover for your fucking pit."

"Well, do it. Don't stand there with your finger up your ass."

Sick, tired, bloody, surely dying, I tugged Novotny along behind me among the burning squad tents, shaking kids out of their holes. Somehow, no, not somehow, but with punches, kicks, and horrible threats, we wrestled ten frightened kids to their rifles and to the protective wall in front of the mortar pit, stood them there with a boot in their butts each time they tried to sit, and made them fire down the trench. We would have had eleven, but I hit one recalcitrant too hard, and left him unconscious in his slit trench. He took a direct hit from a mortar as I herded my group away. One of the herd accused me of murder until I threatened to murder him. But I got ten of them there, and left Novotny in charge.

I went back down the trench to the CP, down and over bodies of the dead and the frightened. The smoke cover was gone, and the burning squad tents made lovely silhouettes of their heads. The automatic fire from the M-60 came at them like a plague of locusts, and they lay in their holes, those alive, firing into the night air. Popping up once, I saw a VC with dynamite grenades blowing the radio vans. Those who hadn't made it back already, wouldn't now. I threw five or six rounds at the VC, but he ducked behind a van, so I moved on to the CP.

Things seemed more ordered there. The air strike and the flare ship were on their merry way, the Vietnamese troops had rallied and sealed their perimeter with heavy and heroic losses, but the Vietcong had breached the western gate again, and would have poured in but for our 81mm mortars, which kept them from massing for a charge. The fire from the edge of the trees and the VC mortars slackened, probably because of a lack of ammo. All we had to do was hold what we had, but there were many VC still in the perimeter contesting what ground we were holding.

"But we have to have that machine gun," Saunders said to me as Tetrick handed me three phosphorus grenades.

"You're both out of your fucking minds," I said, trying to hand the grenades back to Tetrick.

Before either could answer, Lt. Dottlinger stood up in the corner where he had been sitting, saying, "See here, Krummel, that's an order, and you damn well better obey." He had taken time to dress in clean starched fatigues before coming to the CP, and he had walked through the fire like a mad general, and tried to talk to Saunders about leading a charge, but Saunders made him sit in the corner. He was very chipper and clean, but only willing to lead a charge or sit in the corner. Saunders looked as if he had just come off a three-day drunk; Tetrick looked like a dirty old man in his underwear and a dressing around his bald head where a ricochet had peeled a patch of scalp away; surely I resembled death warmed over.

"If he opens his mouth again," Saunders said to me, "kill him. And that is an order." Dottlinger sank back to his corner. "That machine gun is hurting us, Krummel. Take as many men as you want. I'll get you some smoke."

"Get me a fucking tank, will you? Sure. Shit, yes, old crazy Krummel will." I put the Armalite and the shotgun down and walked out of the CP. A burst hit the metal legs of the spotting tower as I stepped out, and lead buzzed about me, plucked at my pants, but missed. Or maybe bounced off. I don't know; I just kept walking.

I arranged with Novotny for some covering fire over the trench, then I slipped into it, hoping they wouldn't shoot me, crawling, cursing under my breath, though no one could have possibly heard me if I had cursed aloud, crawling years just to reach the three bodies of the VC demo men, scrambling months over their slick naked back as noise and light pounded at my head, clubbing my ears, abrading my eyes, pounding, incoming, outgoing, mortars trailing sparks up the sky, flares like flash bulbs hanging fire, fires leaping wild behind me, tracers splitting, screaming the dark shadows above, and as I crept past the latrine, burning canvas fluttered into the earth with me, slow, turning like a red-gold autumn leaf, peaceful. My mind, my body said the attack had already lasted out time itself, but my watch lied in less than an hour. I threw it away, then myself as rounds from the covering fire laced the sides of the trench, scattering dirt and solid fright against my face. Head on bloody arm, I slept, no more than an instant, but surely sleep, for I dreamed of an old hawk-faced maiden aunt of my father's who told him that Americans were bad soldiers because they were afraid. Afraid not of dying, but of getting dirty, and they died because they wouldn't crawl on their bellies, not pride but cleanliness next to godliness, and then I squirmed on under the fire, belly, boots, and chin trailing wakes in the filth under me, and I lived.

By the second van from the end, I pulled the pin, released the handle, then lofted the grenade toward the mortar pit and machine gun. The second I held longer, and the third burst in the air over the compound like a fourth of July nightmare. I couldn't smell the flesh burning, nor the screams of the burned, but the M-60 died with a rattling coughing burst.

A head popped over the protective wall up by the first van, stayed long enough to see me, then disappeared. I crawled forward, then ran in a crouch, and when he rolled over the wall into the trench, I was behind him, thrusting back the slide of the .45. He heard, turned, I fired twice, once wide, the second round into the action of his rifle. His hand jerked away from the butt, but he flipped the rifle and ran at me, screaming, mouth a black cavern in his head, his weapon raised above his head like a sword. I fired again. His left leg flew behind him as if attached to a rope, but even as he fell, he kept crawling. I shot him in the hip and shoulder, and he stopped. I thought that enough (noise, not compassion), so I tried to run past him, but his good hand grabbed my ankle with a grip like a bear trap. I jerked, fired twice at his head, missed, then twice into his back. He grunted, but held. I kicked, tripped, sat heavily on his back. He grunted, but held again. The muzzle blast of my last round, fired directly against his flesh, kicked the .45 out of my hand, but he held what he had, and he had the most frightened man in the world. I sunk the bayonet into the back of his neck. He released my ankle, but the damned bayonet wouldn't come out of his neck. Idiot-like, I jerked at the handle, ran away, came back, jerked again, then ran again as two more heads peeped over the wall. A grenade exploded in the trench one curve behind me, but the concussion only gave me speed, and in less than a moment, I stood in the CP, shouting, "Shit, yes. Fuck yes. Damn right!" at Saunders and Tetrick. They merely nodded, then told me to get as many men in the communication trench as I could find.

The VC commander had about sixty men inside the perimeter, pinched off once more by the militia. He couldn't go back, and probably never thought of retreating, but if he could take the inner triangle, he wouldn't have to. He moved his men out of our wire and behind the vans on the right and the generators and repair shack on the left. The flare ship and the air strike had arrived, and the fire from the trees had nearly stopped, so the M-60s at the north- and south-east points could cover the outside trenches, which meant that the VC had to come right up the middle without even the covering fire of the captured M-60. We had tried to set up another M-60 in the center of the com trench, but three suicide grenadiers had put it out of action. We would either hold with the thirty or so men in the trench who would stand and fire, or we wouldn't hold at all. We had the firepower, but they had the guts.

I went for Novotny and his detail, but found them huddled against the wall, four dead, six wounded, and Novotny hung over the wall, a gutter wound laced black up the side of his head. The sergeant who had stepped on my hand said, "Dead. Direct hit." His left ear was gone and that side of his head covered with blood, but he seemed intact. I herded the mobile members of Novotny's detail into the trench thinking of nothing but staying alive. I didn't even care.

I set up to the right of the CP, the Armalite and the shotgun ready. The VC had fair cover now, Chinese grenades—more bark than bite—coming from behind the nearer generators, some men firing from behind the sandbags on top of the further vans. But we had grenades going out too, the 81mm mortars were beginning to walk in from the outer perimeter west gate. They had to come now.

Twenty or so men spilled out into the open from either side, some crawling, some charging, some kneeling for covering fire. Black pajamas and Jesus-boots flapping, the little men came like hounds of hell, like a forest fire, a crown fire leaping from tree to tree in a mad race of destruction. Those of us who were going to fight were up now, saying at least that we weren't going to die in our holes. At least ten VC fell in the first burst from the trench, but others kept coming.

As they swept past the third van on the right, half a dozen grenades went off among them. They faltered and in that hesitation another ten fell, though not all hit, for they kept firing from their bellies, or tried to crawl to the shelter of the vans. Those left charging were cut down quickly.

I hit a bunch of three on the left at about fifteen yards with the shotgun; they washed into five more, and the mass was ripped apart. Then another one on the right at five yards as he killed the man next to me, then another out of the air as he leapt over the trench. That was the last of the charge. I traded the shotgun for the Armalite, then went down the right after those who had fled to the spare safety of the vans. One in the foot as he knelt, another in a shower of sparks as he poked head and rifle around a van, and a third in the back as he climbed into a van.

Then Joe Morning stepped out of the door of the third van, shot a kneeling man in the back of the head. Then he ran into the midst of them, firing from the hip like a hero, but he hit at least three more before he folded at the waist like a waiter giving a surly bow, folded, fell, lay still.

After Joe Morning, we mopped up. The VC were beat, but

not a single one surrendered. It was over. Oh, the planes chased the VC through the jungle, and the troops stayed on full alert, but it was over.

We collected our wounded, leaving the dead to sleep until daylight. Casualties were high; the 721st ceased to be operational. So many dead, so many ways to die. The mortars had done the worst damage. Dottlinger was the only one I saw without a shrapnel wound of some sort. (I don't mean to imply that he stayed in the CP; he was up firing during the charge, after the charge, after it was over.) Haddad had a black hole in the very center of his bald head, but not another mark on him, the round disappearing as surely as if it had been fired into the sky, and it is buried with him. A nickel-sized piece of shrapnel had torn through Quinn's cheek—in one side and out the other with about fifteen teeth, but not his bad one—and when he was hit, he fell on a tent peg and lost an eye. Peterson had his heel shot or blown off, but other than that he was all right. Cagle, Novotny, Morning, Haddad, Franklin, dead. (Though you know, as I do, that I was mistaken. Cagle wasn't dead, but was on the back side of the aid station, and I didn't see him. He lost two ribs and his right arm, but they saved his lung after it had collapsed. Novotny wasn't dead either, but deaf now.) All the new members of the Trick were still in the vans, dead in the vans where they had stayed. It was over.

I was supposed to be checking the dead VC, but I wandered past Morning's body being dragged away (I knew he was dead), and into the van he had come out of. Eight jumbled positions, four bodies present and accounted for, three new guys whose names I didn't want to know, but the fourth was a VC, a small terribly old man sitting in the corner. He looked like the one with the dynamite grenades that I had missed, but I couldn't tell.

Suddenly I had to pee so badly that tears welled in my eyes. Holding my crotch, I ran out the side door, slipping in blood or coffee at the door, but not falling, then rushed to the still smoldering latrine. All the canvas had burned away and the wooden seat still smoked. I couldn't imagine why I had come to the open latrine to pee, and then I couldn't stop giggling. A paperback collection of Huxley essays and a flashlight also smoked on the seat. I peed on them. Goddamned Joe Morning caught in the can reading by flashlight while the VC shot the hell out of the place. Shit. But he'd fallen too . . . I finished, then wandered back to the van, feeling his loss, feeling the guilt creep in on tiny but sharp-clawed feet.

Lost, tired, afraid, I can't go on. I sit next to the old, the skinny old man, reach for a cigarette in a shirt I no longer wore, or, no, I had quit, hadn't I; I don't know. One of the dead new guys had some in his shirt. How can a new guy be dead? No, no. How can a dead guy be new? I take his package. He's quit smoking for his health. The old man doesn't want one for his health either. Smoking fouls his sense of smell, and he can smell an American five hundred yards away; Americans don't smell like the earth but stink to high heaven. I shove a butt in his mouth anyway. Universal peace offering between men of war, but it won't stay lit, any more.

"There you go, pops," I say. His short flat nose was all mangled and bloody, his eyes were silent as his voice. "No place to get shot, pops, right in the snoot. And in the chest too. One, two, three, four, five, six, seven, and one in the snoot for eight. Somebody had a grudge on you, old man. Say, what's an old fart like you doing mixed up in this shit, anyway? . . .

"Not telling, huh? Maybe you don't know either. By God, old Joe Morning knows. Knew. Generals, politicians, captains of industry want us here, he says. But you could have stayed in your rice paddy, and I could have stayed home. But you weren't meant to be a rice farmer, nor I a college man. We're here 'cause we're afraid, old man. Joe Morning didn't know shit. That's why he's dead. I don't know why you're dead, but that's why he is. He thought he knew. You ever meet him? Too bad, 'cause he's lying out there now, deader than shit, deader than shit. . . ."

But now I slept, my left arm cradling the old man, and I let my dreams tell him all I knew about Joe Morning, all I knew.

I woke in faint light, blinking in the shadows as a shaft of bright air fell across the open door. There were voices outside, Tetrick, Saunders, Dottlinger, making a KIA and damage report, and a loud throbbing of choppers as they lifted out the last of the wounded. The three came in the door, and I started to get up, but Dottlinger shot me before I could stand. The old man's body had fallen across me and took two .30 carbine slugs for me, but one knocked my right arm back against the wall, and another slammed my right leg hard against the metal floor. Dottlinger saw, almost as he did it, who I was, and he dropped the carbine.

"Oh, I'm sorry," he said. "You got the machine gun, Krummel; you'll get the distinguished . . . you know . . . cross . . . something . . . commissioned in the field . . . I didn't. . . ."

Tetrick and Saunders stood on either side of him, fatigue tugging at their faces. Tetrick cried. Saunders turned and knocked Dottlinger back out the door with the clipboard in his hand.

Stunned, sleepy-drunk, but in no pain yet, I pushed the old man off me, and thought I would stand and salute. It seemed the perfect gesture, which is to say, what Joe Morning would have done, but as I shouted Attention! through the tears clogging my throat and tried to stand, the bone grated in my leg, and not the pain but the sound knocked me out with disgust. . . .

. . . and I woke here in this bed, determined to tell someone the truth. All this leading up to the truth. But it has taken too long. I find myself trapped by my own confession. The scene, the moment of extreme truth, swept past without me, the keys of my old machine clacking like knitting needles, and I without blade to cut the thread.

Turn back, turn back, dear reader: "Then he ran into the midst of them, firing from the hip like a hero, but he hit at least three more before I swung my sights across his middle and blew out the base of his spine with three quick rounds, and he folded like a waiter giving a surly bow, folded, fell, lay still."

There it is. I killed Joe Morning. I shot Cock Robin. Rah, rah, rah.

But you already suspected that, didn't you? That's all right. The whole purpose of any confession is to make the confessor, the guilty party, feel better. One whispers his crimes into the ear of a priest, or shouts them at his friends, or lends them to paper. Murderers tend to think they are poets; how distressing to discover that they were poets all along. It wasn't guilt that made me hesitate to confess my murder of Joe Morning, but my vanity. I knew it would affect you if it seemed that I couldn't bring myself to confess. Nonsense. I cared more when I killed him on paper than I did when I killed him for real. I also thought about letting him live. I wanted to kill him for a reason, rather than on a whim. No such luck, you say, He's dead. Nonsense. He's not dead at all.

I've known for three days that the voice screaming down the hall belonged to my friendly enemy, Joseph Morning, but the momentum of the confession, once confided to paper, carried me on, leaving me in the rather absurd position of confessing to a murder that didn't take place, yet. Art deceives as well as History; Life imitates Art as often as Art does Life; History seems to have little connection to either one. I can't apologize for lying, for only an accident of timing kept my confession from being as true as I knew. Should I confess just intent, or should I admit only life-like confusion? Art, History, Life: traitorous knaves. Don't blame me; I'm just their foolish pawn chained to my machine.

That infinite number of monkeys somewhere out there pounding at their machines for an infinite time surely will re-create Shakespeare, Tolstoy, and me, but God knows if they'll ever finish writing the truth.

Please don't despair because it's not over at all.

11

ABIGAIL LIGHT

I must admit that I was glad to see the bastard again. He lay, pale after the long still months in a Saigon hospital, immobilized like a huge turtle by a large cast from toes to chest, thinner, and somehow older, in his hospital bed.

"Off your ass, soldier," I said as I rolled into his room.

"Krummel?" he asked, his head unable to turn to see me.

"Joe, Joe, how are you?"

"Bad, man," he said. "Really bad. Crippled. Can't walk, can't get a hard-on, can't do anything." Tears seeped out of the corner of his eye, the one I could see.

"They'll fix you. Uncle Sam owes you that," I said, trying to joke. I'd rather see him dead than crippled, I thought.

"No, man. All the king's whores and all the king's men can't put old Joe Morning back together again." He forced a chuckle.

"Cut it out," I said. "This guy Gallard is a magician, man. Hell, he tied my leg back on, didn't he? He's all right. He'll fix it up for you."

"There's just nothing left to fix, Krummel. Nothing."

Nothing to say either, so I shut up for a while. Morning talked, but said nothing, and I wouldn't have heard it if he had.

"Well, guess I'll take off, kid. Got a heavy date," I said, but he didn't seem to hear me.

"Krummel," he said. "I need you to help me. You'll help me, won't you? Won't you?"

"Sure. You know I will."

"Get me . . . some sleeping pills or something like that," he mumbled.

"Why?"

"Why do you think? I can't stand this . . . crippled . . . bad scene, man . . . not for me . . . please . . ." he choked.

"Ah, Christ," I said. "To hell with you, Morning, just to hell with you. You're the most melodramatic mother in the world." I rolled away from the bed. "Please help me, Krummel, please," I mocked. "I'm tempted, by God, I'm tempted, if only because you're such a pain in the ass. You want to die, just rot then. To hell with you." I turned the chair, knocked a pitcher off the nightstand, then moved out the door. "To hell with you."

I met Abigail in the hall outside.

"Where have you been?" she asked. "I thought we had a date." In a brown, red, and gold tweed skirt and soft brown sweater with the sleeves pushed back around her elbows and loafers, she was as lovely as a fall coed in autumn. "What's the matter?"

"Wasting my time," I said. "I knocked a pitcher off the table in Pfc Morning's room. Would you pick it up for me?"

"What were you doing in there? You know him?"

"Old friends," I said.

She walked into Morning's room, stayed longer than necessary, and when she came back, her sweet face was wrinkled in concern. Tiny white teeth chewed at her pale lips, and her hands held each other as if no one else had ever reached out for her.

"He's crying," she said, walking behind my chair but not pushing it yet. "He wouldn't answer me. He's just crying. What did you do?"

"I shot him," I said, but she wasn't listening.

"Why is he crying?"

"To hell with him," I said. "He enjoys crying. He's crazy

about it. Leave him alone. He's bad medicine. Stay away from him." Once again she didn't listen, but she did push the chair down the hall. "You're lovely today, maiden."

"Huh?"

I grabbed the spokes and turned the chair out of her hands. "Listen to me," I said. "Is all of you going outside, or are you going to leave half of you in here?"

She took the hand I gestured with, held it with both of hers. "I'm sorry," she said. "But he looked so damned sad. Like a little boy whose dog was just run over. I felt so sorry for him."

"Yeah," I grunted.

"Yeah what?"

"Yeah nothing." I turned, pushed myself on toward the door.

"All right, Billy Goat Gruff," she whispered when she caught me. "Don't bite the milk of human kindness." She pushed me on out the door.

We rolled downhill through the golf course, uphill around the Nineteenth Hole Clubhouse, along the bluff past the Main Club. I took off the blue convalescent pajama top, lay my head back, and let the sun work on me. I kept my eyes closed until we were past the Main Club and into a stand of timber going uphill again on a graveled footpath.

"Where are we going, nurse? Physical therapy in your apartment?"

"Just shut up and help me push."

As we topped the small ridge, we came out on a clearing, a bowl-like depression circled by the ridge. In the center a miniature Greek theater had been built by some bored but imaginative airman, but the rocks were rough-hewn and it recalled something more pagan, Stonehenge maybe. Terraces stepped up the sides of the amphitheater, alternating stone and flower beds, rough stone, exotic flowers, sensual pinks, lush purples, velvet reds and blues, and pure whites. Abigail pushed me down one of the walkways to the bottom of the bowl and stopped next to the stage.

"You're pretty heavy, fellow. I'm not sure I can get you out of here," she said, wiping sweat from her forehead with a bare brown arm.

"You mean we're stranded here?"

"You're stranded here," she said. "I'm not." Then she laughed and ran away, circling the small stage once, then she flopped on the grass, then rolled on her back and stretched. "Isn't it lovely."

"Gaudy as a goddamned Christmas tree," I said.

"Don't be cute," she said. "Admit you're dizzy with beauty, you're stunned with color, knocked out by the air, enchanted with the sky, and madly in love with me."

"It's all right, I guess," I said, smiling.

"Quit that," she said. "I mean it." She sat up, propped her arms behind her, slipped her loafers off, and crossed her ankles. "You never admit anything," she said, not smiling. "Just say it's lovely. Just admit that much."

"It's okay; if you like that sort of shit."

"It's lovely. Admit that."

"Okay, so it's lovely," I said. "So what the hell. Gushing doesn't make it any more lovely."

"I didn't say gush," she said, tilting her head back. (I would have cut my leg off just to kiss her neck just then.) "I just said be honest and not cute and not cynical and admit what is."

"Come off it, lady."

She looked up at me, pouting playfully. "Please."

"No."

She looked down and away, trying to hide a really pouting mouth, and in a small quiet voice asked again, "Please."

"You don't give an inch," I said.

"Neither do you." She rose, pulled the blanket from behind my back and, in a very methodical medical manner, spread the blanket. With a nurse's hands, neutral, efficient, she helped me out of the chair and onto the blanket; then she sat in the chair, held her hands as a child does when she prays, and said, "What are you afraid of?"

"Jesus Christ," I said, nearly shouting. "This is the most beautiful place I've ever been. I'm stunned and enchanted and dizzy, assaulted by beauty, the beast in me is soothed by sky and sun, appeased by flowers, beset by madness, etc."

She said nothing for almost a minute, then, once again between folded hands, "You didn't say you loved me."

I started to shout, though what I never found out, but she

giggled into her hands, stood up, fell beside me, kissed me, then lay her head on my chest.

"You idiot," I said, holding her against me. But I let her be silent too long.

"You didn't say you loved me, Jake," she said, her words muffled against my chest.

I waited, sighed familiarly, then said, "And I won't say it either. I don't believe in love, baby. I'll like you, respect you, and cleave unto you all of my days, but I don't believe in love. I told you that when this started."

"It didn't matter then," she whispered.

"Why not?"

She rolled over, kissed me again, then said, "I only loved you a little bit then. Now I want you to marry me." She blushed, then moved away, and lay face down on the blanket.

I went numb. "What in God's name for?"

"I knew when I saw your face in the sunshine. You need me; I want you. I get out in six months, and I want you to marry me."

"Just be quiet for a while, will you?"

She closed her eyes, and I lay on my back watching the peaceful white clouds fluff the blue sky.

Abigail had been, in her early years, what is commonly known as a town punch, though she was never as promiscuous as she was thought to be—not virtue, but a lack of able candidates, she was able to laugh now. She admitted that she earned the title. Only daughter of a fat merry high school principal and a thin nervous English teacher with a love for Gothic romances, Abigail grew up torn between the castle of eighteenth century love and the battering ram of nineteenth century virtue. Her maidenhead had burst, of its own accord, when she was fifteen, and she slept with twenty or more boys before she was eighteen—dry, senseless pilferings in the back seats of cars. Her reputation followed her the twenty-eight miles down Route 6 from Marengo to Iowa City, and she fell into the sad pattern of repeating old mistakes, until she fell in love. A boy just out of the Navy three years after Korea, a drunk at twenty-two, dated her because her roommate was busy, and because he was more interested in drinking than fucking, and because she enjoyed the same thing he enjoyed, namely sitting by the Iowa River with an icebox full of beer. He found the shy lovely girl under the reputation. He drank less; she fucked not at all; love.

She told him; he suggested that they refrain to refute her past. Three months of happiness, then in January he, drunk, stepped through an air hole in the ice covering the river; the body wasn't found until spring.

She said she spent her weekends parked up there, sitting in the car in the midst of crystal winter, cold blue snow and a pastel sky, cursing, cursing her sin and her untimely virtue. She had no shell to draw about her, but she made herself be careful. There had been a college boy, two pilots, a dentist, and nearly Gallard, but none of them had come to anything permanent.

When she told me I should marry her, I couldn't decide if the knot in my stomach was fear or love. I believe it was love, now, but I couldn't decide then. My life had too many loose strings, and I thought I'd best be about the business of tying them without knotting them. And I didn't believe in love or anything.

"Can you wait and not push?" I asked.

"Not forever," she said, looking up then moving beside me, "but for now." She kissed me, her lips cool on my face, but in only an instant we flamed together.

"Cut it out," I said, "The cast's in the way."

"Nonsense," she said, and she was right.

Gallard came by late that night as I was making pencil corrections in the manuscript I had finished the night before.

"Through with that?" he asked.

"For now."

"May I see it. It was my idea, you remember," he said.

"How little you know, doctor," I said, holding the pages to my chest.

"You told Morning that I was a magician and that I would

raise him from the dead. Obviously, you think I know a great deal."

"Will he get up from the dead?" I asked.

"The spinal column was bruised and pinched, in layman's terms, by a bullet sliver, but I fixed that. He'll walk when he gets over feeling guilty. I understand that you helped that today. Do you know what he is guilty of?"

I laughed.

"I thought you two were friends?" he said, puzzled.

"Joe Morning is guilty of being guilty; he's done nothing."

"Don't make riddles," he said, peeved.

"That's your game, huh? Here, take this mess. Everything I know about Morning is in here." I handed him the manuscript. "I hesitate to let you read it; it tells about me, too, and I ain't always pretty. You understand that I'll deny the truth of it, if you try to do anything about it."

"I don't understand at all."

"You will."

This was Joe Morning's first day.

Gallard took my manuscript, notes, journal, whatever, then left for two weeks in Hong Kong. He put Morning in a neck-high cast, promising that he would walk after two weeks of total rest. He also, after seeing the condition of my cast, took my wheelchair away for two weeks, promising me a smaller cast and crutches in a fortnight. One day of mobility, one taste of Abigail, and chained once more. They also moved me from my room into a ward (where I shall remain until the end) and Abigail and I could talk but not touch; but most of our talk concerned messages from Morning to me.

"He said tell you thanks," she told me the next day.

"Tell him he's welcome," I answered, slipping my hand down the side of the bed to clasp her thigh. She had arranged me with an empty bed on either side. Sharp girl.

"But he also said that you would have to take him seriously someday," she said, moving away from my hand, blushing, smiling. "You horny bastard. I'll have you arrested."

"Don't give them an excuse. They'll lock me up forever if they get the chance."

She fluffed my pillow, trapping my hand between her belly and my bed. "From what Pfc Morning tells me, you should be. He says you're a reactionary moralist at heart and that you believe in ghosts."

"Right," I said, pinching her, "but I'm a lovely guy anyway. Horny bitch, lieutenant."

"Don't hold it against me, sergeant. Rank has its privileges." She poked me in the ribs with a sharp fingernail. "And responsibilities. Good-day." She turned to leave, then handed me a letter. "Your mail." I recognized the handwriting. "Your stateside sweetheart, sergeant?"

"My, ah, ex-wife."

"Tell her she can't have you back," she whispered, then walked away.

"Hey," I said.

"What?"

"Tell Morning I always took him seriously."

"Tell her I take you seriously too," she said, nodding toward the letter.

The jealousy was nice, but the possessiveness worried me, but she smiled a little as she left.

I let the letter sit for a minute as I basked in the love of a good woman, then I opened it, ready for another bout with tolerance and political persuasion.

Dear Jake, she began, *As you can see from the return address, I'm staying with your folks for awhile.* I hadn't seen, though. *I've come back from Mississippi to rest and my father wouldn't have me in the house. After the things I said to him after our divorce, I don't really blame him. I guess I don't blame anyone for anything any more. Just me.*

As I said, I'm back from Mississippi, to rest. I was already feeling old—pushing 29 and childless is old—when I lost a bit of my fervor. (Politics is such a dirty business, in spite of the cliché, just dirty as hell, and I couldn't stand it forever.) Teaching was all right, in fact, I loved it. Fifty- and sixty-year-old women learning to read, even one seventy-year-old man, right in front of your eyes. Jake, it was great. But the other side, the cold planning of who will get their head broken in nonviolence this weekend, and who next. I stayed out as long as I could, but Dick talked me into it.

We tried to block a registrar's office, marched in front of the court house door until they moved us with cattle prods and billy clubs. I never thought they would hit the women, but they did. I fell down and rolled to the sidewalk, but the girl next to me, a lovely girl from Ohio, was hit on the side of the head. Her ear split right in half. I pulled her behind the court house, tried to stop the bleeding, then went for help.

I couldn't get anyone to help, no one, white, Negro, no one. Everyone was screaming and hitting. No one.

When I went back two Negro boys were dragging her between them across the street and into an alley. I thought they were trying to help, so I followed, but when I got there, they were raping her. She came to long enough to try to fight them, then to cry that she would give them what they wanted, she would give it to them, she would love them, but not now when her head hurt, not now. They cursed her, then told her that they didn't want her to give them anything; they'd take what they wanted; then one of them began slapping her while he was on her.

I ran back into the street, grabbed three white men, and screamed at them, "Those niggers are raping her, a white girl, raping her." The white men stopped them, but they also beat the Negro boys so badly they both had to be hospitalized. Dick had the white men arrested for assault, and tried to say that they had attacked demonstrators. The girl from Ohio refused to testify, so I did, and the men got off. Dick called me an ofay bitch, and I caught the next bus home.

Baby, I'm confused. Please write me, please see me when you get home. You used to make such good sense to me. I won't ask you to forgive me, but please write.

She went on, inquiring about my leg and the plane crash, recounting news from home, wishing me a quick recovery, and a speedy trip home.

What do you do? All the good memories came back. The breathless dizzy kiss after a football game, the summer after-

noons on the banks of the Nueces watching a scissor-tail and a
squirrel argue over the live oak above us, the first time she
read Kafka and the lovely perplexity wrinkling her nose as
she said "I don't understand it but I like it." . . . What do you
do?

"Write her," Abigail said after reading the letter. "She
sounds lost. I hate it, but write her." She looked down the
ward, the other casualties, the dismembered kid, both legs and
an arm lost to a mine, the two blind ones, the one with no
face, five with bullet-scrambled insides, three crazy with malaria, one with a virus fever no one could diagnose, assorted
missing and broken limbs, and me. "Write her. Men don't
understand what they do to women. You're all bastards." She
arranged a smile on her face, then walked to the next bed.

I wrote that confusion must be a condition of growing older,
of seeing more, of living, because I must confess to confusion
too. I promised that I would see her when I got home. I told
her that I was in love with a sweet girl, and thinking about
marrying again.
    "You can tell her that you love me, but you can't tell me,"
Abigail said when she read my letter. "Why?"
    "It's different, that's all."
    "Sure," she sneered. "This way you don't risk anything. You
keep her from hoping and you keep me on the hook." She
walked away.
    I tore up the letter, then didn't know what else to do, so I
put the pieces back together and recopied it.

Late the night before Gallard was to return, Abigail came
while I was sleeping. I woke with her fallen on my chest, her
mouth against my ear, her tears on my face. I held her.
    "Jake," she sobbed. "I'm sorry. I'm a fool. I want to break
your leg again, keep you here. I love you. I won't push."
    Her mouth was wet and rubbery with gin against mine, hot,
hungry; her teeth nipped at my lower lip. She had been to the
Club with one of the younger doctors, but had slipped out into
the night and run all the way to the hospital.

"And I'm drunk," she said, sitting up.

"That's okay; I'm asleep. . . ."

"And having wonderful dreams," she whispered. She stood up, her hands smoothing the wrinkled white linen dress down over long tight thighs. "Please," she whispered, then left, quick and graceful with pride, hips swaying slightly with drink and heat. "Please."

12

GALLARD

Gallard came back from Hong Kong, had me rolled into a room, nearly ripped the cast off, threw a smaller one on, then handed me my crutches, saying, "I want to see you in my office, Sgt. Krummel." Then he walked away.

As I stood, my brain reeled a bit and my eyes unfocused, and my first swinging step swung a little loose.

"Let me help you at first," the orderly said.

"Buzz off, jack, I got it under control."

"Well, fall on your ass, wise guy. Nobody'll care."

"You're telling me," I said, swinging out of the room.

He sat, back to the door, feet propped on a typing table, smoking a furious cigar. The blue cloud of smoke whirled about his head as if he had just stepped out of it and his words were as forcefully calm as the orders of a potentate when he said, "Shut the door, Sgt. Krummel." I did, then sat down across the desk from his back.

"I didn't tell you to sit down, sergeant," he said, still facing the wall.

I said nothing.

He turned quickly, pointed his cigar at me, the chewed frayed end, saying, "I didn't tell you to sit down, sergeant."

"You notice I didn't ask you. You got some shit in your ear, man, don't try to lay that military jazz on my ass."

He looked down for a moment, then half-grinned. "If there's any shit, as you say, in my ear, then you put it there, Krummel."

"I seem to remember you saying that it was your idea."

"We all make mistakes," he said. "I don't know if I should turn you over to the Air Police or the psychiatrist. One or the other, for sure, but which . . . Oh, not that it's not good," he said, digging it out of his drawer. "Layman that I am, I still know it's good, you might even call it art, as long as you say art for art's sake, if my jargon is correct. But it is evil, Krummel, a lovely lie and twice as evil for being lovely. Maybe you're like that, but not mankind. I've only been so frightened in quite the same way once before in my life.

"The war had caught me after I graduated from Drake, or I caught the war, you might say, and I joined with flying in mind, but ended up being a medical supply officer. At the end of the war I was on Okinawa while they were still mopping up. A medical convoy had stalled atop a small ridge, and in the valley below I could see Marines chasing women and children through a cane field, shooting them down, laughing, shouting, jumping for real joy. I counted seven women and nineteen children shot down and left to rot.

"The patrol came up the ridge later, to see what was wrong with our trucks. They were young and bright and happy, kids with new toys, a new shipment of carbines, the first they'd seen and they scared me to death." He paused, puffed billows of smoke from the battered cigar. "This," he said, pointing to the manuscript, "made me feel the same way.

"Oh, not that it's not good, but it's just not true. . . ."

"It was meant to be true not beautiful. If it's good," I said, "that's an accident of truth."

"You're mad as the March Hare, Krummel."

He went on at some length about the necessity for truth in art.

"Hey, stop it will you," I said. "All you're saying is that you've met a murderer, found him interesting, liked him, and you're ashamed of that part of you which loves violence as

much as I do, and since you don't know how to deny me,
you're trying to make me feel guilty about something I did
honestly. The trick is to deny actions but never people. Easy.
Actions can be evil; people can't. Joe Morning taught me that,
though he didn't mean to."

"You're right, of course. I just wanted you to see the blackness of your own soul," he said, grinning out of smoke.

"That's what it's all about," I said.

"No hope for you, Krummel. Speaking of hope: Morning's
cast is off, and he still can't or won't walk. He says he has
feeling but no control. . . ."

"No shit," I interrupted with a huge laugh.

Gallard frowned, perplexed, then went on. "I sent the psychiatrist in this morning, but Morning wouldn't talk to him.
The shrink said, 'Well, Pfc Morning, I'm going to talk to you
until you talk to me,' and Morning said, 'Well, Major Shrink,
go right ahead. I was just going to jack off for the first time in
about two months, so it ought to be something to take notes
about,' and he proceeded to do so until Major Psychiatrist left.
And he refuses to go back until Pfc Morning changes his attitude, to which I said, 'If he changes his attitude there, of
course, won't be any need for you to go back.' Most shrinks are
all right; overworked, but all right, but this guy is a real idiot.
Don't repeat that or I'll have you jailed," he chuckled.

"Will he walk?"

"Who? Morning? Sure. He's a healthy kid, and from what
you've told me about him, he should make it. Why don't you
get an orderly to dress him in convalescent fatigues and put
him in a chair and you boys roll and hop down to the Halfway
House for a Seven-up."

"A Seven-up?"

"Tell the waiter I sent you and he'll drop about three fingers
of Scotch in the bottle. Twice, but no more."

"Scotch? Seven-up? You gotta be kidding."

"If you're going to be subversive, you of course have to make
sacrifices." He laughed and waved me out.

"Hey," I said, stopped in the door, "I'm glad you liked it."

"I'm not so sure I'm glad I liked it. Now go on; I've got
healing to do."

As Morning and I made our crippled way along the sidewalk, the sun fell like golden rain on our faces, and the grass
burned green beside us, and the green of the forest along the
fairways was black, and the sky above crackled electric blue.
Morning lifted himself out of the chair with his arms, saying,
"A man could think about living in a place like this. Beautiful."

"It's all right."

"Krummel, you're a turd. A beautiful turd, but a shit all the
same." He laughed and rolled on. "Funny, you know, how
being crippled and maybe dying and even frankly wanting to
die cleared my brain. Somehow, man, my life seemed to sort
itself out while I was down. I began to see order in all the
madness and shit."

"Maybe," I said. "You suggesting compulsory bed rest for the
world till it straightens out."

"Maybe," he said. "There was just one thing."

"Yeah?"

"I'd forgotten about laughing, man. When Gallard told me
you were here and all that crazy crap you got into at the
beginning, I thought, 'Man, if it drags Krummel down, there
ain't no hope for a fool like me.' Then when you came bopping
in like a big crazy cat, full of piss and vinegar and shit, and
suffering for my soul like you were my second mother or
something. I don't know, I felt deserted for a moment, then
when you wheeled around and roared out like Lionel Barry-
more or something, muttering under your breath like an old
woman. I don't know, I cried for a long time that morning—
Morning mourning all morning—but when I came out of it, I
kind of remembered all the shit I put you to, all the times you
saved my ass, and I even laughed about that bad scene right
before Vietnam, all that running, man, and that horrible fucking hole you made me dig, and them thirty thousand push-ups
—my arms got so big I had to get rid of all of my tailored
fatigue shirts—but most of all I . . . I remembered that day
you got the snipers.

"I don't know, man, I saw something that day when you
came back up that hill, something in your face, something I

never realized about you. Mostly it was my fault for not really seeing you, but maybe a little your fault too for always acting like you know everything worth knowing in the fucking world. But what I saw, man, in your face was that you didn't have any more control over your life than I had over mine. You just did what you had to or, I don't know, what something inside your guts made you do. Like me, or something. You didn't like killing those cats, but something inside said that was the right thing to do; even if it was a shitty thing it was the right thing at the right time. And you know, man, I felt for you that day. For the first time since all that shit with the fucking queer happened to me, I felt what it was like to love another man, and I didn't feel dirty about it.

"Course it didn't exactly work out when I went to try to explain it to you. You scared the shit out of me—but you know how our bowels were over there—I thought you were going to kill me. And after I got over being scared, and mad, I thought maybe you would have been right to kill me, and I wondered why you ever bothered to save my ass all those times, why you cared. Then I understood that because you weren't afraid, you were really my friend. . . ."

"You don't have to say all that shit, man," I said, looking away from him.

"Yeah I do. And when I came out of that van that night, I was saying to myself, 'By god that's what Krummel would do,' and I did it."

"Yeah, well, life ain't what you'd call simple."

"That's okay now," he said, spinning the wheel chair, grinning up like a kid. "I'm ready to live, man. It's making sense for a change, and by God I'm ready for it. Bring it on, baby, from now on it's all downhill." No hint of false ring in his voice, no false hardiness, just youth and life.

"Well, just move that chair, cripple," I said. "You're standing 'tween me and my drinking." We went on.

About halfway down the ninth fairway, a golf ball, blinding white against the grass, rolled up beside us like a playful puppy. Morning wheeled out into the grass, picked it up, then popped it in his mouth like a piece of candy. Back on the tee, two tall slim young men and a tanned girl shouted at him to leave the damned ball alone, but Morning just rolled back to the sidewalk and went on toward the Halfway House set just behind the ninth green.

"I ain't never eat me no golf ball," he mumbled, trying not to laugh.

I somehow managed a straight face by the time the threesome caught up with us.

"Hey," the young man shouted who had hit the ball, "what are you doing with my ball?" The other guy and the girl, tall brown and blond, stood behind him.

"Sgt. Jacob Krummel, United States Army," I said, turning and saluting, "sir. Can I be of aid, sir?"

"Huh? Oh, well you could tell your buddy to give me my ball back. That was my best drive of the day, damnit. What the hell did he pick it up for."

"Pfc Morning, sir," I said, and Morning saluted. "Sir, he's not quite right in the head. Hasn't been since he ate all the rats. Not at all well, sir."

"What the hell was he doing eating rats?" he asked. The girl turned white.

"It was rats, sir," I paused, "or our own dead buddies. We were pinned down, no food, no water, for ten days. We're the only two left." I faked a sniffle, but oddly enough real tears seeped out of my eyes.

"Oh, crap," he said. "Just give me my ball back."

Morning quickly took his shirt off. His chest and stomach were covered with a maze of livid red lines where the exploding bullets had plowed flesh. Even the inside of his arms were marked. I also took off my shirt, exposing the side and the arm where the mortar had driven dirt under the raw skin like an exploding tattoo.

"Listen, I'm sorry that you were hurt," he said, and his face seemed to agree with his words, "but could I please have my ball back."

Morning pulled out the waistband of his pants, then spit the ball into his crotch. "Hole in one, mother," he shouted and tried to resume the blank stupid face he had worn before, but a gale of laughter swept him away. He dove his hands into his pants, screaming, "Here it is. Got it. Ahhhh. Wrong one. Yep.

Oops." He flipped it at the young man, saying, "If you drive, man, don't drink."

"What's he, crazy?"

"I told you, sir. The rats," I said, saluting again.

"Stop the rat shit," he said, grinning. The girl laughed, the other guy smiled. "And keep that idiot off the fairways."

"I'm fair," Morning said amidst a giggle.

They played out the hole, then sat with us on the patio of the Halfway House, drinking until dusk. Gallard had been right about the waiters, but he hadn't mentioned that they could be bribed. The young men were both Navy carrier pilots and both in love with the young woman who worked in the American Embassy in Manila. She refused both of them on the grounds that carrier pilots just don't live long enough to love. But we had a good time, a college time, saving the world with loud assertions and booze, loving each other in a wonderfully maudlin way. As we parted, the girl kissed Morning and me, saying she could love us because we were out of it. We exchanged addresses and promised to keep in touch, then they climbed in a cab heading for the Igloo for more drinking, and Morning and I headed back through the long cool shadows to the hospital.

In the ward the mirth of moments before seemed sinful among the broken and twisted men, the blind, the deaf, the dumb. The afternoon became unreal for me, as it seemed all my afternoons were becoming, and as it would seem unreal to the young pilots drifting in at the tiny carrier deck at two, three hundred miles an hour, sweat stinging their eyes and their clammy shorts climbing as their assholes sucked fearful wind and the brassy fear sick in their mouths. Death cannot conceive life, nor life death, and the hint is sometimes more than man can stand. I cried in my bed that night, drink, Morning, death, Abigail, love, and me.

Abigail and I drifted through the two long sweet weeks, discovering love and our bodies during the cool evenings. I had rented a hotel room downtown, and we went there every night for two weeks. Gentle sweet mound of her belly, dimpled, hipbones hard, rib cage delicate as a bird's, red-headed lover of a pussy, legs ever reaching apart . . . and only once did she mention marriage. I answered nothing, she said no more.

Morning would kid her when she came puttering around my bed (Gallard had moved Morning into the bed next to mine), her eyes puffy with nightwork, but her face shining like a fresh apple. He called her Catherine and me Fredrick Henry, and said he was sorry but she would have to die as soon as I deserted. The joke fell quickly, and in a few days Morning, in spite of the afternoon when he ate the golf ball, slipped once more into sullen silence. He went to town every night, and from what he said, was drinking again at The New Hollywood Star Bar with Communist students and unemployed gold miners. His eyes turned cold and secretive when he spoke to me at all, and there were no repeats of that friendly afternoon of the golf ball, no confidences, just superior smiles all day long.

Abigail asked me, one sleepy Sunday afternoon as we lay naked in my hotel room, "What's the matter with Morning lately?" One slim white arm rested behind her head and the other dangled off the side of the bed holding a black Filipino cigarette.

"Nothing," I said, kissing her pebbled armpit.

"Don't do that," she said. "I think he's faking; I think he can walk."

I rolled between her legs, bent to kiss her neck, then bent farther to run my tongue around the nipple of her small left breast. "So."

"Don't do that," she said. "Be serious."

"God knows I am, what-ever-your-name-is honey." I nipped the corner of her mouth with my tongue.

"Don't do that," she said. "You're never serious when I want you to be. Never."

She held her mouth slack as I kissed her and she brought the cigarette and burned the back of my hand propped on the bed. She burned, but I didn't jerk away.

"Shit," she said, "don't do me that way." She twisted, grabbed my hand, and sucked the hole burnt into the skin. "Why do you do that?"

"Why do I do that?"

"Yes," she said, a stray tear dropping on my hand. "You

would have let me burn clear through your hand. You're just crazier than shit, Jake."

I laid my tongue into the stale salty ear.

"Don't do that," she said. "I'm trying to talk to you. Oh, Christ . . . Oh. . . ."

"Can I do that?"

"Oh, Christ . . . yes," she said, falling back on the pillow, then pulling my mouth to hers, whispering against my lips, "oh, Christ, yes, for about two days, ten months, and fifteen years."

"How about something more reasonable, lady, say forty-five minutes." I felt her giggle.

"Braggart."

"Slut." I felt her giggle again.

"You're just never serious when I want you to be."

"I try."

Then one day Gallard took the cast off, issued me a cane, approved fifteen days convalescent leave, and invited Morning and me and Abigail for drinks that night. Abigail and I had planned to fly to Hong Kong on my leave, but hers fell through at the last minute. (Mother-fucking Army, Air Force, Navy, and Marine Corps.)

Gallard had a place off base over behind the Country Club, a house perched on the edge of the bluff like a child's dare, a lovely house with a screened porch running all the way around. A winding walk through a deliberately cluttered garden led from the road to the front door, and two tiny flower-like Filipino maids answered the Thai bells hanging beside the door. They held the door while Abigail and I maneuvered Morning's chair up the steps to the porch, then down to a hall, along the hall past a collection of Negrito weapons, then down into a sunken stone living room, then up through an open dining room with a huge carved mahogany table and buffet, and then at last down to the back porch.

"Split-level houses and wheelchairs go together like shit and potatoes," I said, as I rolled Morning up to the bamboo couch.

"Yes, that's of course why I didn't answer the door," Gallard said from the couch.

"You gotta be kidding," Morning said when he saw Gallard. He wore red silk lounging pajamas. "Fucking indecent."

Gallard looked down. "These wrap-around flys were always the very devil to keep closed. I understand that's their purpose."

"I don't mean you're showing, man, you're just glowing," Morning said. "Pour me a drink, Fu Manchu; eyewash, if you got it."

"Just gin," he said, waving us to chairs.

We sat, drank as the sun disappeared from the ridges across the valley and and darkness fell like a swift blow, ate curry and purple rice and roast pig and sweet and sour ribs and fried rice while moths as large and white as our hands bobbed against the screen like itinerant ghosts seeking work and rice bugs pronged like suicidal maniacs off the wire. Drank again as the tiny lights in the valley expired, drank and talked, mostly about why we were here, Gallard's lack of ambition, Abigail's loneliness, Morning's bad luck, my marriage, drank and talked as if we were never to see each other again, soldiers in a foreign land.

I had just finished my own sad story of love and mistakes and marriage, very drunk, when it started.

Abigail kissed me on the cheek and said, "But we'll do it all right, Jake-baby."

"Better stay way from that ugly bastard," Morning muttered, then grinned. "He's dangerous, lady, mad-dog mother."

"That's right," Gallard sneered. "Professional killer."

"Yep," I grunted.

"Bullshit," Abigail crooned, "he's a lover."

Gallard suddenly stood up, walked to the screen, then turned and nearly shouted, "Fuck. Stop that silly 1940s shit. Woman, this isn't some goddamned movie shit, some romantic Hemingway novel. Oh, yeah, Miss Lonelyhearts, he's your white knight, but he's a fucking killer and I know it." He leaned back against a beam. "I'm sorry," he said quietly. "I'm sorry, but it's true."

"Right," Morning hiccupped from his chair.

"He's a lover," Abigail said again.

"Okay, sure," Gallard said, pouring more drinks. "Say you

do persuade him to marry you. Say you do. He can't stay in the
Army. What's he going to do for a living. . . ."

"He's going to be a college professor," she interrupted.

"Are you?" Gallard roared, pointing his drink at me, gin
dripping onto the mahogany coffee table in front of me. "Are
you?"

"Jesus, I don't know. I hadn't thought about it, but I don't
think so."

"So what's left. An assassin? a mercenary?" He still
shouted.

"Yeah," Morning yelled. "An assimery?"

"I don't know," I mumbled. "There's still work in Africa. I
don't know. I guess I have to do something. Hired killer pays
well sometimes."

"See," Gallard screamed, kicking his chair over, "see!"

"Jesus," Abigail said, moving away from me.

"Well, just why the hell not." Now I was screaming.

All three of them began shouting at me about the holiness
of life, the worth of man, the sin of war, they shouted until my
head roared and my hands sought to cover my face, shouted
until it seemed a waking nightmare, screamed until I shouted
STOP and split the coffee table with one blow then shoved the
pieces through the screen and tore my shirt off and faced
them, crouched, fists clenched, choking back sobs till my
muscles quivered.

"See," Gallard said to Abigail, pointing at me.

"Goddamn you goddamn you," I said, "oh, goddamn you.
You bastards want to tell me about death, about war, about
dying. Shit. Everything you say, I already knew, knew when I
was born. Random risk the sound of that bullet tearing that
kids balls off slapping six inches from my ear meant to blow
off my head my head my blood and brains and life I know
dirty guts looping everywhere every night sleeping night
dreaming snakeshit guts chasing me up and down around my
bed sweating blood across the compound mortars dropping
scattering flesh like rotten tomatoes hot lead fried brains
stinking on my face eyes floating round my night asking why
blood stunned death pupils Franklin a piece of rotten stinking
shit meat me wagonloads of arms and legs and livers and toes

and fingers and heads and guts falling me killing Christ me. . . ." I paused for breath, and sense. "You sent me to Gaul with the Legions then asked me why I became a Hun, you hired me for the Holy Land and called me heathen when I forgot to come back. Fight for my land, my home, you tell me, kill but forget it huh kid when it is all over. You used me you lied you used me you lied you used me, make the world safe for my kind, you say, but *your* kind can eat shit baby cause you are a killer, you say, and I am clean and white and care by God mother-fucker care about human life, you say, but you are not human go back in your cage bird they are not singing the war chant this year—from this day forth baby I fight no more for you but for me, me, me, me!" I walked out, sober now, before they could say another thing.

Abigail caught me because I had forgotten my cane.

"Jake, I'm sorry."

I kept walking.

"Jake, I'm sorry, please talk to me."

"If you don't get your hand off my arm and if you don't shut up I'm going to kill you right here right now."

She stopped, but her sobs followed me down the dark road.

I was drunk when I got on the plane at Clark for Hong Kong the next day and I was drunk twelve days later when I got back and I still hurt.

13

JOE MORNING

What no one understood during Hong Kong time, all the
drinking time, no one, not sweet tiny Chinese whores kissing
bitter wounds, nor Aussie bartenders buying drinks to com-
memorate the horror of Malaya, no one understood that I
loved the nightmare in spite of the fear, the disgust, the
sickness; I loved the nightmares. One of me loved it, another
was appalled. Still another looked on with cool distaste at the
fight; and another drank and fucked to prove he did care; and
even that isn't the whole story. We drink today so we can get
through tomorrow.

Because of an unseasonable fog I had to take the train from
Angeles to San Fernando and a limousine from there, a bottle
holding my hand all the way. I bought another one at the
Main Club before I went to find Abigail. She wasn't at home,
nor in the ward, and Morning's bed was empty. I limped to
Gallard's office, waited until he could, or would, see me, drinking.
    "You want to hang one on me?" he asked as I walked in.
    "Ah, forget that shit," I said. "Where's Abigail?"
    "I don't know. I want you to understand that I am sorry."
    "Sure," I said, "Sure."

"You don't sound as if you understand it," he said.

"Well just wait a while, man. I'll get over it."

"I am sorry. I'll even tell you why. She wouldn't have me, and here she was. . . ."

"Just forget it, will you? Just forget it," I interrupted. I stopped in the door as I left. "I guess I really mean that," I said.

"I hope so," he said.

"Me too." I left.

The unseasonable fog had thickened while I had talked to Gallard. A Pacific front the dispatcher had said; weather in terms of war. Cold heavy fog curling round corners after me. Down the road, up past the Nineteenth Hole, and in the dimness I hear angry golfers curse the visibility, the weather, the unseasonable fog. "Kismit," I shout at them, and my voice disappears in the vapors. Past the Main Club, standing under the damp limp flag, drinking to see through the mists below me. Just the other side of a three-foot stone wall, a bluff dropped away to the same valley Gallard's house clung to the side of. Just three feet up, then seventy feet down to the first ledge, then bounce through the wet green trees, laugh, bounce, fall, laugh again, ringing across the misty valley.

It took four pulls on the bottle before I saw where they were. I ran up the hill by the Main Club, through the trees on a graveled path, then down into the depression among rows of flowers sleeping with wet drooping heads. At the bottom they both waited in the fog so still that they might have been statues waiting years for my return. He lay on the blanket, propped on one elbow; she leaned against the stone stage, arms folded before her.

"How nice," I said, stopping before them to lay my bottle in his wheelchair.

"What did you expect?" she asked, her lips barely moving.

"This, I suppose. That's why I came here. I believe in betrayal."

"He believes in things, love, for instance, and you believe in nothing. It's different," she said, her face still etched in stone.

"You better believe it. Catch the pun. Tell the truth," I said.

"You'd rather scratch your own pussy, have a man for a handmaiden, a legal contract, a toy. . . . You talk a good game, baby, but you can't run with the ball. Well, you've got yourself another cripple. Be sure to convince him that he can't walk; he might want to stand up someday. You couldn't stand that. You gotta have the hurt ones, the drunks, the deserters, the murderers, the slaves, the. . . ." Suddenly I was sitting on my butt. The punch had missed my jaw, but his forearm had pushed me down.

"You don't talk to her like that," Morning said standing over me. "Get up, you bastard, get up."

I rubbed my eyes and face, trying to wipe the whiskey fuzz away. "What you doing, Morning? Shit, you're walking man." I smiled at him.

"You're fucking-A right I'm walking."

"Jesus, that's great. How come you didn't tell me?" I asked.

"You going to fight or not?"

I looked at Abigail; her eyes said please no; I said no.

"Well, get the hell out of here then."

"Jake, he had a right to say those things," Abigail said. "I deserted him at Dick's that night. I should have waited until he got back. Now you stop it."

"Yeah," I said. "Stop it and have a drink and tell me why you can walk."

"Oh, piss on both of you," Morning said, trying not to grin. "I'm sorry I hit you, Krummel, but you shouldn't talk to her like that."

"That's okay," I said; "you missed." I stood up and got the bottle. "Have one on me."

The three of us finished the bottle, then Morning climbed back in his wheelchair, and we took a cab downtown to The New Hollywood Star Bar to drink more. It was a small place, a bar and jukebox on the left, five small tables on the right. We sat at an empty table next to the jukebox. The other four tables were filled by young students wearing faces that glowed with revolutionary ardor and surly middle-aged unemployed gold miners with thick wrists and knotted forearms. Several of both had spoken warmly to Morning as I rolled him in, but more stared at me with hate dark on their faces.

"Hello, Comrades," I said to some of the more sullen ones. They started to rise, but Morning raised his hand and said, "He's just joking. He's all right. He's a friend of mine." To me he said, "Don't mock them, Krummel. They take their politics seriously."

"That's nice," I said, "Let's go some place where they take drinking serious." But Morning didn't answer. I could tell from Abigail's face that she had been in the bar with Morning before, several times.

As we were drinking our third or fourth beer, one of the students walked to the jukebox, which had just stopped playing, lifted the face of the machine, reached inside, and punched off half a dozen songs. Neither of the barmaids even looked up. He walked back past our table, stopped, said hello to Morning, then spoke to Abigail. "How are you tonight American pig cunt? Does it take two of these soft American queers to satisfy you now? You should come to my house sometimes. I fuck two American whores before breakfast, so long they ask me to stop."

"You have a dirty mouth, gook," I said, standing up. Chairs scraped behind me. Abigail and Morning both grabbed at me, saying, in effect, that he didn't mean anything, that he was harmless, but I didn't sit down.

"You don't just fight me, American pig, you fight the party," the Filipino said.

"Oh boy," I snorted. "Well, shit, man, I got God on my side."

"There is no God, capitalistic pig."

"Jesus, son, I hate to tell you that the first thing a revolutionary must do is stay away from clichés."

"Well, you watch it," he said walking away, a superior smile twisting his mouth.

I sat down. "Morning," I said, "You are probably crazy. How come you let him talk to her that way?"

"He didn't mean anything," Abigail interjected.

"That's just his way of telling her he likes her," Morning said.

"You could have fooled me," I said, but let it go at that.

Morning rolled over to the other tables to make peace, but he stayed longer than necessary.

"What's he up to?" I asked Abigail, but the throbbing music covered her answer.

"What?"

"I don't know," she said, louder now. "Trying to get out of the Army, I guess. I don't know."

"You know he's more of a dead-end than even I was?"

"Yes," she said. "Maybe you were right awhile ago. I don't know. I'm just sorry. I've always wanted too much; now I have lost everthing. I'm sorry."

"So am I," I said. "I thought I was going to ask you to marry me tonight."

"Don't say that," she said.

"Okay," I said, so we drank on through swirling smoke and music, silence our only bond.

The hospital began processing my papers one day, then suddenly I had just two weeks left in the Philippines. I was alone now; little to do but drink more in the evenings and limp around nine holes of golf in the mornings and lift weights in the afternoons. Morning still feigned his paralysis, Abigail, her love, and me, indifference. I lifted three hours every afternoon now, hefting weights like a longshoreman on overtime, poisonous sweat squeezed out by the expanding, bursting, exploding muscle cells. My body grew quickly hard again, competent, hard, ready; my limp disappeared. On a quick overnight pass to Manila, I had a fake Swiss passport made, got a Mexican and a South African visa, and called my father to tell him to sell my share of the Santa Gertrudis herd. He didn't ask me why, but he did say he wished I wouldn't. I said I wished I didn't have to. The name on the passport was Robert Jordon; it was a joke; nobody laughed.

Gallard gave another drinking bout, promising to behave if I would. Morning stayed sober longer this time, and he and Gallard argued about the Chinese Communists while Abigail got drunk and I stayed drunkenly sober. When Gallard and Morning walked and rolled to the Main Club for another bottle of gin, together so they could continue the argument, Abigail asked why everyone was ignoring her. I kissed her slack mouth, and said I wasn't. I fucked her on the bamboo couch before she had a chance to protest while one of the maids peeked around the corner of the porch. Abigail, afterward, said I wasn't very nice. I said I wasn't a boy scout, if that was what she meant. Then I fucked the Filipino maid on the kitchen floor while Abigail cried in the doorway. I didn't get any merit badges. When Gallard and Morning came back, I had both maids and Abigail naked in Gallard's big bed. Although Morning had to act crippled, we all jazzed and drank until daylight, then slept until five o'clock. Morning and Abigail argued over breakfast, and it was over between them. She called me a bastard as she left and threw a plate at me; but she missed. Morning and Gallard drank some more, but I followed Abigail home. The next day, I lifted twice, morning and afternoon.

When I had four days left, Morning asked me downtown for a farewell drink. I waited until we were in The New Hollywood Star Bar again before I asked him why farewell drinks now when I had four days left.

"Man," he said, "there has been so much shit between us, and so much good stuff too, that somehow I want to get it straight before I leave."

"No," I said, then pulled on a beer, "before I leave."

He drank, then said nothing. One of the students opened the face of the jukebox, punched some songs, then wandered back to the bar. Marty Robbins came on singing "El Paso" on a scratchy old record, obviously around since the late fifties. When he groaned about "a deep burning pain in my side," Morning nodded, but still kept silent.

When the song finished dying, he said, "No, man, it's me who's leaving first." He waved for more beer. It came, room temperature from a case behind the bar, timid white heads poking over the tops.

"Why?"

"Well, I guess if I can't trust you, man, I can't trust anybody." He looked up very seriously. "I'm joining the Huks."

"So am I," I said, trying to smile.

"Don't joke. I'm not."

"Oh, shit, Morning, get off my ass." But I knew by the sickness in my guts that he wouldn't.

"Man, I know you don't think that the world is worth saving, and in a way, I agree, but I have to do something, I have to try. And this is the only way for me. I can't go back and march in peaceful parades and sing about freedom, man. I can't help register voters for elections that I think are meaningless. I can't work in the slums because I want to tell the people to arm, to burn the fucking country down, to screw the New Frontier and get what they can. Get their guns and run for the hills. But it isn't time for that yet. America is hopeless, and I don't know that this is going to be any better, but it is what I am going to do.

"Man, it is going to take fire for the world to start over again. People have to learn, property has to burn, blood has to run . . . that's all."

"Peace through war," I said.

"That doesn't sound like you." He had stopped trying to convince me that he was going because he knew he was, and he had stopped trying to convince me that he was right because he didn't care. "Shit, man, you taught me about war and about doing what you think is right, so I'm doing it."

"I never said anything about joining the Huks."

"You didn't have to," he said, taking off his glasses. He cleaned them slowly, then handed them to me. "There. I only need them to read, really, and I'm through with that, with reading and talking and thinking, I'm tired of all that. Give them to Gallard and tell him I'm sorry."

"Well, no sweat," I said, drinking and shaking it off, "they probably won't take you."

"They've already taken me. That's funny. Remember that old man you talked to at the wedding down at Blue Beach. He is a Huk. Sometimes you're pretty smart, Krummel, sometimes. Anyway, they'll use me as a pack-mule till they are convinced, and I will convince them."

"I don't doubt it," I sighed, "but I wonder how long you'll last."

"Long enough."

"Yeah. Think about this. You're not a soldier, Morning. Maybe you're tough and smart, but you don't know anything, you haven't . . . ."

"I know as much as you knew," he interrupted.

I had to smile. "Maybe so. Shit, I don't know. I just hate to see you go."

"No other way for us," he said.

"What about your folks?" I asked.

"It doesn't matter," he said. "It doesn't matter at all."

I stood, then wandered to the latrine, peed, wondering how I might stop him, but when I went back to the table, he was gone, the phony wheelchair sitting empty, his glasses gleaming from the tabletop. There was nothing to say. For an instant I wished that he had died in Vietnam, but I knew I didn't. I sat for a moment in the wheelchair, slipped on his glasses, and drank his beer, but it just didn't fit, so I drank my own.

Two, maybe three hours passed, and I thought nothing, said nothing, and drank very little. The Filipino, the student with the dirty mouth walked up to me, and in not an unfriendly voice said "Hello."

I hit him in the mouth and he tumbled backwards into the latrine.

I sat and the music and talk went on for perhaps fifteen seconds, then stopped. I took an easy drink of beer and when the student nearest behind me swung at the back of my head, I ducked, and elbowed him in the ribs. You could hear them break like a bow snapping. He lay on the floor, out of it, and I moved into the corner by the jukebox. There were seven of them, but only two miners, and they were all moving toward me, but I wasn't waiting.

I went for the nearest miner, catching half a dozen punches on my head and shoulders as I went. I had my neck tucked inside my chest and I wasn't waiting. I blocked the miner's roundhouse with a left and his foot with my knee, then hit him in the throat. As he went down, a wave of bodies hit my back, but I rolled as I fell, and came up with my back to the door. The other miner came first and I took two good shots to the forehead before I grabbed his arm and swung him out the door. He rolled over the hood of a car (and a taxi ran over his arm and the driver went for the police).

The bodies again flew at my back and forced me to the wall, but my foot came down on a shin with the edge of my shoe and I caught an inquisitive nose with the back of my head and smashed it like a tomato, and I rolled out again.

They had me in the middle now, swinging, kicking. I missed with a right, hit the top of a lowered head, and felt the bones give way. Kick one inside the thigh, miss another's kneecap, and fall under their hands and shoes. I know I was down and up at least twice, because I remember, and then there was just reeling darkness and spinning lights and sunbursts and darkness. Once, crouched against the bar, I felt broken glass under my hands and knees and wondered why it wasn't cutting. Then someone kicked my head against the bar and the black whirlwind fire blew again.

I came back as the sirens approached, but when I stood, the room tilted and I stumbled across the room to the far wall, then rolled back to the bar. The barroom looked like hell, furniture splintered, blood, glass, a tooth shining in a puddle of beer, an empty shoe under a broken table . . . I closed my eyes, reeled again, then opened them. I felt my face: nose, somehow, intact; a lump as big as my nose on my right cheek; a gap in my lip up through my moustache for my tongue to tiddle; teeth, traditionally strong, still there, but loose; another lump with the skin split across it like a splintered mirror; lumps on my head. Second and third knuckle of the right hand pushed halfway back to the wrist. Half an inch of my left ear disconnected from my head. Flesh on palms and knees sliced. Blood all over. In the mirror behind the bar, I looked as if I had already bled to death, but I was alive, and able to walk now.

As I walked behind the bar, the two girls scooted around the other end and out the door like flushed quail. I opened a beer, poured it in my mouth, then over my head. For some reason I looked around the room for Morning and wondered why he wasn't there, then wondered why I was. And as the police and APs came in the door, the hurting began.

Gallard and Abigail cried and cursed as they repaired me, but I merely sat and endured. The words I spoke were to ask

Gallard to knock me out for a while. I didn't tell them about Morning; I didn't know about Morning.

So there it is.

I told them about Morning the next afternoon, sitting on Gallard's porch watching the shadows leap over the ridges, down the valley, over the ridges, across the sky, just trying to tell them about Morning as moths as pasty as powdered sugar and one butterfly as big as my swollen, bandaged hand and black as dried blood contest the border between day and night; moths out too early, butterfly out too late, white moths, daemons of the night, butterfly black as day, and Joe Morning gone . . . perhaps if he had known that I shot him . . . but then perhaps not, too.

The morning of November 3, 1963. As I waited for my plane to Clark I noticed in the *Stars & Stripes* that the Diem's had been overthrown and killed by a junta of Vietnamese generals. Let shit eat shit, I said.

As I walked out to the small transport a little ceremony was being performed for a casketed body also going down to Clark. A tanned airman held a flag and another played a casual taps as the coffin was loaded by a fork-lift. A high wind came across the mountains, and the flag crackled against the high blue sky, and the wind clipped the sad notes right out of the horn. I thought he might be another Vietnam casualty, but it turned out that his steady shack has stabbed him with a pair of scissors. I kissed Abigail goodbye, hugged Gallard, and threw Morning's glasses in a butt can. There will be nights, I thought as I climbed on the plane, but no more mornings now, just windy afternoons and nights. . . .

And so I flew back home, across the sea, more hopeful than Morning, less hopeful than ever before.

The day after I was discharged at Oakland, John Fitzgerald Kennedy died from an assassin's bullet in Dallas. It took me two months to get home. This was no way for things to end, no ending I could handle, and I carried Joe Morning on my back across the breadth of America, until finally a cold wind blew me home again.

A MOST
PERSONAL EPILOGUE

And that same wind has blown where it might, Africa, South-east Asia, and around for three years since and Morning has been with me all the days, but the manuscript has been gathering dust through that time till now. After he came back to life, I couldn't go on. I'm back home now, recovering from wounds again, just back, from Laos and the CIA, and this letter came last week.

Well, old war horse, I've written pretty often in the past year or so, but haven't had much chance to mail a letter. The postal service out here isn't so great.

It's been tough. I know you told me it would be, and I believed you, but you were right, I didn't know.

It's not the fighting, not at all, in fact I look forward to a fire-fight now days, and I see them often now days too. The army is right behind us all the time now and it is only a matter of time. That phrase works in lots of ways—time weighs more than the base plate of a mortar or five hundred rounds of belted thirty caliber ammo. You didn't tell me about all the time I would spend sitting on my ass under a banana tree, you didn't tell me lots of things. . . .

I'm hard now, man, hard. In spite of the food, I've filled out; got my growth, as you'd say. I steal vitamins whenever I can and, though I can't laugh about it, I know that you do, laugh at the picture of the great revolutionary dashing through the jungles with a bottle of One-a-Day brand vitamins in his pocket. I'm as brown as a gook now, but I'm not one, and they remind me every day. They kept all the shit for me, cooking, washing dishes, until I busted one up who asked me to wipe his ass. God, they're nearly all as dumb as old Dottlinger. They'd rather collect taxes from poor gooks like themselves than rob American bases. They're shit. I guess I'm shit too now. Three days ago I gut-shot an old man who spit on me. He sat in the sun for a long time with his guts in his arms, till I shot him, not out of compassion but out of disgust. Hard.

But somehow easier too. I wish you'd go see my parents, man, tell them that I'm sorry, that I love them (at least the memory of them), and that if I could find a way, I would come home. Don't tell them I'm dead.

But then the hardness is back. I guess you'll get this while teaching at some fat-ass girls' college in the North. The army has been on our tails for four months and I haven't slept much and haven't eaten much and I think maybe I've killed a thousand men and I don't even know why. I haven't eaten beef since I saw you last, haven't had many beers, and don't even know why. I'm not crying, man, because I did what I thought was right, I did it, while most men sit on their fat asses not even caring about right, and though I'm hungry and I've got sores all over my legs and my left arm doesn't work too well since I caught a bullet last May, I know I'm a man now. I don't worry about that. I'm only sorry that there wasn't an easier way.

There isn't much else to say. I just wanted you to
know that I loved you, old horse, and that I was a
fool. I'm not crying, man, but it's been tough, and I
won't be sorry when it is over.

Your friend,
Joe Morning

A note came with the letter, saying that this American had
said that I might send one hundred American dollars to the
person who sent this letter to me. I didn't do it.

I'm glad I was in bed when the letter came, though I'm not
glad to be in bed again. God, the images rush back. Morning
running for the latrine with his ass bobbing white in Dottlinger's face, the mutiny, crying over the dead Huk he wouldn't
spit on six months later. And the things he told me. Fighting on
the university lawn, fighting in Birmingham, fighting. But the
picture that hangs with me: Morning roaring out of that van
on Hill 527, desperate, romantic, mad with hate, sick with
hate, breaking the back of the attack with one fine last gesture, so fine, so fatal that it seems a shame he didn't die there
while he still believed in his hate, seems a shame. But he
didn't. I don't suppose I'll ever know how he died, but I'm sure
it was dirty and painful and impossible to bear, and I'm
certain he bore it well.

It has been tough all over, though. After I drank my way
back to Texas after my discharge, after I dried out for a few
weeks, after I lost Ell again, I did go to Africa, silly as it
may sound, but I met a CIA man in Johannesburg before I
could hire out. I told him, when he offered me a job over two
warm beers, that I didn't care who I killed for, just so the pay
was good and the action often. He didn't answer me, but he
didn't contradict me either. They sent me through Special
Forces training at Bragg, then to language school at Monter-
rey, then to northern Thailand. An Army major and I slipped
into Laos, periodically, to train Meo tribes to resist invasion
from the north. Unfortunately we couldn't train them not to
sell us out to the North Vietnamese regulars operating along

the edge of the Plain of Jars. They must have believed in capitalism, because three different times the major and I ran out of one end of a burning Montagnard village as the North Vietnamese hardhats ran in the other. The third time the major didn't make it and I took a teacup full of shrapnel in my ass then ran three miles, mostly downhill, to the airstrip. And now I'm home again, on my ass, wondering how it all happened, how it will end, why it always happens to me. . . .

But that's Morning's line, isn't it, not mine, but then his letter, sadly, sounded more like me than him. . . .

The mortar round would have killed me this time but for an old Meo woman who stumbled as I ran past, faltered and took the steel meant for me. Pieces of her flesh stuck to the back of my shirt and when I found them on the U-10 flying out, I threw up. The pilot bitched and I told what had happened and he said, "No sweat. Just a fucking old gook broad." When we landed at the base camp back in Thailand, I broke his jaw with my rifle butt before he could get out and lost another government job.

But Joe Morning is dead now, probably, unless the letter fell out of his pocket. Even if he isn't dead, he is surely lost, and that makes me sad. I don't know who to blame, I just don't know who to blame.

When I left Oakland the day after Kennedy died, I drank my way across the Rockies and over to Nebraska. In a service station, the attendant-owner told me that the last owner had been killed by one of those crazy teen-agers in cheap store-bought cowboy boots who spawn in the heartland with nickel-plated .38s and thin excited girls hanging on their arms. The attendant-owner said business had been pretty good. Over in Iowa, I'm told, each spring when the rains fall like Noah's flood, a farmer murders his family with an axe, then hangs himself in the barn like a side of beef. As I passed through Missouri, a man killed his dog, which isn't notable, except that he had spent seven years teaching the dog to yodel. In Oklahoma, twenty-two migrant workers were killed when their truck plunged into the Washita River; passers-by picked their empty pockets before the highway patrol came. And in Dallas. . . .

We've come a long way and the sadness is heavy. Gallard and Abigail finally married and are working for AID in South Vietnam. I saw them in Saigon last year, and though they both still loved me, I had been with the killing too long and made them nervous. Cagle and Novotny have both married, fathered children and prospered, but they both drink too much and talk about war when I see them. Saunders stepped on a mine in the Ia Drang Valley this last summer and died six weeks later at Walter Reed. Tetrick retired two years ago, early, and is drinking himself to death in Grand Island, Nebraska. He told me, when I last saw him, that Dottlinger was doing six to ten in Leavenworth for hot checks. I'm thirty-one years old and sleeping in my father's house again, for now, and don't know what to do, except echo Morning: It's been tough, man, but I'm not crying, and it's not, it's for damn sure not, over yet.

It is November again, and the gray wind and the rain weave at my window. The Mexican Pacific beaches are lovely this time of year, and I'm going there to rest, to drink a little, to eat the sun and dream Joe Morning's dream for awhile. Then I'll be back.

About the Author

James Crumley was born in Three Rivers, Texas, and spent most of his childhood in south Texas. He served three years as an enlisted man in the U.S. Army. Over the years, he has taught at the University of Texas at El Paso, the University of Montana, and the University of Arkansas. Mr. Crumley, who summers in Missoula, Montana, is currently at work on a novel about Texas.

VINTAGE
CONTEMPORARIES

"Today's novels for the readers of today."

—VANITY FAIR

"Real literature—originals and important reprints—in attractive, inexpensive paperbacks."

—THE LOS ANGELES TIMES

"Prestigious."

—THE CHICAGO TRIBUNE

"A very fine collection."

—THE CHRISTIAN SCIENCE MONITOR

"Adventurous and worthy."

—SATURDAY REVIEW

"If you want to know what's on the cutting edge of American fiction, then these are the books you should be reading."

—UNITED PRESS INTERNATIONAL

On sale at bookstores everywhere, but if otherwise unavailable, may be ordered from us. You can use this coupon, or phone (800) 638-6460.

Please send me the Vintage Contemporaries books I have checked on the reverse. I am enclosing $_____ (add $1.00 per copy to cover postage and handling). Send check or money order—no cash or COD please. Prices are subject to change without notice.

NAME_____

ADDRESS_____

CITY _____ STATE_____ ZIP_____

Send coupons to:

RANDOM HOUSE, INC., 400 Hahn Road, Westminster, MD 21157

ATTN: ORDER ENTRY DEPARTMENT

Allow at least 4 weeks for delivery.

VINTAGE
CONTEMPORARIES